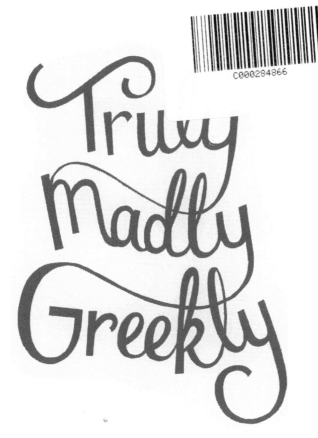

Truly Madly Greekly

Mandy Baggot

Bookouture

Published by Bookouture

An imprint of StoryFire Ltd.
23 Sussex Road, Ickenham, UB10 8PN
United Kingdom

www.bookouture.com

ISBN: 978-1-910751-00-8
eBook ISBN: 978-1-909490-99-4

This book is a work of fiction. Names, characters, businesses,
organizations, places and events other than those clearly in the
public domain, are either the product of the author's imagination
or are used fictitiously. Any resemblance to actual persons, living or
dead, events or locales is entirely coincidental.

To my soul mate, my rock, the man who first took me to Corfu and the one person who always believes in my dreams, no matter how crazy others think they might be! This one's for you, Mr Big.

ONE

She was on a plane. She was going on holiday. Ellen Brooks took another breath. *She had to relax. Breathe slower. Less tantric, more sukhasana. Slowly … slowly …*

Turbulence buffeted the aircraft and she snapped her eyes open, trying to regain balance. How had this happened? How had she gone from wringing the life out of the Inland Revenue, in a meeting that was still referred to in *Taxation* magazine, to counting backwards to keep calm? Had every shred of her former self disappeared the second she'd stopped being able to afford power shoes? She missed her Louboutins more than she missed fine wine. And she practically got the shakes over that.

Ellen put both hands onto the back of the seat in front of her, closing her eyes and holding on. *Focus. Confidence. Imagine you are a tree.*

It was just no good. She felt as far from relaxed as some thought Neil Armstrong had been from the moon. She needed professional help or Paul McKenna himself. Neither of which she could afford. Hypnosis was definitely going on her bucket list. Along with trekking over the Andes and having a go at Segway. When she recovered. When she got herself back in the game and moved on from the doormat phase of her life. Which didn't seem likely yet. She wasn't even close.

Opening her eyes again, she looked out of the window. Here she was, travelling over mountains somewhere in Europe, thousands of feet up in the air heading for sun, sea and all inclusive portions of everything and all she could visualise was her desk. The desk she did secret overtime on. The desk she read *50 Ways To Cope with Hyperventilation* on.

The largest desk in the office, equipped with more stationery than Ryman's, and heaving with paperwork she didn't care about. Plus, the locked drawer hiding all her secrets.

She'd never had secrets until recently. A few short months ago she'd been relatively sane and not at all embroiled in anything she shouldn't be. She'd had a career path, her future all mapped out. Now everything was on the verge of imploding. Breaking rules and order had never been in her nature. She strived for things and she worked hard. Determination and perseverance always won the day. Until the day you took your eye off the ball and got trampled on.

Another uncomfortable sensation rocked her sideways. More turbulence. Ellen put both hands to her pounding head, letting her fingers massage the scalp. She knew she'd left something out of her holiday notes but she had no idea what.

'When the drinks trolley gets to you, get me something alcoholic. Anything will do, but not cider 'cause it gives me wind!'

Tranquillity was lost. She sighed. It was her sister Lacey's bloody fault she was on this plane.

'Apples don't agree with me,' Lacey called. 'Do they do shots?'

Ellen cringed, looking at the woman sat next to Lacey with sympathy.

Lacey was getting married. Not until next year, but these days weddings had to be planned so far in advance even the Gregorian calendar had a job to keep up. So far, Lacey had pushed Ellen around stately homes, castles, churches and racecourses until her sister realised the only way she was going to guarantee blue sky and sun was to have the wedding abroad.

Rhodes had been the island of choice until the hardback brochure for the Hotel Blue Vue, Agios Spyridon, Corfu arrived. Glossy pages full of picturesque scenes of the mountains of Albania, the azure seas, the sandy beach, a close-up of bougainvillea table settings and the one photo Lacey hadn't stopped going on about.

'You get married on a platform in the sea. Actually in the water, Ellie. Well, on the water. You know, "at one" with the ocean.'

'Like a whale?' she'd offered.

After the photo of the water platform, the thrown-petal walkway and the olive tree avenue, Rhodes was nothing more than a once-mentioned idea and Hotel Blue Vue, Corfu was where Lacey and Mark were going to exchange their vows. Provided this taster holiday went well.

Mrs McGoldrick. That was who she'd forgotten from her holiday notes. Posh, picky and a complete pain in the arse. Perhaps she could send a quick text to her assistant, Milo. Could you send texts in flight mode? *Calm. Imagine you are boat adrift on the ocean.*

Ellen pulled in a breath, rolled then straightened her shoulders. *I am not a flake. I could organise and strategize for Lord Sugar if he asked.*

'Can you get me some snacks, too?' Lacey bellowed.

Ellen squeezed her eyes tight shut. The last thing she needed was to be out of the office with a Bridezilla. She turned her head then, to look at Lacey. Earphones inserted, leafing through *Heat*, her newly-coloured platinum blonde hair sat on her shoulders, which were already brown, thanks to a course of sun bed sessions. Instead of the deep frustration she expected, a pang of love waved over her. Why was she complaining? It was her job to suck all this up. She was all Lacey had.

'Not those crisps that smell like fish though,' Lacey yelled.

'Lacey!'

'What?'

'Turn it down!'

Lacey shook her head. 'There's no way you can hear my music from there.'

'I meant your voice.'

This was what happened when you were the elder half-sibling and neither of you had a mother to lean on. Ellen turned her attention back to the sky outside. A 'routine' operation had claimed her mother and suddenly her dad, Al, was a widower.

Al had hated being alone and was no good at it. Seven years later, still struggling to look after Ellen, he'd remarried. Margarette. Who had modelled herself on Maleficent. Nine months on and there was Lacey. A half-sister to chew Ellen's favourite toys and puke over everything else.

Before Lacey's second birthday, Margarette had run off with another man and Al was alone again, this time with *two* daughters. Ellen traced the outline of the plane window. No, their dad might be paying for the wedding but he couldn't be expected to *organise* it. His priorities lay with making sure there was 'proper British grub' at the reception and plenty of Elvis numbers for the karaoke. And that's why the hand-holding and wedding-planning was very much weighing heavily on Ellen's shoulders.

'Would you like something?' the flight attendant asked.

Ellen opened her eyes again and tried to remember Lacey's demands.

'Two gin and tonics and a snack pack, please.'

'Not gin!' Lacey shouted.

'One gin and tonic then, and a beer.'

'Not beer if it's in a tin!'

'Sorry, one gin and tonic, a snack pack, a white wine and an update on the current penalty for murder in European airspace.'

'Not long to go now,' the flight attendant answered with a smile.

'No, just seven nights, forty five minutes and a two hour coach transfer.' She wrenched open the bottle of gin.

'Have they got any chocolate?' Lacey called.

TWO

Yan stood up, the crystal water tracking down his body. Drips and silver slivers channelled down his neck and shoulders, trailing southward. It had been another scorching day and the sun was only just disappearing behind the island.

He smoothed the water over his chest, across his abs and lower, watching it leave him and bounce back into the pool. Running his hands over his close-cropped hair, he roughed it a little, enjoying the sensation. For a second he could forget, have one long breath where everything calmed. But then, as always, a dart of reality stung him back into place. He shook his head.

At least here, in the pool, he felt some sense of peace. The water cooling him down from the day time heat, isolated, without the hordes of holidaymakers invading every space. Here he could relax enough to take stock, evaluate everything that had happened. So much heartache. Leaving behind everything he knew again. This time he had taken nothing but bitter words and bad memories. Why did the bad always override the good? There were softer memories there too, there *had* been times of joy. Those were what he had to cling to now. Those memories were the ones that were going to make him stronger. They were what his dreams were made of.

Pulling himself up and out of the pool he shook the water from his fingertips and looked across at the pastel-coloured buildings in front of him.

It had been two months since he had arrived here and he still wasn't used to it. Corfu and the hotel were so much more than a job to him. He hadn't just *left* his home country, he had escaped. Here, was the start of a new life.

He grabbed his towel from the sun lounger and wiped down his body. *You are worthless*. He shook his head, remembering his hatred of the city and the life he'd been thrown into. The lone option he'd had was to run. Sometimes, to get a second chance, that was just the only way out.

———

'What time is it? It looks like everything's shut,' Lacey yelled at the top of her voice.

They'd arrived and while Lacey was checking out the glass-fronted Blue Vue Hotel for signs of life, Ellen was left to drag all three cases up towards the entrance. Once a project manager, always a project manager.

Until a few months ago she'd been exactly that and highly accomplished at it. She was Miss Focussed, Miss Driven, with plans for her own accountancy practice. There was money to be made in accountancy. It was a good, solid, reliable job that would set up a good, solid, reliable future. Money wasn't to be wasted on the latest trends or the spa, unless work required it. She wasn't clueless about fashion, she just wasn't Lacey.

'I'm freaking starving. D'you think they'll do food?' Lacey asked, checking her watch, one hand on the door.

'Lacey, it's three in the morning.'

'I could murder a kebab.'

'Keep your voice down a bit, Lace.' Ellen puffed as she pulled one case up the ramp and went down for the next.

'It says "A Welcome Drink" in the brochure and I could really welcome a drink right about now. That coach ride was something else. At one point I thought we'd had it. Did you hear the brakes as we lurched towards the edge of that ravine?' Lacey asked, flicking her hair over one shoulder.

'I had my iPod on.' A motivational recording she wasn't about to admit to. Ellen could feel a slick of sweat at the nape of her neck as she heaved Lacey's case. 'Do you have a free hand at all or are you worried you might break a nail?'

'You have no idea how much these acrylics set me back. I need to trial their longevity before the wedding.' Lacey pushed at the glass and chrome door of the hotel.

'The wedding isn't until next year.'

'Yeah, I know and there are twenty five other designs I need to try before then. I'm going to check us in with reception. There's a woman behind the desk looking like she needs something to do. Pass me the paperwork.' Lacey held out a manicured hand.

Ellen let go of the heaviest of her sister's cases and looked through her handbag to locate the documents. She passed them over and Lacey teetered off towards reception on her six inch neon pink espadrilles.

Ellen looked at her watch. What time would it be in the UK? Past midnight. She couldn't phone Milo or anyone else about Mrs McGoldrick now. It would have to wait until the morning – the real morning – when it wasn't dark. When she would hopefully feel less like a close-to-breakdown-thirty-year-old and a bit more just like someone ready for a break. This was going to be her chance to regroup and reinvent. She was going to come back from this better and completely improved – like an update for IOS.

'Lady.' The resonating deep, male voice had her turning around.

Ellen swallowed. The man was right behind her, all six foot of him, dressed in jeans despite the heat of the night and a grey t-shirt that clung to his everything. His visible skin was tanned. Strong-looking brown forearms rested on his hips, a deep V of skin at his neckline caught her eye. He put his hand to one of the cases.

'No thank you.' The words hurried out from her lips as she tried to pull the case away from him. She'd read about this. It was the distraction technique. If she took her eyes off him for a second he'd be helping himself to her handbag.

'Please, I wait for you,' Yan reattempted. He engaged his hand on the bag again.

———

This woman was crazy. He'd never had to fight for luggage before. Holidaymakers were usually only too happy to hand over their bags after the flight and the long coach journey. This person was folding her fingers around the handle of the case so his grip on the other end was loosened.

'I'm fine, thank you. I'm with my sister. She's just inside,' she spoke. Having taken ownership of the case, she had now wound her arm around the strap of her handbag. She looked flustered, her long, brown wavy hair falling over her face, her cheeks pink.

'It is OK. I help with bags,' Yan repeated. He picked up one of the other pieces of luggage.

'I'm fine. We're fine. Me *and* my sister.'

He paused for a moment, looking at her as he picked up the tension in her tone. She thought he was a thief. That he was about to make off with her belongings and disappear into the night. He shook his head without realising he was doing it. In one minute she had formed an opinion of him, just like others had done back home.

He kept his voice even, despite the anger building up in his chest.

'I am Yan from animation team. I show you to your room.'

He picked up the second case and mounted the steps.

'Ooo a man! See, Ellie, I told you there'd still be a party going on. Corfu never sleeps.'

He looked up, seeing another woman appear from the main entrance of the hotel. She was younger, with bright hair and high shoes. She did not look like the woman grabbing at the cases. She was wearing pink on her lips and pouting at him.

He moved then, striding off left towards the terrace bar. The sooner he got these guests to their suite the sooner he could go to bed.

———

He was gone with their cases but he wasn't a thief. Not that he had looked like one, apart from the hint of stubble on his face and the air of strength. Ellen hoped she hadn't offended him by giving the impression she thought she was going to be mugged the second she'd landed on foreign soil.

'Come on, we'd better catch him up.' Lacey eyed her. 'What's the matter?'

'Nothing, I just didn't know he worked here.' She levelled a smile. 'Let's go.' She picked up the handle of her suitcase and prepared to drag it.

'We're on holiday, Sis, you need to lighten up. You do know, if I catch you texting or calling work I will confiscate your phone,' Lacey warned, teetering after the departing Yan.

'Only make threats like that if you can afford to spend seven nights without your hair straighteners.'

Lacey cackled. 'Ooo.'

'Keep up, lady. You are on last row!'

———

'This for lights and air conditioning,' Yan announced, once they were all inside Aphrodite 177. It had been a full five minute walk to their allocated room and Ellen was struggling to catch her breath. *Fitness.* That was another thing she'd neglected a bit over the last few months. The gym membership was the first thing she'd cancelled when the bills started coming. Climbing the stairs instead of taking the lift and the yoga DVD obviously weren't doing enough. She should take up something else. Perhaps Boxercise or self-defence. Hitting Ross physically wouldn't have won the war but it would have made her feel better. Just the thought of it was working now.

She watched Yan put the brass key fob into a slot on the wall by the door and the room was bathed in light, transforming it from darkness and displaying the five-star luxury straight out of the brochure pages. A low hum from the air conditioning unit started up and Lacey let out a squeal of excitement. Large twin beds dominated the room, with a small table and chairs in the centre. A beautiful urn of orchids rested on the table and there was a dressing table against one wall with an illuminated mirror. Matching wardrobes completed the furnishings.

To the right of the door Ellen could see a reasonably-sized bathroom and at the bottom of the room were patio doors she presumed led to a balcony.

Her feet moved of their own accord, taking her up to the glass. She unfastened the latch and pulled the doors apart, letting in a rush of humidity. She stepped just over the threshold, breathing in the scent of the night. Warmth, sea salt, essence of palm tree. She could hear the ocean, a light rolling of waves and in the distance hundreds of twinkling lights shone from the shores of neighbouring Albania. They were here, the village of Agios Spyridon, Corfu.

Ellen stepped back into the room and closed the doors back up.

'Breakfast from seven to ten. Lunch from twelve thirty to two thirty. And dinner from seven to nine thirty,' Yan reeled off, heading back to the door.

'Thank you and thank you for your help with the bags.' Ellen produced a five euro note from her purse and held it out to him.

His expression of disgust was evident. In fact she wasn't sure he could've looked any more shocked if he'd been tasered.

'No, thank you.' He took a step backwards from her and the money.

She was sure she'd read somewhere that it was customary to give tips. She tried again.

'Please, I know how heavy those suitcases were.' She shook the note at him and immediately regretted it. He didn't move a muscle and she was left with a wavering euro note in her hand. Why did she get the impression she'd insulted him?

He nodded his head. 'Water exercise tomorrow at ten. I wait for you.' He opened the door.

Before Ellen could say any more he left, closing the door with a bang. She jumped at the noise and the money fluttered to the floor, unwanted.

Lacey crashed down onto her chosen bed. 'Fancy not wanting a tip! I thought they were all broke over here at the moment. Mark wasn't sure about having the wedding in Greece because of the economic meltdown and everything but I said it would blow over. And anyway, if it doesn't blow over they'll be back to using the drackmark or whatever they had before, won't they? It'll probably be loads cheaper.'

'We should get some sleep.' Ellen checked her watch again. Truth be told, she didn't know why she'd mentioned sleep. She hadn't been sleeping well for weeks and she couldn't see that changing here. The air conditioning might keep the temperature cool but it didn't exactly sing you a lullaby.

Lacey sat up. 'What?! Sleep?! I don't think so. I say we open the mini-bar.'

That was actually a good idea.

——

Back in his room, Yan looked at himself in the mirror. He looked tired and so much older. It was like the last few months had aged him.

It would all have been so simple if he could have stayed in Brashlyan. He had made a difference there. A small difference, but a difference nonetheless. He had filled a void. He had been there for the children when their parents could not. The villagers knew him and they trusted him. There, his honesty and hard work ethic had been enough. The children adored him and, with every year that passed, he grew in confidence. Playing games, football, running in the fields were all such simple pleasures, but vital to his community. It was nothing formal, just teaching the children about friendship and teamwork, giving them a couple of hours a day to run free and be young.

He swallowed, remembering the looks on their flushed faces as the sun went down in Bulgaria. It seemed so far away now. Why did plans have to change? Why did things have to be taken away? *Boyan*.

He pushed back the memory and instead looked at the empty bottle of Rakia on the nightstand, a quarter filled with coins and notes.

He shouldn't have reacted how he had with the holidaymaker and he should have taken the five euros. Saving for something helped keep his focus. He picked up the bottle, observing the contents. How could the bottom have fallen out of his world so easily? Had the life he'd had ever been real or had everything just been paper thin, built on sand?

The situation he had left back home had been half his fault. He might not have chosen to move to the city but he *had* chosen Rayna. He had carved out a life in Sofia he had no passion for. He had directed his enthusiasm and drive into all the wrong places. He had put his faith in someone too easily. He replaced the bottle and sat down on the bed. Getting burnt like that had taught him a valuable lesson. He would never expose himself like that again. Never.

He looked at his watch. There were only three hours to sleep. He closed his eyes. Sleep never came easy to someone reliving despicable things.

THREE

Despite going to bed at just after four in the morning, Ellen was awake before seven. She'd not really been asleep, she'd just dozed, eyes half-open; that irritating state where your lids get heavy, your vision goes blurry and then nothing happens. She'd tossed and turned, counted the fronds in the lilies on the table and waited for the sun to come up.

Lacey was still fast asleep now, her bright, nearly white hair, draped right across the pillow. A protective feeling hit Ellen as she watched her sister breathing, her mouth hanging open, one hand clenching a corner of the sheet, just like it had when she'd been small. She'd often watched her sleeping when they were younger, especially when Lacey had been ill. She had always been the protector, the one making sure everything was how it should be. It was a pity she couldn't do that for herself.

There was light coming through the cream, linen curtains and Ellen got out from under her covers, drawn to what lay behind them. How different would the view look in the daytime? Would it live up to the colour brochure? She put her hands to the material and waited a second. Taking in a deep breath she held it there, paused, poised. Whatever scene was waiting for her it wasn't going to be what she was used to seeing out of the much-hated tiny two bedroom apartment back home. And it wasn't going to be that beach in Majorca either. She closed her eyes. She wasn't supposed to think back. That time was over.

She had to focus on the present, learn from what had happened. *Harbour no resentment, Ellen. Lose the anger.* The last thought just made her angrier. That was the trouble with therapists, especially cheap online ones, if they hadn't actually experienced the pain and humiliation themselves, they only knew how you felt from books they'd read. Even non-fiction could be fiction if it wasn't written properly.

Ellen closed her fingers around the material and got ready to wrench the curtains apart. She let her breath go and it was then, before she could do the grand reveal, her iPhone rumbled into action, the display flashing and alarm bells ringing.

Lacey began to stir and she hurried back across the room to her nightstand. Picking up the phone she saw the reminder she'd set before she got into bed.

McGoldrick – ring Milo.

She checked her watch again. It was only just past five in the UK. She still couldn't do anything yet. Lacey rolled over onto her side and put her thumb in her mouth, sucking like a contented infant.

She was in Corfu. She needed to chill out, relax, not think about anything but the now. She was away from everything here. She was going to use this holiday as a kick-start, to sort herself out when she got home. She was going to take charge, woman-up, believe and achieve. *Find* the money for power shoes.

Marching up to the curtains, she ripped them open with gusto and fell back in awe. The ocean was almost close enough to reach out to. The beautiful, gently rolling Ionian water with the Albanian mountains in the background forced out an audible sigh. Quickly she unlocked the doors and stepped out onto the balcony, the early morning warmth hugging her t-shirt-clad body.

———

From the pool Yan saw her come out onto the balcony. The lady who had tried to give him money just a few hours ago. The one who thought he was a thief. Her brown hair tousled, wearing only a t-shirt that skirted her upper thighs. She was looking out at the scenery as if soaking it all in. He'd done that too. The very first time he'd set eyes on the spectacular view from the incline the rooms were set on.

He watched her smooth her hands along the bar at the front of the balcony as if she was pulling herself into her surroundings. He'd done that also, needing to realise this was his home for the next few months; to know that, if he was sensible, if he didn't do anything stupid, this could work for him. It may not be perfect, but it was a whole lot better than working for a man he despised.

Yan pulled in a breath and dragged his eyes away, turning towards the Albanian mountains as a flashback invaded his consciousness. If that man knew where he was, what would he do? Was their business settled or would there be some kind of payback? The concern was always there, eking into everything, tainting every experience. But was he even worth the trouble to Rayna's father? After all the names he had called him, the cold, hard laughter and the taunts. He'd said Yan was pitiful, not good enough for anything, least of all his daughter. And, in some ways, he was right.

He straightened his arms above his head and launched himself back into the water.

———

To the right of the view was a lagoon of a swimming pool, exactly as the brochure had depicted. A waterfall rushed sparkling crystal clear water into the pool, palm trees skirting its perimeter. Wicker easy chairs faced the ocean, Greek music played and maids busied themselves, sweeping, cleaning and righting sunloungers. Ellen could just make out the beach if she stood on her tiptoes. There was promise of golden sand and blue umbrellas.

Over to the left was an outside eating area – white wood tables and matching chairs - and further towards the sea was the wedding-themed pergola and that now infamous water platform. Blue and white drapes, flowers blowing in the breeze, the wooden structure her little sister was planning to get married on.

Thinking about Lacey and Mark making vows of eternal love to each other caused a hit of something close to jealousy to cascade over her. She shivered. She wasn't jealous of her sister. She was happy for her. Mark was part of their family and Al thought the world of him. The men competed in golf tournaments and drinking contests together. They could even belch in unison. Mark was the son Al had never had.

Looking out at the water, there was just a tiny gnawing inside Ellen, when she thought about the impending celebration, a feeling that made her wonder if she would ever be as happy as Lacey was.

Straightaway she was transported from Corfu to an ill-fated trip to Majorca with her last boyfriend. Ross Keegan had asked her to marry him on a secluded beach near Alcudia and she hadn't known what to do. He'd got the knees of his chinos covered in sand, the words had come out of his mouth and she hadn't answered. She'd stood there, looking at the ring, then back at him, then at the sunset. Finally, she'd pointed at a boat on the horizon. Eventually, he'd got up.

The crux of it was, she hadn't thought it was a real moment. And that had spoken volumes. They'd never talked about the future further than whose turn it was to stay the night. Marriage, being together forever, had never been on her radar with Ross. He was a career guy like she was a career girl. He liked her, she liked him, they cross-sold their services and they both worked long hours. She told him her dreams of owning her own business and he hadn't thought she was crazy. He'd sat up. He'd looked interested. He'd said encouraging, supportive things. Accepting a proposal would mean changing things, being together. All the time. Every time she'd thought of sharing her life like that she had visions of her father and Lacey's mother. The shattered relationship, the clothing store bills long after she'd gone. But one thing Al and Margarette had had was passion. Most of the time it had involved fighting long into the night, fuelled by alcohol, but it was passion all the same. The only thing she and Ross had got passionate about was interest rates.

But did she see herself being alone forever? Getting her kicks from chick-lit novels and trial balances? It was fine being a determined, lone wolf, full of ambition and big plans, but was that all she wanted? Because here she was, thirty, single, broke, a chief bridesmaid at her younger sister's wedding, with rubbish hair and an obsession with the accounting needs of a horse trainer. There had to be more. She wanted there to be. But what extra something would fit with her 24/7 work ethic? Because work was all she knew and she wasn't about to give up her everything for something with no guarantees, was she?

Ellen shook herself, sending a flying beetle off her forearm and down over the balcony. It was then, as she continued to soak up the scenery, that she saw an even more pleasing view than the Albanian mountains. Pulling himself up the pool steps was a Greek Adonis. Ducking her head slightly, to get a better view and to make her voyeurism less obvious, Ellen watched as the man got out of the water. All taut thighs and abs, he grabbed a towel from the nearest sun lounger.

He had dark hair, wet from the pool and shorn fashionably close to his head. He was tall, with a broad chest, nipped in at the waist followed by very small black trunks.

The man rubbed at his body with the towel, droplets of water bouncing to the ground and changing the terracotta tiles from a dull auburn to a bright orange. Then he raised his head and she found herself looking directly at him. It was *him*. With fewer clothes on. The man who had helped them with their bags. The one she had shied away from like he was a mugger.

———

She was looking down at him from the balcony, watching him dry himself off. She probably thought he had been up early checking under the sun loungers for lost watches or loose change. He shook his head. He was overreacting. This was about *his* perception of people, not hers. He had to remember this wasn't Bulgaria and these weren't the type of people he had been forced into associating with over the past year.

He looked up at her. She averted her eyes, as if she was suddenly finding the tiled floor a more interesting stimulus.

Last night she had been a newcomer, a woman alone on foreign soil and he hadn't introduced himself straightaway. She'd been cautious and he'd been rude. He shouldn't judge too soon.

He raised a hand to her.

'Hello, lady!' he called. 'Do not forget, water exercise here, at ten. I wait for you!'

———

Ellen froze, still watching him rub himself dry with his towel. He waved again and she fled, stepping back inside the doors and closing them up. The air-conditioned atmosphere restored her temperature and she took a deep breath, trying to bring her heart rhythm back down. *Relax. Breathe. Focus.*

'What the hell are you doing?' Lacey asked.

She jumped. Lacey was sat up in her bed, staring over at her.

'Nothing.' Ellen moistened her lips. 'I just had a look outside. Shall we go to breakfast? I really fancy some toast.'

'Are you serious? It's only just gone seven. It's all inclusive. They aren't going to run out of food or anything.' Lacey flopped back down on her pillows.

'I know but we need to check out all the facilities, don't we? See how they operate. See if Dad's going to cope with hardboiled eggs and hams when the wedding's here,' Ellen continued.

'They do full English, Ells. It says in the brochure,' Lacey yawned. 'What's the matter with you? You're acting really weird.'

'I'm not, I'm just hungry.'

'It's work isn't it? You've been on the phone to work already! What did I say, Ellen? You shouldn't even think about work when you're on holiday, especially when you're on holiday with me!' Lacey threw back the covers and got out of bed.

'I haven't. I'm not and I definitely won't.' Apart from the one call she was going to make as soon as Lacey was caught up talking to someone in management about seating plans.

'We're not getting up at seven every day. I might be here to organise my wedding but I'm also here for a good time and I intend to make sure *you* have a good time too,' Lacey announced. She pinged the elastic waistband of her Little Miss Naughty pyjama shorts to emphasise the point.

That meant one thing. Ellen would be drinking her dad's eighteen stone body weight in cocktails and being made to do party dances. She never remembered all the moves to 'Agadoo'.

She nodded rapidly at Lacey in an attempt to end the conversation.

'Good, well, I'll just have a shower, do a recovery and rescue pack on my hair, choose a bikini and an outfit … I should be ready by nine,' Lacey informed.

'Fine, I'll read.' Ellen smiled, picking a paperback up from the nightstand and hugging it to her.

'And no calls to work,' Lacey said, pointing an accusing finger.

'No.' Ellen shook her head. 'None.'

It was going to be a very long week.

———

'Hello, handsome.'

Yan looked up from his bowl of cereal and met with the green eyes and over-tanned face of Monica. The woman snaked an arm across his shoulders, reached into his bowl and plucked out a chocolate cornflake, popping it into her mouth with over-emphasised lip action.

'Good morning, Monica. How are you?' It seemed like she had been shadowing him for days now.

They taught you about over-familiarity with guests on day one of the animation training course. You should always smile. You should try your very best to learn names and use them, but physical contact was an invitation to trouble.

'I'm wonderful now I've seen you. Water exercise this morning, isn't it?' Monica asked. She whipped her black curls onto her shoulder and planted one hand on her hip.

'Yes, at ten,' Yan answered. He kept the smile fixed on his face. If she stayed too long his cheeks were going to hurt.

'Wonderful.' She let out a dreamy sigh. 'I find it does one such a lot of good to indulge on holiday, as long as you balance it up with some form of rigorous exercise.'

She was leaning over his chair, oblivious to the half a dozen holidaymakers, forming a queue behind her, waiting to squeeze past on their way to the hot buffet.

'You should Zumba. It is with Sergei, at five,' Yan suggested. He got to his feet.

'I might just do that,' Monica answered, her voice low and husky.

'Water exercise!' he shouted. 'Water exercise everybody! At ten!'

Monica reached for her ears and, seizing his chance, he made his escape. Being busy had its advantages. It left you little time to think.

FOUR

'How many types of eggs were there? I'm making notes for Mark and Dad. 'Course, if it wasn't for this stupid golf tournament, they both would have come with us,' Lacey said, jotting notes on a Hello Kitty pad which was leaning on the edge of her sun bed.

'Hard-boiled, fried, poached and scrambled.' Ellen turned the page of her novel. 'It wasn't just the golf. They both have to work to pay for this wedding.'

They'd found sun loungers to the right of the deep end of the pool, next to the stunning view of the ocean. Lacey was sporting a barely-there tangerine two piece that made her look like an elongated Wotsit. Still, better to look like a well-loved snack than someone in a burqa, like she did.

'It isn't costing *that* much. Did you know Niamh's wedding cost twenty-five grand? I mean, she didn't even have proper live entertainment or anything. They do Greek dancers here with plate smashing and fire.' Lacey smiled and raised an eyebrow.

'I have a feeling Dad will love that.'

Ellen's phone trilled and a couple lying on loungers next to them looked over.

'For God's sake, Ellen, we're on holiday! Turn it on silent or it's going in the pool,' Lacey threatened.

From the display Ellen could see it was the office. Lacey hadn't left her for a second since it had become a civilised enough time to call the UK and she was betting Mrs McGoldrick had been on the phone to Milo already. Maybe she'd received a late submission penalty in the post. Or maybe it wasn't that. Maybe it was something to do with Keegan Manufacturing. Ellen swallowed. It couldn't be. She'd been careful. Being careful was about all she had left in her ammunition.

'Hi there! Water exercise in a few minutes with Yan.'

At the sound of accented tones, Lacey sat up from her prostrate position. 'Oh my days, who is that?'

Ellen was still looking at her phone, the display flashing on and off. She couldn't answer it.

'Ellen, look at that bloke! He's bloody gorgeous.' Lacey pulled herself further up the lounger and adjusted the bra of her bikini.

The phone stopped ringing and Ellen watched, waiting for the voicemail message to appear.

'Ellen,' Lacey hissed, plastering a wide smile on her lips. 'Look!'

'Hi! Are you joining in the water exercise?'

Ellen looked up to take in a tall, tanned, athletically-built, dark-haired man dressed in a navy-blue polo shirt and matching shorts, standing beside Lacey's lounger. He was smiling down at her sister, a clipboard to his chest, all perfect white teeth and dark eyes.

'Are you the instructor?' Lacey asked, with more than double the required pout for attracting the entire male species.

'Sometimes, but not today. Today it is Yan. I am Sergei. Serg,' he introduced.

'Well hello, Serg. I'm Lacey,' she purred. 'So, what *do* you instruct?' She played with a tendril of her hair.

'Water polo, boules and Zumba. Sometimes volleyball,' he informed, his clipboard casting a shadow over Lacey's midriff.

'I do Zumba back home. I might join in. What time?'

Ellen turned her attention back to her phone.

'Five, by the stage,' Sergei informed.

'Great.'

Sergei turned to Ellen. 'How about for you? Some water exercise?'

Ellen knew he was addressing her but she couldn't look up now. She was waiting for the voicemail icon. Something was wrong, she just knew it. Her horoscope in Lacey's magazine had mentioned an unexpected phone call.

'Ellen! The lovely Sergei is talking to you! Are you going to do water exercise?' Lacey barked like a sergeant major.

Ellen dropped her phone back into her bag and shook her head at the man.

'No thanks. I'm not really very good in the water.'

'Now I've heard it all! She's actually a fantastic swimmer! She saved a boy from school when he fell into the river. She got a commendation from the fire brigade and everything,' Lacey exclaimed, loud enough for the whole pool area to hear.

'This isn't a swimming competition,' Ellen snapped back. 'Sergei has foam sausages.'

'I put your name down. We maybe see you in a few minutes,' Sergei said, giving Lacey another smile before searching for other interested parties.

'Thanks a lot, Lacey. Now he knows my name he's going to be getting me to come up on stage for this and join in with that,' Ellen stated angrily.

'What's the matter with you this morning? You're more uptight here, in thirty degree, blue sky weather, than you are at home when it's pissing down with rain and Milo's ballsed something up with someone's accounts,' Lacey snapped.

At the mention of the office Ellen stiffened. *Swallow down anxiety.* Or drown it with cocktails. The bar was looking more appealing by the second.

'Hello, lady. You come to water exercise, yes? I wait for you.'

At the sound of *this* voice Ellen looked up and found herself staring into the most incredible pair of eyes. They were blue, an almost indescribable blue. Clear, yet deep, intense and hypnotic. Yan was dressed in the same style of uniform Sergei had been sporting and he was smiling at her. Perhaps he had forgiven her for thinking he was a bag snatcher.

She shook her head at him regardless. 'No, thank you. It's our first day.' Her cheeks were heating up under his scrutiny.

'You learn today for tomorrow,' Yan told her, unfazed.

So he wasn't a thief but he was determined. And it didn't sound like he was going to let her out of joining in. Another bully of a man who thought he knew what was best for her. She let out a snort of displeasure.

'For God's sake, Ellen, get off the sun lounger and go and enjoy yourself. You love the water.' Lacey smiled at Yan. 'She loves the water.'

'This is not hard for you. I help,' Yan insisted.

Her face maintained the same expression and she felt her cheeks solidifying with the effort. Why couldn't everyone just leave her alone? Wasn't it enough she had to hear all the intricacies of wedding favours while she was here? Now she was expected to be a happy holiday joiner. All she wanted was some quiet. A chance to plan a restructure of her life. She didn't want ringing phones or any of … *this*.

'I understand.' Yan nodded. 'You want to just eat and drink for all of holiday, not have fun.' He made to move off.

'What? You can't say that,' Lacey remarked, almost spitting out a mouthful of drink.

Ellen gritted her teeth together before answering him. 'Some people can have fun without needing to have it with the entire holiday complex.'

'You have fun on your own with book,' he responded, nodding.

'Yes, actually.'

'And to read story of other people is more fun than to make story of own?'

His broken English seemed to make the statement all the more cutting. She was being sliced right through the middle in broad daylight and she had no response.

———

Yan had no idea why he'd said that. If people said no to joining in with animation there was no penalty to pay. You moved on, found others eager to participate. But he was standing there, his hands on his hips, staring at this English woman and waiting for her to react. Why? Because she'd judged him the second she'd set eyes on him? He had to move past that. People judged people. It was flawed human nature but it was reality.

Now his breathing pattern had altered. He was fired up, adrenaline starting to hum. He watched her put her thick paperback down onto the table and stand up.

She was facing him now, her eyes narrowed as she tied her hair back into a bunch.

'I want you to know that I'm doing this once,' she stated. 'A one-time only thing and you don't ever ask me again.'

He said nothing and watched her look over the water where other residents were collecting the foam spaghettis.

'I mean it can't be *that* hard,' Ellen continued. 'I've been swimming since before foam sausages were even invented.'

He nodded. 'Good. Then let us go.' He swooped a hand towards the water.

———

She was struggling. In the couple of months Yan had worked at the hotel he had never seen someone so unrelaxed. Every movement Ellen made was restricted by concern – for space, for accuracy. Her eyes would dart left and right at the other participants, checking their form and repetition, every part of her body tight and stiff. She kept a straight face the entire time, her brow furrowed in concentration as everyone moved around the pool following his instructions. What caused someone to be like that? What made her so closed to what was going on around her? It was as if she didn't want to interact with anyone at all, couldn't break a smile. At that thought he gave a swallow. If his job didn't require it, he probably wouldn't have been interacting with anyone either. But he had his reasons. Maybe she had her reasons too but he could almost guarantee she didn't have the head of the Bulgarian mafia on her tail.

———

Ellen's arms were aching and the water that had looked inviting was actually freezing. She'd been sandwiched between a frighteningly made-up woman in a white and gold sequinned one-piece called Monica and a six foot six mountain of a Russian called Uri.

She didn't know if her arms were really hers and she was still holding them in the air, her hands grappling with a foam sausage.

'Pump arms up like this!' Yan instructed from the side of the pool, thrusting his muscular arms skywards.

Pump your arms up in the air seemed like an everyday request for Uri. For Ellen, on the other hand, it was a task that made her pits strain like hell. If she wasn't careful she'd be unable to operate a knife and fork at lunch. Yoga did not prepare you for this kind of torture.

'And run. Run around in water. One-two-three, *eins-zwei-drei,*' Yan continued, demonstrating.

This had been such a mistake. What was she thinking? She shouldn't have had some sort of face-off with a hotel employee just because she felt guilty about thinking he was a luggage mugger. It was an easy mistake to make. He'd been a stranger with his hands on their cases. She was simply a single woman abroad being cautious.

She splashed her hands into the pool. She wasn't enjoying this either. She was hopeless at it and her mind was still on her job. A job she hated. A job she wouldn't be doing if it hadn't been for that one, big, fat mistake. Saying no. How could saying no ruin your entire life? But she wasn't dwelling. No, no dwelling, just living in the moment.

The water rippled around Ellen's thighs as she ran in a circle, following the giant strides of Uri. As she came back round she looked to the poolside just in time to catch Yan pulling his polo shirt over his head.

There was that perfectly sculpted brown abdomen she'd been admiring from the safety of her balcony earlier. And, as he dropped his shorts, the small trunks were revealed. Without any hesitation he jumped into the pool and joined the group, ordering everyone into a circle and putting his arm around Uri on his right and then Ellen.

She jolted. She had a man's arm across her shoulders; a man with a gorgeous thick accent and scorching blue eyes, a rude man who was making her pay for an innocent reaction in the middle of the night. How had she got here? That was the trouble with going through a personal crisis, every little feeling was magnified, everybody's actions questioned.

———

'OK, that is end of water exercise. Thank you everybody. Next, we have cocktail game, *cocktailspielen,* with Sergei, by the bar,'

Yan announced, removing his arm from around his participants.

Ellen let out a sigh of relief and ducked her shoulders down
into the water, tipping her head back and wetting the whole of
her hair. Despite it being ridiculous, she did feel like she'd had
some exercise far superior to stretching into a table-top position
in her living room. She closed her eyes and tried to hold a breath
and count like she'd been taught in her online meditation class.

'You like the water exercise?'

Yan's voice snapped her out of relaxation and she opened her
eyes. He was standing next to her, close. What was it with this
guy?

'It was fine. I survived, like I knew I would.'

'We repeat tomorrow,' he said, smiling.

'Ah, well I said one time only and it wouldn't be so adventur-
ous if I did it twice.'

'I see you tonight? At the show? We have Greek dancing,' Yan
continued. He scooped water up with his hands and let it trickle
from his fingers, showering down his body.

'Oh great, your national pastime.' Had that sounded sarcas-
tic enough?

'What?'

'Greek dancing? You're Greek.'

'I am not Greek. I am from Bulgaria.' He dribbled more water over his body.

As hard as she was trying, she couldn't stop her eyes from
reverting to his well-built chest. *Raise your head, Ellen.*

'So you will be there?' he asked.

'Yes, we'll be there. No need to come and hunt us down.'

She watched his features harden a little at her chosen words.
She was doing so well with the insults, with such minimal effort.

'I'll try and get Lacey to join in,' Ellen continued. 'That's *Lacey* over there. My sister.'

Lacey was game for anything. Animation was much more suited to her than Ellen. And if she got Lacey involved in activities she could get that quiet time she craved.

'What is name?' Yan asked.

'Lacey,' Ellen repeated, twice as loud.

'*Your* name,' Yan asked.

'My name?' She hadn't forgotten it but she didn't know why he'd asked or whether she wanted to give it. But it was just her name, not the town she was born in or her PIN.

'Ellen.' Her cheeks flamed. 'I'm Ellen.' Now she felt stupid.

'Ellen,' he repeated in his heavy accent.

The second he rolled the word around in his mouth it caused her to swallow, involuntarily. He was looking back at her, still cupping water in his hands and depositing it down his body.

And then he was out. In one quick move he hauled himself from the pool and stood up on the side. 'I see you tonight.'

She bit her lip. Was it too hot to wear Spanx?

FIVE

Despite his best intentions, Yan found himself looking for Ellen. Why, he had no idea. He was only there for light encouragement, to assist the hotel residents who *wanted* to join in. It wasn't his job to pester people. They'd been firmly told that pestering people led to low reviews on Trip Advisor.

Still, he couldn't help noticing how different she was from the usual prostrate women who had no inclination for animation. Ordinarily, along with the sun worship and the cocktails, there was laughing, letting go, not caring how you look when doing things that weren't routine. Ellen was not laughing.

For the most part of the morning she'd sat on a lounger, but was never still. She had her phone, and books, so many books. A pile of thick paperbacks had been on the table next to her all day. She liked words, stories – that was all he really needed to know. Like Rayna she was from another world. One he didn't belong to. There seemed to be so many scenarios like that for him.

He filled a plastic cup with lemon and lime and sat down under the shade of the outside restaurant's canopy. His eyes began to shut and he snapped them open. He was so tired. Lack of sleep, too much sun, not enough water and that constant feeling that he had to stay on his toes. One slip, one reason for team leader, Tanja, to scrutinise him and he could be in trouble.

'Yan, you OK?'

He flinched as Sergei slapped him on the back and joined him on an adjacent seat.

'Yes, OK. You?'

'I am now.' Sergei lowered his voice. 'I have very sexy girl in Zumba today. I mean, very sexy.' A wide smile formed on his colleague's mouth.

Yan shook his head. Most weeks there was a sexy participant reported in the Zumba class. He was sure Sergei had done more than South American moves with most of them too. He would not choose Sergei for a friend but he was part of the team. You couldn't dislike anyone in your team even if you didn't agree with the way they conducted themselves.

'She had it going on up here *and* down there,' Sergei continued. He put one hand to his chest and planted the other on his rear.

'You know the rules,' Yan told him.

'You think I am scared of Tanja?'

'You do not need job?'

Sergei shrugged his shoulders. 'Yes, I want the job but … ' Sergei stopped talking, focussing his eyes across the restaurant. 'There she is, the sexy girl.' Sergei nudged Yan's elbow.

Yan looked over in the direction his colleague was staring and saw Ellen and Lacey making their way from the sun loungers towards the steps to the hotel buildings. He swallowed. Still there was no smile on Ellen's face. She was looking into her bag, hair falling forward, hands rummaging through the contents. She was never comfortable. He had spent all day watching her, seeing the distracted actions that were in complete contrast to the fire in her responses to him. For whatever reason she wasn't at ease here.

'Wow, wow, wow,' Sergei sighed.

The repeated word had Yan tightening his core and shifting on his seat. 'You look at Ellen?'

'What? No. Her name is Lacey,' Sergei answered.

Yan got up. 'I have football.'

'Hey, we have drinks on the beach tonight, yes? After show?' Sergei asked.

'I need to sleep.'

'Oh come on, you can sleep when you are dead. We need to party,' Sergei answered.

———

'D'you know, the whole time I was doing Zumba, that Sergei was checking out my arse! I mean, you'd think he'd never seen someone shake their arse before, the way his eyes were out on stalks. And *this* is a Zumba *instructor*!' Lacey opened the door to Aphrodite 177.

'You *were* flirting with him,' Ellen remarked. She gave a soft sigh and trailed into the room behind her sister, dumping her bag on the floor.

'What? I was what now?'

'I said you were flirting with him. Every time you did a turn, you shook your arse in his face.' She flopped down onto her bed.

The sun had been relentless all day. As they were on a Greek island she should have expected it but she hadn't been abroad since ... Majorca. Bloody Majorca! She kicked the foot of the bed and her flip-flop fell to the tiles.

'Flirting with *him*! *He* was flirting with *me*! He obviously doesn't know I'm an engaged woman!' Lacey fanned a hand at her throat.

'No, probably because you didn't tell him and because you're not wearing your engagement ring.' Ellen sat up, her brow creasing in suspicion. 'You're not wearing your ring. *Why* aren't you wearing your ring?'

'It's being sized,' Lacey replied, not missing a beat.

'Sized? You've had it over a year.'

'I did that cabbage diet. It took ounces off my fingers.'

Ellen watched her sister's expression in the mirror. She saw the doe eyes, the nervous tilt of her head and the lump moving up and down in her throat as she swallowed. Lacey was a terrible liar and this was it. This was the moment Ellen had been half-expecting for months now. Lacey was wearing the same expression she had worn at the castle in Kent when the curator had wanted to talk dates. She had dismissed the look then, put it down to tiredness, being overwhelmed, Mark not being there … but here it was again. Lacey was having doubts about this marriage.

'What's going on?' Ellen rasped.

'Nothing's going on. The ring's being sized. Serg the Perv was letching over my arse and that's it, end of story.' The answer had come a little too quickly.

Ellen leapt to her feet and grabbed at something on the dressing table. 'Right, I'm confiscating the hair straighteners.' She strode towards the safety deposit box in the wardrobe.

'No! Ells, stop!' Lacey screamed, turning and chasing her across the room.

'Either you tell me what's going on or they're in here for the duration,' Ellen threatened. She put the appliance into the safe and hovered her hand over the keypad.

'All right! I'll tell you. Just give them back,' Lacey begged.

Her sister's voice cracked and Ellen could see there were tears threatening to spill. This was serious.

'Lacey, what is it?'

'I don't know. Just everything. I'm not … ' She shuddered. 'I'm not sure I want to get married anymore.' A tear escaped, slipping down her cheek.

For a second, Ellen couldn't speak. Her sister had said the words out loud and now it was out she couldn't really believe it was true. Lacey had been planning this wedding for over a year. They'd almost finalised the cake flavour and settled on a raisin colour for the bridesmaid dresses. She talked constantly about dressmakers, horse and cart hire, the Red Arrows doing a fly past.

'I love all the planning and we've had a blast, haven't we? There isn't a venue in the south of England we haven't visited but ...' Lacey paused. 'Well ... when I saw that platform in the sea it really made me think. This is it. Marriage is it, you know ... forever. Is that what I want?'

'But, Lace, now?' *Mother mode.* Ellen had to get into mother mode right now and make sure she said all the right things. She braced herself, sat up straight and prepared for whatever was coming next.

'That's just it. I don't know. I'm not sure.' Lacey sniffed.

'Have you said anything to Mark?' She passed over a tissue.

'What?! Are you mad? Of course I haven't said anything to Mark! How can I say anything to Mark? We're engaged and I'm out here supposedly checking out our wedding venue. I can't exactly say *hey babe, you know I'm off to Corfu to check out our wedding venue? Well actually I'm not really sure I want to get married. I'm just going for the cocktails and to check out the Zumba instructor.*'

This was really bad. 'Were you?'

'Was I what?'

'Checking out Sergei.'

'Maybe,' Lacey admitted. A loaded sigh left her lips.

'God, Lacey.'

'Yeah, I know.'

Ellen put a hand over one of Lacey's and gave it a squeeze. She mustn't judge. She mustn't tell her to buck up her ideas and she definitely mustn't tell her how lucky she was to have someone like Mark. No one wanted to hear that when they were going through a crisis. Although, right now, the thought of not having the wedding, her one distraction from the sorry state her life was in, was tilting her axis.

'I wish I was more like you, Ellen. You're sorted aren't you?'

Lacey's words put a strangle hold on her. 'Sorted' was not a word that could be used to describe her life at the moment. Her lack of response to Ross' proposal hadn't just been the end of their relationship. It had been the end of everything as she'd known it. Because when she'd said no it had all become crystal clear. Ross had never been interested in *her,* he'd only wanted what he could get from their alliance. Then when it all fell apart, he had helped himself anyway. He took the inheritance her mother had left her. The money she'd been going to use to start her own accountancy practice. And she was so mortified, so ashamed and embarrassed that she hadn't seen it coming, she had told no one.

She should have gone to the police the second she found out, but she could practically hear their words when she told them he'd had access to her account. She'd been naïve. She maybe couldn't have seen him as a life partner but she'd trusted him when it came to money. She'd had no reason not to.

'I wouldn't say I was completely sorted.' She dropped her eyes to her lap and glugged back the boulder in her throat. This was uncomfortable, dodgy terrain.

'You are. You've got your own place and a great job. You're just happy doing what you do,' Lacey continued, toying with Ellen's fingers.

'I wouldn't put it quite like that.' Her heart was already picking up speed and a vision of Milo taking an Allen key to her locked drawer flashed through her head.

If only Lacey knew she was still sitting on a bean bag she'd reclaimed from her dad's house and eating discounted food. She bought paperbacks from Scope. She wouldn't have been able to come on the holiday if her sister hadn't begged her *and* paid. She had had to sell an old mobile phone to buy her euros. Everything went on bills and credit cards. She'd cancelled Sky months ago.

'What am I going to do?' Lacey asked, her eyes widening.

'Maybe it's just pre-wedding jitters. That's quite normal. *Woman* practically has a quarterly feature on it.'

Lacey let out another sigh. 'I do *love* Mark.'

'Then what are you worried about?'

'Loving him enough, I guess. Do I love him enough?'

'Only *you* can answer that question.' Ellen stopped, realising she actually sounded like an agony column. 'But don't answer it now because I've got a stinking headache.'

'I have a cure for that,' Lacey leant down and produced a bottle from her bag. 'It's called *ouzo*!'

'Where did you get that from?'

'Oh I got talking to that cute waiter, Spiros, the one who cleared our table at breakfast. He said he'd do Greek dancing with me tonight.'

Greek dancing. With the hot Bulgarian animator Ellen insulted every time she opened her mouth. Maybe he would smash a plate over her head while he had the opportunity. She really needed a refresher on her people skills as well as everything else connected with interaction. Here, she felt like she'd spent the past year in a nuclear bunker. When had she got so completely self-absorbed?

'So, have you done *any* wedding planning while you've been here?' Ellen asked.

'I asked Spiros about table covers and napkins. Here, *yamas!*' Lacey toasted, raising the bottle.

And there she was. Her sister, marriage concerns forgotten about thanks to a Greek aperitif. If all life's worries could be washed down so easily, she'd be up for a bucketful.

SIX

He spoke Bulgarian, some English and German, but Yan still couldn't get all the moves right in the children's disco. He loved the children. Like the children he'd helped in his village, their infectious nature and enthusiasm made everything a little better. But dance wasn't really his thing. He preferred sports, games, something with a purpose. Dance was just moving with no winner at the end. He liked there to be a point to things. A goal. Just like in life.

It was thankfully the last song and tonight he wasn't performing. For the Greek night there was a professional band of dancers. The animation team just had to introduce the act and stay visible, encouraging holidaymakers to participate.

He'd seen Ellen and her sister sit at a table about ten minutes earlier. She'd looked over at the stage before choosing a seat. Now she was crossing and uncrossing her legs, fidgeting on the chair and ripping up a serviette. Not relaxed. Her mind obviously somewhere else. This feeling he could relate to.

———

'Oh my days, have you seen Serg the Perv? He's wearing a magician's suit! What does he look like?!' Lacey exclaimed, putting a hand over her mouth and belly-laughing.

'He's entertaining the children. What did you expect him to be wearing? More Lycra?'

'Now that's an idea.'

Ellen wasn't looking at Sergei in his pink, star-emblazoned cloak, she was watching Yan. He looked uncomfortable. His eyes were trained on Sergei, copying his every move like a shadow, trying to keep pace. Despite his garish trousers, green t-shirt and red nose, she still found herself checking out the way his top rode up a little as he moved. She swallowed. What was she doing? Checking people out was Lacey's department. But he *was* nice. Attractive, despite the clown clothes.

'What was his name again? The one you thought was going to rob us?' Lacey spluttered, briefly removing the straw from her mouth.

'Yan … I think. I don't really need to remember the name of the animation guy.' Even if she was ogling his athletic form every chance she got.

'Oh yes, Yan. He has gorgeous eyes. I remember from speaking to him at the ping pong table.'

'Have you spoken to everyone in this entire hotel already?'

'If I'm going to be having my wedding here it will pay to get to know the staff. When you make a connection with people it all helps galvanise the business relationship. I learnt that on a customer service course,' Lacey told her.

'Wow, New Style Fashion have taught you something then. What's next? Government office?'

'Don't be patronising. I'm very good at what I do. I got a woman with absolute keyboard buttons for breasts to buy one of their new Enhancer bikini tops. She said she'd never felt so good.'

'Lacey!'

'Her husband's face lit up like the Vegas strip. Ooo good, the kiddie's music has finished. D'you want another drink? What am I saying? Of course you want another drink. I'll surprise you.' Lacey got up from her chair, pulling her neon green dress back over her thong.

As soon as her sister was out of sight, Ellen grabbed into her bag for her phone. Another three missed calls and now there was a voicemail. She knew she should call, or at least listen to the message. It might have nothing to do with Mrs McGoldrick. It could be something else – something worse.

'You have to make call? You want to be at home not on holiday?'

She looked up to see Yan. The red nose had been taken off and he looked slightly less like someone who had been bouncing around to a mix of German/English/Spanish euro-pop with toddlers.

'That's a bit rude,' she answered defensively. She felt her shoulders stiffen. She didn't like his direct talk one bit.

'What is rude? That I ask you question?' His brow furrowed. 'I get to know you.'

'I'm here for my sister and, I'm enjoying myself very much if you must know.' She gripped the phone in her hand, looking at the screen out of the corner of one eye.

Yan let out a snort. A noise that seemed to say he hadn't believed Ellen's last sentence. He pulled out the chair beside her and sat down.

Right away her cheeks began heating up. What was he doing? She didn't want to talk. About anything. She wanted to listen to a message that could change the course of her life.

'I do not believe this,' Yan continued, his eyes studying her.

Ellen let out a sigh. 'What would you like me to say? It's lovely here. The scenery is beautiful, the food's great and Lacey's sampling every cocktail on the menu.'

'And you?'

He was studying her and Ellen could now see what Lacey had meant about those eyes. They were so blue, so clear and ... enchanting. She swallowed, willing her mouth into action.

'I'm fine. I just have a lot of things on my mind.' She clenched the phone even harder in her hand.

'But you enjoy the water aerobics?' he asked. The eyes were still firmly fixed on her.

'I don't know whether "enjoy" is the right word, but it definitely made me feel a lot less guilty about having two puddings at dinner.' She smiled.

———

When Ellen smiled, her eyes widened upwards and outwards revealing milk chocolate brown irises underneath thick lashes. If he was honest with himself he'd noticed her eyes in the pool earlier. Warm, no notes of the superficial like Monica. But why did that interest him? Why was her behaviour intriguing him? Because she was at odds with her surroundings? Unsettled here, like him? She didn't want his attention. That irked him even more and made him want to know what was going on with her. At that thought he felt a shot of warmth hit his cheeks.

'Yan! What's with the threads? Not a great look, I have to say. If you need any fashion tips I'm the person to speak to. I practically run my branch of New Style Fashion at home.' Lacey was back, returning to her seat with two glasses containing fluorescent-coloured liquid.

'Please don't listen to her. She's already had far too many Apricot Coolers,' Ellen interrupted.

He looked down at his bright clothes. 'This is for uniform,' Yan said.

'So, what's going down after the Greek dancing tonight? Where's the party?' Lacey asked, playing with her straw.

He watched Ellen sit back in her chair and toy with the material of her dress.

'On the beach,' said another voice.

Bouncing into the conversation, Sergei pulled up a spare chair from an adjacent table and sat down next to Lacey.

'Sergei,' Yan said. He loaded the reply with a note of warning. He knew what was coming next. Sergei had been doing this ever since Yan arrived at the hotel and probably for weeks before. Another week, another girl taken to the beach. He wasn't about to be a part of this tonight.

'What?' Sergei asked. He threw his hands up in a protestation of innocence.

'Ooo a beach party! That sounds like my sort of place. What time?' Lacey questioned, turning her attention and body to Sergei.

Lacey's interest was obvious and Yan looked to Ellen. She was shaking her head, slowly, deliberately but also resigned. As if she had been expecting the reaction.

'Sergei, you cannot ...' Yan began. He had to say something.

'Relax, Yan.' Sergei turned to Lacey. 'You can keep a secret, can't you?'

'I'm just about the most expert secret keeper I know.' Lacey giggled.

Ellen was still quiet, not saying anything, one hand tightly holding her phone in her lap.

'It's not a secret. After things close here we head to the beach for fun,' Sergei informed the pair.

Yan leaned forward on his chair and directed his gaze at his comrade. 'It is not for holidaymakers.'

'Oh relax, Yan. What is the worst that can happen?' Sergei asked him, inching his chair a little closer to Lacey's.

'*I* need this job,' Yan responded, looking over his shoulder.

——

The real concern in Yan's voice made her act. Lacey was being an over-the-top flirt and for whatever reason Yan wasn't happy with the beach party invitation situation.

'To be honest, we're still tired from the flight yesterday. We'll probably be making a move back to our room when the Greek dancing's finished.'

Ellen watched for Yan's reaction. There was none. He was still looking at Sergei.

'Are you crazy? There is no way I'm going back to our room any earlier than dawn and it's your duty to accompany me. Besides, you can't play cards on your own, you're useless at Solitaire,' Lacey announced. Her sister followed up the attempt at humour with an attention-seeking shriek of laughter.

'We must go ... see other people,' Yan said, standing up.

'Wait for me, after the dancing,' Sergei said to Lacey, locking eyes with her, his teeth reflecting in the half-light.

'Sergei,' Yan ordered roughly.

Lacey waved her fingers at the departing Zumba instructor and then turned back to her cocktail.

Ellen gritted her teeth. 'He looks like Mateo from *Benidorm* and you are *not* going anywhere with him.'

SEVEN

Yan couldn't concentrate. He stood with his back to the bar watching the musicians set up on stage, his every ion tense. He tried to dispel it, look at ease. Sergei was an idiot. His lack of restraint with women was going to get them both in trouble and he didn't need that. It was fine for Sergei. He didn't have to pin his whole life on this one opportunity. If Sergei lost this job, there would be others for him. If *he* slipped up there would be no second chances.

But he didn't want to keep running forever. He wanted this fresh beginning in Corfu to be a stepping stone. Once he had the means, he could look into a new venture, like trying to recreate what he'd had in the village back home. But until that time, he had to do good work here, for both the money and the experience.

'Here, lemon and lime.' Sergei passed him a plastic cup filled with white fizzy liquid.

'What is this?' Yan took the cup but looked up, questioning.

'I tell you, lemon and lime.' Sergei held his hands up. 'Just lemon and lime, I swear.'

'You should not invite girl to beach.'

'Oh relax, you think too much of everything.' Sergei slapped his back. 'We're here for another *three* months, Yan.'

'And you have girl back home,' he hissed. He did not share Sergei's philosophy that whatever happened in Corfu stayed there. It was dishonest and it didn't sit well with him.

'Yes and when I return, all will be well. But until then...' Sergei began.

'Until then what? It is OK to ... п р а в и с е к с with girl?' The use of his native language would surely make Sergei realise he was serious.

'Whoa, whoa, whoa. No one say anything about sex.' Sergei held his hands up again.

'You do not need to,' he answered flatly. 'It is written all on your face.'

—

'You're not going to be a party pooper the whole week, are you?'

Lacey asked the question as Ellen was swirling her straw around in yet another brightly coloured cocktail. It wasn't anything like fine wine but it was hitting the spot. She'd been gazing out from the entertainment arena at the arrival of the Greek *bouzouki* players and the dancers. The women were wearing brightly coloured dresses with underskirts, elaborate hats with lace, flowers and gold beading. The men were in black trousers, white shirts and waistcoats with red cummerbunds. So much tradition.

She turned to Lacey. 'There isn't meant to be any party. You're supposed to be planning a wedding. Isn't there meant to be a hotel wedding coordinator?' Ellen snapped the question out like an angry shark.

She understood that Lacey was having jitters about the wedding but exactly how unsure was she? As much as the marriage chat got on her nerves she'd rather her sister was talking about that than a beach party with someone from animation. The wedding was real. It was something written in ink in her paper diary and marked out as 'busy' on her iPhone. A booked, not-to-be-changed window.

'I saw her at lunch. She looked a bit odd,' Lacey said.

'What?'

'She had a moustache.'

'Oh, Lacey.'

'What?! I'm not having my wedding organised by a woman who thinks it's acceptable to have a moustache!' Lacey exclaimed, poking out her tongue.

'It's any excuse, isn't it?' Ellen swiped up her drink.

'No. Of course it isn't,' Lacey insisted. 'You need another drink. I'll go and get one.' She rose from her chair.

'I don't need another drink. I need you to be honest with me about this wedding. About your obvious need to go partying with Mr Zumba.'

This was much more than pre-wedding nerves. It wasn't just the look at the castle in Kent, or the not wearing the engagement ring, Ellen also knew it wasn't the first time Lacey had lapsed. And that had never been addressed either.

'I just want to have some fun.' Lacey slumped down into her seat.

'That's fine, but I'm concerned about the need to have fun with someone like Sergei.'

'He's different and he makes me laugh.'

'He's on holiday for six months of the year. He's well-practised at making people do lots of things.'

'I just want to ... let loose, you know. Be free for a bit.' Lacey chewed on her straw.

'I'm not sure I like the sound of that.'

'I love Mark but you know what he's like. It's golf this and used cars that. Sergei, he likes the same music as me and he listens when I talk.'

Ellen picked up the far-away look in her eye. This was bad. 'Raining attention on people is Sergei's job, Lace.'

'I know that and it doesn't matter. Because I don't want to *marry* Sergei. I just want to ...' Lacey started.

'I don't think I want to know.' Ellen was milliseconds away from clamping her hands over her ears. Lacey was a livewire, but she and Mark as a couple had always been solid. Well, apart from the one faux-pas she knew about. What if that wasn't all? What if there were other episodes she didn't know about?

'I want to know he isn't what I want and that Mark is,' her sister blurted out.

'Oh Lacey, that's a dangerous game to play on holiday.' Ellen let out a sigh.

'But it shouldn't be, should it? Not if Mark's the one. It shouldn't be dangerous at all, that's the whole point,' Lacey confessed.

'You're testing yourself for no reason. And I've seen his dark eyes and those moves. Put it this way, if you were on a diet you wouldn't walk up and down the street past McDonalds would you?' *A food analogy.* She was really scraping the barrel.

'I probably would,' Lacey answered.

'Look, the Greek dancing's about to start. We'll watch that, have a few more drinks and then we'll go back to the room.' If she kept Lacey away from temptation then nothing would happen. But should she really have to shut her in their suite playing card games to stop her being unfaithful?

'What? Before midnight? Ells! We're on holiday!'

'I know, but ...'

'Come with me.' Lacey's eyes widened and got dewy. 'Come with me to the party on the beach. You could get along with that Yan.'

Get along with? What did that mean? She didn't like the tone the three words were spoken in. It almost sounded like Lacey wanted to pair her off with a random man just so she was occupied and not paying attention to her activities.

'*I* wasn't invited,' Ellen reminded.

'*I'm* inviting you.'

She shook her head. This wasn't fair. Double bolting their room and keeping Lacey entertained with the mini-bar was one thing, to attend something they really weren't wanted at, to stop her from cheating on her fiancé was quite another.

'I think you need to talk to Mark. It's not vital this wedding happens yet. You could take a step back. It isn't like you've made any final decisions on anything. We've had nothing back from the Red Arrows,' Ellen said.

'I can't talk to him. Not from here – not now.'

Ellen felt the apprehension in her sister's words. 'Why not?'

'I just can't.' Lacey stood up. 'I'm getting another drink.'

Before Ellen had a chance to think any more about her sister's predicament, her iPhone began to ring. The Lassiter's logo flashed up and she swallowed. The office – at six thirty UK time – this wasn't good. She looked at the icon, flashing brighter then darker, brighter, then darker. She inched her hand nearer to the phone, her fingers hovering over the 'answer' key.

'*Oopa!*'

The loud male voice shouting into the microphone had her nudging the table in reaction. The phone signalled a missed call and she slouched back down, waiting for the red spot that meant more voicemail.

There it was. Another message she should really listen to but couldn't. *Breathe. Float down into a calm bubble.* It had to be about Mrs McGoldrick's accounts. All she needed to do was call the office and tell Milo to get it done. One little phone call. He didn't need to go into her desk. It was locked and she had the key. There was nothing to worry about. There was no way in the world anyone could know she had embezzled funds from Keegan Manufacturing.

'Hi, hi, hi! *Kalispera!* I am Dasha, new in animation. Are you having good time?'

Ellen jumped, looked up, then up some more. Dasha was well over six feet tall and was dressed in drag. A tight black mini-skirt teamed with a bright yellow vest top. The whole ensemble was set off by a feather boa in pink and a broom he was treating like a microphone.

'You dance the Greek with me?' Dasha said, taking hold of her arm.

'No thank you. I actually have a bad ankle,' she responded. Trust this to happen when she had been on the very verge of taking charge.

His strength pulled her instantly from her seat.

'Dance is good exercise! Come!' He vaulted towards another table, taking a vice-like grip on a woman's arm. 'Hi, hi, hi! Come for dancing!'

As with Lacey, it was going to be easier to just give in.

EIGHT

As he watched her, Yan could almost feel it from across the room. Ellen was smiling, her lips parted, her mouth wide and up-turned. It was like she'd been transformed by the *bouzouki* music. Her cheeks were flushed too, a reddish hue with a sheen to her skin, from the humidity of the evening and, he expected, from the exertion of the Greek dancing. Yan clapped his hands together in time to the beat and prepared to encourage more dancers to join the group on stage.

He liked Greek night. Everyone got involved, all worries were forgotten and, if you got the steps wrong, no one cared. You all whooped and fell about and started all over again. If only life were like that. Everything in this world had turned so solitary. Insular. He *would not* live that way. He would recreate the security he'd had back in his home village somehow.

'I think you owe me a dance.'

Monica was at his shoulder, a tight, white dress hugging her every curve and her wavy, black hair sat on her shoulders.

'I ...'

'I insist.' Monica took his hand, giving him no choice.

Caught in a position he didn't want to be in. It was becoming all too familiar.

—

'That Dasha is just hilarious, isn't he?' Lacey tightened her hold on Ellen's waist and joined in with the Conga-style line.

'I'm not sure about that. He has a death grip when he wants you to do something. Where did he come from?' she asked.

'Bulgaria. They're all from Bulgaria. I don't think there can be very many people left there if they're all in animation.'

'Listen, Lace, about the party ...' Ellen started.

'It's going to be great. I told Dasha we were going and he squealed like a girl and rubbed my cheeks with his hands.'

'Please tell me you're talking about your face.'

'He's my new BFF,' Lacey announced.

'You've known him two songs.'

'Friendships are formed so much quicker over here. I like that continental attitude.'

Ellen moved around the corner of the stage and caught sight of Yan joining the line. Monica was clutching his hand, a pout on her lips that hinted at possession. Ellen's eyes met with Yan's and she swallowed. Perhaps it was possession. If Sergei's actions were anything to go by there was a lot of free love to be had at the Blue Vue Hotel, perhaps Yan wasn't fussy about age gaps.

'Will you look at her in the white dress? Rough as.' Lacey nodded in Monica's direction.

Ellen opened her mouth to launch into a not-judging-a-book-by-its-cover speech but closed it up again. Sometimes it wasn't appropriate to be nice. And Lacey was right. The dress was far too tight and far too young for Monica. Not that Yan seemed to care.

Ellen shook her head, diverting her attention back to the professional dancers who were trying hard to get the stage full of residents swaying in time to the *bouzouki* music. Monica clamped her hands onto Ellen's hips, joining the line.

'I love to dance,' the woman declared, letting out a whoop and digging her nails into Ellen's skin.

She glanced over her shoulder and caught Yan's eye. He smiled at her and she quickly turned back around.

'So, what's the real reason you don't want to go to the party?' Lacey called over the music.

'You might not care about gate-crashing something, but I do.'

'Are you worried you might actually enjoy yourself, Mum?'

'What did you call me?'

'You need to chill out, Ells. I appreciate all the big sister love and advice and everything, but you don't have to be the grown-up all the time. In fact I don't *want* you to be.' Lacey ended the sentence with a shout as she turned the corner and fell off her shoe.

Ellen held her tongue. Lacey had no idea. It wasn't that she *wanted* to be her mother-figure. There wasn't a queue forming or an audition process with people eager to fill the position. Not even Margarette had wanted *that* responsibility and she'd gone through the whole labour thing.

At the root of the swaddling was Ellen's love for her father. His life had been one long line of let downs on the personal front. She would always pick up the slack, keep things on an even keel. Al was proud of her. He had always beamed with admiration at her every achievement. She didn't want to let him down.

Ellen swallowed. He wouldn't be so proud if he learnt she'd used her intelligence to pilfer funds from her ex-boyfriend's business.

She steadied Lacey as they turned another corner on the dancefloor, her mind at odds with the tempo of the *bouzouki* player.

After Ross had taken her money and she'd just about picked herself up off the floor, she had got a job at the firm that handled his business accounts. Over the past few months she'd used every piece of accounting know-how she possessed to divert funds, to get her revenge. She wanted to make sure he paid for every penny he'd taken from her and suffered the same kind of humiliation. Some days she knew she'd made poor choices, other days the satisfaction of payback made her grin evilly like a Bond villain. Right now, the Corfiot air felt stifling. Keeping secrets was exhausting.

'So, d'you fancy that Yan, or what?' Lacey shouted.

Ellen felt the temperature rise even more and her cheeks heated up as her sister gave an elaborate wink and hitched her head back towards Yan. Subtle as a breeze block.

'Are you joking? He thinks I'm miserable and haven't the first clue how to have fun at an all-inclusive resort.' And he was right but she wasn't ever going to admit that.

'You just told me why *he* couldn't possibly fancy *you*. So you *do* fancy him! I knew it. He's just your type,' Lacey exclaimed.

'What? My *type*? I don't have a type!'

'Still not hearing you don't fancy him!'

Ellen sighed. Men were categorically off her agenda. She'd well and truly learnt her lesson. Her mission back home with the disappearing money was almost complete and after that she was going to re-evaluate, re-carpet the living room and buy back her jewellery. The only dates she had planned involved whatever Freeview had to offer and Ben & Jerry's.

She wiggled her hips out of Monica's grip. 'I'm going to sit down.'

'You mustn't break the line, it's bad luck,' Lacey yelled.

'What?'

'It's true, I read it in a guide book. If you break the Greek dancing line your life is blighted by a thousand curses from Aphrodite,' Lacey insisted.

'She was the goddess of love.'

'Well, maybe it wasn't her. Who's the scary-looking one with the beard?'

'Gandalf?'

'Oh, whoever it is, it's bad luck. Keep in line!' Lacey ordered.

—

Monica kept adjusting his hands every time he moved them up and away from her hips. He wanted the music to stop now. All he wanted to do was get back to his room and have a try at sleeping. He wasn't in the mood for drinking and having Sergei's type of fun.

'So, I'm only here for three more nights.' Monica twisted her head to look up at him. 'I think it's time I got to know you a whole lot better.'

'I am Yan, from Bulgaria. I speak some English and German, a little Russian,' he responded quickly.

'A run-down of your linguistic achievements wasn't exactly what I had in mind.' She licked her lips. 'Zeus 202 in half an hour. Don't be late.' She batted her heavily made-up eyelashes.

Before Yan could open his mouth to reply, Monica had shimmied out of the line and made her way down from the stage and back towards her table.

They didn't teach you how to politely decline direct propositions at animation training. And he wasn't sure whether he had the patience for polite with Monica. She was another woman with money who wanted to use him. Maybe he didn't want to go to the beach party with Sergei but he definitely needed a drink now.

Without thinking any further, he put his hands on Ellen's hips and closed up the line.

—

A new sensation on her hips, a touch much firmer but not altogether unpleasant made Ellen look around. Here she was again, eye to eye with someone so good-looking he could be model material. A man who seemed to find it amusing to question her behaviour. Someone Lacey wanted to hook her up with.

He spoke. 'You dance very well.'

'Is that a joke?' Ellen shot back.

'A joke?'

'I was man-handled by a cross-dresser and made to join in.'

'You would like to be sat back at table poking screen of your phone?' he asked.

It was annoying to have someone insult you when you were facing away from them. It was even more annoying when the person seemed to have you completely sussed from a few brief encounters.

'You should come ... to the party on beach,' he called.

'The party you don't want residents to go to?'

She felt his breath on the back of her neck as it released from his chest. In a second her spine was zinging.

'You look like you need fun,' came his reply.

'Really? I thought I looked like someone who had no idea how to enjoy herself on holiday.'

And then he laughed. A deep, chocolate-coated, full-bodied roll of a laugh that came from the depths of him. Her comment hadn't been that funny. And she'd only made it because she was sick of him making close-to-the-mark remarks about her every vacation enjoyment.

'Come to beach and I will forget you think I am thief when we first meet,' he remarked.

Ouch. She really had insulted him with her desperation to anchor down their luggage when they'd arrived.

'I even stop telling you about your frown face,' he added.

Ellen moved her mouth subconsciously. Was it on a permanent downward slant here too? She turned her head to look at him.

'One drink and no stupid animation games.'

NINE

Bo's Bar was only about a hundred yards from the Blue Vue Hotel. It was a one level building, open on three sides with pop hits blasting out from speakers positioned around the main room. Lacey and Ellen had taken a table in the centre and were halfway down a cocktail each. Despite the noise in the bar, there were actually very few customers. A couple of old men with a dog sat in wicker easy-chairs by the entrance and a twenty-something girl and boy were entwined in each other's arms on a corner sofa.

'Totally loved-up,' Lacey remarked, her eyes on the same thing as Ellen.

'Yeah.' Ellen couldn't take her eyes from them as the drum and bass pulsed through her body. Either drunk or very much in love, their passion was evident and something in Ellen reacted to the scene. Just how did that feel? To be caught up with someone so intensely the world could stop turning and you wouldn't know?

As the track changed to something by Ed Sheeran she noticed Sergei, Dasha and Yan enter the building.

Ellen stuck her face into her cocktail glass and watched as they went to the bar.

Lacey propped her elbows on the table and rested her head on her hands. 'Sergei's certainly scrubbed up well.'

Ellen closed her eyes. What was she doing here? Why had she gone against everything she knew was sensible and accompanied

Lacey on this man-fishing expedition? Lacey was engaged and *she* didn't want anyone.

———

'I get us some drinks here and then we go to the beach,' Sergei said, beckoning the barman.

Yan had noticed Ellen the second they'd walked in. She was sitting on a high stool, her long wavy hair loose, her legs bent up, feet on the footrest, stirring her straw in a cocktail. He saw her look at her watch. Was she bored with attempting to have fun already? Did she want to be somewhere else? Was she waiting for him? The last thought did something to him. He looked away and took some peanuts out of the dish on the bar.

He wasn't sure why he'd asked Ellen to come tonight. But he did know he wasn't going to stay back at the hotel and wait for Monica to realise he wasn't coming to her room. She might have started a search to find him and he didn't want to take any chances. But why ask Ellen here? A distraction. That was the answer. She was a distraction from everything else that was going on in his life. He could be distracted as long as it wasn't in the same league as Sergei.

'Yan, beer,' Sergei said, passing him a bottle. 'Everyone, let's go to the beach.'

He accepted the drink and lifted it to his lips.

———

Even in the dark of the night, the beach was stunning. Tealight candles were glowing on half a dozen tables set up just before the water's edge, creating a warm, hazy atmosphere across the sand.

A makeshift bar was being erected out of beer barrels and planks of wood, underneath two large palm canopies.

As Ellen followed the party she recognised a lot of people from the hotel. The restaurant manager was jigging up and down using a chair as a dance partner, three or four waiters were there, a couple of women who worked in reception, bar staff, the man she'd seen cleaning the pool. It was beach party central for employees of the Blue Vue Hotel.

'Ellen!' Sergei called.

She looked across, saw Sergei and Yan sat at a table. And where was Lacey when she needed her? One shriek later and she saw her, a little way away, performing a dance routine to Pitbull with Dasha.

'Come! Come sit down!' Sergei beckoned.

Kicking off her sandals, she made her way over to them. The second she got near she noticed the bottle of *ouzo* and three plastic cups. She put her shoes on the ground and sat down in a chair. She eyed the Greek drink like it was a hazardous substance. Or contained Rohypnol.

'It was so hot today and I am so tired,' Sergei said, pouring alcohol out for each of them.

'I get some lemon and lime,' Yan offered, making to leave.

'What for? Come on, a couple of *ouzos* and we'll all start to unwind,' Sergei insisted.

Sergei held a cup out to Ellen. She hesitated as a memory came to the fore. Neat alcohol, not out of a plastic cup, but out of her 'Accountants never die, they just lose their balance' mug back home. Morning drinking for a week at her lowest ebb. That was rock bottom. Alcohol past midnight in a plastic beaker was positive sanity. She took the cup.

'*Yamas!*' Yan said. He raised his cup, knocking it with Sergei's before downing the drink in one.

Ellen threw the drink down and let the burn travel across her tongue to the back of her throat. It would probably eat away at her stomach lining but wasn't that supposed to be good every now and then? Cleansing – a kind of Greek detox. *Ouzo* had to be better for her than Aldi's own brand whisky.

'I see Dasha is getting into party spirit.' Sergei rolled his eyes towards his colleague.

Ellen turned to see Lacey and Dasha pumping their arms in the air in time to the music.

'He is OK. I meet him at training. He is hard working.' Yan poured the three of them another drink.

'Did you all train together? Is there some big animation school?' Ellen asked.

'We do training, we come together, then we get teams and hotels,' Yan explained.

'So, is this what you want to do? As a career?' She was wide-eyed with interest. She didn't dare not get involved with conversation when her habitual email refreshing would be scrutinised by Yan.

Sergei let out a loud laugh and poured more drink into his cup. 'Shit, no! I don't know what I want to do yet. I am only twenty-three years old. I am too young to know what I want to do for career.'

'I like to work with children,' Yan broke in. 'Maybe with sport. Football or swim. I do this before, in Bulgaria.'

'Pa!' Sergei exclaimed. 'You want to work with children all the time? One afternoon of kids' club is too much for me. Paint on their hands … they scream … they make mess.'

—

Yan swallowed. Perhaps admitting that in front of everyone here was a mistake. The fewer people that knew about him, the better. The more information you gave people the more they had to hurt you with later.

He looked at Ellen then, unsure of her reaction. Would she think it was mad? That someone who organised water aerobics and crazy competitions could be entrusted with the care of children. That he had the ability to achieve it.

'I think working with children is one of the toughest jobs there is. You have to have so many attributes to make a success of it,' Ellen spoke. 'Getting English tourists to play games is great practice for it.' She smiled.

He fixed his eyes on her, waiting for the 'but', the hint that she was saying what she thought she should, not what she felt. There was nothing else. Just warmth and honesty in her tone.

———

'I think you all work so very hard. I don't know where you get the energy from,' Ellen said.

'From *ouzo* of course,' Sergei announced. Laughing, he knocked back another drink.

'We do not drink *ouzo* for all of the time. We drink much water in the day,' Yan added.

'Who's for something else? Metaxa cocktail?' Sergei offered, standing up.

'Not for me thank you,' Ellen said. The *ouzo* was already taking effect; mixing mysterious Greek drinks together so rapidly was going to be buying a first-class ticket to the hangover from hell.

'Is good ... we have one,' Yan said, nodding in suggestion.

Live a little. Baby steps. Small risks. 'Maybe just a tiny one,' she agreed.

TEN

Sergei left them and made his way over to the bar. Ellen adjusted her dress, crossing her legs and leaning back into the sun chair, the strong beat of Rihanna coming from the sound system. The *ouzo* had made her feel just a little bit blurry around the edges and it was nice. Here she was, on a beach on a beautiful island, drinking after midnight, thousands of miles away from every problem she'd ever had.

'What do you do for job?' Yan asked.

The bright blue eyes were studying her and she moved a little before answering. Ellen cleared her throat. 'I'm an accountant.' She followed the statement up with a deep sigh.

It was only after her elongated noise of discontent that she realised Yan was looking a little blank.

'An accountant.' She stopped to think of other words and a better description. 'It means I help people with their finance.' He looked none the wiser. 'Their money. Taxes?' she offered, slowing her speech a little.

'Ah, the bad people.' He nodded his head.

'Oh no, not the Revenue. I try to help people avoid giving them too much.' Laughing, she shook her head. 'I like my job, well …' She paused. 'I'm good at what I do.'

What did she really mean? She liked it? She *used* to like it? She wanted it back? She cleared her throat.

'You are … how you say … very intelligent,' Yan concluded, an air of finality in his tone.

'I wouldn't say that exactly. These days everything's computerised. I just have to load the figures into the program and it's done,' she told him.

It was only at that point she noticed Lacey next to her chair.

'She's lying her arse off. Not only is she clever, she got a hundred percent in her final exams. A hundred percent. That's not even a full stop out of place! And she won South Wiltshire Business Woman of the Year.' Lacey plonked a cocktail glass onto the table.

'Lacey...' Ellen's face was alight with embarrassment. She really didn't want to be clever here. Clever sounded logical and boring. It wasn't laid-back and fun. It was everything Yan thought of her already, stiff, grumpy, English. She hiccuped.

'It is good job,' Yan replied, nodding his head.

It didn't sound like he really meant it and for the first time she wished Lacey was ensconced somewhere with Sergei and not butting herself into the conversation.

'Ellen was headhunted for the job she does now at Lassiter's. She was made an offer she couldn't refuse,' Lacey carried on, pursing her lips around the straw.

Ellen had no idea how to salvage this other than to press on. Ever since she had met this man she'd humiliated him – all but called him a bag snatcher, offered him money which he found offensive and said she hated his water aerobics.

'Listen, I think animation is so much more interesting and you get to travel, to see the world.'

The words had supposed to come out heartfelt, firm and encouraging. Instead, the tone she'd nailed was patronising.

'Oh yeah, animation is far more interesting. I'd much rather be dancing than adding up. But the clown suit would have to go.' Lacey cackled.

'I find Sergei.' Yan stood up.

'He's by the bar. See you in a bit,' Lacey said, waving her hand.

Ellen watched Yan walk across the sand, away from her and towards a collection of good-looking women at the bar. One put an arm around his shoulders and whispered something in his ear. Ellen turned away but a bubble of anger was rising in her as Lacey threw herself down on a chair next to her, all legs and high shoes.

'I wish you wouldn't do that,' Ellen hissed. She took a large swig of her drink and put the plastic cup down with such a thump the bottom crumpled.

'Do what?'

'You were boasting about me.'

'I don't know what you're talking about.'

'He was asking about my job and you made out I was the female equivalent of Stephen Hawking.' She spat the words out.

'Well, you sell yourself short.'

'I wasn't selling myself at all.' She narrowed her eyes at her sister. 'I was just talking and you ruined it. How was he supposed to tell me about *his* job when you've just depicted me as the next big financial aficionado? Like, I don't know, Lord Sugar with breasts!'

'We know about his job. He dresses as a clown and counts to three in four different languages.'

'And there's *nothing* wrong with that!' She stood up in a rush, planting her feet firmly on the sand, hands on hips.

'What?' Lacey had a childish, bemused expression on her face she always wore when she was being deliberately stupid. Ellen didn't want to look at it a second longer.

She left, on shaking legs, heading off towards the bar in search of the brandy cocktail she'd been promised, or anything else that was going to help her forget everything. It was always about Lacey. Lacey had to be the centre of attention. Bigging up Ellen's achievements wasn't for Ellen's benefit, it was for Lacey's. *Look at me! I have a clever sister!* The reality was she had a spineless, pathetic, sister who was fighting hard to retain her dignity, working a pointless job and trying to work out what to do next. A fist-sized lump arrived in her throat and no amount of swallowing was getting rid of it. Before she was truly aware of it, she was clinging to a parasol, tears rolling down her face.

———

He should have guessed she was intelligent. Most of the women who came to the five star resort were smart. They were either rich or successful of their own making or they had rich, successful husbands. Why did it worry him? Because it brought it all back. The beautiful woman he'd fallen for. The one person he'd put his trust in. And the man who'd treated him like a son until he had expressed an opinion, stood up for what he believed in.

He took another *ouzo* down in one and turned away from the bar. On instinct he looked for her. Lacey and Dasha were standing on a bench, practicing balancing. Ellen was clinging to a beach umbrella, tears rushing down her cheeks. Something in him stirred. What could be so wrong in her life that she was crying on a beach in Corfu?

He turned back to the bar and ordered another drink. It was not his place. She was not his business.

ELEVEN

'I have crazy golf score card and drinking straw ... no napkin,' Yan said.

The deep baritone jolted her and Ellen sniffed loudly. Before she could stop herself she'd wiped at her nose with her bare arm.

'Go away,' she said, as firmly as her tear-coated voice would allow. She cleared her throat and shifted her stance, standing up straight and feigning emotional maturity.

'I could get napkin,' Yan offered.

'No, it's OK. I'm fine. It's definitely the *ouzo* not me.'

'You would like more?' he asked.

'No, I don't think so. But, thank you.' The damn tears weren't going away, no matter how hard she blinked.

'Some lemon and lime?' he offered.

'Don't be kind. Us Brits don't like it. We're copers.' She gave him the best smile she could muster. 'Honestly, I'm fine.'

Even to herself she sounded slightly unhinged. And now he was just looking at her, probably not understanding the word 'coper', and wishing he'd never invited her to the party.

'I should probably round Lacey up and go back to the hotel,' Ellen said, shifting her feet on the sand.

'It is early,' Yan stated.

Ellen looked at her watch.

'In a few moments there will be limbo. Is fun,' he added.

'It sounds difficult.'

'I teach you. Come on, one more drink,' he suggested, nodding his head towards the bar.

Ellen looked at her watch again, then focussed her gaze on Lacey and Dasha, their arms stretched outwards, balancing on the narrow bench and squealing like girls.

'Just one more drink, but not *ouzo*.'

Right on cue, from by the bar, Sergei held aloft an umbrella-festooned drink and beckoned them over.

———

'Come on, Dasha, let's get this limbo started,' Lacey said, pulling the man up from his seat by his feather boa.

'We need people to join in. Come on everybody!' Dasha announced.

Ellen looked to Sergei as Lacey led the way to where other members of staff were setting up a frame and canes on the sand. His expression gave away all his intentions towards her sister. Before she could think any more she was talking.

'Lacey's getting married. That's why we're here.' It was best he knew the score now. There was no place for him in her sister's life.

Both men looked at her as if waiting for more detail. Perhaps 'married' wasn't a universal word. Sergei's teeth disappeared behind tight lips.

'Um, married, you know. Matrimony, a wedding,' she attempted to translate.

'We know what you speak of,' Yan told her, his response stiff.

That announcement had somehow killed the atmosphere completely. A wedding was supposed to be an occasion filled with joy and happiness, a mention of it shouldn't have people looking into their cocktail glasses not knowing what to say next.

'So, she's having it here, I think. At the Blue Vue Hotel,' Ellen finished up.

Yan nodded and picked up his glass.

———

A wedding. Someone else planning an event to start the beginning of a new future. His stomach turned and it was nothing to do with the alcohol he'd consumed. He'd given Rayna a ring, promised her forever, before he had known exactly what her father's business was. He swallowed back a mouthful of bile. This was why he was single and looking to stay that way. It wasn't just the rules of his job, it was self-preservation.

'Her fiancé's called Mark. He's really nice. He sells cars,' Ellen continued.

'She did not say she have a wedding,' Sergei said.

Yan wanted the wedding talk to stop. He looked over to the limbo, trying to ignore the ugly feeling rising up in him. It was stupid. He couldn't have a physical reaction every time someone mentioned a wedding, or whenever he saw a couple in a happy relationship. He needed to strengthen up in these scenarios, instead of letting his mind wander back to somewhere he really didn't want to be.

'Are you OK?' Ellen asked.

He turned to her, saw the expression on her face. He realised then he had crushed the plastic cup in his hands, splitting it in half.

'I am OK.' He stood up quickly.

'Limbo, baby! We start!' Dasha locked his arms around Yan's waist.

———

The limbo appeared as natural as walking to the workforce of the hotel. Their chests flattened, their backs bowed and contorted until they slipped under the pole with ease.

Ellen was going to do her very best not to make a complete idiot out of herself. She could do this. She was flexible. She'd done yoga, proper yoga, before she'd cancelled the classes. The teacher had said her cow was one of the best she'd seen.

She glanced over at Lacey. Her sister was sharing yet another cocktail with Dasha. One of two things would happen in this upcoming situation; either Lacey would be an expert at limbo and win, or she would be useless and not care. Either way, yoga or no yoga, Lacey would be more of a success than Ellen.

'I think I'll sit this out. You know games aren't really my thing,' she stated, turning to Yan.

'Sit out?'

'Yes, sit down. Not take part. No limbo.'

'No?'

'No.' That had sounded forceful. She hoped she hadn't offended a Bulgarian national pastime.

'You would rather look to your phone or read giant book?' Yan asked.

'Some people might think your knowledge of my behaviour was almost stalking,' she responded.

'I do not understand what you say.' He looked at her. 'I see you roll from one side of lounger to the other many, many times. Then put book down, pick up phone, drink cocktail, get mad with sister …'

'And here I was thinking you actually paid attention to those stupid games you organise.'

'They are stupid? Because you do not want to do them? Many people enjoy this.'

Another insult had managed to fire out of her mouth without her even realising it. But he had started it, commenting on her every move. Just because she wasn't coated in coconut oil, fanned out in a star position facing the sun, unmoving until her bladder needed release, it didn't mean she wasn't having fun.

'Limbo is fun. We do together.' He reached for her hand.

The contact took her by surprise but she didn't have time to think about it. He interlocked their fingers and tugged her out of her seat.

———

A woman Ellen recognised from clearing tables at the hotel restaurant bent herself almost parallel to the sand and flicked herself up with style to rapturous applause. Ellen might be able to get herself down into a crescent lunge but this looked more like medieval torture.

'I'm going to look stupid. I'll make *you* look stupid.'

Yan smiled and shrugged. 'I dress in clown suit for my job.' He laughed and tightened his grip on her hand. 'I know all of stupid.'

'OK! Now we have current limbo champion, Yan from Bulgaria and from England ... Miss Ellie,' Sergei announced.

How did this happen? Now she was going to be humiliated *and* sound like a character from *Dallas*. *And* Yan had neglected to mention that he wasn't just good, but brilliant.

'Lower the bar,' Yan told Sergei.

'You want to start lower?'

'Sure.'

'Is that such a good idea? I mean this is my first time ...' she reminded him. Paranoid about making an arse of herself and a limbo virgin – this whole thing was not boding well.

'Lower the bar,' Yan repeated.

Sergei and Dasha moved the pole until it was resting only two feet from the sand.

'I can't do this. Look at it,' Ellen said. She could feel the muscles in her back tightening as every second ticked by.

Lacey started to chant like a stand of football supporters. 'Ellen ... Ellen ... Ellen ...'

'Hold my hand. Don't let go,' Yan instructed.

With her sister whipping the group up into a frenzy and their encouragement ringing in her ears, Ellen stepped towards the pole.

The music was turned up louder, something by Shaggy kicked in and before Ellen could think about it anymore, Yan was pulling her downwards. She inhaled and willed her body to move in ways she'd only ever asked it to move to the sound of whale song. The pole was close. She was nowhere near low enough. She knew she ought to do something bendy with her ankles, but that area had never been the most flexible and she'd torn ligaments once falling off a wall on a mission to rescue Lacey's Barbie-With-The-Hair-That-Grows.

The firmness of Yan's grip was kind of distracting too. His hand was warm, heating hers up with the contact, their fingers interlocked tight. It was such an unfamiliar sensation. She wasn't used to contact like that. Ross hadn't been a hand-holder. Bloody Ross! Ross would never limbo. He'd be too worried about messing up his hair and getting sand in his Vans.

Ellen needed to do this. She didn't want to show herself up. For some reason she didn't want to let Yan down either, even though he'd forced her into it. She had expertly negotiated million pound company mergers before the dawn chorus. She should be able to do this. Perhaps her new start would begin by getting her body under a bamboo cane.

She darted her eyes sideways, watching to see what Yan was doing. He was completely horizontal. She needed to put some more effort into this. Using every muscle she possessed, she straightened herself out, leaning back and trying to keep balance. An inspirational poster of flamingos came to mind.

Ouch! Her spine was going to snap any second. Her face was coming up to the bar and Yan's grip on her hand was strengthening. His ankles were at ninety degrees, flat in the sand. That couldn't be right.

Ellen licked her lips, trying to concentrate. This was nothing to do with physical ability, or contortion, this was mind over matter. She ducked her head back as the pole came upon her and then she fell backwards, pulling Yan over with her.

She hit the sand and he fell down on top of her.

Even before she could register the weight of him she was looking into those eyes. Bright, clear, gazing into hers. His breath was ragged, a smile forming on his lips. She felt her mouth move, her lips upturn into a smile, then a laugh escaped her.

'Oh my God, that was totally stupid.'

'You smile.'

He hadn't moved an inch, was still laying over her. She could sense the heat of his body seeping into hers, feel the thud of his heartbeat.

'I can do it. I'm just a bit out of practice,' she whispered.

———

Yan's hand was still in hers and he had no desire to end the connection.

'I like it,' he responded softly.

Adrenalin was coursing through him as he looked at her. Those big, brown eyes, the full lips now widened as she appraised him. He wanted to put a hand in her hair, stroke it away from her face.

Before either of them could react there was an uproar of cheers and applause. Lacey grabbed Ellen's free hand and began pulling her from the ground.

'You aced it, Ells! You're a freaking limbo queen!'

'What?' Ellen struggled to her feet, brushing grains of sand from her dress.

'Lowest height of the night and the pole didn't even get a wobble on! A cocktail for my big sister! Over here! Right now!' Lacey yelled.

Yan watched Ellen look back at the limbo station. There was the pole, sat where it should be, unmoved.

A smile spread across her face and she turned to him. He got to his feet, brushing the sand off his clothes.

'We did it,' she breathed. He could sense the satisfaction in her tone.

'You think we do not?' he queried.

'Yes.' She laughed, nodding her head.

'I *know* we do it,' he responded.

———

Her heart soared as a feeling of heat and triumph wrapped her up. She knew it was partly the alcohol she'd drunk but it wasn't *just* that. For tonight, Yan had managed to make her forget her issues back home. Her shoulders felt looser, her ankles were killing, but that familiar knot of tension she carried around was nowhere near as tight.

'Thank you,' she whispered.

He nodded, putting his hands into the pockets of his jeans. He looked uncomfortable and wouldn't meet her eyes. She opened her mouth to fill the silence with something.

'I …'

'We are champions, my friends!' Dasha's off-key singing broke the moment. He slapped a large hand on Yan's back and slinked an arm around Ellen's shoulders.

'Brandy cocktail. Get it down you,' Lacey said, pushing a glass at her. 'I love you, Ells. You're the best sister in the whole bloody world!'

Now Ellen *knew* Lacey had drunk too much. The declarations of love came only just before the puking up. It was going to be a long night.

———

Yan watched Ellen being made to sway in time to the music with her sister. Despite everything he knew to be right, he'd felt it. A rush. A shot of arousal when he'd got close to her. Her body with his on the sand, their hands entwined. He needed to stay away from her. She could not be a distraction because he couldn't guarantee his actions. Besides, if his instincts were right, the very last thing Ellen needed was a love affair. She seemed to be carrying the weight of the world on her shoulders.

'She's getting married,' Sergei remarked, watching Lacey and Ellen.

Yan shrugged.

'I do not want her to be getting married.'

'Why not? You do not look for relationship.'

'No, but …'

'What do you want me to say?' Yan's anger at Sergei was fuelled up by his own apparent weakness for a beautiful woman. He was going to be sensible enough not to act on it but Sergei was Sergei. He didn't think of anyone but himself.

'Hey, Yan, come on, what's up?' Sergei put an arm around his shoulders.

'Nothing. Nothing is up.' He shrugged Sergei's arm off. 'You know what? Do what you like as always. I do not care.'

TWELVE

The sun was coming up and Yan hadn't slept again. So many things were going around in his mind. He'd had *ouzo*-induced hallucinations spiralling around in his head all night. Rayna, his village, his children, how things had been left. He put his finger and thumb to his forehead and tried to ease the headache. Too much alcohol. Too much talk of weddings. Then, Sergei, asking him about Lacey. Sergei took chances and he didn't think. In contrast, all Yan *did* was think. It was slowly driving him crazy. Like thinking about Ellen and the bolt of desire he'd felt for her. That could not happen again.

He sipped water from the plastic cup in his hand and focused on the outlook. He didn't have a sea scene, they were reserved for paying customers. But he did have a view of Mount Pantokrator. Set against the already cornflower blue sky, rising up towards the early mist of the morning it never ceased to amaze him, its core set amongst the green olive groves and the crags towering upwards. It was two thousand, nine hundred and seventy-two feet of solid rock, knowing its purpose in life, doing exactly what it had been doing for thousands of years. And here he was, Yan Aleksandrov, one hundred and sixty pounds, twenty-eight years old, knowing less now than he'd ever done.

Seeing movement in the car park he squinted his eyes to get a sharper image. It was Monica emerging from a car. Out of the driver's seat came Spiros from the pool bar. Within seconds they were locking lips. He watched them, shaking his head. He didn't understand women at all.

———

'This is all your fault. You let me drink brandy!'

'I *let* you drink brandy? You and the new drag queen entertainer were practically embalming yourselves with it.' Ellen's finger was hovering over the voicemail application on her phone. Should she listen to it now or after breakfast? If they *made* it to breakfast. Lacey had been vomiting on and off for an hour.

'Did I do anything stupid? Just tell me now, get it over with.'

'Let me see ... you danced a Conga line into the sea ... er ... you told someone called Spiros he looked like Bradley Cooper – which he definitely doesn't by the way – and you tried to bring a stray dog back to the room because you said it had sad eyes.'

'Oh, God, my head is proper killing me! Why doesn't this Ibuprofen work?' Lacey leant her head against the toilet and shut her eyes.

Ellen had ordered her sister to keep the bathroom door open. One time, when they'd both lived at home, Lacey had locked the bathroom door on a vomit trip and passed out. Al had kicked the door down after Ellen raised the alarm and Lacey had been taken to A&E for a stomach pump. It wasn't happening again here on her watch. Al would kill her.

'I suppose you're feeling chipper! Why didn't you drink more?' Lacey moaned.

'I don't feel quite a hundred percent if I'm honest.'

'I feel like something marked way low down at a Primark sale.'

'Well, the only way is up then. Shall we go and get some breakfast?'

Lacey's answer to that was a gut-wrenching hurl into the toilet bowl. Ellen moved out of the room and onto the balcony for some fresh air.

It was humid and the sun was already high in the sky. Down by the pool there were a few tourists out moving sun loungers into the best positions. She took a breath of the warm air and looked back to her phone. She was being stupid. She was strong enough to deal with whatever Milo had to say to her. Forgetting voicemail, she hit the contacts button and pressed on the Lassiter's profile.

It connected and began to ring. She checked her watch. It would be just after eight in England. Milo was always in by eight. Unless the coffee shop was busy. He couldn't start his day without a double espresso.

The answer phone cut in and she ended the call. This was typical. She'd summoned up the courage to ring and no one was there. She pressed the voicemail key and put the phone back to her ear. She may as well hear what the emergency was.

———

'Hi, Ellen, sorry to bother you. Hope you're having a great time in Corfu. Mrs McGoldrick's been on the phone. She's received another reminder from the Revenue. I told her not to panic and I've sorted everything. You must have left it out of your holiday notes but fear not, it's sorted ...'

———

Ellen shook her head. Trust Milo to make himself out to be the hero who saved her skin. She was grateful he'd controlled the situation, though.

———

'... *so you have a fantastic time and we'll see you when you get back. Oh, one other thing, Ross Keegan from Keegan Manufacturing called and wanted to set up a meeting with me and Brianne. You've done most of the work so you should be in on that. Think it's an ASAP so expect something in your diary the day you get back. It'll be welcome home and back to the hard graft! Anyway, enjoy your break. Ciao!'*

———

Her hand was shaking so much she couldn't move the phone away from her ear. He knew. She was positive of it. Ross knew she'd been stealing from him.

———

There was a board outside the restaurant. A picture of a rock formation in the azure sea, a perfect blue sky behind. Ellen could almost feel the relaxation draping over her like a cloak. There was a trip that morning, leaving from outside the hotel, it was only ten euros.

'This is *not* a good idea. I can't see us being popular if I puke up in the scrambled egg,' Lacey groaned.

Ellen turned back to her sister. She had stuck Lacey under the shower, made her dress and marched her down to the restaurant before breakfast ended for the day. Lacey might be too hung over to have something to eat but she needed to do something and the bar wasn't quite open yet. She looked again at the board on the easel. Sidari. It promised blue skies, pretty beaches and peace once she'd lost the other people on the coach. It would take her away from Lacey's hangover and the phone call from Milo.

Lacey let out a belch.

'Oh, Lacey, just go and sit down. I'll make a pot of tea,' Ellen said. She indicated a free table behind the glass doors.

She couldn't cope with Lacey being a pain in the arse today. Ross was coming into the office. Ross Keegan, entrepreneur, the ex-boyfriend who proposed in Alcudia, the one who had ripped up her business dreams, the one she'd stolen from. It was her worst fear come true. He must know. But what was he going to do about it? He was just as guilty as her, if not more so. And that was all the defence she had. She followed Lacey into the restaurant and headed for one of the teapot stations.

'Good morning, the queen of the limbo.'

The unfamiliar voice startled Ellen out of her thoughts. She looked up into the face of the restaurant manager. He was smiling at her and offering a tea pot. She remembered him clapping at her and Yan's performance a mere few hours ago.

'Oh, good morning.' She tried in Greek. '*Kalimera.*'

He began to simulate a limbo technique much to the amusement of a pair of elderly ladies at a table nearby. A blush was well on its way.

'Thank you.' She didn't know quite what else to say. As he was called away by a member of his team, she concentrated on making tea for two.

'Ellie! Could you make me some toast? And I'll try some bacon. Just a bit,' Lacey hollered across the room. 'And a croissant! Get me a croissant!'

The trip was sounding more and more tempting.

THIRTEEN

'Up ... down ... up ... down ...'

As he was encouraging participants of water exercise to raise their arms, Yan was watching Ellen and Lacey arrive poolside.

Tanja had caught him at breakfast and asked him to collect names to join in with that night's quiz. He needed to pass that job onto Dasha or Sergei and he'd just about decided Dasha would ask fewer questions and would enjoy the extra attention. Tanja had also asked him to accompany the coach trip to Sidari later that morning. Being given more responsibility was a good thing. He needed his experience and willingness to count above everything else.

Lacey didn't look very well. She seemed to be finding putting her towel down and lowering herself onto the lounger hard work. Ellen had a tray of drinks in her hand, all of them with straws and umbrellas. It was only half past ten. Under her arm were two large paperback books. She raised her head and caught his eye. He turned away. There had to be boundaries.

———

'Turn the sun down, will you? Or preferably off. Was it this strong yesterday?' Lacey moaned, screwing up her eyes.

'I don't know,' Ellen replied. Sitting down on the lounger, she swung her legs up and put a straw in her mouth. She sucked as hard as she could, wanting the instant hit from the strongest mix of drinks she'd ever seen the barman deliver.

'I think you're actually feeling just as bad as me but you don't want to admit it.'

'I feel fine.'

'You're needing a hair of the dog.'

'Hairs actually.'

'What have you got in there?' Lacey struggled to sit up.

'Half an Alsatian and an Old English sheepdog.'

'Is it nice?'

'It's very alcoholic.'

'What's the matter?'

'Nothing a score of these won't cure.'

'God, how long are you going to keep this up? I wanted to stay in the room. You're the one who dragged me out here.'

'Because you're supposed to be planning a wedding and all you've done is have one vague conversation with someone about table settings.' Ellen had raised her voice so much her throat hurt and a topless woman to her right lowered her magazine to look their way.

'That's mean *and* untrue. I've looked at the bridal suite. It's like our room but twice the size with a Jacuzzi bath,' Lacey informed.

'When did you do that?'

'Yesterday, when you were asleep on the lounger with your mouth open drooling like a rabid Old English sheep dog.'

'I wasn't asleep.'

'You didn't even notice I'd gone.'

Ellen sucked harder on the straw, hoping the alcohol would numb every sense.

'I see your limbo partner's in the pool limbering up. I'm surprised you aren't in the water with him. He's the only man here that actually looks hot in trunks,' Lacey remarked.

Ellen took her mouth away from the straw and flicked her eyes left to look at the pool. Yan was congregating everyone into a circle, ready to jog around in the water.

Yan had been so lovely. She hadn't planned on lowering her defences with alcohol and crying like an idiot but he'd been nice, consoling. He hadn't seemed to judge. The jolt of lust she'd had when he'd fallen on top of her hadn't been on the agenda either. And she'd thought about little else since they left the beach last night – until Milo's message.

'Sergei's not around,' Lacey said. She followed the comment up with a soft sigh.

'It's volleyball soon. He's probably sorting out his balls. Anyway, why do you care where he is? He works for the hotel and you have a fiancé,' Ellen reminded her.

'I know.'

'Then why does it matter where Sergei is?'

'I don't know! I'm just making conversation.' Lacey held her head with both hands.

'I think you need a conversation with Mark, about the wedding. The wedding you're supposed to be planning this week.'

'I *am* planning it. As soon as I've got rid of this headache I'm going to go and fix an appointment with the wedding planner. You were right. Just because she has a slightly hairy face, doesn't mean she isn't a marriage planning guru,' Lacey responded.

'Quite.'

'So, what do you think, so far? Is it the place? For my wedding?' Lacey asked. She dragged her body into a sitting position.

'It's a beautiful spot. The mountains of Albania just across the water, the sea, the sand … not forgetting the water platform.' She levelled a smile at her sister.

'It's pretty special,' Lacey agreed, nodding.

'But no matter how special the place, it has to be right. You and Mark have to be right.' Ellen faltered on the last part of the sentence. This was so hard. How could she understand how Lacey was feeling? And what qualifications did she have for guiding her? Years trying to be the mother she really wasn't. That was it. Nothing else. It was exhausting.

'It feels like we've been engaged forever,' Lacey admitted.

'It feels like we've been planning the wedding forever.'

Lacey sighed. 'I need to be sure that when the cake's been cut and eaten … when the doves have been released and all the goody bags have been given out … when the disco's playing "Run" by Leona Lewis … I need to be sure it still feels special.'

'Volleyball! We have volleyball in five minutes over on the sand court!'

Sergei's voice had broken into the conversation, booming the next part of the animation program through the microphone.

'Lace, if you need the thought of a big wedding … if organising the party of your life is the only thing making your relationship special, then …' Ellen started.

'It isn't … I don't think. I'm just not sure how to be sure.' Lacey stopped talking and put a smile on her face at the sight of Sergei striding towards them.

'Why are you smiling at him like that?'

'Like what?'

'Like a drunk celebrity on *Alan Carr: Chatty Man*.'

'Drink your drink. Good morning,' Lacey purred as Sergei arrived next to them.

'Good morning. How are you?' Sergei's eyes were fixed firmly on Lacey's bikini top, his dark hair perfectly gelled back, sunglasses on his face.

'All the better for seeing you looking so energetic and ready for action.'

'Don't stand too close, Sergei. She's been vomiting since seven.' Ellen put her empty cocktail cup down.

'You have too much last night?' he inquired.

'Too much what?' Lacey batted her eyelids.

'Please! Just tell us what you'd like us to sign up for before *I* start being sick.'

'Volleyball. In five minutes.'

'Lacey'll play.'

Within a couple of minutes her sister's mascara would be running down her face and her hair would resemble Seal in his dreadlock phase. Surely that would make her less attractive to Sergei.

'I won't. I can't. I don't know how to,' Lacey protested.

'I teach you,' Sergei assured.

'Great. That's you occupied. I'm going to see if they have space left on the coach trip.' Ellen got up from the lounger.

'What coach trip?' Lacey asked.

'It was on the board outside the restaurant.' She began to gather her things up together. 'Some place beginning with "S". I'm not sure. I don't care. It looked nice and it isn't volleyball,' Ellen stated.

'But we've only just sat down,' Lacey protested.

'And until you're ready to make decisions one way or the other about this wedding I'll be in the place beginning with "S".'

'Well, what am I going to do?'

'I don't know. Just try not to get pregnant.' She slipped her bag over her shoulder.

'Well, when will you be back?' Lacey asked, looking affronted.

'This afternoon some time.'

'Then I'll make an appointment with the wedding planner,' Lacey blurted.

'Fine. Text me the time.'

Ellen turned away, closing her eyes and taking her first steps towards abandoning her sister for a few hours. Being an emotional prop wasn't working, perhaps some solitary time would help them both figure things out.

FOURTEEN

Why did going on a coach trip just for a few hours feel like she was running away? Ellen let out a sigh as she moved herself into a window seat and settled her bag on her lap. She'd felt like this the day she'd moved out of home into the gorgeous three bedroom house with river views. Lacey had acted like she'd bought a place on the moon and Al had behaved as if she was severing one of his limbs. So much guilt. Al wanted her to be a success, a golden girl to show off at networking events, but he also wanted her to be the stalwart of the family, the one who kept things together, straightened out Lacey, solved the personal crises. How could any one person pull all that off?

And that was why she hadn't moved back home when things turned bad. Even though the house with the river views was long gone and the apartment she had now felt smaller than Harry Potter's cupboard under the stairs, there was too much emotion attached to living with her dad and Lacey. If there was one thing she truly still valued, it was her independence. And despite all that had happened to her, it was the one thing she was still holding on to, tightly, with both hands and white knuckles.

The engine of the coach started up and Ellen looked forward as the final passengers boarded. The door started to swing shut and there he was, looking for a vacant seat. Yan. For one brief second their eyes connected and her insides twanged like an elastic band. Just a few hours ago he had been on top of her on the sand.

Subconsciously she inched herself closer to the window, making more room next to her. She looked out to distract herself. Urns of clematis and bougainvillea surrounded the hotel entrance and international flags billowed in the breeze. Olive trees and perfectly clipped bushes of green made up the foreground, with lusher vegetation leading to wooded groves behind. Where one end of the hotel was all about the beach, this part was all about the rural countryside.

Ellen turned her attention back to the bus and she swallowed, waiting to sense Yan coming up the aisle. She hadn't known he was going to be on this trip but a little piece of her was hopping up and down at the thought.

And then the coach moved off. She looked over the backs of the seats in front of her and saw he'd taken the jump seat up front. The hopping up and down sensation turned into one, quick, fall back to earth.

—

After a forty minute ride along the northern coast of the island, the coach finally came to a stop. Yan got to his feet, clipboard in hand and addressed the tourists.

'We are here, everybody, outside Nik Nak bar on main strip of Sidari. Sidari have many good shops, restaurant, bar and café. There is also excellent beach and the famous landmark of Canal d'Amour.' He checked his watch. 'We will meet back here, at this same place, Nik Nak bar, at three thirty.'

His eyes went to Ellen as he said the same thing over again, this time in German. She was here alone, without her sister. He had not expected this. He had assumed she would be staying at the hotel, lying on a lounger reading another of her thick books.

The driver opened the coach door and he stepped down, ready to ensure the guests all disembarked safely.

'Where's the best place for pie and mash?' a middle-aged man asked Yan as he stepped down onto the pavement.

'The English food?' he checked.

'Yes, pal.'

'There are many restaurants with British flag outside. The best I think is the Smugglers Inn near the Canal d'Amour. You should walk this way,' Yan said, pointing along the strip.

When he turned back Ellen had got down from the bus and was standing beside him. Her hair was loose, and she wore a peach-coloured summer dress over her swimsuit, sandals on her feet.

'Hello,' she greeted.

'Good morning.' He smiled. 'You decide to get away from stupid animation games.'

'Oh, are you not doing them here? It was the only reason I came,' she teased.

'You make joke,' he stated, unable to stop a grin invading his face.

'Maybe,' she admitted, readjusting her bag on her shoulder. 'So, where should I go here? What are the best things to do?'

He hesitated for a moment as more clients came down off the coach. 'What do you look for?'

'I don't know really. Maybe the famous landmark? I ought to see more of Greece than the food and drink.'

An elderly couple looked to him for assistance. 'What time did you say the coach goes back?' the man of the couple asked.

'Three thirty,' Yan looked at his watch again. 'It is three hours' time.'

When he turned back Ellen was still there. He had a choice. He could give her directions or he could go with her. What had he planned to do with his three hours here? Have a drink? Some lunch? Sit on the beach and worry? She was here alone. It didn't feel right to ignore her. He swallowed, hesitating for a moment before speaking.

'I could walk with you?' he suggested. 'I just need to make sure everyone is off bus.'

'OK,' she said.

—

The heat of the sun was intense as they walked along the road through Sidari, heading to the Canal d'Amour area of the town. Although Ellen had applied factor thirty sun cream before she'd left the room that morning, it felt as if it was already being lasered off.

Sidari was a proper town, with far more going on than Agios Spyridon. There were rows of shops on both sides of the road, interspersed with bars and restaurants, blackboards stating the day's specials in multi-coloured chalks outside them. There was a buzz about it, different from the laid-back atmosphere of the Blue Vue Hotel and its quaint surroundings.

Differing styles of music filtered from several bars as they walked, all amalgamating into one mixed up fusion that highlighted the varying tastes of the town's visitors.

There were shops selling souvenirs, traditional Greek cafés and *gyros* grills, plus quaint little stores offering olive wood items, dream catchers, linen and lace. If only Ellen had enough money to purchase gifts. Still, browsing and inhaling the exotic mix of scents – from aromatic wood to spicy meats – was a completely free treat she could indulge in.

She looked to Yan. 'Do you like it here?'

A moped zoomed past them, beeping its horn in response to a stray cat.

'I have only been here once before,' he responded.

'Oh.'

'Most of time Tanja go with the trip. She is my boss,' he answered.

'Is she a good boss?' Ellen asked.

'She is much better than last boss.'

'What did that boss do to you?'

'He make me leave Bulgaria,' Yan responded. He stopped walking. 'It is there. See?'

Ellen followed the line of his arm and looked in the direction he was pointing. There, just a few hundred yards away, were distinct fingers of rock jutting out into the ocean. Their make-up was pale, a biscuity cream colour and, even from this distance, she could see the stacking effect, layers and layers of sandstone, one set upon another. She hadn't seen anything like it before. It was mesmerising.

'You have drink?'

Yan's question brought her back to the pavement on the edge of the beach.

She shook her head. 'No, I left in a bit of a hurry.'

'I get this,' he said, indicating the shops across the street.

———

Ellen carefully negotiated the rocks as she followed Yan's long strides up the pathway to the top of the rock formation. It wasn't a steep climb but there was no let-up in the ferocity of the sun. She really needed some of the water Yan had purchased.

'You are OK?' he called over his shoulder, turning slightly to look at her.

'Yes, I'm fine. Just hot,' she replied, trying hard not to pant.

Speaking of hot, it wasn't just the sun that was increasing her temperature. The only thing she'd had to look at in the last fifteen minutes was Yan's taut thighs and calves as they powered up the incline. She'd taken part in highly inappropriate ogling Lacey would have been proud of.

'We are here,' Yan announced, stopping.

Ellen caught her breath and took the final steps up to join him. The view made everything else fall away. From this vantage point, the almost chalky consistency of the rock underneath her feet, she could see for miles. Across the water the width of a sandy beach was visible, with people sunbathing under umbrellas, then rows of magnolia and terracotta coloured apartments and houses, before finally the vibrant greens of the pine trees on the hills.

'It's beautiful,' she whispered.

Yan took a step closer to the edge, looking over into the swell in the middle of the rock where water was thundering in and out, filling and emptying with the tide. 'I think of how many people have stood here over the years. How rock has changed or how it has not.'

He was right. How many people had stood in this very spot over hundreds, even thousands, of years? What had changed? What had stayed the same? This resilient striped rock, both eroded and bound together by the sea, put everything into perspective. She closed her eyes, drawing in a breath, letting the whisper of the waves soothe her. When she opened them again Yan was wearing a wistful expression as he looked out over the water.

'Do you miss Bulgaria?'

—

Ellen's question tugged at him and he took a step back from the edge and moved to a flatter piece of ground. He sat down on the floor, opened his rucksack and held out a bottle of water to her.

She moved towards him, accepting the drink.

'I miss village where I live,' he finally replied.

'You have family there?' Ellen asked, drinking some of the water.

He nodded. 'My parents and my brother.' He opened up his bottle of water and took a swig from it. 'I have not lived there for some time. I have to leave to work in the city. More opportunity. You understand, yes?'

'Yes, I understand.'

He looked at her, standing in front of him while he sat. He pulled off his t-shirt and lay it down beside him. 'You want to sit?'

'Oh, thank you.'

She moved then, carefully folding herself down onto the shirt, crossing her legs.

'I tell you last night, in Brashlyan I work with children. When parents work I teach children sport, games, to fish and to swim,' Yan said. He swallowed. Why was he telling her this? This was something so important to him. Sharing things had turned out so badly last time he had done it. And he barely knew this woman. *Shouldn't* know her.

'But you had to leave?'

He nodded. 'There was fire in factory where most people work. They do not need for someone to look after children anymore.'

'And that's why you're in animation,' Ellen stated.

'It is better than meat factory.' He smiled. 'But not like your job with money.'

———

Her job with money. It wasn't something to be held up and admired at the moment. But it would be again. One day.

She opened her mouth to reply but stopped as her eyes settled on his body without the covering of his t-shirt. What was there to say when you were in the presence of a man who looked like that? She admired every nuance of his physique as he drained some more water from his bottle.

'You like this job?' Yan asked her.

'Yes.' It was a quick, positive response that came from her gut. But in her current situation it wasn't entirely the truth. She tried again. 'It's what I've always wanted to do. But I'm sort of between situations where I am.'

'What does this mean?' Yan asked, studying her.

'Um, it means I probably won't be working at the same office for much longer but that hopefully I will be doing the same kind of work somewhere else.'

'For more money?' he asked.

'Maybe.' She took a sip of her water. 'I don't know. It isn't always about the money, is it?'

He nodded. 'To be happy is better.'

'Yes it is,' she agreed.

Yan locked eyes with her. 'You are older than your sister?'

'A little bit.' She wondered whether the sleepless nights were finally beginning to show on her face.

'But you are not to be married?' he enquired.

She shook her head. 'No, not yet.' That wasn't a definitive answer for someone who didn't have English as his first language. 'I mean, no, not at all yet.' English didn't seem to be her first language either at the moment.

He nodded. 'Me too.'

Rightly or wrongly, his reply made it felt like someone had dropped an Alka Seltzer into her stomach juices.

Yan scooted forward towards the edge of the rock and looked down. 'You know, they say if you swim in the Canal d'Amour you will find your true love.'

Ellen swallowed and tried to quell her pulsing heart.

Yan let out a laugh that completely dispelled the electric tension coiling inside her.

'I do not believe this! It is story for holidaymakers,' he exclaimed, still laughing.

'Yes, of course. Silly, gullible tourists,' she responded, forcing a smile.

'But we should swim,' Yan announced, getting to his feet.

'Oh, I don't know,' Ellen said, staying put.

'Come, we jump,' Yan said, holding his hand out to her.

'From here? Are you crazy?'

'Yes, crazy is good thing sometime,' he said.

'Not when it involves a rock metres above the sea.'

'Come, we play animation game. It is called "jump into the water",' Yan teased.

'What does the winner get?' Ellen asked.

'Last one into water must … '

'Buy beers on the beach?'

'You will not do this, I know.'

She got to her feet then, stepping a little closer to the edge. It was high, it looked at least a hundred metres. The turquoise water was moving in gentle waves against the base. This was something Lacey would do without a second thought. But not her. She focussed on the sea, watching it reel back and forth.

She might not have ever taken physical risks before but her whole life lately had been one risk-taking move after another. And she wasn't afraid of the water. *Determination*. She had plenty of that.

She turned to look at Yan, challenge in her eyes. 'I'll meet you down there.'

Without thinking a second more, she ripped her dress up and over her head and leapt up and out into the air. There wasn't time to think about the distance she was going to fall, this was *living in the moment* taken to the extreme.

The warm salt water compressed her body as she landed and when she eventually surfaced she was coughing it out of her lungs, trying to get her breath back. Her whole body was tingling, every nerve crying out from the rush and the adrenaline. Her hair was clinging to her face, the sun beating down as she searched the water for Yan. Where was he?

'Ellen!'

She heard his voice but she couldn't locate him. It was taking a lot of effort to tread water.

'Ellen!' he called again.

She looked up and there he was. He was still standing on the rock metres above her. He hadn't jumped.

'You are crazy lady!' he hollered. 'I bring bags and buy beer!'

FIFTEEN

Ellen stretched herself out like a contented cat, turning her body towards the sun and letting its heat roll over her like a blanket. Here she was, on Sidari beach. A reggae tune was coming from somewhere close and there was the sound of mopeds buzzing by, the constant peep of their horns. Before she had closed her eyes and given in to the sun's rays, she had stood and admired the ocean. It was glittering, endless, a blue carpet laid out beyond the taupe-coloured sand just asking to be enjoyed. Ellen had let it wash over her as she swam to shore knowing that Yan was waiting for her.

Now, lying here, it was all about tuning out, forgetting about everything else, just relishing this time. It was like she was sixteen again, isolating herself under the apple tree at the bottom of Al's garden, with a book, a Diet Coke and prawn cocktail crisps. Books and the quiet had been her escape from the pressure of exams, the demands of Lacey, Al's constant pushing towards academic excellence.

She was almost completely dry now and, having drunk a large bottle of Mythos, she was in that sleepy, drowsy, dreamlike state where she was almost unreachable. It was a bit like a deep meditation only miles better.

'We should get back to bus.'

Yan's voice drew her back. That thick, sultry accent sliding between the words. She didn't want to open her eyes yet. She wanted to replay his voice, remember the way his hand had fitted into hers last night, let the sun merge the two together wrapping her up in a beautiful mix of warmth and desire until it was one delicious daydream.

'So I can tell everyone that you were too scared to jump into the water,' she said, a smirk on her lips.

'You have done this before. They have rocks like this in England. You practice and cheat to win drinks,' Yan said.

She let a laugh leave her lips. 'Do you have an idea how cold the water is in England?'

Finally, slowly, she rolled her eyelids upwards. And there he was, standing just in front of her, his body accentuated by the light. Abs, pecs, she didn't know where to direct her gaze first. She meant *redirect* her gaze. She wasn't the man eater of the Brooks family.

She sat up, reaching for her dress and pulling it over her head.

'Here.' Yan held his hand out to her.

She accepted it, letting him pull her to her feet. She smiled at him. 'We don't have to run, do we?'

'You would like to run?' he asked.

She laughed, shaking her head. 'After my water-jumping trick I think I've earned a rest.'

'What would you like?'

Her cheeks heated up as all manner of things came to mind. She spoke quickly. 'Tell me more about Bulgaria.'

———

By the time they had walked back to the Nik Nak bar then travelled the twenty plus kilometres back to Agios Spyridon, Yan had told her about his move to Sofia. But he had deliberately kept things back. *Boyan*. He didn't want all the harsh realities he'd been faced with in his country's capital to taint Ellen's view of anything … including him. She didn't need to know how he'd struggled to make ends meet and what he'd almost been forced into to survive. He had a clean slate here. He didn't have to be the person Rayna and her father had tried to turn him into or the worthless individual they said he was. Besides, Ellen was a holidaymaker, interested in him only because he was from a different world. That had to be all.

The coach pulled to a stop outside the marble steps of the hotel and Yan got to his feet.

'Thank you everybody. I see you for quiz tonight at the pool bar.'

——

Ellen got to her feet, sliding her body out from the seat and into the aisle. Lacey had texted on the journey home. She had ten minutes to get to the gazebo where her sister had arranged an appointment with the wedding planner.

She smiled at Yan. 'Thank you for today. I had a nice time.'

'I had nice time too.'

Her stomach was churning and she suspected it wasn't from missing the all-inclusive lunch.

'I see you for quiz tonight?' Yan asked her.

She nodded. 'Do you take bribes?'

He looked confused. 'Is free to play.'

She laughed. 'I'll be there.'

He touched her arm and for a second she sizzled from her toes to her reddened shoulders.

'I wait for you,' he told her.

She swallowed, a quick-witted remark not forthcoming.

'Are you getting off, dear?' an elderly woman asked from behind Ellen. 'Because it's toasted sandwiches at half past four.'

She smiled at Yan. 'Bye.'

—

'So, you would have wedding on water platform, looking over beautiful sea and mountain of Albania. Then you come to beach-side restaurant all decorated in colour of choice for reception.'

Zelda the wedding planner did have a moustache but she was nice.

'And how many does it seat?' Ellen asked, looking at the tables and chairs under an ornate wooden gazebo-style structure.

'One hundred.'

'Is that going to be enough, d'you think?' Lacey asked. She looked to Ellen for an answer.

'Goodness, Lace, how many people are you going to invite?'

'Well, there's all the girls from the shop and my mates. Then there's all Mark's mates from the golf club and his work. Plus Aunty Fil and Eric, Aunty Pearl and Robin, our cousins ...'

'I'm not sure they're all going to be able to come.' The hotel wasn't cheap to stay in, despite a wedding party discount, plus there were the flights. Al couldn't be expected to cough up for travel arrangements for half of Wiltshire and not many people had that amount of spare cash for someone else's wedding. She knew *she* didn't. She'd already planned what she was going to sell to cover the cost. If she wasn't back in the professional saddle by then.

'But it's my wedding. Of course they'll come. Auntie Fil'll love it. She'll bring a hat for every day of her stay.'

'If you like, I show you water platform now,' Zelda said, preparing to lead the way.

Ellen watched the expression on her sister's face. Was that joy or a sense of being overwhelmed? Neither of them moved and Zelda turned back.

'I shall give you a moment, yes?'

'Yes. Yes, just a moment to … look at the glasses and the cut-lery,' Ellen jumped in. She could see Lacey's eyes had a certain sheen to them and she was worried it wasn't because she was overawed by the vases of bougainvillea.

'It didn't feel real in that castle in Kent. I liked the Tudor banqueting hall but it just seemed like it would be a fancy dress party. Here, it feels different,' Lacey blurted out.

She knew exactly what her sister meant. Everything here in Corfu was heightened by the island's beauty. But it wasn't just the flora and fauna or the stunning scenery, there seemed to be an ambience about the place, a deep romanticism. It was the perfect place for being in love and falling in love.

'Of course they don't have a hog roast or go karts.' Lacey sniffed loudly and broke the tension.

'No, this is true.' She didn't really know what Lacey wanted her to say. She was just going with it, letting it play out, being supportive and encouraging. Hoping it was a blip.

'I think I've seen enough for today.' Lacey's voice was soft as she raised her eyes to meet Ellen's.

'Are you sure?'

'Yeah. I mean, it's cool isn't it? Anyone would be lucky to get married here.'

She sensed Lacey's reservations and moved towards her. 'They would. If it was right.'

Lacey nodded and Ellen slipped an arm around her shoul-ders.

'We've got four more days. That's loads of time for decision-making.' Ellen lifted her sister's chin with her finger, forcing her to look at her. 'Let's go and get a drink.'

'And cheese pies? They do cheese pies at the outside restau-rant at half past five,' Lacey said. She sniffed.

'Good, I'm starving.' Ellen waved a hand at Zelda and encouraged Lacey back towards the path.

'How was the place beginning with "S"?' Lacey asked, looking up at her sister as they walked.

Made even more stunning by a person with a name beginning with "Y". Ellen smiled. 'There wasn't one shop that did fake designer shoes.'

'Waste of time then,' Lacey answered. 'Should have done volleyball.'

'Absolutely. I won't make that mistake again.' She couldn't keep the smile from her face.

SIXTEEN

'OK everybody! Tonight, we have music quiz for you! Lots of questions of many different bands. To enter, collect sheet from Yan, Dasha or Sergei, choose team name and get ready to win wonderful prize!'

Tanja was standing on the stage with the microphone, taking charge of the quiz. For Yan, Dasha and Sergei it was almost another evening off. All they had to do was talk to the guests, help with any queries about the questions and ensure everybody had fun.

Yan took a swig of his lemon and lime and looked over to the tables at the front. Ellen and Lacey had come into the entertainment area about half an hour ago. Ellen was wearing a short cream dress with small flowers on it and her hair was loose on her shoulders, her face a little tanned from the Sidari sun that day. The sight of her had made his throat dry up. Spending the day with her had been one of the best days he had had since he'd been here. He'd felt relaxed, carefree, all the things he craved, all the things he'd lost. But she had to be out of bounds. Inappropriate feelings weren't part of his plan for the future.

'Tanja want you to collect team names.' Sergei thrust a clipboard towards Yan.

'What? We do not collect team names in quiz before,' he responded, making no move to take the offering.

'She has prize for a draw,' Sergei repeated, pushing the clipboard against his chest.

Why was Tanja changing things? They had a routine, things worked more smoothly with a routine. There was no way he was going to do it. He shook his head at Sergei.

'No, I do not do this.' He crossed his arms over his chest.

Sergei studied him as if he was working out what he was thinking. 'What are you afraid of? Is it the English girl? Ellen.' A grin spread over Sergei's mouth. 'She go on trip to Sidari today. You like her!'

'Sergei, I am not like you. I do not want a relationship here.' He could feel the beads of perspiration forming on his brow. The more he said it, the more it might sink in.

'It is OK, my friend. You know I know how to keep things secret.' Sergei nudged his arm.

'I have to help Dasha.' Yan pushed the clipboard back at Sergei and fled. It was the only thing he could do.

———

'We need a team name,' Lacey said, pen poised over the quiz sheet.

Ellen didn't respond. She was looking across the tables at Yan departing. He was tipping up chairs, squeezing himself by in some desperate hurry to leave. She carried on watching, right up until he disappeared along the passageway that led to the kitchens.

'Ells, we need a team name for the quiz.' Lacey tapped her pen on the table. 'I know. How about "Brooksie Babes"?'

'No.'

'Bootilicious?'

'No.'

'Rule Babe-tania?'

She shook her head at Lacey. 'How about something normal?'

'Something boring, you mean.'

'Yeah, something boring that won't make Sergei think you're giving him the come-on.'

'It's a team name, not an invitation to our room.'

'Then why does it have to sound like we're offering escort services?'

Lacey dropped the pen on the table and swiped up her drink. 'Fine, you think of something then.'

Ellen picked up the pen and wrote something down at the top.

'"The Dynamic Duo"? It's lame and dull and everyone will think we're Batman and freaking Robin,' Lacey protested.

'Half the people here are German or Polish. It won't matter.'

'It matters to me.'

'Because it doesn't immediately sound like we're going to get our tits out?'

Ellen knew she'd raised her voice just a little too much and was now drawing attention from Uri and his table of relatives, as well as the stag party who had arrived that day.

An appointment had arrived in her iPhone diary while she'd been getting ready. Keegan Manufacturing. The date and time were fixed and she was terrified. Her wonderful day with Yan in Sidari, her crazy jump from the rocks surrounding the Canal d'Amour seemed like a beautiful dream that had never really happened. Real life had flooded back and was threatening to take over.

'What's wrong?' Lacey asked.

'Nothing.' She didn't want Lacey asking questions. Her sister had enough to think about and confiding her own problems wasn't going to help. She'd done this. She'd known the risks. It was all on her.

'Have you called the office today? Are you going over some-one's audit in your head?'

'No, of course not.'

'I know when you're lying, Ells.'

Did she? She hadn't picked up on anything over the past few months. She offered her sister a small smile. 'Too much sun and not quite enough wine ... yet.'

And that was her grand plan. Pretend it wasn't happening and drown the knowledge out with alcohol. Perhaps she had more in common with the half-blood princess than she'd ever realised.

'I'll get us some more drinks! With your knowledge of the Eighties we're going to ace this quiz no matter what we're called.' Lacey paused to think. 'How about "Bikinied Out"?'

'No!'

———

'Question fifteen,' Tanja started. 'What band have a hit with "It Must Have Been Love" from the film with Julia Roberts and Richard Gere, *Pretty Woman*?'

'Ooo I know this! I know this!' Lacey shrieked, leaping off her chair and waving her arms.

'Sshh! Uri's been trying to listen to our answers since the start. His chair's been creeping closer and closer.' Ellen put an arm across their quiz paper, shooting the Russian a warning glance.

'I know this one. I really know this one!'

As she waited for Lacey to come up with the answer her eyes caught sight of Yan returning. He looked calmer, no longer rushing. She watched him meander through the crowds, stopping to speak to people, assisting them with their papers.

'Ellen, pay attention!' Lacey barked.

'I don't need to pay attention because you said you were going to give me the answer.'

'Oh, what was their name? She had white hair and he was a bit geeky. A bit like Annie Lennox and the one who played the guitar. Dad liked them. Can't remember his name. It'll come to me ... give me a second ...'

'Roxette.' The whisper came from Sergei as he ducked his head into their huddle.

'Oh bloody hell, you've spoiled it now!' Lacey exclaimed crossly.

'What?' Sergei looked affronted. 'I help you.'

'Thank you but we don't want to cheat,' Ellen answered.

'And I *knew* the answer, it just wasn't coming to the tip of my tongue right away.'

Tanja called through the microphone again. 'Question sixteen ...'

'You come to Bo's Bar tonight?' Sergei asked.

Ellen watched as Sergei rested a tanned hand on Lacey's bare arm. This was getting really dangerous now. Touching, where her sister was concerned, was the start of turning harmless holiday flirtation into something more. Lacey raised her eyes to meet Ellen's. She wasn't quite sure what Lacey was subconsciously telling her to do. Do something? Say something? Neither?

'I ...' Lacey started to reply.

'If you like me to repeat question ...' Tanja called.

'What? We missed the question?' Ellen scraped her chair back, standing up. 'Please! Please repeat the question!'

'Or perhaps we could go somewhere else,' Sergei continued.

His long, lean fingers were stroking Lacey's arm now and her sister was doing nothing to stop him. Ellen banged her fist on the table.

'Sshh! We need to listen to the question! Lacey, pay attention.' She gave her sister a look that had her retracting her arm from the table.

'"Gangnam Style" was big hit all around the world. But what was name of artist who sing it?'

Lacey sighed. 'PSY.'

'I see you later,' Sergei said, taking a step back away from the table.

'How do you spell it?' Ellen asked.

'I.T.'

'Very funny.' She watched her sister eyeballing Sergei as he left. There was absolutely no doubt in her mind now, her sister was extremely close to forgetting all about her engagement.

'I would like to go to Bo's Bar again,' Lacey said wistfully. 'You've got to admit the limbo was fun.'

'But you don't want to go for the limbo,' Ellen said. She looked up at her sister, trying to read her expression.

'But if you were there ...'

'Lacey, I'm not a chaperone!' She needed to spell it out. 'If you need me there so you can resist the charms of Sergei then there's definitely something wrong with your relationship with Mark.'

'Don't say that.' Lacey sounded shocked.

'I'm actually sick of saying it! You're not wearing your engagement ring and I saw the look on your face when we were at that water platform today. It wasn't the expression of someone excited about marrying the person they want to spend the rest of their life with.' Ellen looked directly at her. 'It was fear.'

She watched Lacey shrink down into her seat, wrapping her hands around her cocktail glass and twisting the straw with tense fingers.

She opened her mouth to speak again. 'Lace ...'

'OK, question seventeen ...' Tanja moving on with the quiz put an end to the conversation.

SEVENTEEN

Uri was standing on the stage, proudly holding his canary yellow cocktail above his head like it was the World Cup. His team had pipped the stag party to quiz glory and the Russian was milking it.

'How the hell does a Russian know the complete back catalogue of Cliff Richard?!' Lacey huffed, downing her third shot of the night.

'Google. Didn't you see him tapping away on his phone?' Ellen asked.

'Well if he's linked up with the Albania network that little win's going to cost him a fortune.' Lacey stood up. 'D'you want another drink?'

'No, I'm OK.' Ellen was watching Yan. He was holding hands with a girl of about six or seven, swinging her around on the dance floor to a Boney M number. The girl was giggling, her pig tails flying out behind her and he was laughing, grinning at her and pulling funny faces. His enthusiasm was evident. What was also evident was the snug fit of his jeans over his buttocks and down his taut thighs. She swallowed.

'Listen, maybe we should get a bottle of wine and take it back to the room,' Lacey suggested.

The children adored him. Ellen carried on watching as a small boy ran up to give him a high-five and join in with the dancing. Good-looking, fit, kind, funny in an annoying type of way.

'Are you listening to me?' Lacey's voice, only one decibel below the sound of a Boeing Rolls-Royce engine, drew Ellen's eyes away from him.

'Sorry. What did you say?'

'I said maybe we should get a bottle of wine and go back to the room,' Lacey repeated.

Ellen watched her sister blink moist eyes before dropping them down, her expression landing in her lap.

'Is that what you *want* to do? Or is that what you think you *should* do because I badgered you about Mark?'

'Does it matter?'

'Yes, Lace, I think it does.'

Lacey let out a sigh and slumped back in her chair. 'I don't know what you want me to do, then!'

It was like a response from an angst-ridden teenager. Ellen looked at her sister. Lacey's lips were pouting, her arms folded across her chest, pushing up her breasts in the bright pink vest dress she was wearing. Looking at her now she didn't seem mature enough to drink alcohol responsibly, let alone commit to a lifetime relationship.

'I think you should go to the beach with Sergei,' she stated. 'If that's what you want.'

Lacey sat forward on her chair, her eyes widening, a mixed expression of shock and excitement coating her features. That said everything she needed to know.

'What?'

'Only *you* know what's right and maybe it isn't Mark.' Ellen stopped. She could hardly believe what she was saying? Why was she saying it? Because she was fed up of keeping close tabs on Lacey like a private investigator? Because she couldn't be bothered fending off Sergei's amorous suggestions to her sister anymore? Because Ross Keegan who hadn't broken her heart but had ripped her life apart was going to do it all over again when she got home?

Ellen spoke quickly, before she had time to do any more thinking. 'Maybe it isn't Sergei either but ... you do what you want to do, Lacey.' She smiled. 'And if you work anything out along the way then all the better.'

The sound of chairs being scraped back from their tables and people departing quickly from their places took her attention away from Lacey. Residents were off like bees, buzzing to different spots on the complex, looking around sun loungers, in undergrowth, behind the ice cream stand. It was the biggest flurry of activity she'd seen since the queue for toasted sandwiches that afternoon.

'Is there some sort of weird treasure hunt we're missing out on?' Lacey remarked, looking up.

A thirty-something woman was diving in and out of tables, wringing her hands, a look of horror all over her face. Ellen's stomach knotted, then her heart dropped. She recognised the woman from the restaurant. She had two sons. One was about eight and was with her, hanging on to her cardigan. The other was smaller, perhaps four or five. He wasn't there.

'What's going on?' Lacey repeated.

'Have you seen my son? He's four. He was dancing by the stage, just a few minutes ago and now I can't find him anywhere.' The woman's voice was addressing Uri's table of friends. 'His name's Zachary. He's got blonde hair and ...'

'A kid's missing?' Lacey exclaimed.

Tanja's voice came over the microphone. 'Attention, everybody. We are looking for small boy. His name is Zachary and he is four year old. He is wearing green t-shirt and brown shorts. He have the blonde hair and blue eyes and ...'

'I don't like this,' Lacey said, pushing her glass away from her.

'The pool,' Ellen said, jumping up from her seat.

Lacey shivered. 'Oh don't say that.'

Ellen began to move, pushing through tables and heading towards the lagoon pool.

'Ellen!' Lacey called. 'Wait!'

'Help look for him, Lacey and then go to Bo's Bar! I'll meet you!'

———

Yan had had the lights brought up and he'd scoured every inch of the pool with a powerful torch he'd grabbed from the dressing rooms. The boy was not in the water.

'He's in the water,' Ellen stated, running breathless toward him. 'You hear about it all the time. It's what happened to that boy I saved from the river.'

'He is not,' Yan replied, waving the torch over the pool again.

'He must be. There's nowhere else he could be. They're turning over the place back there.' Ellen hitched a thumb back toward the entertainment area.

She didn't seem able to catch her breath. She was panicked, nervously standing on her toes, stepping from one foot to the other.

'He is not here. I promise to you,' Yan insisted.

'Then he must have been ... taken. Do you think he's been taken?'

He heard the words catch on her lips and knew what she was thinking.

'No.' Yan shook his head. 'That is not possible here.' It was a small village outside of the complex, a close community, from what he had learnt from the locals who worked at the hotel. But the gate to the beach was never locked. It was a possibility someone could come in.

'Is there anywhere else down here? How about the kids' club?'

'Is all locked.'

'The play park.'

'The mother say she has been there to check.'

Ellen's eyes grew larger. He heard her breath stop. 'He could make it up towards the restaurant in five minutes or so.'

All at once he understood. 'The adult pool.'

Before he could stop her, she was sprinting across the complex.

EIGHTEEN

'Help!'

The words were barely making it out of her mouth. Her lungs were burning with every stride as she ran, full pelt, up the stepped incline towards the adult pool. 'Please! Check the pool!'

She knew every single second counted. If she could get some-one over there before she made it, he might be in with a chance. *If* he was actually in the water. But, as she rushed through the half-light, desperate, snatching at every mouthful of humid air, there was no one around. People inside the lobby bar couldn't hear her and everyone else was down by the lagoon pool, searching.

She ran up the short flight of steps, her legs wobbling with nerves and anticipation. The moment the pool came into view she saw him. A tiny form, out in the centre of the water, face down, motionless. Before the sick feeling had even a second to start overwhelming her, she shook off her sandals and dived into the water.

Despite the stickiness of the night air, the pool was unheated and the cold bit at her skin. This was nothing like the tepid wa-ter at the bottom of the rocks in Sidari. She drove on through the water until she could grab him. Treading water, gasping for breath she turned him over, looking at his pale, lifeless face for anything, any slight indication of recovery. There was nothing. No movement, just stillness, limpness, white skin, closed eyes, light and laughter gone.

'Ellen! Bring boy here!'

———

Yan was not going to give up. He had spent a week with Zachary already. He painted everything green at the kids' club. Green sun, green car, green flowers, even the picture he had done of his mother and brother was green. Like a family of aliens.

'Ellen! Bring him to me!' he yelled to her.

She was shivering, holding the boy and looking at his face as if there was no hope. There *had* to be hope. If there was one thing he wanted to believe in it was hope. And this boy had his whole life in front of him.

Ellen swam, one arm leading her through the water, the other wrapped around the boy's neck, keeping his chin up and his head above the surface. As soon as Yan could reach, he plucked the child from the water and lay him down on the tiled floor.

'He's gone, isn't he?'

'Sshh! You must call for the doctor,' Yan ordered, opening Zachary's airway with a tilt of his head. 'Then go and get mother.'

He knew she hadn't gone anywhere but he had to concentrate. Everything he'd learned about resuscitation on day five of the animation course he had to remember accurately now. Zachary needed him to get this right. There was no second chance when you weren't working on a plastic dummy.

'Ellen, get help!' he ordered roughly.

He heard her leave then, the soles of her bare feet scudding across the tiles toward the lobby bar. Although he knew in his heart there would be none, he listened and looked for signs of breathing. Finding nothing, he pinched Zachary's nose and pressed his mouth to his.

———

The barmen and the restaurant manager had followed her back down the path towards the pool, along with a gaggle of guests. The receptionist was phoning down to the entertainment arena to alert Zachary's mother. Ellen had never felt so sick. All her problems from home, Lacey's indecision about her marriage, everything, it all paled into absolute insignificance when put alongside what was happening right now by the water's edge.

Ellen was biting her nails, willing something to happen. She'd take just about anything right now. Yan was pressing down on the little boy's chest, battling to bring him back. There was nothing anyone else could do but watch, look on at the struggle, feeling utterly useless and insignificant.

Then, suddenly, a small cough broke the tension. Had she heard the noise or was she just hearing what she was hoping to? Another cough followed and then the sound of vomiting. She couldn't help herself, she rushed forward, broke from the congregated group and went to Yan. She dropped to her knees, a euphoric feeling welling up.

'He's alive!' she exclaimed, looking down at the boy.

Yan had turned him into the recovery position and now Zachary was emptying his lungs and stomach contents all over the flagstones. Yan was stroking the boy's hair, whispering words of reassurance to him. She saw that his hands were shaking, his forehead beaded with sweat, his jeans wet from the water on the floor.

'You saved his life,' she stated.

He shook his head. 'No. You did.'

He raised his eyes to match hers. Those clear, fluid, ice-like eyes delivered a loaded look that resonated deep inside her. Shivering, she put a wet hand over his, needing to make a connection.

'Oh my God! Zachary! My baby!'

Yan removed his hand from hers, hauling himself up to his feet. 'He is OK. The doctor will be here soon.'

His soft, unflappable tone did nothing to calm the mother who was down on her knees, cradling her son as he gasped small rapid breaths.

A mother's love was seeping out all over the terracotta tiles and filling the muggy air with a tangible density. A love she'd never known. A love Lacey hadn't had, either.

The sobbing was both joyful and tinged with nervousness, guilt, concern. It was hitting her, pummelling her insides for a response. *You're on your own. You've got nothing and no one and no one knows what happened except Ross Keegan.*

Ellen started to shake. Her arms prickled with goose bumps as the water on her skin began to dry. Her hair was dripping down onto her already saturated clothes, her teeth chattering and every part of her feeling like it might seize up.

———

Yan's insides were churning, his body pumped with adrenalin. The boy had been so cold, so white, so full of death that even as he had pushed to restart his heart, he'd thought it was too late. But hope, belief that life couldn't be that harsh, that cruel, to an innocent child, had driven him on. He had to bring Zachary back. The boy was counting on him. He'd had to step up.

And he had. They both had.

He looked at Ellen and balked. She was shaking uncontrollably, from her bare feet up through her drenched dress to her wet hair, falling in dripping strands in front of her face. It was a warm night but there was a breeze strong enough to bring down the temperature. Her skin was pale too, her lips bluish and trembling. He moved to her.

'Ellen.'

She didn't respond, just stood, her body vibrating into the puddle of water she was creating on the tiled floor.

Yan put a hand to her arm. It was cold to the touch. She seemed to have to drag her eyes towards him and away from the scene in front of them. The doctor had arrived and was assessing Zachary.

'You need to be warm,' he told her.

———

His voice was firm but the mellow tone sent a sliver of heat across her skin. She opened her mouth to speak but her lips were stuck solid, like cubes of ice, stiff and unresponsive.

'Come,' he ordered.

She could do nothing. Her hips felt immobile as he looped his arm around hers and urged her into a walk. How did she make it happen? Could she actually walk?

Ellen faltered forward, feeling absolutely none of the flexibility from the limbo the previous night. She sensed that if she didn't lean her entire body weight against Yan then she'd be on her knees in seconds.

'It is OK,' he said reassuringly. 'It is not far.'

One foot in front of the other was too far at the moment. She'd never felt so incapable. It was as if her entire body was closing down and she couldn't do anything to stop it. Every part of her was numb. Her legs moved as if they were wooden lumps with no give or bend. She had no idea where she was going, just making her limbs create motion was taking every resource.

Yan was holding her with his upper body, half propping, half carrying her along the path towards the block of rooms to the immediate left of the main restaurant. She was still shaking when he manoeuvred her down a short run of steps towards a line of doors on the bottom floor.

Holding onto her upper arm with one hand, he reached into the pocket of his jeans. Pulling out a key he fitted it into the lock and turned, opening the door.

NINETEEN

Ellen's breath was collecting in her throat now and everything was dark. Yan led her into the room and inserted the key fob into the slot on the wall to activate the lights. As she wavered he caught her.

'It is OK,' he whispered.

She shook her head as tears filled her eyes.

He didn't know what to do. He knew what he *should* do and that was to get her out of the soaking wet clothes before the temperature started to do some real damage. But could he? It would mean undressing her. She was barely standing without the wall of his room for support. The only sound, apart from the air conditioning unit, was her teeth juddering together.

He reached for the remote control on the countertop next to the sink and switched the cold air off and the heating on.

'You should …' He'd started talking but he didn't know whether he could finish the sentence. He took a breath. 'Take off clothes.'

'I'm … so … cold,' she stuttered.

'I know. I will get more clothes,' he stated, moving quickly.

Yan opened the wardrobe and pulled out the warmest thing he'd brought with him to Greece, a plain black roll-neck jumper. It would be good enough but what did he have for the rest of her?

'Yan …'

Her voice sounded so desperate that he slammed the wardrobe doors closed and hurried back to her side.

'It is OK,' he insisted. 'It is a hard thing to see but, the boy is OK? Yes?'

He grabbed a clean towel the maid had left that morning and then paused, unsure what to do with it.

'I can't get this ...' she started.

Her hands were at the buttons of her dress. Her fingers looked swollen and wrinkled and she couldn't seem to unfasten the buttons. Tears were seeping out of her eyes now as the emotion overflowed. He knew what she was feeling because he felt it too. What they'd done. What might have happened if they hadn't arrived in time.

'I just can't ...' she sobbed.

'It is OK.'

She nodded, her teeth still knocking together, her motions unstable. The first button remained fastened and she dropped her hands to her sides as tears slipped down her cheeks.

Yan reached up to the button, putting his fingers around the hard plastic circle and quickly slipping it inside the material and out. He raised his eyes to her, hoping that if this wasn't what she wanted him to do she would say something. He paused, his fingers poised by the second button.

She moved her head in another nod and he acted quickly then, unfastening all the other buttons until the dress was completely undone. Without hesitation he swept the light cotton off her shoulders and carefully placed the dress on the table to his right.

Just a bra and panties. This beautiful woman was in his room in nothing but her sodden underwear. He bit his tongue, unable to take his eyes from her. It was inappropriate to be reacting to her like this to it but he couldn't deny he felt something. There was an attraction there, a pull he had no control over.

As if feeling his scrutiny, she wrapped an arm across her breasts and he moved then, whipping the clean towel around her back and closing it in front of her.

'I will put on shower,' he stated.

———

The rivulets of hot water hit her skin and she let out a cry of anguish before she could stop herself. It stung. It burned. It was only when the warmth began to seep through her frozen skin that it started to feel better. She closed her eyes, standing under the steaming shower, letting the heat defrost her mind as well as her body. Nothing felt quite as it should be. How could a night out under the stars in humid Corfu have turned into an evening of almost tragedy? She snapped her eyes open as the numbness began to ease. And what was she doing in Yan's room? In his shower? She had her own room. Why hadn't she just gone back there? And Lacey ... she said she'd meet her.

Shaking her head, Ellen lifted up one of her hands and looked at her sausage-shaped fingers as they began to adjust to a more normal temperature. She didn't have the energy to worry about her sister right now.

She hunched herself over, letting the water cascade down her back. The most important thing was that they had saved a little boy's life. There was time to think about everything else later.

———

Yan could hear the shower still running. He was on his second drink. The chaos had stopped, everything had stilled and he could finally get his thoughts in order. A boy had almost died tonight.

His mind immediately strayed to a place he kept shut off. Not a boy, but a young man, someone in the prime of his life. Someone he had loved so much. He took another swig of his drink and pushed the memory away.

He refocused, filling his lungs with air. A tragedy had been averted tonight because of him. Because of Ellen. Life of any kind was better than no life at all, that much he knew.

The water in the bathroom stopped and he took a swig of his neat Metaxa. She would be coming out, joining him here. His heart was thumping in anticipation and he knew it shouldn't be. He had no right to feel anything for her. He'd made promises to himself, promises he'd meant to keep.

Why then had he taken her here, back to his room? Was it just because his was the closest place for her to change and get warm? Or had he acted on that shot of attraction he felt for her? Whichever it was, something about her had got under his surface.

He heard the door of the bathroom open and he slugged down another mouthful of drink.

———

Pulling the black roll-neck jumper down over her thighs Ellen stepped barefoot out into the room. Yan was facing the doors at the end of the room, a glass in his hand. He'd changed, she noticed, his damp clothes replaced by another pair of jeans and a white t-shirt.

'I hung the towel up in the bathroom. I didn't know if ...' she started.

He turned around. 'The maid will change.'

'That's what I thought.' She nodded.

He raised the glass he was holding. 'Drink?'

'Yes.' She had no idea what it was but it looked alcoholic and warming. She just wanted to be warm and tepidly numb instead of freezing and frighteningly solid.

She watched him move over to the kitchen area to prepare the drinks and she didn't know what to do. Should she sit? There were two wooden chairs at either end of a table, plus the double bed. It was nothing like the suite she shared with Lacey. Everything was fighting for space here.

'You can get in bed,' Yan called.

The statement drew a breath out of her and, as soon as the words hit the air, he swung around, his eyes wide.

'I just mean ... for cold ... to cover legs with the blanket,' he hurried out.

She nodded. She moved across the room to the bed, *his* bed and pulled the covers off slightly. She sat down on the edge of the mattress, bunching the counterpane around her until she was covered and tucked up like it was a sleeping bag.

He brought her a half-full tumbler of brown liquid and she took it.

'Thank you.'

He nodded and stood still in front of her for a second, watching her take a sip of the brandy.

'It's good,' she responded. The first reassuring drops of warmth began to make their way down into her stomach and up to her cheeks.

'I have two of these already,' Yan announced. He gave a small smile.

Ellen smiled back but it felt awkward. He was standing in the middle of the room just a little way from her as if he didn't know what to do. Should she move along the bed to let him sit down? Or was that too close? She looked at him, feeling a charge of attraction. It had crept up on her.

'I get a chair,' he stated, moving to the table. Decision made.

Yan brought the chair down the room and placed it opposite her. He sat, cradling his glass in his palms.

Ellen broke the silence. 'Where did you learn to resuscitate someone like that?'

He shook his head. 'We have training before we come.' He drank some more of the brandy. 'We do not expect to use.'

'No, I suppose not.'

He matched her gaze. With those eyes. The eyes that caused her stomach to whirl around like a tornado. She self-consciously pulled at the jumper with her free hand, *his* jumper, the only thing she had on.

'You make the difference,' he said. 'You think very fast. Where boy is, how to get there.'

'Children are fascinated with water. It's a flaw in them at that age; they're all about the fun and not realising the dangers.'

'You are clever.'

She shook her head. 'I've just spent a lifetime with Lacey who never thinks about anything she does. I was lucky, that's all.' She looked back at him. '*We* were lucky.'

Yan nodded, breaking the eye contact and taking another drink.

'I thought he was dead,' Ellen blurted out, a wave of emotion hitting her, making her hunch forward, catching a sob in her throat.

———

The fear and sorrow in her voice dug its way inside him.

'You must not think this.' He sat forward a little. 'In few days Zachary will be back in kids' club making green pictures.'

Ellen's sob turned into a half-laugh then and she raised her head. 'Is that what he does?'

Yan nodded. 'I ask him why this is. He tell me he like colour green.'

'Children,' Ellen said, sighing. 'Everything is so simple to them.'

'This is truth,' Yan replied. 'In my country children do not know of what goes on. The things that make bad change.'

'In the city? With the boss that made you leave?' she asked.

Her beautiful eyes were wide now, looking at him, waiting to hear what he was going to say next. She wanted to listen. She wanted to know about his life. Despite the fact that it was a dangerous area of conversation, a murmur of excitement was rising in his gut.

'Parts of Sofia are very beautiful. There is much history and famous building.' He let out a sigh. 'But there is also much ... gangs, bad people ... corruption in leaders,' he explained.

She was still looking at him, waiting for him to carry on. He remembered, not too long ago, no one listening, no one caring what he had to say, no one bothering to try to understand. Could it be different this time?

'There is no jobs for some people. No money except for with mafia. It is with danger,' he continued.

'I ... I had no idea.' She gulped down her brandy.

He straightened out his body, sat higher in the chair. He shrugged. 'Everyone have to make change some time.'

'Yes, they do,' she agreed.

'So I come here. I get experience in animation, with children, then maybe one day in future I have place like in my village.'

———

He had a plan. A simple business plan to work for himself doing something he was passionate about. It was resonating violently with her because it was what she had been aiming for since her first job as an accounting junior. Their target market was very different but their desire to succeed seemed to be so similar.

'Is hard for men with children,' Yan continued. 'Because of how things are in the world. Bad things that happen.' He shook his head. 'Children here told not to hold hand, not to make friend. I know this is for safety but it is sad.'

She felt a lump in her throat, arriving in response to more of Yan's impassioned words. This man wasn't just good-looking, he was deep and sincere. How she had misjudged him on that very first meeting. A shiver ran through her bones and suddenly the glass she was holding dropped to the floor.

Ellen leapt up off the bed and the cover fell from her legs.

'I'm so sorry!' She put her hands to her head. 'I'll get something to clean it up.'

'No!' Yan slapped a hand on her arm to stop her moving even an inch. 'You have nothing on feet. It is glass.'

———

His hand on her arm had meant to be a warning not to leave her position, but it was now sending shockwaves of longing through his veins. He couldn't let her go. His fingers were coiled around her forearm, firm but overpowered by the contact with her skin. This shouldn't be happening. He was meant to be shut off, his emotions cauterised. *You are worth nothing.* A voice he still heard. He shouldn't be standing here with his hands on a guest. Yet still he couldn't move.

'Yan.'

Ellen was looking at him. Thick eyelashes, still a little wet from the shower, over chestnut brown eyes, beautiful, pure, innocent ...

He lowered his head, moving his hand slowly, tracing the skin on the underside of her arm with his index finger. Two glasses of brandy and a near death and he was losing hold of his restraint. But her skin felt so good beneath his fingers, so soft, so right. He stopped at her wrist, looking back up, wanting to see from her eyes if this was what she wanted too.

———

Ellen had closed her eyes. As soon as Yan touched her she'd felt it, an electrical pulse, a hot glow, growing quickly and moving, heating her from the inside. Yan caught her hand in his, entwining their fingers, gently connecting them together with every tiny movement.

Was this because of what had happened with Zachary? The gravity of what they'd shared, the moment, her being half-frozen and him being well-meaning? Or was it something else? Something more?

Yan was holding her hand in his like it was a precious Greek artefact newly-discovered and liable to break if touched too heavily. She could barely breathe. What should she do? Did she *want* to do something? It wasn't sensible to engage in hand-holding with someone on holiday, was it? She'd been telling Lacey as much since they arrived. But Lacey was engaged and she wasn't. She was as single as any person could be.

Ellen looked up at him, trying to convey every emotion that was travelling through her. Attempting to let him know through pupil dilation alone that she felt something too.

As if reading her mind he spoke in a whisper. 'Is OK?'

She didn't trust herself to reply and not sound like a prim English thirty-something. She wasn't just a career woman. There was so much more to her than that. She had feelings. Feelings she'd locked away for months and Yan was attacking the barricades with his touch, his attentiveness, his caring nature – those eyes and that body.

She unlinked their hands. For a second, she could see it in his eyes. He was worried she was going to back away, put an end to their connection. Ellen smiled at him and reached up. Finding his jaw she touched a hand to his cheek, taking pleasure in the feel of him as he leant his face into her palm.

———

Ellen's fingers on his face were setting him alight. Was it just the fact it was forbidden? He didn't think so. He had never wanted forbidden. He just seemed to want her. Her touch, so real, just simple, honest perfection. He closed his eyes as she ran her fingers slowly down his neck, pausing at the rimmed collar of his t-shirt. He wanted to kiss her right now. He wanted to take her in his arms and put his mouth to hers. He wanted to forget what he ought to do and find solace with her. Time could stand still. He could forget home and everything that had happened there and be with this beautiful woman. A beautiful woman who was seeing him as he was.

Yan opened his mouth to speak, but before he could get the words out Ellen was pressing her lips to his in an open-mouthed kiss that rocked him. Almost as soon as they had touched she was drawing away, her cheeks red, her eyes bright, but a look of concern furrowing her brow. Did she have regrets? Was it not what she wanted?

He inched forward, reaching for her hand and slowly lowering his face back towards hers. Would she pull away? Should he do this? Their lips came together again and the second it happened everything else fell from his mind.

TWENTY

His lips left hers and he took a whole stride backwards and away.

'I am sorry.'

Ellen didn't know what to say. Why was he apologising? Had she done something wrong?

He stepped further back.

'Ah!' A yelp left his lips.

She looked to the floor and his foot. He'd stepped onto the smashed glass.

'Don't move. I'll get something.' She stepped sideways, squinting at the marble floor and trying to pick out any shards that could be waiting to embed themselves in her feet.

'No. I am OK,' he insisted, warily shifting back to the chair.

'Don't be stupid. You're bleeding all over the floor and you might have some glass in there.'

She was heading for the kitchen area and the sink, although she wasn't sure what she was going to do when she got there. Water was all she could think of and something to wipe the cut.

'You should go,' he called.

She stiffened at his words. One kiss and now he wanted her to leave. She sighed and concentrated on running the water into the bowl. Until he'd pulled away she thought, well, she'd thought he was feeling what she was feeling. Now he wanted her to go, even with the threat of half a tumbler of glass stuck in his skin.

'I am OK,' he said again.

She turned the tap off with force and swung around to face him. 'I get it. I'll go. Just as soon as I've checked out your foot.'

She hadn't really meant those words to come out so harshly but there they were, spinning through the air between them. She kept her eyes steady, watching him, one leg crossed over the other, his hand holding the injured foot as it continued to bleed.

—

She didn't understand and how could she? He'd kissed her, taken her mouth with his and broken every rule of his job and every self-imposed one too. The second their lips met he should have pulled away. But he hadn't. He'd kissed her again, deeper and fuller and she had reacted. Reacted with a passion to match his.

'Tsk!' He let the sound out in reaction to his thoughts without meaning to. Raising his head he saw her shoulders sag. This was for the best.

'I cannot ...' he started. He needed to say something to end it, to let her know this would not happen again, for his own protection and to make sure she didn't tell.

She was walking towards him now, the bowl from the sink in her hands together with some paper towels, ignoring his words. This wasn't good. She was intent on playing nurse and he knew if she touched him he would crumble. He took a stronger grip on his foot to make it clear he wasn't going to give it up to her.

Ellen knelt down on the hard floor and looked up at him. 'Give me your foot.'

Just the thought of her hands on his skin sent shivers through him. He held on and kept his expression hard.

'I can do this,' he stated.

'Why are you being like this?'

He could feel the frustration and annoyance in her tone and for a second he relaxed. This wasn't him. He wasn't someone who would treat a woman badly. That was Sergei's well-practiced role.

He watched her sink back onto her haunches. 'If you regret kissing me that's fine. I'm a grown-up.' She let out a sigh and the guilt coiled inside him.

'Ellen ...' he began.

'I don't know exactly how old you are, but I'm thirty which means I'm definitely past all the teenage stuff.' She looked up at him. 'It was a just a kiss. One moment of holiday madness. I can go right back to not enjoying my holiday tomorrow.'

As she talked and he listened, he felt his feelings sway out of sync. This was good. She was letting him out of the situation, getting him off the hook, closing the door on it. But there was another part of him that didn't want her to dismiss the kiss. He'd felt more in that kiss than he'd felt in any other kiss in his life. How could that be so?

'So, we don't have to talk about it or think about it or ever mention it again.' Her voice sounded steady and determined. 'I'll just check out your foot and then I'll go.'

She was making it so easy for him. She'd given him feelings tonight that at one time he thought he'd never experience again and he was treating her so poorly.

'Ellen,' he started again.

'Listen, I can do a holiday kiss and move on.' She gurned. 'I might even try my luck with Spiros tomorrow.'

———

That wasn't the right thing to say at all. She was such an idiot. She didn't want to cheapen what they'd just shared. Because it *had* been special. And she didn't want to repeat it with Spiros or anyone else on the holiday complex despite her insistence otherwise. It was one thing not to turn their kiss into something it wasn't, but entirely another to say it hadn't mattered a bit and she was up for snogging anyone she could get her lips on.

'I didn't mean that,' Ellen stated quickly.

'It is OK.'

He sounded completely pissed off now and she didn't blame him. *Well done, Ellen.* Share a wonderful, passionate kiss with someone hot and pretend it was no better than locking lips with a random on New Year's Eve. Even animators with experience in no-strings relationships had feelings, didn't they? It wasn't all pass the *ouzo* and drop your knickers, was it?

She grabbed his foot and, as she did, he removed his hand from around it. There was a large slice of skin open on the left side of his sole and a smaller cut at the very bottom. She narrowed her eyes, looking into the wounds as best as she was able in the dimly-lit room. She couldn't see any glass shards but that was the nature of glass, transparent and hard to detect. She wet a paper towel and pressed it to his foot.

He didn't flinch or make a sound so she looked up, checking his expression. The blue eyes met hers and a warm, fuzz of feeling fell like a light fluffy cloud around her.

'I ... I can't see any glass,' she said, trying to break the spell.

'Good.' He shot his foot away from her so quickly her hands fell into the bowl and water sopped onto the floor.

'I am sorry. I clear up.' Yan stood up.

'Don't!' Her voice came out on the very edge of angry. 'It's just some water.' She got to her feet, pulling the top down over her thighs as she rose. 'If you tell me you have a bandage or some plasters somewhere, I'll go.'

He nodded his head but didn't sit. He was looking at her as if he didn't know what to do or say.

'Right then.' She picked her sandals up from the floor and slipped them onto her feet. 'I will see you for water aerobics tomorrow.'

She marched to the door with all the nonchalance she could muster and placed fingers on the handle.

'Ellen, I do not mean for you to go this way.'

His voice, velvet-coated, made her insides curl. She had had that mouth on hers, experienced pleasure so intense … But she mustn't get emotional. It was over before it had really begun.

'Thank you for the drink and the loan of your shower.' She couldn't look at him. She mumbled to the floor. 'Get a bandage on that foot.'

She pulled at the door handle and slipped out of the room with no turning back.

———

The breeze was chilling her bare legs as she hurried down the sloping path at the side of the buildings towards her and Lacey's suite. She'd left her dress and underwear in Yan's room, but there was no way she was going back. If she arrived back at his door minutes after leaving he'd think she was desperate and clingy, that she wanted to start some sort of relationship. And she didn't. She liked him, yes, but she was on holiday and he worked there, saw different women every week, probably fell in lust a hundred times a season. And that was OK. It really was OK. And the kiss had been wonderful. She could hold onto that memory. She'd been desirable to someone who hadn't wanted anything else from her. That was enough.

As she rushed up the flight of steps to the room she realised she had no key. Running off in pursuit of a missing boy had been far more important than handbag, phone or keys. Just as she noticed a crack of light at the bottom of the door there was the sound of conversation from inside. Her heart faltered. Lacey was entertaining. And there was only one person she'd invite back to the room. Balling her hands into fists she hammered on the wood.

TWENTY ONE

'Lacey! Let me in! Let me in right now!'

Ellen's hands were just beginning to hurt from the pummelling when the door opened.

'Hi! Hi! Hi! Miss Ellie!'

Dasha greeted her, all six foot four of him in high sequinned platforms and a red mini-dress she was sure was Lacey's. Her mouth hung open and she didn't know what to say. She'd been expecting Sergei. She'd thought she was going to walk in on naked writhing and have to disconnect them somehow. Being greeted by a cross-dresser in one of her sister's outfits was so much better. She managed a smile.

'Hi. I forgot my key. I left my bag at the table and ...' Ellen began.

Lacey appeared at the door, bright pink lipstick covering her lips and her hair in multiple bunches, like elastic worms, coiled around her platinum strands.

'Oh my days! Look at the state of you! What's that jumper you're wearing?'

At Lacey's reminder of her lack of clothes she shivered. 'Can I come in?'

'Ooo I am sorry! Come in! Come in!' Dasha opened the door wider and put a strong hand on her shoulder, pulling her into the room.

'Where've you been?' Lacey narrowed her eyes. 'And where are your clothes?'

'I got cold after getting in the pool and had to ...' she started. She didn't know where to sit. There were dozens of outfits laid out on both beds and hangers of clothes dangling from every available vantage point, including both chairs.

'Getting in pool? Are you crazy, lady? Pool is unheated. To swim at night time is very too cold,' Dasha announced, his eyes wide.

'You went swimming?' Lacey exclaimed. 'In your clothes?!'

They didn't know about Zachary and the rescue. She thought news would have travelled quickly around the hotel but it seemed these two had been swamping everything out with fashion if the room was anything to go by. She perched herself on the arm of one of the chairs next to a green sequinned dress she knew wasn't Lacey's.

'The missing boy, Zachary ...' She paused, remembering his pale skin, his lifeless form as she dragged him through the water. 'He was in the adults' only pool. I pulled him out.'

'Fucking hell! Is he dead?!' Lacey exclaimed, wide-eyed.

Ellen shook her head. 'No, he's fine. Yan did mouth-to-mouth and brought him round.'

'Yan save life of boy? This is amazing!' Dasha exclaimed.

'I had no idea! Everyone left the entertainment area so we went to Bo's Bar. I waited but you didn't turn up so we came back. Are you all right?'

Ellen nodded although she felt anything but all right. She was still cold, bitter to the bones and tingling a little from her encounter with Yan. She tightened her lips as she looked back at her sister. She wasn't going to tell Lacey anything about the kiss. She and Yan had both needed a bit of human contact after a traumatic event that had shocked them. It was a natural reaction to seek solace and consolation and neither of them had anyone else to turn to. They'd been within easy reach of each other, the inevitable had happened, that was all. Another shiver ran over her.

'I get hot drinks?' Dasha offered.

'I could do with something stronger. You've got a bruise the size of Wiltshire on your thigh,' Lacey remarked, pointing.

Ellen looked at her leg. There was a dark mark on her skin. She presumed she'd got it from the pool when she was struggling to get Zachary out. She couldn't feel it. But then she could barely feel anything.

'I go to bar for drinks,' Dasha decided, heading for the door.

'The bar will be closed now it's ...' Ellen started.

'Bar is never closed if you know right people,' Dasha replied, batting his eyelids. 'I will be quick. I will find handbag.'

Lacey's dress whisked through the doorway on his broad frame and he closed the door behind him. Ellen let out a breath and her shoulders sagged.

'So you're a heroine again. Just like you were with Dennis Jones,' Lacey remarked, throwing herself down on the bed and scattering a gold polka dot trouser suit.

'No, I just got myself in the right place at the right time, that's all. It was Yan. He did all the hard work.' She gazed into the mid-distance. 'He brought him back from near death.'

'And what time was this?'

'I don't know. Just after Zachary's mum was out of her mind searching every square inch of the entertainment area. Half eleven?' Ellen guessed.

'And it's almost half past one,' Lacey stated, looking at her watch.

Lacey had turned into one half of *Scott & Bailey*. Within seconds her sister's suspicious looks and unbelieving stance were going to have all the details of her exchange with Yan falling from her lips if she didn't think fast.

'Where are your clothes?'

She didn't have an innocent explanation. 'One of the maids took them to dry and gave me this.' She hoped that was plausible.

'Urgh! A Greek roll-neck! I can't even look.'

Ellen picked up a tiny neon blue bandeau top from the table and held it up between thumb and forefinger. 'And what d'you call this?'

'Fashion. Me and Dasha have had a little frock therapy,' Lacey admitted.

Ellen caught the blush on her sister's cheeks and it was *her* turn to look suspicious.

'You know, I half expected to find Sergei in here with you. Dasha and dresses were a welcome alternative,' she remarked.

She saw the redness rise on Lacey's cheeks and she knew. Sergei may not have been in the room when she'd returned but something had happened between them.

'What happened?' she asked.

'What? What d'you mean, what happened?' Lacey got off the bed and started to pace around the room picking up outfits and laying them across her arm like she was Julien Macdonald at a fashion show.

'Lacey, you're the world's worst liar.'

Lacey let out an annoyed grunt and threw the dresses to the floor. 'Why do you always have to freaking do that?!' She slumped back down onto the bed.

Ellen kept silent. She'd opened the door and now it was up to Lacey to let the truth out. She silently prayed it was no more than flirtation but in all honesty she suspected bodily contact.

Lacey flicked her legs back and forth off the bed like a child on a swing. 'Sergei and I…we kissed.'

Ellen's stomach plummeted. This was bad. This was her fault. She should have been there keeping an eye on her. But if she had, if she hadn't run for Zachary, something far worse would have happened. And Lacey was twenty three, she had to keep reminding herself of that. She should fight the instinct to baby her.

'One minute we were fighting over a cocktail umbrella and the next ...' Lacey let out a long, high-pitched sigh that Ellen tried to interpret. She wasn't getting regret.

'The next I was looking into his brown eyes and ...'

'Lacey.'

'What?'

'Don't romanticise it.' Ellen blew out a breath and attempted to push any thoughts of Yan to the back of her mind. 'You kissed him. You didn't sleep with him. We can move on from this.'

Lacey dropped her eyes to the floor. *Oh God this was bad.* It looked very much like it had already been romanticised *and* created into a Hallmark movie. Lacey was practically sepia and blurry around the edges with romance.

'It felt nice,' her sister whispered.

Ellen closed her eyes as visions of Yan's face lowering onto hers battered their way into her head. Her sister had kissed another man and all she could do was wallow in the delicious feelings she'd been wrapped up in not more than half an hour ago. This was serious.

Ellen opened her eyes back up and looked across at her sister. She didn't look twenty-three, she looked about sixteen and completely lost. There was only one thing she could do.

Ellen moved across the room and sat down next to her sister, enveloping her in consoling arms, coddling her blonde head against her shoulder. Lacey started to cry but she had nothing to give her this time. No words of wisdom, no tellings-off, no instructions on how to sort it all out. Her advice had mainly been based on common sense, not experience and right now she was floundering in every respect.

'I shouldn't have done it,' Lacey blubbed. 'But I wanted to. So I did.'

Ellen ran her fingers through her sister's hair and let the tears fall.

———

Yan swept the last of the glass into the dustpan and stood up, flinching a little as his bandaged foot met the floor. It was sore but it hurt a lot less than his pride. He'd treated Ellen terribly from start to finish. He'd invited her back to his room. That had been his first failing. Then, what had followed, was one mistake after another.

Undressing her, inviting her to use his bathroom, offering her a drink, sharing conversation, touching her ... kissing her. Where was his self-control? Why did this one holidaymaker affect him so badly? If he wanted no-strings gratification, he could easily obtain it from Monica. Was that what he wanted? Someone to fulfil a basic need? He didn't think so. He wasn't like that.

He put the dustpan on the table and slumped down onto a chair. She'd listened to him. She wanted to know about his aims. She was genuine. A curling ache built in his stomach as reality bit. She only liked him because she didn't know. Rayna had *loved* him before she'd found out. Rayna was going to marry him and her father had given him a job. They'd been promised a house of their own in a time when things were so dire in his home country. He'd felt not just hopeful for his future, but excited about it. What a fool. He should have known there would be strings attached.

He shook his head as the panic grew in his chest. He'd taken the only option available. He'd stolen what he needed and told a wealth of lies to escape. He couldn't lose sight of what was most important now. It wasn't any feelings he might be developing for someone on holiday. It was his survival.

TWENTY TWO

'What am I going to do if he's at breakfast?'

It was the third time Lacey had asked the question during the walk from their suite towards the restaurant. The first time they'd been interrupted by having to break-up a fight between too anorexic-looking cats that were going at it over a thankfully dead beetle. The second time Lacey'd asked, two old ladies had approached them and thrown their arms around Ellen. *You're the heroine. I heard the boy was whiter than Michael Jackson. Pulled from the very jaws of death.* And now, time number three, Ellen still didn't want to answer.

'Ells, what am I gonna do?'

'Well, I'm going to have an egg and bacon roll.'

The truth was she was just as nervous about seeing Yan. How awkward was it going to be? Although she'd told him she was very capable of handling a kiss on holiday for what it was, her stomach was in knots with the sickening morning-after-the-kiss-the-night-before feeling. And it wasn't just that. It was the day in Sidari. The smell of the olive groves and sea salt, the laying on the sand, listening to the reggae music and the hum of the mopeds…She'd been so warm and content, so comfortable with him. None of which she could mention at all to Lacey.

'I don't know what to say. What do I say to him?' Lacey asked.

'*Kalimera*? *Guten morgen?* What other languages does he speak?'

'I thought you'd be crosser than this.'

'Would you like me to be?' Ellen strode on and there it was. The adult only pool. At the moment still empty, but with towels on sun loungers around the perimeter waiting for just another day of sun-worshipping.

She was holding her breath, trying not to think about what might have been and focus on the fact that everything was OK. Zachary had survived.

'D'you think anyone will actually swim in it? I mean, don't they need to do forensics or something?' Lacey interrupted her thoughts.

'It wasn't a murder.' She couldn't help rolling her eyes at her sister. 'And it will have been cleaned like normal.'

'I'm not going in it. It's creepy.'

Ellen shaded her eyes from the sun as they carried on up the short run of steps and moved under the canopy of the outside bar, following through into the lobby and reception.

'Oh God.'

Ellen's exclamation was in reaction to the banner, balloons and streamers straight ahead of them and the full animation team stood in front of it, wide smiles on their faces.

'Oh my days, he's here. He's here! What do I do? What do I say?' Lacey went into full-on panic mode.

Ellen looked at Yan. His smile wasn't as wide as those of the rest of the team. It seemed like it was a struggle to look at her. Dasha strode forward, crushing her in a bear-hug and, as her ribs bent, all she could do was let it happen.

'Hi! Hi! Hi! You are hero! Miss Ellie, you are special person for our day today! We make for you delicious cocktail and please come for special breakfast!'

She didn't know what to do. She didn't want this fuss. She just wanted to keep her head down and get it straight.

'Everyone at the Blue Vue Hotel would like to thank you for your rescue of little Zachary last night,' Tanja spoke.

Ellen nodded, her eyes slipping sideways to Yan as Lacey grabbed hold of her arm.

'Don't let me go,' Lacey hissed in her ear.

This was awful, people were starting to stare from inside the restaurant. Uri and his family were near the door and he had the loudest voice known to man.

'Thank you but really it was ...' She looked to Yan but he shook his head as he stepped forward, pressing a cocktail glass into her hand. He stepped back quickly, making sure not to nudge her fingers on contact, looking keen to keep his distance.

'Is that bits of chocolate in there?' Lacey asked, looking at the drink.

Then, from across the lobby, a little boy was walking towards her. Ellen recognised him immediately. His blonde hair, a face with more colour than the night before and a smile. Zachary.

'Hello,' he greeted, a little subdued.

'Hello, Zachary.' She bent down to his level, dropping to her knees.

'Thank you,' he whispered.

'Oh, you don't have me to thank.' She wasn't going to take the credit for all this with signs, cocktails and fanfare. 'Yan over there saved your life.'

She pointed to him deliberately, for her own benefit as much as Zachary's. He deserved the praise and attention much more than she did. Yan dropped his head, refusing to look up.

Zachary handed her a piece of paper.

'What's this?'

'It's for you.' He grinned and pointed at the drawings in green pen. 'That's me lying on the water with my tongue sticking out and crosses for eyes. And that's you.'

Ellen looked at the person in the picture, a woman with a square head wearing a cape and doing what seemed like the butterfly. 'You've made me look like a superhero.'

'You are.' Zachary's mum reached out and touched Ellen's arm as she got up.

There were tears on the brink but she couldn't let them out. She didn't want to frighten Zachary and give away just how close he'd been to being lost.

'We spent most of the night in hospital but, as you can see, he's a little fighter,' she said.

'I'm so glad he's OK.' The words stalled and an emotional snort came out.

'Thanks to you,' Zachary's mother said. She gave Ellen's arm a squeeze and, as she did, Ellen pressed the cocktail glass to her mouth to stop the teary onslaught.

—

Yan felt sick. As he watched Dasha lead Ellen and Lacey into the restaurant he knew he should have done something more. He'd handed her a cocktail and averted his eyes every time she looked his way. What sort of person was he turning into? It was bad. It was rude. She had done nothing wrong except accept everything he'd pushed her way. Affection. Lust. Whatever it was it had been on him, not her.

'Yan, did you hear what I say?'

He hadn't heard anything and he turned to his team leader with a blank expression. 'I did not hear.'

'I will need you to fill in report for the incident with Zachary. For hotel and for head office. To explain what happen and what you do. All the details,' Tanja said.

All at once it felt like every drop of blood in his whole body was racing to his head. A burning, pressing sensation was moving upon him like a weighty cloud. He couldn't respond. But he had to say something. Say anything.

'I will bring you papers,' Tanja informed.

He could feel his heart, hard and heavy against his chest, banging a violent rhythm. It thumped in his ears, echoed through his mind, rolling its sound to his very core.

He nodded at his boss and the effort of making the movement, going against everything his body was telling him to do, had him reaching for the banner stand for support.

'You OK?' Sergei physically steadied him as Tanja left them, following Ellen and Lacey into the restaurant.

He nodded, trying to restore some air to his lungs and some normal patterns to his body's engine. 'Yes.'

'Lacey would not look at me, you know,' Sergei stated, sighing.

Yan turned his head to Sergei, an expression of disgust on his face. The guy had no idea what a real problem was. He pursed his lips and spoke. 'The problem is not with her looking at *you*. It is with *you* looking at *her*.' He pointed a finger. 'Stay away.'

With those words hanging in the air, he headed out of the lobby.

———

'Is that a watermelon?' Because it looks like a work of art or something.'

Dasha had led them to a table for two by the window overlooking the lagoon. That alone wouldn't have been an outstanding occurrence but the table was laid with crisp white linen, usually reserved for the evening meal, a bougainvillea display and an intricately carved watermelon.

'It's too much,' Ellen said. She picked up the cocktail umbrella infested orange juice in front of her.

'Oh my days. I think that waiter's bringing us fruit salad,' Lacey exclaimed.

A dark-haired waiter approached the table, placed bowls in front of the pair, then left with an elaborate bow. Ellen turned her attention to the landscape out of the window. The lagoon stretched out towards the sea in the distance, the sun dappling the water with spots of bright light. The beach of Acharavi was also just visible. Its terracotta, cream and whitewashed buildings dotted like toy houses amongst the green fields and dusty tracks. It was all so beautiful, untroubled, relaxed. Everything she'd strived for with her free online life coach.

'Ellen.'

She looked up just in time to see a slice of pineapple fall out of Lacey's mouth.

'I've been unfaithful. And I'm not even married yet.'

Lacey's hair was falling forward all over her face, there was syrup from the fruit salad snaking its way down her chin and her large eyes were primed to leak. She had to say the right things, the sensible things. She just wasn't sure she had it in her.

She spoke. 'I know about Gary Barlow.'

Ellen watched her sister's face turn from confused and tearful to shocked and disbelieving. Lacey's lips fell open, losing a grape and her hands reached for the comforting solidity of the table.

'I don't know what you're talking about.' Lacey shook her head. 'He's never been my favourite member of Take That.' She flicked back her platinum mane. 'I was always a Howard Donald girl.'

Ellen nodded. She'd expected that reply. She knew Lacey would try and lie, gloss over everything, despite her expression and reaction already giving her away. That's just how Lacey was. Talking her way out of situations, saying anything so as not to give the game up, even if it was as bloody obvious as Jason Gardiner's hair transplant.

'You know who I mean. Gary Barlow from school. The Gary Barlow you idolised from the second he joined. The Gary Barlow who never asked you out.'

'Oh!' Lacey slammed her hand on the table and tilted her head back in a laugh so fake it should have won an award. 'Oh, *that* Gary Barlow!'

Ellen shook her head at her sister and the overreaction. 'I know you kissed him last year.'

Lacey's tan came off her face quicker than a waxing strip pulled by a well-qualified beautician. Her sister opened her mouth to speak but had nothing. Ellen watched her close her lips again and direct her eyes at the flower arrangement.

Ellen let out a breath and felt slightly regretful. She shouldn't have brought the subject up. She hadn't done it for the right reasons. She'd done it to stop Lacey talking about Sergei as if he were a soul mate she'd discovered. It wasn't going to help things. It was probably going to make things worse. But it was too late now.

'Amy told me,' Ellen drove on. 'Remember how drunk she got when we went to the pizza restaurant for your birthday? She said if your tongue had been any further down Gary Barlow's throat you could have licked his appendix.'

Lacey shook her head, dropping it further toward the table.

'I'm not judging you here, Lace. I just ...' Ellen paused, considering what she really wanted to say. 'It's the second time this has happened and ... Maybe it's a sign.'

She wasn't sure that was really what she'd wanted to say at all.

Lacey raised her eyes from the tablecloth and the look Ellen found there wasn't good. It was a mash-up between furious and bewildered, like a child about to have a full-blown tantrum. She wasn't sure she wanted an angry baby unleashed at breakfast.

'F.Y.I., Gary Barlow kissed me first and it didn't mean anything. And, if you must know, he had that many ulcers it was like snogging a gherkin.'

The picture being conjured up made Ellen's already tender stomach rotate. 'You're missing the point. This isn't about whether you *enjoyed* the experience or not, it's about the actually doing it in the first place.'

'If you knew, then why haven't you said something before?' Lacey accused.

'Lacey ...'

'No! If you knew I'd snogged Gary Barlow why haven't you ever mentioned it?'

'Well ... because Amy told me months after it happened and you were happy then. Happy with Mark, like normal. I assumed that meant it was just a mistake, a drunken kiss that meant nothing.'

'So instead of saying something to me at the time, you thought you'd put it in a box at the back of your mind and bring it out to slap me in the face with when it suited you?'

'Lacey ...'

'No. This isn't anything to do with me and Gary Barlow or even Sergei.'

Lacey's voice was increasing in volume with every word. Ellen could see Uri's group turning their attention away from their mountainous plates of food.

'This is to do with *you!*' Lacey jabbed a finger across the table towards her.

Ellen couldn't stop her eyes from reacting to the pointing and the tone from her younger sister. Lacey had fixed her eyes on her and wasn't letting go.

'What d'you mean it's about me? *I've* never kissed Gary Barlow.'

'This conversation isn't about kissing anyone.' Lacey narrowed her eyes. 'It's about you being jealous.'

'Jealous? Jealous of what?'

'Jealous of me. Of me having Mark and a wedding and everything that goes with it. I saw you in the wedding boutique back home. You held a dress up to yourself and admired it in the mirror!'

Lacey made it sound like looking at your reflection in a wedding dress shop was a sin that should have been top of the Ten Commandments.

'You're getting worked up. Take a breath.'

'No, I won't take a breath. That's your stupid thing – the breathing and the focussing. I know exactly what all this is all about. It's about you wanting me to be single, because *you are.*'

Ellen didn't know what to say. The mood Lacey was in there was little point saying anything. She was on the defensive, rattling out anything she could to deflect the conversation away from the fact that she'd cheated on Mark ... again. Ellen picked up her orange juice and took a sip. Out of the corner of her eye she watched Lacey fidgeting in her seat, picking at the fruit in her bowl with her fingers.

'Of course only a few months ago you *had* a boyfriend. Well, at least we think you did. You *said* you did. Except for the fact we never met him,' Lacey carried on.

Ellen put the glass down in a rush, turning back towards the serene view out of the window. *Breathe and focus.* She pulled in air, trying to suck some peace inside and ignore everything Lacey had said.

'Now I don't even know if he *was* real. 'Cause one minute you were *supposedly* going off to Spain with him and the next you're back. You cagily say you've broken up and you don't tell us anything.'

'There's nothing to tell.'

'Because he wasn't real?'

'No.' *If only.* If he'd been a figment of her imagination she wouldn't be in the dire situation she was in now, with her locked drawer, lack of furnishings and possible fraud conviction pending.

'Then what?'

'We're not talking about me here. We're talking about you and Mark. What you did with Sergei and Gary Barlow.' Ellen sighed. 'I don't *want* you to be single, for God's sake. I've spent the last year of my life trawling wedding venues.' She paused. 'I just want you to be happy, Lacey.'

'You're avoiding the questions. I knew he wasn't real. Mark said he wasn't real and I told him he was being dumb.'

This was impossible. Or a blessing. If Lacey believed Ross had never existed she might question Ellen's mental health but she'd stop asking. Then again, she didn't want to completely lie to her sister. Maybe it was still too soon to share *everything*, but holding her hands up to being delusional was another thing altogether.

'He was real.' The words came out through tight lips. 'He *is* real.' Ellen sighed. 'We went to Majorca and he asked me to marry him.'

'Fuck.'

Ellen let out a breath. 'Yes, something like that.'

'And you said no.'

'Worse than that.'

Lacey creased her brow.

'I pointed at a boat.'

What was he going to do? How was he going to avoid it? Yan should have known something like this was always going to be a possibility. But if he'd known, would he have done things differently? Would he not have pulled the boy from the pool and saved his life?

He'd been mad when he'd left Sergei. There was his colleague, concerned about a meaningless relationship, like the world would end around them. It infuriated him. It was such a waste of everything. If he was in Sergei's position, without so much hanging over his head, he wouldn't be spending a second worrying about things that didn't matter. He'd be living life, enjoying life, making the most of every second. Perhaps that's what he should do anyway. Take a few chances, bend the rules. The clock was ticking anyway.

Yan glanced through into the restaurant, his eyes searching out Ellen. Her beautiful eyes, the way her lips had reacted to his last night ... It had felt like a little piece of freedom. But, as with everything in his life, it just seemed that little bit too far out of reach.

TWENTY THREE

Yan still couldn't concentrate. Already that day he had spilt paint all over the carpet of the children's clubhouse and had an awkward moment with Monica during aqua aerobics when her bikini top had come undone. Ellen hadn't joined in with water exercise like she had said she would. He'd seen her and Lacey pull up sun loungers in their usual spot but neither of them had interacted. They'd taken it in turns to walk to the bar and Ellen had read another book. She hadn't even looked his way. Not that he should be surprised at this. Not after his behaviour of the night before and again this morning. She was doing the right thing. He, on the other hand, couldn't stop looking for her.

'We should start the darts.' Sergei's voice broke his thoughts.

Yan looked at his watch. It was already after midday and participation in the day's activities had been significantly reduced. He was low on energy and completely lacking in enthusiasm.

'Is late. It is time for food.'

'This is not from me. This come from Tanja. Guests ask for darts,' Sergei said.

'What guests?'

'I do not know but she say we must do this.' Sergei grabbed up a clipboard and passed it to him. 'You collect names.'

Yan didn't touch the board and shook his head.

'Come on, Yan. I always take names,' Sergei moaned.

'You have more languages,' he answered quickly.

'Is easy. *What is name?* Write down. *Thank you. In five min-utes by bar.*'

'Good. You go.' He took a step back.

'I cannot.' Sergei dropped his eyes over to the left. 'I cannot speak with Lacey.'

Regarding his friend's slouched stance he really didn't know what to say. He didn't know exactly what had happened be-tween them and he wasn't sure he wanted to know. He'd learnt too many times it was often better to know as little as possible.

'Last night, we ... me ... and Lacey ... '

Before Sergei could say any more Yan grabbed the clipboard. 'I will take names.'

—

'Was he crap in bed or something?'

'What?' Ellen looked up from her book at Lacey's question.

'Ross. Was he rubbish in the sack?' Lacey sniffed. 'Because you didn't actually say why you didn't want to marry him.'

No. She hadn't said. She'd washed over the details and given as brief information as possible. She couldn't open up. She still felt so stupid and so humiliated over the whole affair.

'It wasn't one thing,' Ellen finally responded.

'He was crap in bed *and* he didn't get *Hollyoaks*?'

'That's your criteria is it?'

'Mark likes *Hollyoaks*,' Lacey said, shrugging.

'It wasn't either of those.' Ellen sat up, noticing Yan heading out from under the bar area and towards the pool. She felt the childish urge to hide. She'd already been put on the spot with Lacey, she wasn't sure she could cope with anything else. She was still trying to work out in her head how best to get her clothes back and return the top he'd loaned her.

'So, what was it if it wasn't sex or TV? Money?'

An icy sensation ran up Ellen's spine and she cooled instantly despite the heat. *Money*. Something she'd never had to worry about before was now all she could think about ninety nine per cent of the time. She watched Yan moving along the line of loungers encouraging the occupants to participate in something other than sun worship. He was limping slightly. She'd felt a niggle of guilt when water aerobics had taken place earlier. Uri and Monica had even glanced in her direction right before the jogging up and down. She just hadn't been able to face it.

'Was he on the dole or something?' Lacey continued.

'No. Look, do you want another drink?' Ellen got up, snatching her sarong from the small plastic table separating the two sun beds.

Lacey didn't respond but eased herself up a little and slid her sunglasses down her nose. 'Looks like they're about to do a game.'

Yes. And Yan was about to come along and ask them to play and she couldn't face him.

'I'll get you another Apricot Cooler.' Ellen didn't stop and wait for Lacey to reply but headed off, skidding on the wet tiles as she raced to the bar.

———

Ellen had finished an Apricot Cooler before the barman had even poured Lacey's. At this rate she was going to develop a dependency. It was unnatural. A normal woman her age should not be leaning on local liquor for support just because she'd kissed a member of animation and left her clothes in his room. What she should do was chillax like Lacey had been telling her since they'd arrived. Lacey was chilled. Lacey was so relaxed she was forgetting promises of eternal devotion to her fiancé and wrapping her limbs around a Bulgarian. Just like she had. Like sister like sister. Both with the reckless tongue gene.

A hard slap on the back brought her back into the moment.

'Hi! Hi! Hi! Miss Ellie, you play darts!'

Before Ellen knew what was happening, Dasha was clamping her hand into his, moulding it like it was play clay and dragging her towards the stage area where Sergei was setting up the dart board.

'No, I don't play darts.'

She'd barely squeaked out the words before Dasha laughed – that roaring, booming canon of a laugh that drowned anything and everything.

'Everybody play darts. See, Miss Lacey is here.' Dasha pointed at Lacey and Yan arriving from poolside.

Ellen's stomach dropped and she dug her nails into Dasha's hand making him squeal like a girl and let go.

'Sorry,' she offered, not meaning it. 'I've got a massage booked.'

She took one last look at Yan and headed towards the steps.

TWENTY FOUR

Ellen had eaten far too much at dinner. She'd undone the zip on her skirt a little as soon as they'd sat down at a table in the entertainment arena. No one could see and she didn't intend to get forced into dancing again.

The night was muggy. It had been another thirty degree day and out of the air conditioned building it was every man for himself with the mosquitoes. She picked up her glass of water and took a sip.

'No you don't. One alcoholic drink to every soft one like you promised.' Lacey pushed the jug of the night's special cocktail towards her.

'Have you called Mark?' It was a low blow she knew but when Lacey was scrutinising her drinking habits any distraction technique had to be put into operation.

'Yes.'

Ellen sat forward on her seat. 'Really? You really called him?'

'He *is* my fiancé. Of course I called him.'

'And?'

'And the golf tournament's going well. Dad's in sixteenth place and Mark's twelfth.'

'Lacey.'

'What? What did you want to know? Whether I'd told him I kissed the Zumba teacher last night? No, I didn't and strangely enough, he never asked.'

'Well, what *did* he ask about?'

'Nothing much. We were just touching base.'

Lacey's eyes turned sheepish and were re-focussed, away from Ellen and into her drink.

'Touching base is a term people use when they have nothing to say to one another. You and Mark have a wedding to plan.'

'You're getting boring now.'

'Lacey, the only reason we're here is for the wedding.'

'No, you're wrong.' Lacey put her glass down on the table. 'That was the reason we came here in the first place, but now things have changed. We're having fun without all the planning, aren't we?' Lacey smiled, a lipstick sheen of a smile that seemed to transmit that she didn't have a care in the world.

'Welcome everybody to the Blue Vue Hotel! Tonight for your entertainment we have Miss Blue Vue Hotel competition!'

Tanja yelling into the microphone stopped the conversation.

'Ooo Miss Blue Vue. Shall I enter?' Lacey's face became a picture of youthful excitement.

Ellen shrugged. 'I'm certainly not going to stop you.'

———

Yan had her clothes in a plastic bag. He'd gone to drop them at reception before he came down to the entertainment area but he just hadn't been able to do it. It seemed wrong, impersonal, inappropriate after what they'd shared. Now they were in the backstage dressing area on the table next to his discarded clown outfit and the forms Tanja had passed him earlier. It was a sheaf of paper. At least four pages with questions and boxes and lines to fill up with words he didn't have. How did he begin to explain what had happened with Zachary? How could you describe such an incident? All he felt now was fear, a cold dread, the black cloud back again, waiting over his head to break the storm.

'What do you do back here?' Sergei poked his head around the door.

'I ... make sure costumes are ready for contestants.' Yan pushed the forms away and picked up a pirate's hat.

—

Ellen saw Yan come onto the stage from the backstage area. He began to arrange chairs into place, all tight forearms and toned obliques through the thin material of his shirt. Her stomach moving at that precise moment had nothing to do with the stack load of *dolmades* she'd consumed and she knew it. He caused that reaction in her and she was almost sure he felt the same. Really, the way she was feeling now, she wanted to dive straight into whatever was happening between them. She felt lost here, never more alone, despite having Lacey and her infidelity issues. She was like a boat cast off from the shore, being battered by the tide and drifting, being carried further and further away from everything she thought she knew about life. She needed something.

'And our first contestant for Miss Blue Vue Hotel is ... Miss Lacey from England!'

Dasha's announcement had Lacey squealing, jumping from her chair and trotting off to the stage where Sergei, Tanja and Yan were waiting.

Ellen downed the remainder of her drink and looked toward the beach. The towns and villages of Albania twinkled from across the water and a ferry, lit up with white lights, sailed past the bay, following the path of the moonlight. The cicadas started their song from the palms and the scent of citrus invaded her every sense. How could she be somewhere so beautiful and feel so tied in knots? She was stuck, trapped and most of it was her making. If she hadn't even dated Ross, if she hadn't shared anything with him, or if she'd dated more seriously in the past, gained experience of love and trust a little sooner she might have been less naive, less susceptible.

She jolted from her reverie when her phone rumbled into action. Swiping it up she pressed icons until she found her emails. There was one new one from Milo.

All her senses halted at once, a full-on all together ceasing. Her thumb was hovering over the email as she read the subject line. *Keegan Manufacturing.*

A lump the size of Ayers Rock was blocking her throat as she lightly pressed the screen of her phone to read the email. With blurred vision she started to pick out words – *discrepancies, modifications* – and the contents of what Milo was talking about. He'd been through the Keegan Manufacturing accounts. He knew there was something wrong. And by the time she got home, everyone would know it was down to her.

———

Something was wrong. Yan could tell. Although the three competitors for the Miss Blue Vue Hotel contest were swishing bits of themselves over chairs in a bid to perform the sexiest moves, his eyes were focussed on Ellen. She'd finished her drink quickly, her hands shaking as she held onto the mobile phone in her hand. Her eyes, those beautiful, brown eyes, were filled with alarm. She was only a few yards away but completely out of reach. He had a job to do. He swallowed to relieve his dry throat as he watched her. He wanted to go to her, find out what was happening, what was making her look this way.

He watched her stand, pick up her bag from the floor and make towards the steps. She was leaving.

TWENTY FIVE

Ellen had to do something. She couldn't just sit there, stuck, her whole professional future whirling around in her head like a cinematic merry-go-round. Everything she'd built, everything she'd strived for, followed by visions of it all crashing down around her. She'd got her vengeance on Ross but she had committed a crime in doing it. Why hadn't the seriousness of that hit her before now?

Ellen could hear the laughter from the stage as she walked around, past the steps to the suite and down the path toward the beach. Lacey squealing, Dasha exclaiming, the sound of balloons bursting. It wasn't real life. It was a holiday, an alternate world and right now she couldn't cope with any of it.

'Ellen.'

She heard Yan's voice but she couldn't stop walking. She just needed to keep on moving, stepping away, distancing herself. She focussed on the night sky, so full of stars, so vast and dark …

Yan grabbed hold of her arm and pulled her to a stop just before the gate.

———

He turned her around where she stood, forcing her to pay attention to him. But instead of looking into his eyes as he hoped, she focussed her gaze lower, at the bag he was holding. The bag containing her clothes.

He swallowed, the air between them sharpening.

'They are cleaned,' he stated, breaking the tension.

The words sounded stupid and inappropriate. They were nothing like what he wanted to say.

'I don't care,' Ellen responded. 'You can keep them if you want. Give them to the next girl.'

Her voice sounded detached, like the words had come from her but she hadn't been the one saying them.

'You are upset,' he offered, putting the bag on the floor.

'Yes, I *am* upset.' Her eyes narrowed. 'And there's nothing anyone can do to fix it.'

Ellen turned away, shaking her arm free from his touch.

'How do you know this?'

———

She'd expected him to give up. She wanted him to give up. She just needed to reach the sand and the sea, press her toes into the ground and try to stop the world from turning.

'It could help to talk,' he offered. 'I could listen and it could help you.'

Ellen turned back to face him. He was looking at her, those aquamarine eyes studying her face, his hands in the pockets of his jeans now, his chest rising and falling with each breath.

She relented. 'I don't know what to say.'

She felt her breath collect in her lungs, pooling there, not knowing whether to rise up and out or sink back down into her abdomen. He was looking at her, those eyes resting on her.

'You do not have to say anything if that is what you want.'

She watched him place the bag on the ground and take a step closer to her.

Her body reacted to his movement. It was an involuntary motion that started slowly deep inside her and then grew, spread out, widening itself into something forceful. As it overwhelmed her every sense, she rocked on her heels, imbalanced, off centre.

'I behave so wrong last night,' he began.

She shook her head. 'No.'

He hadn't done anything but retreat. And retreating had been the sensible thing to do. She'd craved his attention in the moment. It had been a natural response to being involved with something so terrifying that she would remember it forever. She shivered.

'Yes, I do.' He shifted further forward. 'I know this.'

He was close now, face to face, looking at her with a hot intensity. She wet her lips with her tongue as every ion of her woke up to his proximity.

Her eyes matched his, her breath accelerating against the humid air between them. She didn't want to talk. Right now she wanted to act. She wanted to feel lost, weightless, spiralling in the moment, ungrounded and just a little chaotic. Where had all her thinking ever got her?

———

Yan knew this was going against his self-imposed embargo and every one of the rules of his job but he couldn't stop it. He felt something for her and he hoped he could sense a matching sentiment from her. He had his new beginning here but where was the meaning? He could work harder than anyone else and this still might not be the answer to his future. She liked him. She liked him for him, as he was now, with no need for shaping or change. That meant so much.

But still, he was nervous. The whole of his body was supercharged, jolting his insides as he stood before her, wanting to act but trying to be calm, needing everything to be just right.

'I do not do this …' He paused, his eyes holding hers captive. 'With any other woman here.' He tried again. 'There is no next girl.'

———

The sincerity in Yan's tone hit her far more than the words. She really believed him. She knew he was telling her the truth. And the fact he wanted her to know that, wanted her to feel she was special – it touched every sense.

Ellen pulled in her core as he raised a hand and grazed it down her hair. As each strand filtered through his fingers she felt it more keenly.

The warmth of his breath, the taste of the heat in the air, it was overpowering everything. A heady, erotic mix assaulted every inch of her as he drew himself closer still.

She couldn't hold off any longer. She didn't want to waste another second in this half-state. She was so close to feeling more than she had ever felt. It wasn't just arousal from a sexual reaction, it was a call to her soul. Here was her chance to open herself up, with no ulterior motives, just her feelings and a good, kind, gorgeous man reciprocating.

———

Yan couldn't wait. His heart was pulsing hard, the fine hairs on his arms standing to attention. Ellen was there in front of him, her mouth slightly open, her full lips moist and tempting. All sense had left him. He had no choice now. His body was in control but it was much more than just chemistry. Right at that moment it felt like destiny.

He took her mouth with his, hard, assured, nothing like the kiss they'd shared in his room. This time he wanted there to be no doubt. He wanted her to know just how much he longed for her. Her beauty, her simplicity, the goodness in her. She was raw, pure, untainted.

With both hands cradling her face, their mouths connected, he walked her backwards.

———

Ellen let out a gasp as her back hit the wall and they came apart for a second. He looked at her, his face only a centimetre from hers, his eyes alive, his breathing ragged. She moved her mouth to his again, pulling him into her, closing the gap and pushing her back against the cool of the wall as the weight of him pressed onto her. She wanted this so much. She wanted to get to know this feeling, believe in it, have faith that it was all for her. It didn't matter for how long, it just mattered that she experienced it; wanting someone so much, being desired by a man for who she was, not what she had.

He moved his mouth from hers, leaving her feeling suddenly bereft. But as his tongue touched the outside of her neck and his lips travelled across her bare shoulder she coiled up inside. Every inch of her was on the highest alert, each section of skin being set alight by the touch of his lips, the pull of his mouth.

She ran a hand over his shoulder and down his back as far as she could reach, riding over the muscles through his thin shirt, relishing the solidity of his form as the weight of his body moved against hers.

———

Ellen's skin was like the softest caramel, smooth and sweet under his tongue. His thumb trailed a circle down her arm as his mouth followed the path. He wanted to experience every part of her, slowly, gently, making each second count. His eyes were closed but as she reached up and under his shirt he opened them, drawing back slightly, looking at her. He had to be sure this was what she wanted. He did not want to push her to do anything she did not want to do.

Yan opened his mouth to speak but, before he could, she had caught his mouth in another hot kiss. Her lips told him all he needed to know. She wanted this, wanted *him*.

———

The sound of conversation moved him back a little. He looked at Ellen. She was breathing hard, her cheeks hot but she stilled, sensing she should.

It was Dasha, Yan was certain and someone else he couldn't recognise from voice alone. One of the guests perhaps? There was no way he wanted to be found out like this, with Ellen, but not for all the reasons he usually thought of – his new start, his job. His only thought was for her.

'Let's go,' Ellen said.

Her whispered, anxious tone brought him back to the present and he felt her fingers slip between his.

'Let's go,' she repeated, tugging his arm towards her and away from their precarious position.

The voices started to increase in volume and he looked at her flushed face, her eyes swimming with moisture. Her fingers were still locked with his.

He moved then, tightening his grip on her. With one stoop to pick up the bag of clothes he hurried with her, towards the gate.

TWENTY SIX

They'd left the complex behind and Yan had turned them left, the opposite direction to Bo's Bar. His hand was still in hers with no sign of backing away or retreating this time. It was warm, comfortable there, felt right. But he hadn't spoken yet. They were just walking, hands locked together, sedately moving along the track.

'Where are we ...' she started.

'The beach,' he jumped in.

'But ...'

Before she could argue that this wasn't the way to the beach, she saw it open up in front of her. The grassland fell away and at the edge of the bank was yet another beautiful beach. Completely deserted, sun loungers stacked in a high pile by an old wooden shack and, overlooking the sand, was a tiny white chapel. Tall trees flanked the sand, their leaves rustling and fluttering like paper fans. The only light was from the moon, creating a silver glow across the water's edge.

'Oh, Yan, it's so...' She didn't have any words adequate enough to describe the breathtaking scene.

'Guests always go to other beach. It is near to hotel more,' Yan told her.

He was still holding her hand and she squeezed it now, wanting him to realise she was still there, still touching him.

He turned to look at her and smiled. A wide smile, one that looked like it came from the heart of him.

He brought her hand up to his lips and with a feather light touch he skimmed the skin with his mouth. She felt her insides melt like warming chocolate. She didn't wholly understand what was happening between them but, right now, somehow, explanations just weren't required.

'You like to walk on beach?' he asked her.

She nodded.

———

They walked the length of the beach, an easy silence between them, just content with the sound of the gentle waves lapping the shoreline. Then Yan stopped, moving to sit down. Ellen followed his action, lowering herself onto the sand. She smiled up at him and he slipped an arm around her shoulders, drawing her into his body. He felt her warmth seep into him and he ran a hand down her hair, stroking softly.

'Something is making you worry,' he stated. 'That is why you are upset before?'

He felt the immediate tension in her torso in reaction to his words. Maybe it wasn't his place to ask her these questions so soon.

'Yes.'

Ellen's voice had come out one notch above a whisper and emotion was evident. He remained still, his hand moving to gently caress her opposite shoulder. If she wanted to tell him more she would.

'I had a difficult message from a colleague about one of my cases.' The voice was stronger now. 'When I get back home there's going to be a lot to sort out.'

He nodded even though he didn't understand. *When she got back home.* Another reminder that this something between them, would not last, was not *meant* to last. It was inevitable. Yan nodded again.

'But that's then, not now. And I don't want to talk about it.' She moved on the sand, turning to face him full on, taking his hands and linking them with hers. 'Tell me what you like best about here, about Corfu.'

She was smiling at him now, her eyes full and glistening, her expression set with excitement.

'What I like best about Corfu?' He paused, tilting his head as if in thought. 'I like you. When you do not wear the frown face.' He paused. 'When you smile.'

She laughed then and her whole face lit up as she rocked forward and swiped at his arm with her hand. 'I'm not from Corfu. I'm from England.'

'What do you like from England? Does it rain all of the time?'

'Most of it. And when the sun does shine everyone complains it's too hot and they ban hosepipes.'

He furrowed his brow and she reached up and gently pressed the crease between his eyes. 'We like to water our gardens. Not me, I don't have a garden. But my dad and all the other English people.'

'I like nature here,' he told her. 'There is a lagoon just there.' He pointed down the beach and Ellen turned to look.

'Maybe we could go there ...' She stopped herself. She didn't really know the rules for this holiday flirtation she was having. A night of kisses might be all that was on offer. Just as she was beginning to wonder how she would feel about that he spoke.

'Maybe tomorrow?'

'I'd really like that,' she told him.

———

'You have more family?' Yan asked her, releasing his fingers from her and shifting his body a little.

They were laying on the beach and more than an hour had passed. The sand was cool against Yan's back and the only sound, apart from their conversation, was the ebb and flow of the tide and the breeze through the trees that lined the road behind.

'Just a dad,' Ellen answered. 'My mum died when I was young.'

'After she have your sister?' he queried.

'No, she has a different mother. My dad married again.'

He noted her tone. 'You do not like this woman?'

Ellen sighed. 'No, I didn't like her and she didn't like me. I don't even think she liked Lacey very much. Still, she's gone now. They divorced, years ago.'

She tilted her body towards him, reengaging their fingers. She smiled. 'Say something to me in German.'

'What?'

'Please. I like it. Say something.'

'I don't know what it is to say.'

'Anything.'

He smiled then and spoke. '*Ich bin Ellen. Ich liebe Wasser-Aerobic.*'

Ellen squeaked and let his hand go. 'That isn't proper German.'

He laughed, enjoying her frustration.

'I wish I could speak more languages,' she said.

'You speak only English?' he asked, turning on his side to face her.

'I did a bit of French at school but the only words I remember are *croque monsieur* and *voleur*. What does that say about me?' She laughed.

'I do not know of French,' he answered. 'Only German and a little Russian. I work in café and bar. I pick up what they say in other language. I learn.'

'That's so clever to be able to do that.'

Prickles ran up his arm and he felt the now familiar sense of unease dragging at him. He swallowed the bitter taste away. He couldn't say much more. 'When you want to not work in meat factory you use everything you can to stop it.'

'I would learn Russian if it meant escaping the meat factory. It sounds horrid.'

'Sshh.' He held still, listening, then sat bolt upright.

———

Ellen pulled herself up too, holding on to his hand as he turned his head towards the entrance to the beach. 'What is it?'

'Sshh.'

She heard it then too. Voices, a little way off, but still audible and getting closer.

'What should we do?'

Yan pursed his lips as if preparing to 'sshh' her again. But before he could, every hair on her body rose up at the sound of female laughter.

'Oh my God,' she whispered. 'It's Lacey.'

Yan turned away from the approaching couple and back to her. 'With Sergei.'

She didn't know what to do. Should she do anything? What was she more worried about? Lacey being alone on an almost deserted beach with Sergei, or *her* being discovered with Yan? At that precise moment she wasn't certain.

'They can't see us,' she said quietly.

'No, is dark.'

'No, I mean I don't want them to find us.'

'No,' he agreed.

———

Yan wasn't sure how he felt about her statement. She must know that he couldn't be seen with a hotel resident. Or was it she was just ashamed to be found with him?

Yan turned his head, watching Lacey and Sergei moving along the beach behind them. They were arm in arm, chatting excitedly, laughing too loudly, uncaring as to who saw them, like they were the only two people in existence.

'Where are they going?' Ellen asked.

'Ellen ...'

'Is there another bar or something near here?' She stopped before continuing. 'Or just the lagoon?'

The worry in her voice was evident and he didn't know what he should say. He knew how Sergei operated but telling Ellen would serve no purpose but to concern her more. He also did not want her to think that he and Sergei were the same. He had never brought someone here before, had never had that intention in mind.

'No,' he stated. 'No bar. Just more beach and mountains.'

He watched her nod her head as if expecting the answer he'd given.

'What do I do?' she asked, turning to him, her eyes wide and questioning.

—

Ellen put a hand to her head, rubbing the skin over her brow, as if it would help her find an answer.

'She does not want to get married?' Yan asked.

Ellen let out a non-committal sound pitching somewhere between a sigh and a snort. 'I don't know what she wants.'

'Sergei. He has someone back in Bulgaria. A girlfriend. He talk to me of this.'

She had thought as much. Lacey was throwing her relationship with Mark away on a meaningless fling. Should she try and stop her making a fool of herself? Here was her golden opportunity to wade in, tell her the Zumba instructor was attached, embarrass them both with some home truths.

'You want to meet with them?' Yan asked.

She didn't know what to do. Whichever way she chose threw up dilemmas.

Another high-pitched shriek of a laugh from her sister made up her mind.

She looked up at Yan. 'Will you walk me back to my room?'

—

Yan loved the hotel at night. Everything was subtly lit up by the glow of the lantern-style lamps dotted around the hotel grounds. It was perfectly peaceful apart from the hum and buzz of the night time bugs.

The air was warm but a slight breeze shifted the humidity, riding over them. He saw Ellen shiver.

'You are OK?'

She nodded, rubbing her arms to stave off the chill.

He should put his arm around her. He wanted to but he couldn't. He'd already taken one risk that night and if they wanted to spend more time together there would be others. But here, in the complex, out in the open. It was too risky.

They continued to walk but it wasn't far. The women had one of the gold star suites facing the sea and the mountains at least a ten minute walk from his room.

'So, here we are,' Ellen said. She'd stopped outside the door to the room, slotted the key in the lock and edged it open. He watched her hug her arms to her body.

Here they were, the night over. It seemed too soon.

He desperately wanted to pull her towards him, hold her against him, feel her hair between his fingers ...

Then she spoke. 'Do you want to come in?'

—

It felt awkward. Both of them standing on the balcony walkway, neither knowing what to do. She didn't really want him to go yet. They'd not had long enough, but she couldn't have stayed on the beach knowing what Lacey and Sergei were doing.

Yan shook his head then and a flutter of disappointment manifested inside her. She shouldn't feel that way. What exactly was she inviting him in for anyway? More of the red-hot kisses he'd given her or something else? Not that it mattered because the shake of his head had already turned her down.

'I would like this ... very much but. ..' he started.

'It's OK. You don't need to explain.'

'Ellen, I am not like Sergei. Please, you have to believe this.'

Yan caught hold of her hand then and massaged her fingers.

'You shouldn't. Someone could see. And I don't want to get you into trouble.' She tried to let go but he held on and stepped forward, backing her into the room.

'Yes, but this is important also,' he insisted.

'I understand.'

'Sergei has many girls, Ellen.' He looked at her, sincere. 'I tell you I do not.'

Her heart warmed at the statement but straightaway she checked herself. They only had three more nights. It was temporary.

They were in the room now and he pushed the door closed. 'I do not say this right.' Yan sighed.

'No, you're saying everything fine.' She nodded, toying with his fingers as he clasped her hand.

He reached up with his free hand and swept her hair back from her face. As his fingers made contact with her cheek she closed her eyes, letting the feeling wrap her up. His lips found hers and she widened her mouth to let him in deeper. A sigh escaped as he moved a hand to her chest.

He wanted to touch her, go further, let her realise just what her presence did to him. Was it too much? Was it too soon? He moved away, but the second they were disconnected she took hold of his hand and replaced it, tracing a path, encouraging.

His mouth left hers and his fingers reached for the hem of her top. All the while he fixed his eyes on her, wanting to see her reaction, wanting to know this was what she wanted too. Tentatively he hitched up the material, exposing her midriff and the edge of her bra. A tiny noise came from her and the sound sent a shard of white hot heat through him. He couldn't hold off, couldn't think straight. He pulled the material over her head, discarding it.

———

Ellen watched her top fall to the marble floor. She'd lost all breath, together with every scrap of sensible she'd stored up. His gaze was penetrating. The way he was drinking her in was like he could see right through the cotton and lace to the arousal beneath.

And she *was* aroused, squirming with it, her back rigid, the rest of her liquefying under his scrutiny.

Yan wasted no more time, reaching around her back and unclasping her bra, pulling the material away from her and dropping it to the floor.

A gasp flew from her when he dropped his head and his hot mouth found her nipple. Turning her body slightly, she braced herself against the table, anchoring one hand on top of a chair.

She drew his head further, guiding him deeper. She didn't recognise herself or the responses she was giving. It was almost unchartered territory. She wanted more, wanted to get high on the buzz she was experiencing. Life could be exciting. She had a right to feel this way.

'Yan,' she said, breathy with lust. She drew his head away.

———

With the taste of her skin still on his lips he let go, raising his head to her command. His eyes met the rosy glow of her face, the wide eyes and dilated pupils, the pert blush of her mouth. He was breaking every rule for this woman and it had happened so quickly.

She spoke. 'I want you to stay.'

His body contracted at her words, the meaning so obvious it burned him. It was too soon. Even though their time together was going to be short, he didn't want it hurried. It had to mean something and that meant slowing things down.

He caught her mouth with his again, his fingers at her breast, teasing the skin with short, gentle strokes.

He wanted to hold her, all of her, naked against him and just forget everything else. But that wasn't fair, not on her, not on him.

'Not yet.' He didn't know what else to say. It wasn't enough. It didn't explain anything but it categorically told her no.

He grazed her breastbone with his fingers, travelling upwards and away from the skin his touch had scorched.

He could see the disappointment in her eyes and it affected him. He didn't want to disappoint her. He wanted the same thing but ...

'I understand,' Ellen spoke.

Her voice was laced with emotion and he watched her swallow. What was he doing? She was bare-chested in front of him, looking beautiful and he was backing away. He bent to the floor and picked up her top.

———

Everything was sensitised. He'd lit up every inch of her with his tender touch. But now he was going, when she was alert, needy and desperate for more. She watched him pick her blouse up and hold the fine material in his hands. She didn't move, just looked at him, pensively.

He straightened it, shaking the material loose and holding it out. Gently he placed it over her head and she slipped her arms into the sleeves. Minus a bra but covered and almost proper again. Suddenly she felt abandoned.

'I do not want to leave,' he started. A loaded sigh left his lips. 'Then ...'

'I must.' He nodded. 'But, I see you tomorrow?'

He was really going and she shouldn't act like a child who'd been denied sweets. He was doing the sensible thing. She nodded back.

He pulled the door open and as he stepped back he walked into something. He picked the bag up and held it out to her. 'Your clothes.'

She took it but said nothing.

'Ellen ...'

She threw her arms around him then, holding him tight. Even if it was only a holiday romance it was important to her. It was so important.

He drew away, kissing her mouth. 'Goodnight.'

'Goodnight,' she whispered.

TWENTY SEVEN

'Good morning.' Yan high-fived a passing child as he made his way to breakfast. 'Hello, good morning Uri, we have water exercise this morning at ten.'

The Russian waved a hand and headed left.

The sun was sizzling hot already, the sky was cloudless and he felt amazing. Better than ever. He had a spring in his step, his thoughts only of today. He'd pushed everything else to the very corners of his mind. He wondered if Ellen would be in the restaurant at breakfast now. He wanted to see her. To see her and remember what they had shared together the night before. Affection, mutual passion. He felt goose bumps start on his arms despite the heat. He had to keep his feelings for her under control. They only had a few days together and he wanted to make the very most of it. If they were found out that would be the end, for the relationship and for his job.

'Yan!'

Tanja's shout had the excited goose bumps turning into chills. He turned just before the steps leading to the main hotel complex and faced his boss.

She was dressed in uniform, her dark hair clipped back, an unreadable look on her face.

She began to talk speedily in their native tongue. 'Good morning to you. I have you for water exercise, trip to Perithia and football today.' She checked things off on her clipboard.

'Yes. No problem.'

'And you have done report, yes?'

Yan knew she would ask this. That's what the chills over his skin were about and he had no answer prepared. He needed to think on his feet, something he was well-practiced at. He wet his lips.

'Not yet.' He paused, watched Tanja's face fall into not amused. 'It is so very hard to go back.'

'What?' She creased up her forehead appearing not to understand.

'It was a ...' He paused, looked down at the floor then back up again. 'I have bad dream. The look on face of the boy ...'

He watched Tanja's face soften a little, saw his performance was working. A part of him contracted, knowing it wasn't right, but self-preservation was paramount here.

'I realise it was a very sad and difficult situation. It is something we all hope not to go through but reports have to be filed.'

Yan nodded his head and ground his teeth together. It wasn't going to get him out of it completely – he knew that – it was just buying time. He just needed the day.

'I will let you off the football. I will ask Dasha. You will do report before evening animation program.'

She'd given him what he wanted. He could have kissed the ground in relief. Now he just needed to speak with Ellen.

'Yes, OK,' he replied, keeping his tone sober.

'Good.' Tanja nodded then turned away, heading off in the direction of the kids' club.

Yan let out his breath and realised then just how tight he'd been holding on to it. He wiped the perspiration from his brow and looked toward the restaurant.

A hand squeezed his forearm.

'Hello, lover. I think you've been avoiding me.'

Monica's scent invaded every sense.

———

Ellen ran a brush through her hair, looking in the mirror. With each stroke she glanced to the side, looking over at Lacey's empty bed. Her sister hadn't come back to the room the night before. The strangest thing was, instead of feeling angry or agitated, she didn't really feel anything. No worry, no disappointment, nothing.

Lacey had made a choice and Ellen wasn't to blame. It wasn't her job to guard her from all life's crossroads, not matter what their father might think. Whatever path Lacey was going to tread was on Lacey.

Ellen put the brush on the nightstand and picked up the sun cream. Squeezing some onto her fingertips she closed her eyes, rubbing the lotion across her shoulder and down the top of her arm. All the places Yan had caressed the previous night.

She was still glowing inside from what they'd shared. This holiday had taken on a whole different perspective and it was saving her. She had three more nights to squeeze the life out of it before she faced her fate back home.

And what was that exactly going to be? Facing the consequences of her relationship with Ross? Looking for her dream job? Reclaiming her business executive mantel?

She looked down at the cheap sandals on her feet. In this heat Louboutins would pinch and stifle. There was no call for power shoes on this idyllic island. And here, under a cloudless sky, the only thing spiking her memory was how free she'd felt when she'd jumped off the rocks in Sidari.

She looked at her watch. It was almost nine. She wasn't going to wait for Lacey to appear, not when there was a chance she could catch Yan.

———

The sun was ferocious and Ellen was glad she'd applied sunscreen. She joined the main path that led to the dining room then stopped. Just up ahead, to her right, was Lacey. Unashamedly dressed in last night's outfit, laughing out loud, platinum hair tossed back, Sergei holding her hand. *Holding her hand. In the complex. For all to see.*

Ellen swallowed as the full, simple intimacy of the scene hit home.

Instead of calling out, instead of shouting and waving and catching her up, Ellen let her go. What was there to say that hadn't been explained in what she'd seen?

'Good morning. Lovely day, isn't it?'

She looked at the approaching person and her eyes met with Monica.

'Yes, it's lovely.'

'Will you be joining us for water exercise this morning?'

Sergei didn't seem to care who saw him and Lacey together. He was an archetypal holiday lothario. She watched the couple disappear behind the main building of the hotel.

'Water exercise?' Monica repeated.

'Sorry, yes, maybe I will,' she answered.

Monica let out a sigh. 'I'll be sorry to leave tomorrow. Yan is so sexy, isn't he?'

Now Ellen focussed on the woman, taking in the heavy make-up and cherry red lips.

'If only I could take him home with me,' Monica added.

Ellen swallowed, not knowing how to respond.

'Still, I'm hoping our last night will be one to remember.' Monica smiled and lasciviously licked her lips. 'If you're going to breakfast I'd avoid the hams today. I saw a toddler with his grubby, little fingers all over them.'

TWENTY EIGHT

'Hello.'

Ellen didn't even bother to lower her sunglasses. She could see, even through the tinted lenses, that Lacey was already playing Little Miss Contrite. It made her nauseous. 'Hello.'

She didn't flinch, just carried on reading her book. It was only twenty minutes before water aerobics and she was both gut-wrenchingly nervous and excited about seeing Yan.

'*Hello?* Is that really all you're going to say?' Lacey stuck her hands on her hips and looked affronted.

'Are you going to sit on the lounger? Because standing right there you're blocking my sun.'

Lacey let out a loud snort and dropped her towel to the sun bed.

'Well, this is nice. I spend the whole night *not* in our room and you're not even interested. I half-expected the Greek army to be starting a search party.'

Ellen shook her head. This was typical Lacey behaviour. She'd spent all night cheating on her fiancé and she wanted a Mexican wave.

'I would have sent the Greek army straight to Sergei's room.' She paused. 'Or is Gary Barlow on Corfu?'

'What?' Lacey turned her body towards Ellen and stiffened up.

'What would you like me to say here, Lacey? Would you like me to clap you on the back for sleeping with Sergei or berate you for cheating on Mark? You tell me which and I'll do all the words and the corresponding faces.'

'It isn't like you think ...' Lacey began.

'No? Wait, don't tell me, you didn't sleep with Sergei, you spent all night swapping nail varnish tips with Dasha.'

'No, I ...' Lacey started again.

'Oh no. No. Don't say what I think you're going to say.' Ellen removed her sunglasses to get a better look at Lacey's expression. 'Don't say Sergei told you he loved you. Don't tell me he said you were the only one for him and declared eternal devotion.'

'It wasn't those exact words ...'

'Oh Lacey! You're a fool!' She stood up. 'He says that to everyone! He no more loves you than he loves ...' She looked around the pool area. 'The grandmother of that family from Scunthorpe.'

'Sit down,' Lacey hissed. 'You're making a scene.'

'And you're making a big mistake. Lacey, he's a Romeo. And not the loyal Shakespeare kind, the love-them-and-leave-them kind. The kind that hurts girls.' She swallowed, choking back the emotion that had arrived. 'Girls like you.'

Lacey tutted. There was only one thing for it.

'And he has a girlfriend. There! I've said it. Sergei has a girlfriend back in Bulgaria!'

'Will you stop? I know that. What d'you think I am? Dumb or something?'

Ellen sank back down to her lounger, stunned. What did she mean?

Lacey sat down and crossed her legs under her, turning to face Ellen.

'I know exactly who Sergei is, Ells. He gave me all the lines, the moves, but I knew that. I knew he was going to give me that.'

Ellen had no idea what was going on here. She had to be misunderstanding. It sounded like Lacey had gone into this fling with her eyes open, knowing the score and didn't need protection from her elder sister.

She didn't know what to say. A wasp hit her parted mouth and she swiped at it with her hand.

'I slept with him. So what? It was sex.' Lacey unfurled her legs, stretching them out over the lounger. 'He says it's undying love and I laugh because I know he's talking out of his arse. But it doesn't matter.'

'But it's not right,' Ellen stated. She'd hoped to think of something better to say but she couldn't find the words.

'I know that, too. If I want to have sex with Sergei, if I've cheated on Mark, then that isn't fair.'

'Well ...' Ellen began.

'So I've done the only thing I could do. I've told Mark it's over.'

The book fell out of Ellen's hands and hit the floor. She couldn't stop the gasp escaping or her stomach from falling to somewhere near the Earth's core. 'What?'

'It's all thanks to you, Ells. You were right. About what I was feeling for Sergei *and* about Gary Barlow. The relationship isn't right if I'm going about snogging and sleeping with other men.'

'That wasn't ...' Was that what she'd said? Was this the conclusion she'd been hoping for? It certainly wasn't the one she'd been expecting. She'd thought Lacey would get the infatuation out of her system and then be ready to commit to Mark. But that wouldn't have been right – to hide what had happened, to let everything that happened in Corfu stay in Corfu. She was just so shocked. 'What did he say?'

Visions of Mark weeping into his golf bag and their dad having to deal with the fallout came to mind. Mark was a crier.

They'd watched *Watership Down* at Christmas and he'd excused himself from the room for twenty minutes after the end credits.

'He didn't say anything. I left him a message.'

It was all Ellen could do not to hurl. 'What? Lacey ... you didn't ... you can't. You broke up with him on ... voicemail?!'

'iMessage actually. No kisses, not even a smiley face because I didn't want him to think there was a chance of getting back together. Because there isn't ... not ever ... like, ever.'

'Oh my God, Lacey. You can't break up with him by text. You've been going out so long and ... He deserves better.'

'I couldn't actually speak to him.' Lacey's determined façade began to slip just slightly. 'He would have cried. You know he's a crier. When we watched *Harry Potter* he cried for a week when Dumbledore copped it.'

'And you don't think he's going to want to talk when he sees that message? The very first thing he's going to do is call.'

Ellen didn't believe this was actually happening. Through every hour of uncertainty in her life there had been Lacey's big, fat Greek wedding to cling to. It had been her distraction, her purpose, her chance to redeem herself. Was that why she was so shocked and a little angry? For her own loss, not for Lacey and Mark's?

'Phone's off. And that's the way it's going to stay until we land in England.'

'Lacey, you can't do that.'

'It's done. It's my decision. If he starts calling you you'll have to switch your phone off too.'

—

It took less than fifteen minutes for Ellen's phone to start ringing. Mark. She knew she should answer it, speak to the poor guy, but she really had no idea what to say. The phone throbbed again and she looked left at the caller display.

'Don't you touch it. Turn it off,' Lacey ordered.

'I can't turn it off. I need it for work.' A small lie, since she'd avoided just about every call from Lassiter's so far.

'You're on holiday!'

'Yes and what a great one it's turned out to be! So far I've watched you throw away your relationship, won a limbo competition and saved a drowning boy.'

'And there are so many positives in there.'

Ellen grabbed the phone and turned it to silent. She felt so sorry for Mark. Dumped by iMessage and now everyone was ignoring him when he needed answers.

'Water exercise for you?'

She hadn't even noticed Yan approach, that was how much this was affecting her. And there he was, her one chink of light in this whole sorry mess. Standing just in front of her sun bed, looking tanned, toned and gorgeous.

'Yes,' she replied, standing up. 'Yes, please.' She looked to Lacey. 'We'll finish this conversation later.'

'It is finished. The conversation ... and everything else.'

—

'You are OK?' Yan whispered as she followed him to the edge of the pool.

'Yes. It's just Lacey.' She blew out a breath. 'Everything's Lacey.'

'It is about Sergei.'

She stopped walking and raised her head. 'She's dumped her fiancé.'

'Dumped a what?'

'Sorry. The man she was going to marry. She's ended things. Said goodbye and *auf wiedersehen*. It's over.'

'You speak German.'

He wished he had not made a joke when he saw her close her eyes. She looked so sad, as if it was *her* relationship that was over. They were standing so close and he just wanted to touch her, to give her the comfort he was sure she needed.

'You would like for me to speak with Sergei?' he offered.

She shook her head. 'No. This isn't his fault. Not really.'

Yan didn't know what else to say. He was angry with Sergei. He had no real feelings for Lacey and now, because he couldn't keep himself in check, a marriage would not happen.

'Sorry, I shouldn't be telling you all this and ...'

'It is OK. I like to know.'

Ellen was looking at him as if she didn't know what came next. He didn't either. He desperately needed her help but she was looking so lost. The timing was all wrong. But time was the one thing he didn't have. Tanja needed the report. He swallowed.

'I take trip to Perithia today. You will come?'

She let out a sigh. 'I don't know if I can. Not with Lacey doing what she's done.'

This was not good. He didn't want to push her but if he didn't it could spell disaster for him. He had to be at least a little bit honest.

'I would like for you to help me.'

'Help you?'

He nodded. It was all he could manage as he hadn't thought of an explanation yet. She looked confused.

'Yan! Are we starting?'

Monica again. Only one more day to put up with her constant interruptions and advances. He tightened his core.

'You should join others.'

'What time is the trip?' she asked.

'At two this afternoon.' He was holding his breath now, both hopeful and desperate.

She nodded. 'OK. I'll come.'

———

The first time Ellen had done water exercise she'd been so self-conscious, as unrelaxed as a person could be. Now things were so different. She was enjoying it, wholeheartedly. She stretched her arms high and gazed at Yan as his polo shirt rose up to reveal a small section of midriff.

Next to her Monica let out a lusty sigh. Ellen saw her eyes were also locked on Yan and she didn't like it. She didn't believe there was anything between them but Monica's desire was more obvious than Amy Child's cleavage.

'That is all for today. We meet here again tomorrow at ten.' Yan ended the session.

Ellen dipped her body down into the water and looked over at Lacey. Sunglasses on, ear phones in, prostrate on the back. She resembled someone completely chilled, not someone who had just ditched their fiancé.

Ellen pulled herself up out of the pool and shook the water from her body. She felt refreshed, relaxed, almost like she could cope with anything life threw at her.

Lacey didn't stir when Ellen made it back to the loungers. Drying her hand on her towel she reached for her phone. She hadn't turned it off, just slipped it onto mute and now there were twenty missed calls. She clicked on the list and life threw her something else. Nineteen of the missed calls were from Mark. The last one was from Ross Keegan.

TWENTY NINE

'I don't know how you can eat like that after everything's that's happened.'

Ellen's own stomach was as unsettled as an anti-fracking protest. It didn't quite know how to react. Half of it was grumbling with something like fear about the fact that Ross had called and the other half was whirling with anticipation for a rendezvous with a man who made her tremble with longing. Catching everything life was throwing at her? She wasn't sure two hands were enough.

'Upset gives you an appetite,' Lacey responded, pushing another spoonful of cake into her mouth.

'And you *are* upset, are you? Because the way you were huffing and puffing in the ping pong game and throwing the shots down I didn't realise.'

'Of course I'm upset. I'm going to have to call all the people we've booked stuff with. I don't know how I'm going to tell the dove lady. She'd never been anywhere more exotic than Croydon.'

'Is that really all you're upset about?'

'Of course not. I love Mark, I do, but I don't want to settle down yet. There's too many things I want to do like ...'

'The plank with Sergei.'

Lacey screwed up her face and put her spoon down. 'I don't know why you're making jokes. It isn't funny.'

'It wasn't a joke.'

'Anyway, you did the same thing. You told that Ross you didn't want to marry him. At least I didn't laugh and point at a Sunseeker.'

'That was different.' Ellen swallowed. So different. With no love from either side. Just a business transaction. Networking with benefits.

'It would be, wouldn't it? Because you couldn't possibly make the same mistakes I do. You're clever, intelligent Ellen Brooks not stupid, thick Lacey.' She swiped up her wine glass.

'What?'

'You don't do anything wrong. You don't make mistakes. You don't have a crappy job at New Fashion helping breast impaired women sort their cleavage out. You work for the top accountants in the area doing clever shit with numbers.'

Ellen could see the tears in Lacey's eyes and something inside her revolved. Was that what she thought? That she was perfect, that she had no obstacles to face, didn't know how it felt to fail at something?

Lacey didn't stop. 'Those bloody school prize-giving certificates are yellow with age but Dad still polishes them and runs his fingers over your name on them.'

Ellen didn't want to hear this. It was causing her insides to spasm.

'When I passed my Level One in Customer Service he patted me on the head and said he'd buy me a new dress.' She raised her voice a decibel. 'I work in a clothes shop!'

'I don't know why you're saying all this. Dad's parted with hundreds of pounds already for a wedding that isn't going to happen.'

'And that's what it's always about. Money. *I'll get you a Barbie-with-the-hair-that-grows, Lacey. You deserve the best, Lace, let's forget about the Leona Lewis CD, let's get Leona Lewis.* All my life he's paid me off because you're the daughter of the woman he really loved and I'm the reminder of the bitch that left him high and dry.'

She had to leave. She was sorry Lacey felt like that but she couldn't hear it. Ellen stood up, unsteady on her feet.

'What are you doing? You're not going to say anything? Tell me I'm wrong? Say it isn't true?'

Visions of Al's face when she'd shown him her ACCA certificate came to mind, the pride in his expression. It told the tale that despite all the ups and downs, he'd done something right with her up-bringing. He was proud of Ellen and that pride, that fear of disappointing him, was what had led to all her actions after she'd turned Ross down and he'd taken her money.

'You can't say anything because you know I'm right.'

'Dad loves you for you, Lacey.'

'How patronising is that?!'

'Stop it.' Ellen couldn't catch her breath. Her heart was beating so hard. 'Don't make this about me.'

'It's always been about you. How could I possible compete with Little Miss Perfect?'

She picked up her bag and looked at her over-emotional sister. Fierce expression on her face, eyes narrowed but shiny with unshed tears. For once she didn't feel sorry for her. Because she'd always been sheltered from everything. Lacey hadn't seen how Al had struggled, hadn't noticed all the things Ellen had done for her. She'd been so young and they'd protected her. But that had made her oblivious and now it was backfiring.

Ellen lowered her voice. 'It isn't a competition.' Her voice started to break. 'It never was.'

THIRTY

The ancient town of Old Perithia, according to the leaflet Yan had handed around on the bus, was a protected heritage site and a designated area of natural beauty. Its collection of ruins and ongoing restoration were the oldest examples of traditional mountain villages.

Situated at the bottom of Mount Pantokrator, it afforded a full, stunning view of the huge peak that loomed over the island, green in part, grey craggy rocks commanding the rest and the communications tower at its pinnacle.

Ellen surveyed her surroundings as Yan gave guidance to others on the trip. Like the rock formations in Sidari, everything here was so old. It was like looking into the past. Rough, cobbled pathways, homes built by hand, a few stray sheep wandering around. Her eyes settled on a taverna. Sucking in history could definitely be done better with the benefit of a cold lemonade.

'You wish for drink?'

She turned and Yan was beside her, a clipboard in his hands.

'I think I do.' She nodded. 'If only to get over the drive up here.'

He smiled. 'Panos does this two times for a week for six months of year.'

'I'm reassured.'

'Come, we sit,' Yan said, leading the way towards the taverna.

———

Yan liked Old Perithia. In a lot of ways it reminded him of his village in Bulgaria. It was simple, quiet, people were working hard to maintain the deserted buildings, save little pieces of the past.

They sat under the vine-covered pergola at a table for two and ordered lemonades.

Something was still on Ellen's mind. He could see the distraction written on her face. He inched his hand across the table and placed it over hers. The connection made her jolt, and look up at him.

'Someone might see,' she whispered, moving her hand back a little.

'Most people will try to climb to top of mountain.' He turned his wrist, looked at his watch. 'We have hour before they know they cannot do this.' He linked his fingers with hers. 'You want to tell me what is wrong?'

She shook her head quickly.

'This is all about Lacey?' he asked.

She let out a sigh, aligning their hands, moving her fingers through his.

'We had an argument before. It was stupid.'

'You worry a lot about her. Because of the no mothers?' he asked.

She nodded. 'Yes.'

He took a breath before continuing. 'I know all of this.' He paused. 'I tell you I have younger brother, yes?'

She nodded.

'I have older brother too.' He hesitated for a moment. 'He die.'

Ellen directed those warm brown eyes at him then and he swallowed as all the memories rode over him. He thought about

Boyan often but never spoke about him. He had looked up to him. Boyan had been two years older and when he was twenty five he had been murdered in the street for his wallet and phone. Gang related, they'd said, but no one took the blame.

'How?' Ellen asked.

'Killed in the city. Beaten until he was dead.' He rattled the statement out without emotion. That's the way it had been, even back then. To show emotion was weak, even when the very worst thing had happened. He needed to be strong for his parents, for his younger brother. He had become the eldest sibling and the responsibility that brought was huge.

Ellen shook her head and her reaction to this sent something spiralling inside him. The revelation had affected her deeply. Someone who had never known his brother was grieving a little just hearing he had passed.

'And here I am crying over my little sister being a diva.'

———

Yan shrugged and she swallowed as snapshots of her mother from the photo albums at home came to mind. There was so much loss between them.

'It happen. I never forget him but there, he is gone.'

There was both finality and tenderness in his tone. She squeezed his hand tightly in hers.

'That is why I have to do something with my life.' He sighed. 'To make it better. For Boyan and for my family. I wish to make them proud.'

Making people proud. Was that what life was about? It seemed to be a constant echo in her own life. She had done the making proud part and now it was a fulfilled legacy that was hanging over her like an executioner's guillotine.

Yan took a sip of his drink then let go of her hand. He reached for his clipboard and turned it over. She watched him detach some papers and hold them in his hand.

'I do not want to ask this but …' he began.

'What is it?' Ellen asked.

'Tanja, my boss, she need me to fill in report about accident … with Zachary.'

'Yes, I expect there will be a lot of reports to fill in about that. The insurance company and …'

'And for my company too. Because I save the boy.'

The papers in his hands shook a little and straightaway he stiffened up, clearing his throat. 'It have to be in English.'

Ellen didn't say anything, unsure what he meant.

'The report have to be in English. Is language all of company understand. Will you help?'

———

Quick, direct and straight to the point. That was the only way he was going to be able to do this. He didn't even want to think about it too much. He didn't want to have to use her but what other choice did he have? He couldn't ask anyone else from the team. They would not understand. Ellen was the only one he trusted enough.

'You want me to write it for you?'

She'd understood but he had to make this sound light. The moment he let any nervousness or emotion into the request she might sense something was wrong.

'My English for writing is not very good. I am ashamed of this.'

'Ashamed? I think it's marvellous you can speak so many languages.'

She was being so nice and so kind. He felt guilty for lying to her. 'I will tell you what I see and do, if you could write? I do not want to ask but Tanja, she ...'

'Of course I'll do it.' She smiled. 'We can do it now if you get me some of that cake like the couple over there.' She indicated the table to their left where a man and a woman were tucking into huge wedges of a sticky brown sponge.

'You know if you eat this I will make you play volleyball,' he joked.

'You know if you don't get me cake I won't fill in the forms.'

———

She had meant it to be funny but the concern coating his features made her wish she hadn't fussed about cake she didn't need. He had paled, was wetting his lips with his tongue. He picked up his glass of lemonade and drank it all down.

'I will get cake,' he said, getting to his feet.

'Yan, we don't have to have cake,' she blurted out.

'No, is OK. You help me. I buy cake,' he responded.

'Let me pay,' Ellen offered, bending to pick up her rucksack. Perhaps money was the issue here. She'd made him buy beers on the beach. Now she felt guilty.

'Ellen, stop.'

His tone had her dropping her bag to the floor and looking at him, eyes wide. She didn't want to upset him. He was the best thing she'd ever had and in a few days she'd never see him again. Their first row after only just getting together couldn't be over cake in a deserted village.

He stepped towards her and, without any prelude, he kissed her lips, his hand in her hair, pressing her to him. When he finally let her go her head was swimming.

He looked at her, a serious expression on his face. 'I am to buy cake.'

Ellen nodded, her lips still fizzing. 'OK.'

———

'... after heart ... to push ... I do not know how you say this.'

They had eaten the cake and for the last half an hour he had talked, Ellen had translated and they had almost filled up two sheets of paper.

'Heart massage? Er, I'll put resuscitation.' She wrote down the words and he watched the letters forming. She wrote so quickly, with such confidence. She'd understood what he was trying to say and made it into proper English sentences.

'I thank you so much for this.'

'Believe it or not, I like filling in forms.'

She smiled as he frowned.

'How could anyone like to do this?' he asked.

'I don't know, I suppose some people are good at certain things and other people are better in other areas. Look at you, with animation, with the children – that takes so much patience, an understanding of human nature even. I'm just good at paperwork.'

'Ah but now you are expert at water aerobics and you jump from Canal d'Amour and then there is Greek dancing.'

'Which I was particularly rubbish at.'

'I do not think this is true. I watch you.'

'Did you now?'

She was smiling as their flirtatious banter wove around her like a magic spell.

Yan cleared his throat. 'You say you are not to be married.'

'That's right.'

'Is there someone for you?

'I don't know what you mean.'

She watched him take another moment.

'Do you have boyfriend at home?'

'No! No, of course not.'

'I am sorry to ask, I just … I do not want for there to be anything between us like this.'

'I'm really nothing like my sister,' she said with half a smile.

'You are close to someone once?' he asked.

Ellen's thoughts immediately went to Ross.

'There was someone, some months ago. But it didn't work out.' She dropped her eyes to the cobbled stones of the floor.

'What happen?'

Ellen watched a team of ants head off towards a discarded bread roll. She didn't raise her head before replying. 'He asked me to marry him and I said no.'

———

She'd mumbled the words out but he'd heard every one and his insides responded by tightening up, knotting together at the mention of marriage.

'I didn't love him and he didn't love me and it's wrong to marry someone for tax breaks.'

'For what?'

'It doesn't matter. It's not important.'

He nodded.

'Right now, this week, the most important thing to me is being with you.'

He watched her expression as she took both his hands in hers. It was what he wanted to hear, wasn't it? He wanted to eke out every second enjoying the way it made him feel in her company, didn't he?

He let go of her hands and softly touched her face with his fingers, cupping her jaw.

———

At his tender touch she wanted to cry. She was over-emotional because of her fight with Lacey, because of the missed call from Ross.

Yan let out a heavy sigh, his eyes locked with hers, their faces close together across the table.

'It would be more easy for me to not feel this way with you.'

'I know.'

'I have to keep this job, Ellen. It is all I have.'

'I know that.'

'If I do not have this job for the summer I do not know what …'

She moved her lips to his and kissed him hard. She wanted to let him know how much she had started to care.

'Ellen.'

Him breathing out her name only made her kiss more insistent. She wanted to feel his mouth enveloping hers, wanted his hands on her skin, to feel the throb of his heart against hers. It was special. He was special. And England couldn't have been any further away.

A gentle throat clearing had them breaking quickly apart. The waitress was standing at their table, a smile on her face.

'You would like more cake?' she offered, collecting up their plates.

'Oh, no thank you. It was delicious but if I eat any more he's going to make me do Zumba,' Ellen responded.

Yan shook his head. 'I do not do this.'

'No?'

'No. After we finish drink we walk to top of Mount Pantokrator.'

Ellen nodded. 'I know you're joking.'

He let out a laugh, shaking his head.

Her eyes shot left and upwards, scaling the almighty mountain. She turned back to Yan. 'Isn't there a cable car?'

THIRTY ONE

Ellen was glowing. Yan hadn't made her walk to the summit of Mount Pantokrator but when they'd returned to the Blue Vue Hotel they hadn't gone back inside the complex. Instead they'd walked along a track down to the beach and then further, along a few miles of dusty, rocky dirt road towards the town of Acharavi.

They were tracking the edge of the turquoise water, woods to their left, shingle beach on their right. The sea was rolling white crested waves onto the rocks of the small inlet, licking the stones clean before turning to bubbling surf. A little way out, a blue and white fishing boat was buffeted by the ocean's force as a dot of a sailor attempted to pull in his catch. Apart from the lone fisherman, there was no one else in sight.

'Goats, see,' Yan said, stopping suddenly and pointing into the trees.

Ellen shielded her eyes from the sun and followed the line of his arm. 'Are they wild?'

'You are scared of goat?' he asked.

'No, of course not, we just don't have wild animals like that in England.'

'Goat is not like tiger or lion.'

'Very funny.'

Yan grinned and slipped his hand back into hers.

'I can't remember the last time I went on a walk.' She let out a sigh. 'You definitely couldn't do this in a pair of Louboutins.'

'I do not understand.'

'They're designer shoes. Expensive.'

'You have these?'

'Not anymore.'

This time when she said the words there was no yearning pang for them.

'The man you were with. He buy you shoes?'

Ellen shook her head. 'No.'

'He has not money for these shoes?'

'Money was one of the reasons it went downhill.'

'Downhill?'

'To crap. Ended. Finished. *Kaput*,' she offered.

'You know more of German,' he exclaimed.

She laughed. 'What about you?'

———

'What about me?' He'd said the words too quickly because he was worried about what else to say.

'You asked me if I have someone back home. Do you?' Ellen asked.

Her tone was so gentle, so concerned.

'No.' He needed to stop there but he could feel the words automatically coming to his lips. 'But there was someone.' He stopped walking.

A moment ticked by before Ellen spoke again. 'What happened?' Her voice was quieter now, subdued maybe because of his answer.

He shook his head. 'It is difficult.'

What could he say to her? He did not want to lie but he did not want to tell her the truth either. He had to keep it from her. Not just to protect himself but to protect her. He didn't want to let her down. They only had a few days and he wanted her to remember him as someone she had felt strongly about, not someone who was challenged.

He watched her swallow.

'You don't have to tell me. If it's still raw, then ...' she began.

'It is but ...' He was getting emotional. He hated the fact that even now, after all this time, the thought of what had happened affected him so much. He straightened his shoulders, lifted his head a little.

'Yan, I'm sorry, I shouldn't have even asked.' She touched his arm.

'No. It is OK.' He felt for her hand. He wanted to hold it while he told her at least some of it. Because she was important to him and she had shared her story with him.

'I was to be married.'

He looked up then, waiting to see what the statement did to her reaction. Her face tightened, her mouth closed up and her eyes widened just a little.

'We were together for two years and very happy ...' He stopped. 'I think we are happy. So I ask for her to marry and she say yes.'

'What happened?'

———

Ellen couldn't help herself. She had to know. Yan's girlfriend had accepted his proposal, had wanted to marry him, unlike her situation with Ross. What could have changed?

'Was there someone else?' The words blurted out of her mouth as they rolled over her mind. 'Sorry, I don't know why I said that.'

'No ... I do not think.' He picked up a stone from the track and moved it between his fingers. 'It was her father.'

'Her father?' she queried.

He nodded. 'He is very rich man. He give me job but at the end … I could not do this.'

'So, you couldn't do the job and that meant you couldn't marry his daughter?' It sounded like something out of a film.

'Rayna have a choice. She can decide to be with me or stay with father.' His tone was sober. She didn't need to be told his girlfriend's decision.

'I'm sorry, Yan.' She *was* sorry. Although she was glad he was here with her, she had come to know he was not the type of person to give his love lightly. Everything she'd seen him do in the time she'd known him had been measured and thought about. The way he was so conscientious about his job, how he was with the children, how he had stepped up to save Zachary.

'We can make plans but if others think of different then …'

'I've made plans all my life and look where that's got me.' Ellen smiled.

———

It was a smile from her heart. When she had first arrived in the resort he wasn't sure if he would ever see her smile.

'So plan is to not make plan?' he asked her.

'Yes, I think so. I think it's all about taking every day as it comes.'

Now she looked excited. Had he done that? Had he given her that sparkle in her eyes and that glow on her cheeks? Just by getting to know her. By spending time with her. He hadn't planned for any of this to happen, a connection the very last thing on his mind, but it *had* happened and it had grown – was still growing between them.

Perhaps it was time to trust a little more.

THIRTY TWO

Yan grabbed hold of Ellen, picking her up and throwing her over his shoulder with minimal effort. She screamed as her head hung upside down, bumping up and down, taking a closer view of the dirt track than was safe.

'Yan! Stop! I'm going to fall!'

'You will not fall.' He started to sprint off into the greenery. Bushes and olive trees, tall grass and flora flipped past her line of sight as he ran into the wooded area.

'There are snakes here. I've read about them in the guide book. Put me down!' Her voice jolted as she thumped up and down on his back.

'Snakes are not to worry for. Like goat they will not hurt you unless you scare for them.'

'I'd rather not risk finding out!'

'This is not planned. You say not to make plan. I take you into wood.'

Yan lowered her down off his back and spread his arms wide at the surroundings. She blew out a breath, brushed her hair back behind her ears and looked at the building just in front of them half hidden by vines and leaves.

'What is this place?' She walked forward towards the building, pushing weeds and undergrowth out of her way.

'Church. It was church. Now it is nothing,' Yan replied, following her.

Ellen put her hands on the peach coloured plaster that was crumbling and coming away from the structure. Even in its current state of disrepair it was beautiful.

'How did you find it?' She went towards the wooden door.

'Sometime we take kids' club on nature walk.'

She expected it to be locked but she pushed at the door anyway. It opened. 'It's not locked,' she said to him.

He stepped ahead of her. 'I will go first. There could be goat.'

She thumped his shoulder as he led the way into the body of the building.

Yan pushed open the inner door and as she followed him she raised her head to the roof. A gasp escaped her lips. The ceiling was still in one piece, a starlit night sky in dark blue, carvings and paintings marked out in white and gold.

'It's beautiful,' she breathed.

'I like to be here,' Yan responded.

Ellen took her gaze away from the ceiling and focussed on the rest of the room. The seats were split and broken, the floor covered in dirt, dust and plaster from the flaking walls.

'When I dream, I think of making kids' club here someday.'

She moved towards him. 'What do you mean? Like in your village in Bulgaria?'

'People have always to work late here, for shop and restaurant. After the school they could come here until parents finish,' he said.

—

He knew in his heart he would never be able to get a job at a school. When he first saw this place the idea had formed. After the summer season he could lease the old church, earn money from looking after the local children, teaching them sport and games. If it was wet they had the building, once he had done repairs, and if it was nice weather they had the woodland and the beach.

'I think it's a brilliant idea.'

Her eyes were shining.

He nodded. It was a good idea, he knew that, but he wasn't sure it was an idea he could implement very easily. Setting it up would require skills he just didn't have.

'Are you going to do it?' Ellen asked. She looked eager and excited.

'I do not know.' He tested one of the seats with his hand before sitting down on it. 'I have the rest of season at Blue Vue Hotel first then ...'

'Afterwards, then. You could spend the winter making repairs and in the spring ...'

'It is not so easy. I would need to get job to pay for church and repairs. To fix will take time and ...'

'I know but think what you could achieve.' He watched her looking around the building. It was as if she could already see the room transformed into a place for children to play.

'It is big job. To make new.'

'I can see that.' She turned around and looked to him. 'But just imagine what it could be like. And how much good it could do. Have you asked local families? Is there demand?'

Ellen was so animated, looking at him with both affection and excitement. His small dream, the dream he'd held for so long, was invigorating her. She thought it was important. She thought it could be done. She believed in him.

'There are people at the hotel who need for this,' he responded.

'Of course there are. The waiters and the bar staff, the cleaners, everyone.' She sat down next to him. 'You should make a list of people to ask. The people who run Bo's Bar and the other bar just down from that. What about the supermarket next to the hotel entrance?'

'There are many things to arrange. To work here I must have permit,' he reminded. 'I have one until end of season but then …'

'Oh. I didn't think about that.' Her happy expression dropped for a second.

'And there are papers you need to work with children. In my village people know my family, they trust me. Here it is all different.'

'Oh. I didn't think of that either.'

'But maybe this can be done,' he suggested.

Ellen smiled again. 'I think it would be brilliant. If you could do it. If you have the time and the right paperwork and the money.'

—

At the mention of money her insides clung together as they plummeted. Everything came down to it, no matter what you did. And a few months earlier she would have been in a position to help him. But would they have ever met? Even if she had still come with Lacey on this holiday she wouldn't have been the same person. Would she have been open to Yan? Or would she had spent the time glued to her iPhone typing emails to work?

'I have some money but I do not know if enough.'

'You could ask, about the church. Who owns it?'

'There is a man. He lives not far from here. Thanasis.'

She nodded. 'Then you should ask him.'

He turned his head to look at her. 'You think I can do this?'

'I think you can do anything you want to do.'

He let out a long breath. 'I am …'

'A little scared?' she offered.

She understood how that felt. Visualising what you wanted, even coming up with the plan, that was the easy part. Taking those first steps to making it a reality was the hard bit.

'I do not want to feel this.'

'I could help you, if you like. I could go with you to see the man?'

'You would do this?'

'Yes, of course.'

Yan put his hand over hers and interlocked their fingers. Then she raised her head and met his gaze. There were tears in his eyes.

THIRTY THREE

Ellen had looked for Lacey but she wasn't out by the pool. She was probably somewhere with Sergei or sulking down on the beach. The one thing Ellen could guarantee Lacey wouldn't be doing was sparing a second worrying about her. And that was just fine. She could shrug it off too. Lacey had made her decision. The wedding was off and it was one less thing on her plate. She'd never really liked the colour of the bridesmaid dresses anyway.

Ellen sat down at a table by the bar and looked out to sea. On this clear day you could make out the shapes and colours of the buildings on Albania. Only the wave of heat over the land distorted her vision slightly. A yacht, it's large, white sail fanning out above the deck sailed into the bay, ready to drop anchor.

Corfu was such a beautiful island and this place, this spotless complex and the village of St. Spyridon was a tranquil oasis untouched by the rest of the world – if you could manage to forget real life for a week. She was glad she'd come here. She wouldn't have missed it for anything.

———

They were just singing a goodbye song in German when he got to the kids' club. Yan opened the door and clapped as they ended the tune.

'Yan!' Zachary exclaimed excitedly.

'Hello everybody! That was great singing.'

'You come to join us, Mr Yan? Does everybody want Mr Yan to sing with us?' Dasha asked the children.

All of the children responded favourably but he shook his head. 'I cannot. I have to help Sergei move tennis nets.' He looked to Tanja. 'Can I speak with you?'

The team leader moved a little girl down from her lap and stood up. 'I will be one moment,' she spoke to the children. 'Why don't you see if Dasha can remember moves to "Gangnam Style"?'

Yan backed up into the lobby of the kids' club, the report in his hands.

'Is everything good?' Tanja asked, her brow creasing as she joined him.

'Here is report.' He held the paperwork out to her.

Tanja took it and looked at the writing. 'Is in English?'

He ignored the question in her sentence. 'Yes.'

'It would be easier for you to write in Bulgarian?'

'I think ... because boy is English and paperwork will be needed in English ...' he began. He hoped this would work. He was sure it would not matter in which language the report had been written as long as Tanja did not guess that he had not written it.

'You think hard about this. That is good. Very good.' She nodded at him. 'Thank you.'

He looked back into the kids' club room and saw Dasha leaping about mimicking lassoing a rope over his head. The children were copying him, laughing and having fun. This was where he wanted to be all the time. With the children, helping them be happy, giving them joy.

'You should go. Sergei will need your help.'

Yan checked his watch. 'Yes. Thank you, Tanja.' With a nod he headed back to the door.

———

Ellen saw Yan come into the bar area and straightaway her body reacted. She was practically humming with excitement whenever he was in the vicinity. She was no Little Miss Celibate but she'd never been so affected by a man before. And, after more sensual kisses in the olive grove that afternoon she was practically ready to combust with longing.

She took a sip of her Metaxa and Coke, knowing he was approaching.

'I give Tanja the report,' he whispered, standing next to her bar stool.

'Was everything OK?'

She spoke like a Russian spy, the nearness of other hotel employees preventing anything else.

'Everything is OK,' he responded.

She could listen to that accent all day. Preferably with him naked beside her. That was it. She didn't want to wait any longer. She wanted to spend the night with him. Tonight.

'Are you doing a show tonight?' she asked, her voice a little raspy.

'Celtic show. Like *Riverdance*,' he said. 'There is fire.'

'And after the show? What would you like to do then?' She turned on her stool so she was facing him, keeping her voice low.

'What would you like to do?'

He had asked a question but it had sounded like one they already both knew the answer to.

It was now or never. She swallowed, opening her mouth to speak.

'Hi! Hi! Hi! Miss Ellie, you must come!'

Something in Dasha's high-pitched voice hit her emotional panic button. As he raced to them she saw his usual jovial smile was missing, replaced by a look of concern, his eyebrows almost up in his hairline.

She knew. 'It's Lacey isn't it?'

'What has happen?' Yan demanded to know.

'You must not make the panic. She is OK. We look after her,' Dasha stated as he played with the lace on his top.

'Where is she?' Ellen asked, looking at Dasha.

'She is with Sergei. They wait for doctor in reception area,' he informed.

'Has she had an accident?' Now she was a little bit scared.

'She has bucket.'

That reply told her all she needed to know.

———

'She's drunk too much and now she's playing her favourite game, I Love Lacey,' Ellen announced.

She was stomping at speed through the hotel complex towards the main building and Yan was going with her. He had many things to do but he couldn't leave her until he knew she was going to be all right.

'Game?' He didn't understand.

'Attention-seeking. That's what she's best at.' She puffed out a breath. 'She was like it when she was planning the wedding and she's like it now there isn't going to be a wedding.'

'She is sad?' Yan suggested.

'No, just a pain in the arse.'

'Arse? What is arse?'

Ellen didn't answer him but carried on marching up the steps.

———

It wasn't hard to pick out her sister in reception. Lacey had turned into a lobster, her pink bikini camouflaged against her glowing skin. She was sitting in a massage chair, reclined back, a small white towel pressed to her forehead. Sergei stood beside her, holding an ice bucket.

'Oh my God, look at her.' Ellen couldn't help exclaiming. Lacey's flesh was bright red and angry and as she stepped up to the scene her sister leant to the left and threw up.

'How did she get like this?' Her voice was accusing and she directed it at Sergei.

'You look at me?'

'You're with her, collecting her puke.'

'Ellen,' Yan broke in.

'She lie in sun all the day and drink too much of cocktails,' Dasha informed.

'The first one is something that stupid children with no responsible adults looking after them do. The second one she's done every day of this holiday so far.'

'Make it stop,' Lacey groaned, holding a hand to the towel on her head.

'Make it stop?' Ellen took a step towards Lacey. 'I'll make it stop. Get off that chair and get back to the room. All you need is after-sun and painkillers.' She grabbed at Lacey's arm and pulled her forward.

Lacey screamed and a passing waiter dropped his tray of glasses to the floor. Ellen let go of her sister's arm and looked at the blanch marks left on Lacey's skin. The three finger-shapes were not disappearing and Lacey was now blubbing uncontrollably.

'We wait for doctor, Miss Ellie,' Dasha said, putting an arm around her.

Did Lacey really need a doctor or was this all acting up as usual? She no longer had people to dance around entertaining her with wedding apparel at the hotel. Sergei had been working all day and she had ... she had left her. Was this really a reaction to breaking up with Mark? Was the earlier nonchalance a mask? Had Lacey now realised the devastation, sat in the sun uncaring about her own health and safety, alone and hurting while Ellen had been halfway up a mountain?

She didn't know what to do. She was in a foreign country and her sister needed medical attention. She looked away from Lacey, seeking Yan.

'It is not your fault,' he whispered.

She nodded, letting the words and his tone comfort her.

'She do this all herself,' he continued.

She nodded again, but it was somewhat half-hearted this time.

'I feel sick,' Lacey yelled, turning in her seat and hanging her head towards the bucket.

'Lacey?'

Ellen balked, darting her eyes in the direction of the voice. A familiar voice. Her dad's voice.

And there he was, Al. Larger than life, dark hair slicked back, pale chinos on his legs and a Cotton Traders polo-shirt in XXL. He had a giant holdall in each hand and was looking toward his ailing daughter.

'Dad,' Ellen greeted, rushing towards him. She needed a hug. She needed his consolation.

'Ellie, what's goin' on 'ere? What've you done to your sister?' Al dropped the bags.

The hug didn't come. And the blame was placed firmly at her door.

'Nothing,' Ellen mumbled.

'It don't look like nothin' from where I'm standin'. What's goin' on here? Is this what all this cancellin' the weddin' nonsense is about? She been drugged or somethin'?

'Drugs? No, sir, we have no thing like this here,' Dasha chirped up, toying with the florescent yellow beads around his neck.

'You a man or a woman?' Al barked.

'Dad, for Heaven's sake, stop it,' Ellen begged.

'Stop it? I've only just started, girl. Me and Mark have come over 'ere to find out what the bleedin' 'ell's goin' on.'

'Mark.' The whimper came from Lacey.

'Mark's here?' Ellen whispered. She swallowed. This was a disaster.

———

Their father was here and Mark, the man Lacey had been going to marry. Yan looked at Dasha. The man had his hands on his hips now and was pouting at Al, probably cross his gender had been questioned. Sergei had paled significantly.

'Of course Mark's 'ere. You don't get a text tellin' you the weddin's off and not do nothin' about it.' Al glared at Ellen. 'Why 'aven't you done somethin' about it?'

'I ...' Ellen began.

'Please, sir,' Yan began. 'No one is to blame.' The second his words made contact with Al's consciousness he realised he should have said nothing.

'No one is to blame? My daughter's sittin' 'ere looking like a bleedin' tomato, 'urlin' her guts up and no one's to blame?' Al boomed. 'Who served 'er too many bloody cocktails?'

'Dad, stop shouting. This isn't anyone's fault,' Ellen begged.

Ellen looked completely shell-shocked. She was trembling and instinctively Yan put a hand on her shoulder.

'Dad,' Lacey moaned, holding out her hand to him and trying to sit herself up in the chair.

'Don't tell me what to do, Ellie.' Al grabbed hold of Lacey's hand and helped her off the chair. 'It looks like you've done quite enough already.'

Angry, bitter words, pushing the fault onto Ellen. Yan already disliked this man. He felt Ellen's shoulder sag and he removed his hand.

'Mark,' Lacey whispered through sore, tight lips.

'He's taken the cases to our room. Let's get you down there and get some coffee.' Al glared at Sergei. 'Get us some coffee and get someone to carry these.' He pointed at his holdalls, abandoned on the floor.

———

Ellen was redundant, unneeded and unnecessary. Her dad had walked in and taken over and he blamed her for everything. She didn't know why she was so surprised. It had been like this her entire life. Yes, he might be proud of all her achievements, both academic and professional, but she was also the first person he blamed when things weren't perfect. Especially when it came to Lacey.

She watched Al walk away, propping Lacey up, while a porter trailed behind, struggling with the weight of the holdalls.

'I feel sorry for Miss Lacey,' Dasha remarked, moving the necklace through his hands like worry beads.

Ellen couldn't stop a snort coming from her nose. That was the problem, everyone always felt sorry for Lacey. No matter what she did, it was never Lacey's fault.

'Dasha, you should go for food,' Yan told him.

'Yes, big show tonight, Miss Ellie.'

Ellen looked at Dasha, not really acknowledging what he'd said. The reality was just about starting to sink in. Her dad was here, with Mark. Here. In Corfu.

'Get for me some salad. I will be there in one minute,' Yan said.

What was she going to do? How was she going to fix this giant mess? It hadn't been in her three day plan to sort anything out until they got home and now home was here.

'I do not like the way he speak to you.'

Yan's words broke into her thoughts and she raised her head, meeting his eyes.

'He does not listen and he does not know what happen,' Yan continued.

She shook her head. 'He always does that. It's just his way.'

'It is wrong way.'

'He's my dad, Yan. The only family I've got except Nan and she's barely there at all now she's in her nineties.'

'That mean he can speak with you like that? To not listen and to try to make your fault?'

Ellen shrugged. She didn't know what else to say. She had promised Al she would look after Lacey on this holiday, just like she'd told him every other time she'd been left in charge of her. Except nothing had ever happened before. There hadn't been a broken relationship or sunstroke, just a case of head lice and a melted Barbie horse.

'I have to go,' she said.

'No. Not like this.'

'I have to. I have to make sure she's all right and ... I have to be with my family.'

Not that she would really be noticed. Al and Mark would circle Lacey, flocking and fawning, while she fetched whatever Lacey wanted. She'd always been the one who kept hold of normality whenever Lacey's chaos descended.

'I want for you to eat with me.'

—

It would be noticed, him sitting with a hotel resident, but he needed to say something to stop her from going. She couldn't leave feeling so badly about herself, her father's words echoing in her ears, believing she was at fault. He wanted her to go away happy from their afternoon together, looking forward to the night. He didn't want things to change. They had so little time, what if this shock arrival changed things between them?

'Give them time to ...' he paused. 'Give Lacey time to stop ...'

'Puking?' Ellen offered.

'Is that the word?' he asked.

She nodded, putting her hands into her hair and sweeping it back. 'I can't.'

'You are sure?'

'Even if I'm not needed for Lacey now I should get ready for later.'

She took her hands from her head and gave him a small smile. There was more colour on her cheeks and she had stopped shaking.

'I will see you at the show?' Yan queried.

'I expect so, once Dad's over the initial fright of seeing Lacey that way ...' She stopped to take a breath. 'He likes entertainment.'

Yan swallowed.

'And after the show?'

Air escaped Ellen's lips and she joined one hand with her other, toying with her fingers. 'I don't know, Yan. I don't know if I can. I mean, I should be with my family and try and sort all this out.'

He'd expected this reaction, was ready for it, but it didn't stop him finding it hard. 'I understand.' He said the sentence quickly, so there could be no going back.

'Do you?'

He didn't trust himself to say anything else. He did understand but he didn't want to. He wanted to be with her because he knew in a few days he would never see her again and that pulled at him.

'I want to see you so much but ...' she started.

She sounded like she was sorry. He didn't want to make things difficult for her. Perhaps it was best to just let go.

'I understand. You have to go,' he breathed out.

'Thank you,' she whispered.

She turned then and he watched her go, rushing through the lobby, each step taking her further away from everything they'd shared.

THIRTY FOUR

'So, tell me this time, what the 'ell's been goin' on 'ere?'

Al's question was directed at Ellen.

It hadn't been hard to find Al's room. She'd headed down the main path until she heard his voice shouting commands – at Lacey to stop crying, at Mark to pour coffee, at a poor maid for no particular reason at all.

Now she was sat on one of the dining chairs, twining and untwining her fingers. Lacey had passed out on Al's bed with the air conditioning on full pelt and Mark had been sent to the bar on a beer run.

'Nothing's been going on, Dad.' She knew that wouldn't be a good enough answer but it was all she had and it was the truth.

'Do I look like I was born bleedin' yesterday? Something must 'ave 'appened.' Al put his hands to his hips and held in his paunch. 'One minute she's 'ere checkin' out the amenities for the weddin', the next she's textin' Mark it's over.'

'I know.' What else could she say?

'*You know*? Is that it? *You know*.'

She was never going to be able to shirk the blame in her father's eyes. Al was already confident that Lacey's decision was Ellen's doing and he didn't even know the half of it.

'I don't know what I can say,' she tried. The fact was, it didn't matter what she said. Al just needed to shout and, rightly or wrongly, she had to wear it.

'You could say that she wasn't in her right mind when she sent that message. You could say she was drunk on cocktails and she didn't mean it,' Al suggested.

'I could say that,' Ellen responded. 'But it wouldn't be the truth.'

'That's not helping, Ellie.'

She watched him put both his hands to his head and suck in a giant breath.

'I told her she shouldn't have ended it by text. I said it was cruel and ...'

'Why the 'ell didn't you phone me? If she was 'avin' these pre-weddin' nerves or what-'ave-you ...'

'It isn't pre-wedding nerves, Dad. There's a lot more to it than that.'

'Like what? I've been bloody well askin' you for the last 'alf hour.'

'It isn't really for me to say.' Ellen paused, watching for his reaction and knowing what it would be.

'*It isn't for you to say?* Are you windin' me up? What d'you think you're 'ere for?'

She swallowed. And here it was again. It was her fault because her role in the family was looking after Lacey. It was her responsibility alone. No one else took ownership and if things went wrong she was held accountable.

There was a knock on the door.

'That'll be Mark,' Al stated.

Ellen didn't move. She was actually terrified about seeing him. He would probably take the same tack as Al. She hadn't shielded Lacey from her own opinions. God knows what would happen if they found out about Sergei.

Al let out an exasperated noise at her lack of movement and crossed the room. He flung open the door and there was Mark, a tray of plastic cups filled with beer in his hands. Sandy-brown hair spiked up with hair products, puppy dog grey-green eyes. She'd forgotten just how boyish and vulnerable he looked.

'Come on in, son,' Al welcomed.

Ellen stood up and angled her body towards the open door. She didn't want to meet his gaze, let alone answer any questions. 'I have to go ... I need to have a shower and ...'

'You're not goin' anywhere until this lad 'as 'ad an explanation,' Al boomed.

She fixed her eyes on the grey floor tiles. Even though none of this was her doing she still felt a cloak of guilt on her shoulders, the weight of which was crushing her.

'It's all right,' Mark said, his voice soft. He sniffed and she heard the tray of drinks go down onto the table.

'No, it's not all right. We need to be kept in the loop 'ere. No one's tellin' us anythin',' Al carried on.

She had to face this head on. She had to look him in the eye. She hadn't done anything and she felt sorry for him. She raised her head.

'Hi, Ellen,' he greeted soberly.

'Hi,' she replied. 'Listen, I just want to say that when I didn't answer my phone yesterday it wasn't because ...'

'You never answered your phone to 'im?!' Al made it sound like she'd committed treason.

'No. I wanted to but Lacey ...' Ellen sputtered.

'Lacey told you not to,' Mark guessed.

'Christ, she's just a kid, Ellen. You should 'ave taken control of this situation the minute it started goin' tits up.'

She needed to get out. Her head was beginning to ache and she wasn't helping. Her very presence was adding fuel to the fire. Mark needed to speak to Lacey who was in a sun and booze inflicted stupor and was likely to remain that way until the morning. No one could give him the answers he wanted except her sister.

'If I had any idea that this was goin' to 'appen I wouldn't 'ave let you come 'ere.'

Something inside Ellen twisted at his words.

'*Wouldn't have let me*,' she stated, her voice deadpan.

'I wasn't fully on board with 'avin' the weddin' abroad as it was. Foreign food and Delhi belly. There's no way you'd ever get an 'alf decent sausage roll,' Al continued.

'It isn't *your* wedding,' she said, focussing her eyes on Mark.

'I was bleedin' payin' for it.'

Al had no idea that what he was saying was offensive. His lack of filter usually didn't bother her this much but now, with every harsh remark, she was getting more and more prickly.

'Because you wanted Lacey to have the best,' Ellen responded. 'Because she wanted to make a show of the wedding and you were letting her.'

Her words had come out hard and loaded with an emotion she didn't recognise. Angst. Jealousy. Disappointment. These were feelings she'd hidden so well she hadn't acknowledged, even to herself, that she truly felt them.

'I'm not apologisin' for wantin' the best for my girls.' Al folded his arms across his chest.

'And I'm not apologising for letting Lacey make up her own mind about her marriage.'

She'd shouted the retort and as soon as the words were out she looked to Mark. He swallowed and turned his head away. This must be so hard for him. All she'd thought about was Lacey's life, what Lacey would do once she'd made her choice, but there was so much more to it. There was Mark and right now she felt so sorry for him. But *she* couldn't make it right.

'I have to go,' Ellen stated, stepping towards the door.

'Go? Go where?' Al exclaimed.

It was tempting to say *anywhere* because that was the truth of it. 'Dinner's from seven until nine thirty and the show's on straight after. It's a Celtic night.'

Both Al and Mark were now looking at her like she was demented. She swallowed. What did they expect? For them all to sit around Lacey's bed all evening like they were waiting for a priest to give her the Last Rites? She had sunstroke, not malaria.

Ellen put her hand on the doorknob.

'But, we've got things to discuss,' Al started.

'No, Mark has things to discuss with Lacey.' She engaged her father's gaze. 'And none of this was my fault.'

Before Al could have the chance of the last word she opened up the door and left.

—

'You do not eat,' Sergei observed.

Yan had prodded and poked his meal around the plate for the past half an hour and only a couple of forkfuls had met his mouth. He couldn't relax. He could only imagine what was happening with Ellen. Her father shouting and being angry for no reason. He put down his fork and pushed the plate away.

'It is nerves for the show. It will be fine,' Sergei reassured. 'First time we do new show there are always mistakes.'

'It is not show.'

He didn't know why he had said that. It would have been much easier to have Sergei believe it was just pre-performance nerves, now he might ask questions.

'I should be the one not to eat,' Sergei said, sitting back in his chair and putting his hands behind his head. 'Lacey's father is here and the man she is to marry.'

'The man she not marry anymore,' Yan added. He watched for his colleague's reaction.

'You think this is because of me?'

He sensed something in Sergei's tone that sounded almost pleased that he could be the cause.

'You want this girl? For girlfriend?' Yan spat the words out. He knew what the answer would be and he saw nothing to be smug about.

Sergei opened his mouth but no words came out.

'Well?' Yan asked, picking up the water jug.

'No. She leaves in a few days. She live in England.'

His words hit home. But not in connection with Lacey, with Ellen. He cared for her and she too was going home so soon.

'Yan?'

It was only when Sergei spoke he realised he had overfilled his glass and water was flowing over, wetting the table. He leapt up, grabbing napkins and pressing them to the spillage.

'You are nervous for the show. I can see this,' Sergei answered, moving his plate back from the wet puddle.

Yan wiped the table and gathered up the wet cloths, rolling them into a ball in his hands. 'Yes, you are right. I am.'

Why was it always so much easier to lie?

THIRTY FIVE

Alone at a table with four chairs. It was almost like being back at home. The only difference was the temperature and the smell of insect repellent combining with citronella candles.

Ellen took a sip of her Apricot Cooler cocktail and stared at her phone on the table. It was still switched off and she wasn't entirely sure why she'd taken it out of her handbag. Mark wouldn't ring. He was either at the lobby bar drowning his sorrows or locked somewhere with Lacey trying to make sense of the mess of their relationship. But Ross had rung. There was no doubt in her mind about the number. And he could ring again, perhaps already had, maybe he had even left a message. What would it say?

She swallowed back the nauseous feeling that lined her throat. What was there to say, really? He'd done what he'd done and so had she. It was just a case of what they were both going to do about it. She hoped he was feeling at least some of the humiliation she had experienced, some of the hopelessness she was still coping with. But it wasn't just about what he'd done. It was what it meant. He'd taken something from her that was irreplaceable.

She picked the phone up and dropped it back into her bag.

———

Yan wasn't in the right frame of mind for the show. It was the biggest showcase they'd had to do and they'd been practicing every chance they'd had for the last six weeks. He pulled the black vest top he was wearing down lower over his black jeans. Silver swirls of glitter paint were on his arms, his eyes outlined with dark liner. He looked more like a would-be comic crime fighter than a Celt. And, standing in the dressing room, he just felt miserable.

'Don't you look gorgeous?'

Monica's smoky tones had him looking towards the door. She was leaning against the door jamb, one hand on her hip, her eyes roving from his top to the floor.

'You must not be here. This is backstage area for people that work,' he told her.

She made a noise, halfway between a growl and a laugh and put one stiletto foot in front of the other, moving closer.

'It's my last night,' she purred.

'I know of this.' He stood his ground but she was already so close he could smell her sickly perfume. 'I hope you have a good holiday at Blue Vue Hotel and you like to come again.'

'Oh, I'd definitely like to come again.' She waited a beat. 'And again and again.'

Her face was now so close to his, the heat of her breath hit his cheeks. He leant back and grabbed the closest thing to hand.

'You should sit in the crowd.' He brandished the baton he would be twirling in the show, jerking it towards her like a cattle prod. 'We are about to start show. With fire.'

Monica grabbed the stick from his hands and dropped it on the floor.

'Darling, we could make fire together.' She planted her hands on his chest. 'I'm so bored of this game of cat and mouse. I'm quite happy to sweeten the deal. Shall we say five hundred euros?'

Yan put his hands on top of hers, ready to remove them from his body. Then he stopped. *Five hundred euros.* His mouth went completely dry, like someone had come along and filled it up with sand. What he could do with five hundred euros. The church rental, the money needed to start the refurbishment, the makings of a brand new life once the summer season was over.

'Aren't I even beginning to tempt you?' Monica continued, her fingers flexing the thin material of his t-shirt.

He should stop her, he knew that. He should make her leave before someone came in. He knew what she was asking and it was a vile suggestion. Giving himself to someone he cared nothing for, in exchange for money. It was prostitution. Something desperate people did to survive. Back home he could have done exactly the same. He could have taken the money Rayna's father had offered him and carried on the work he'd been ordered to do. Turning a blind eye to evil and corruption. This was not as bad. This was one night for the right reasons. For his future, for the after-school club, to live.

'Six hundred euros and that's my final offer,' Monica purred. He swallowed. He could do this.

———

'Ladies and gentleman, we have very new show for you tonight. Please putting your hands together for the Blue Vue Hotel Animation Team 2015 in "Celtic Calling".'

Ellen put down her glass of water and clapped her hands together as the lights went up on stage. There was Yan, standing behind Dasha and Sergei, Tanja to his left, dressed all in black with silver patterns on his skin. In any other lifetime she would have thought he looked daft, but here, in the midst of atmospheric lighting and music, it was perfect. *He* was perfect.

'Get us a pitcher of whatever's the strongest.'

She barely had a chance to acknowledge her dad's presence before he was pulling up one of the empty chairs and lowering his bulk onto it. Mark was drifting towards the bar area.

'Bit small, these chairs, ain't they?'

Al was obviously directing the question at her, since there was no one else within range, but she didn't know what to say. How did you pick up polite conversation after the car crash of their talk only a few hours ago? Besides, she wanted to watch the show. She turned her attention back to the stage. The troupe was dancing, flags whirling around their bodies as the speakers blasted out violins, guitars and drums.

'This it, is it? The five star entertainment?' Al let out a scoff for good measure.

'Sshh!'

His voice was louder than the *Riverdance* music and she couldn't concentrate on it.

'Did you just *sshh* me?' Al's reply was prickly.

'Sorry, Dad, but I really want to see this. It's the first time they've done this show and ...' Now she sounded ridiculous. He had no clue how important it was that she watched Yan. Why would he?

'Shall I go and sit somewhere else? I wouldn't want to *disturb* you.'

Ellen shook her head. 'No, don't be silly. I'm sorry.'

She couldn't bear anymore arguments and confrontation. It was obvious Al was really concerned about the situation between Lacey and Mark. He'd travelled thousands of miles to join in an uncomfortable scenario.

'Any karaoke?' Al asked.

'I don't know,' she responded.

She looked at Yan. He was dancing with Tanja, lifting her high up into the air, spinning around, then putting her down and catching her in his arms. Had she been harsh with him earlier? He had been trying to be nice and she had dismissed his efforts and told him she couldn't see him later. Was that the right decision to make? Did she need to be with Al, Mark and a half comatose Lacey? Before her dad had arrived, she'd wanted to spend the night with Yan.

'The doctor came. Gave your sister somethin' for the pain. She's 'ad a cool bath. Feelin' a bit better.'

'That's good,' Ellen said, nodding. 'I'll go and see her in a while.'

'Nah, don't do that. She needs 'er sleep. We're keepin' 'er in our room for tonight. There's three beds so ...'

She kept on nodding. Of course they were keeping her with them. *She* couldn't be trusted to look after Lacey now. She had abandoned her, left her alone for a few hours to get half-fried by the Greek sun. Also, keeping Lacey with them would allow them both plenty of time to brainwash her into putting the wedding back on the table. Her dad wanted her married to take the pressure off. That's why Ellen had never moved back, even after everything fell apart. She wasn't Lacey's twenty-four hour carer and she shouldn't have to be. With Ellen gone, far too much responsibility had fallen on Al.

A whoop went up from the audience and she looked back to the stage to see Dasha, Sergei and Yan with flaming torches in their hands.

'Ho, the entertainment just got better.' Al clapped his hands together. 'Everyone loves a bit of the ol' fire.'

———

The crowd were roaring their appreciation and Yan felt so good. The show had gone well. No one had got burnt and apart from the one near-accident with the accelerant, it had all been completed without a hitch. Dasha pulled his hand downwards for another bow as the audience continued to clap. It was their best reaction yet. Small moments like this, when he felt worthwhile and appreciated, were what made everything a little better.

Without really realising it, he looked for Ellen. He hadn't seen her at the beginning of the show, with the lights on him and the crowd in darkness, but now he scanned the tables. There. There she was, halfway back, sitting with her father and a younger man. Before he could think logically a wave of jealousy rode over him. He bit it back, shook sense into his thoughts. This had to be the man Lacey was to marry. Not someone with Ellen. He swallowed, hot and concerned about someone else being with her.

His eyes found another person in the audience. Monica. Sequinned from mid-thigh to mid-breast, moistening her slick lips as she smiled at him. His stomach lurched and he dropped Dasha's hand as if it were contraband, bolting for backstage.

———

Ellen saw Yan leave the stage and sat back in her seat. There was little hope of speaking to him with her dad and Mark here, even if he managed to get some time in between entertaining. So much for this being *the* night. It was like the Greek gods were conspiring against them.

'I fancy a Jager, Markie. Do they 'ave any?' Al piped up, pumping his plastic cup down on the table.

Mark was looking into the mid-distance and didn't appear to hear Al's raucous baritone. Ellen got to her feet.

'I'll get some drinks.'

'Crackin' stuff. Get a couple, bein' as it's all in, will ya?'

She smiled at her dad and made her way over to the bar.

The air was so humid that the mosquitoes were out in full force. Ellen slapped at her arm and another one bit the dust. She brushed the body to the floor and joined the queue at the bar.

'Wonderful performance tonight wasn't it?'

She turned her head to see Monica joining the line behind her.

'Oh yes, it was very good. I loved the tricks they did with the fire. Quite glad I wasn't in the front row though.'

'A new way to get your legs waxed, maybe?' Monica tittered out a laugh.

Ellen smiled. 'This is your last night, isn't it?'

'Yes and I'm determined to make the most of it.' She lowered her voice a notch. 'I've finally managed to pin down the delicious Yan.'

'Oh.' She had to remember this was all in Monica's imagination.

'I hope it's going to be much more than an *oh*. It's going to cost me six hundred euros but what the hell? I can do without a designer handbag in exchange for a night of passion with him.'

Bile flooded Ellen's throat and she couldn't respond. Monica was making this up. Yan felt nothing for Monica. She was a resident he had been keeping at arm's length the entire time she'd been there.

'Those biceps and those eyes! Oh, I can imagine it's like looking at the ocean and feeling the hard rock of the mountains all at the same time.'

She had to remain composed if she was going to extract the truth from Monica. As much as she wanted to be sick and burst into tears this wasn't the time or the place for overreacting. She took a deep breath.

'So how did you manage that?' She swallowed. 'Did you just ask him or ...'

'I can be very persuasive, you know. But, to be honest, although it isn't very flattering, I think the money did the talking.' She brushed her hands down the front of her dress. 'These poor boys from these *lesser known* countries are so desperate for money they'll do literally anything.'

He wouldn't. Yan wouldn't. She knew him. He'd told her he wouldn't do that. But he needed money. He'd shown her the church, told her how much it meant to him to work with children. Six hundred euros was a lot of cash.

'I'd forget about taking home any tacky souvenirs for relatives. Spend what you've got on one of them.' Monica pointed towards Dasha and Sergei, who were talking to a large group of people at a table near the stage.

Ellen wanted to leave. She didn't want to hear another thing that came out of Monica's mouth. It had to be a lie. It just had to be.

'Can I please help you?'

She felt like the humidity was stifling her. She couldn't think straight. A manicured hand tapped her arm.

'The barman is asking for your order. Don't be too long about it, I have a Long Slow Comfortable Screw Against the Wall on my menu.'

'Jägermeister,' Ellen blurted at the bartender. 'Can I have the bottle?'

THIRTY SIX

'Beautiful this place is. Isn't it, Markie? Beautiful.' Al necked another shot and slammed the cup on the table.

'Stunning. Just like my Lacey.'

It would have been romantic if Mark's words weren't slurred and if Lacey was still *his* Lacey. As it was, Ellen was too numb to comment. After three shots, that made her throat and stomach burn in quick succession, she was back to water and wondering when she could leave.

'Gets 'er looks from 'er mother. That's all she 'ad though, Markie. Margarette was much better at looking pretty than she was at getting on in the world.'

'Like Lacey,' Ellen chipped in without meaning to.

'That's a bit harsh, Ellen.'

It was Mark who had spoken up and as he shifted in his chair he knocked his half-empty plastic cup over, spilling alcohol onto the table.

'Sorry, it's just that you two don't seem to have really grasped the fact that the wedding's off,' Ellen said.

Al snorted and followed it up with a laugh. 'Course the weddin's not off.' He shook his head as if the very idea of that was preposterous. 'Your sister 'as never known what's right for 'er. That's why we came out 'ere. With Markie 'ere she'll soon see sense.'

Ellen nodded. 'That was your plan, was it? Not to listen to what she wants and why she feels she has to cancel the wedding, just to bully her into going through with it?'

She looked at Mark then. His eyes were closed and he was slumped sideways in his seat. Alcohol and tiredness had obviously taken over.

'She needs guidance, Ellie. I thought she might 'ave got that from you but ...'

'I'm not her mother.'

She'd blasted out the words far too loudly and regretted it immediately.

For a second, Al looked wounded. The usual reddened glow to his cheeks dulled and he sucked his lips into his mouth like they'd just been tainted by a lemon.

'I'm well aware of that, Ellie.'

'Are you?'

What was the matter with her? She really needed to shut her mouth and stop talking, before this became a lot more about her than about Lacey.

'I think you've 'ad too much to drink.'

'Why? Because I'm speaking the truth?' Ellen could feel her expression getting harder.

Al shook his head and averted his eyes. He was dismissing her. He didn't like what she had to say so he was trying to ignore it, pretend it wasn't happening.

'It wasn't my job to bring Lacey up. But you made it that way.' She was almost panting now, her body working itself up into a frenzy. 'I've done what I can for so many years, years when I was learning how to do things myself.' She sighed. 'She's not a child any more, she's a young woman. She's able to think for herself and know what she wants.'

'She's not like you, Ellie.'

Al's voice was pitched a little lower, his tone a little bit kinder. Was that pride she could detect there? Pride in the way she had turned out? He wouldn't be so proud if he found out what had happened back home.

'No, because she's her *own* person. That's what I'm trying to tell you.' Ellen sighed. 'She's not a little girl anymore, Dad.'

She saw the shift in Al's body. He deflated before her eyes, dropping his chin to his chest, his shoulders rolling forward. His grief for his failings was evident. He'd lost one wife, the other had left him and he'd had to bring up two daughters on his own. He'd struggled, was still struggling. Life was no longer Irish stew out of a tin and the television as a babysitter, but even after all these years, emotionally he was no further forward.

'You can't keep putting out your arms to catch her. She has to learn to take the fall.'

Al looked up. 'Like when she rolled all the way down the 'ill at Old Sarum when she was four.'

'She got up, covered in bramble scratches and screamed about her ice cream.' Ellen smiled, remembering.

'Bit different when it's a weddin' though,' Al mused.

'But it is *her* wedding, Dad. If she isn't ready, she isn't ready. You can't force her to go through with it just because you think Mark will look after her.'

He nodded, gave a hearty sniff and plucked a paper napkin from the holder on the table.

'She's really not ready to get married. I believe she cares for Mark but she's still young. She has her whole life ahead of her and she doesn't have to make plans yet.'

Ellen could hardly believe she'd said that. Just a few short months ago making plans was all she'd done. She'd had a career timeline and a five year plan.

Mark gave a snort. His head jerked upwards and he opened his eyes as he came back to consciousness.

'I'm going to leave you to it,' Ellen said, standing up.

'You be all right getting back to your room?' Al asked her.

'Yes, Dad.' She smiled. 'I've never been the one you have to worry about.' The words resonated but she held on hard to the expression.

———

Yan saw Ellen stand, pick up her bag and get ready to leave. She was going somewhere without her family when she had said she would not be able to see him.

'We have more drinks. You get for us, Yan,' Dasha said, placing a firm hand on his arm.

He didn't want her to leave. He wanted to see her, to be with her. She was weaving her away through the tables, heading towards the steps that led back to her suite.

Yan diverted his eyes. Monica was sitting a few tables away from him. She'd latched herself onto a family who had arrived that day. She was talking animatedly but looking to him every now and then, most likely to check he hadn't run away. In truth, that's exactly what he had always planned. He stood up.

'More *ouzo*, Yan,' Sergei said.

He left the table but didn't head for the bar.

———

Ellen was so tired and, as she left her dad and Mark, her thoughts turned to Yan. Had he really arranged to meet Monica for a night full of goodness-knows-what?

She stood on the last step before the path to her room and took in the view. The mountains of Albania were nothing more than shadowy outlines pin-pricked with twinkling lights. She could hear the sea, waves breaking. A paradise, a retreat, for anyone relaxed enough to enjoy it.

'Ellen.'

Yan's voice coming out of the darkness sent a shiver over her body. She turned towards the sound and there he was, his hands in the pockets of his black jeans, a white t-shirt hugging his torso. All traces of glitter and sparkles were gone from his body.

'I know you say you need to be with family but …' he started.

'I'm really tired. I need to go to bed.' She tried to keep her voice level but failed.

'You are mad with me?'

He sounded confused. She should just ask him outright but she wasn't sure she could take the answer.

'I just need some sleep. It's been a bit of a hectic day,' she said.

'What is *hectic*?'

She wished she'd chosen 'busy'.

She let out a sigh. 'Are you going to sleep with Monica?'

There it was, out in the open, blunt and to the point, the sort of accusation that couldn't be ignored.

Yan started shaking his head but no words came from his mouth. He wouldn't meet her eyes.

———

He felt sick. Everything was shrinking inside of him. Each single word she'd said was stinging like a mosquito bite. Because he *had* thought about it. Really thought about it, just for a second.

'I think your silence says everything I need to know,' Ellen jumped in. She turned to go and the thought of her leaving like this made him act.

'No,' he grabbed her arm. 'I do not do this.'

'Six hundred euros. Ring any bells?'

He shook his head again. Monica had spoken to her. Ellen had heard it from the woman herself, who was clearly still holding on to the hope that he would change his mind. In the end, he had said no, but he'd deliberately left her with enough hope that he might change his mind just to get her out of the dressing room.

How could he put this right? How could he make her see?

'So she didn't offer you six hundred euros for a night of passion and you didn't say yes?'

The way Ellen was saying it made it sound like the worst crime imaginable. And it was, here it was. Because he cared for Ellen, truly cared and he didn't want her to think this of him.

'I do not say yes. I tell her no.' He held onto Ellen's arm, his fingers smoothing the skin. 'For a very small time I think of this. For the church, for a new life ...'

'You thought about it?'

He saw horror coat her features and his stomach turned. Hearing the tone of her voice now, seeing her reaction, how could he have even thought about it? And how could he have just told her that truth? Because he was an honest person, because the truth was everything. Perhaps she would never have known how close he had come to accepting Monica's offer, but *he* would have known and that wasn't right.

Yan nodded. 'I have done things I wish to not do again, to survive in life. I am not from your country. We have not the same troubles. I work very hard but sometime working hard, it is not enough.'

The disappointment lay in every inch of Ellen's expression. He knew that to even think of giving in to Monica was wrong, but Ellen didn't understand. She had never been in this position. Without hope, without money. She was at an all-inclusive resort on holiday with her good job and her comfortable life to go back to.

'Why would you do that?' The words were choked up with emotion and they beat into his heart.

'I did not do this,' he reminded.

'Is money everything to you? Is that what your dream is about? To achieve it as quickly as possible, even if you have to sell yourself to someone?'

'No, this is not it.' Yan let go of her arm and put his hands to his head. 'Why I do not do this … is for you.'

Ellen caught the emotion in his voice but it felt different. Wrong. What was he saying? Had he turned down the money and Monica because he *knew* it was wrong or because he knew *she* would think it was wrong? There was a world of difference between the two.

'Ellen, it is because I care for you. You come here and show me so much.'

She tightened her core. She would not let his declarations affect her. All he really cared about was himself and his plans for the after-school club. He didn't care for her. He barely knew her.

'I warned Lacey about falling for the patter of foreign men the second she started going doe-eyed over Sergei.' She shook her head. 'I should have listened to my own advice. Instead I played right into your hands.'

'I do not understand all of what you say.'

'I have no money to offer you, Yan. Nothing. So if it's funding for your project you want, then Monica is the best bet.'

She was going to cry. Despite her valiant attempts to not show emotion she was falling apart on the inside and it was leaking out of every tan line.

'I do not want your money.'

'That's what they all say at the beginning. They take an interest in you even when you're not looking for anything to happen. They pursue you, they woo you, they don't stop until you give in and then, when you think you know them, when you think this isn't maybe a burning passion like the films but something solid, something reliable, they pull the rug out from under you, destroy everything, take it all.'

She knew she was ranting but she couldn't stop. The tears were rolling, falling out of her eyes and starting to track down her cheeks. This wasn't just about Yan. This was Ross too. What she had let him do, how he had hurt and betrayed her trust in such a terrible way.

'I do not do this to you,' Yan spoke.

'It doesn't matter. Don't you understand that? How could it matter when in a couple of days we'll never see each other again?'

'I do not want for this.'

'What?' She sniffed.

'I do not want not to see you again,' he responded.

'You don't care about me. I have no money, didn't you hear that? I have nothing for you!'

Ellen burst into tears and he held on to her, took her arms and braced her as she cried. She didn't want the bubble to burst but it well and truly had.

'I know I am not good for you. You are clever lady and all I do is dance.'

His hands were holding on so tight but his voice was soft, washing over her senses, calming, soothing. She swallowed. She shouldn't listen. She'd listened to Ross against every instinct she had and look what had happened there.

'I have never tell anyone about ...' He paused. 'I never tell anyone about ... my brother. About Boyan.'

———

Yan needed her to know that she wasn't just a holidaymaker to him. What they were sharing, physically and emotionally, was as real as it got. It was more real to him than anything he'd ever had before.

'What?' The word was a vague whisper on her lips, barely a sound at all.

He took a deep breath. There was so much else he hadn't told her but telling her about Boyan was more than he had shared with most. It meant something to let that out and share it with her, even if at the time he had brushed over it like it barely registered. It *was* important. Boyan's memory was the part of him that kept him driven, gave him strength, urged him on.

'I share this with you ...' He didn't know how to explain himself. 'Of who I am.'

He struggled over the words but hoped the sentiment had been conveyed.

'I thought I was getting to know who you were but after this ...' Ellen began.

He couldn't believe this was happening. He was going to lose her here, now, not in two days when he was prepared for it. He had been wrong to trust again, stupid to believe someone could think something of him. She believed what a sex-crazed rich woman had told her. Money doing the talking yet again.

She shook her head and pulled her arms free from his grasp.

'No,' he stated roughly. 'You do not do this.'

'I'm going back to my room,' Ellen stated. She started to walk.

'Yes, go!' he shouted. 'You go, Ellen. You go back to where you hide.'

———

Ellen stopped moving and turned to face him again. His hands were by his sides, his eyes directed at her, lips formed in a tight line. Did he understand what he had said to her?

'You judge me very first time that we meet,' he said. 'You look at me now and you judge again. What about you?' he asked. 'You do not tell me anything of yourself.'

'What?' For a second she didn't think she'd heard correctly.

'You tell me nothing,' he repeated.

'That's not true,' Ellen started. 'You know about my job and you know about my sister.' She took a breath. 'You know my mother is dead and my father is here making a drama out of everything.'

She was struggling to think of other things she'd told him. She must have told him something else.

'You tell me your mother is dead but you do not tell me how this make you feel,' he bit back. 'You read books and you work, why do you do these things? What are the things to make you laugh?' His voice was low and level. 'What are the things to make you sad?' He let out a sigh. 'I tell you all of my dream. What of yours?'

Ellen swallowed. Her dream. Her completely shattered dream of being her own boss and running her own firm. She couldn't give him details without sharing the very worst things she'd done in her life.

'I don't have any dreams,' she stated.

He nodded, like he was resigned to her answer, like he had almost been expecting it. 'Then I judge you.' He sighed. 'I judge you do not trust enough to tell me.'

'No, I ...' she started.

'Goodnight, Ellen.' He turned then and walked away.

THIRTY SEVEN

Yan watched the barman pour another large measure of Metaxa into his glass. He was alone, sitting outside at the only bar in Agios Spyridon other than Bo's. A left turn out of the hotel gate, past the beach and it was there, just hidden behind a cluster of lemon trees. The citrus fragrance, the buzz of the gnats and the ocean lapping at the shore were the only things piercing the dark of the night.

He didn't know what to do. Part of him wanted to throw the glass at the wall of the bar and watch it smash, the other half wanted to cradle it to his chest and sob. He should never have got involved with a resident. He knew that. Why had he broken the rules? Why had he risked not only his job but his heart again? He had made promises to himself to go things alone, to concentrate on building his better life, away from Bulgaria, to mark out a different future.

But perhaps it was impossible. Maybe, after the summer season, he should just go back to Sofia and live as he had done before Rayna. Bar work, casual labour on construction sites, the meat factory, places that didn't ask too many questions.

He raised the glass to his mouth and took a swig of the liquid. He didn't want return to that. He couldn't even stand the thought of it. The ugliness of the city, the threat of men like Gavril Danchev. Life had to mean more.

Something invaded his line of sight and he turned his head just slightly. Ellen. He swallowed, turning back to the bar. What was she doing here? There was nothing left to say.

———

This was the very last place Ellen had looked. He'd told her before there was nothing but the lagoon and the mountains once you got past this bar. For a brief second she'd worried he might have thought again about spending the night with Monica. But she'd known in her heart that he wouldn't. And now here he was, sitting at the bar, a glass in his hand, his body turned away from her.

Despite the humidity of the night, she was shaking. What she was about to do was going to alter everything. She took a tentative step forward, forcing her body to move.

She wasn't sure whether he had seen her approach, but if he had, he wasn't making any reaction to it. Perhaps she was too late. Maybe she should have swallowed her stupid pride and said something sooner.

She arrived at his side and took a breath. 'Yan.'

The sea breeze blew her hair and she shivered against it. Yan remained stoic.

She tried a second time. 'Yan.'

This time he turned, slowly tilting his body around on the stool until he was facing her. Those perfect blue eyes looked jaded, lacking in light, showing nothing of their usual vibrancy.

'Can we talk?' she asked, her voice disjointed over the words.

'What is there to talk about?'

His reply was bordering on cold but it was scorching her insides. She had to make this right.

'Please, Yan.'

She was quaking now, nervously threading her fingers together, waiting, hoping for something. After what felt like an age, he slipped down from the bar stool, moving past her towards the beach. She hurried to follow.

'Listen, you were honest with me about Monica and I should have accepted that better. You didn't have to tell me that you'd thought of ...' She paused as she tried to take longer strides to keep up with his pace. 'You'd thought of taking the money. You could have lied to me or worse still, gone through with it. But you didn't do either of those things.' She wet her lips. This wasn't coming out as well as she'd hoped.

He looked at her then and she felt a tiny shard of hope spike. She cleared her throat and prepared to say what she'd really come to say. He'd stopped on the sand, just short of where the tide was licking the shore. She stood next to him, looking out across the water, trying to take comfort from the tiny, twinkling lights of the towns and villages of Albania.

'I'm not very good at talking about myself, like you said. In fact I do the very best I can to avoid it.' A nervous laugh escaped her lips. 'But I'm great with a spreadsheet.' She closed her mouth and her eyes. 'You probably don't even know what a spreadsheet is and why should you? They're the most boring thing on Earth.' She sighed.

He turned to her then, looking at her quizzically. He was probably wondering what the hell she was going on about. But this was vital. It was one of the most important things she had done in her life. She was conquering a fear, letting someone in, giving herself fully for the very first time.

Still Yan didn't speak and all she could hear was her own rapid breath and the soft waves. She could do this. And when it was all out of her mouth, whatever happened next, she would had done the right thing. *Breathe.*

'The man I was with … Ross. He asked me to marry him and I said no. I told you that,' Ellen started. She felt the fear building up inside her chest but she kept her mouth open and continued. 'Well, I said no for lots of reasons but mainly because I didn't love him. I couldn't imagine spending a whole week with him, let alone a lifetime. When I said no I knew things would change. I knew he would probably end the relationship and we would both go our separate ways and … I was fine with that. But he wasn't.'

—

He turned fully then, facing her instead of the water, the breeze rippling his t-shirt.

She looked terrified, the material of her skirt wavering slightly as her legs trembled beneath it. He swallowed and slipped his hands into the pockets of his jeans.

Ellen flinched at the movement, appearing jarred for a second before speaking again.

'Well, for about a week he pretended things could go back to the way they were. I was in the middle of this big acquisition and I really had no idea what he was going to do. I took my eye off the ball, Yan. I trusted him to be just a decent, genuine person and he betrayed me in the worst way. And he *knew* it was in the worst way which makes it so much harder to come to terms with.'

He could see the tears forming in her eyes, the pattern of strain on her face. He had no idea what she was going to say next.

'He stole from me, Yan. He stole every penny I had saved and all the money my mother had left me when she died.' A sob escaped then and it was all he could do to stop himself from reaching out to her. He couldn't, not yet, something was telling him to wait.

'I'd kept every penny she left me and saved everything I could from my wages for as long as I can remember and he just took it. He took it for his dream. Keegan Manufacturing. He used my mother's legacy to fund his unbreakable packaging idea.'

———

He'd broken something that she had thought unbreakable. There was a certain irony in there somewhere. She swallowed another sob before it made it out of her mouth. All this time, keeping this secret, this hatred and hurt, buried under the surface. How had she done it? *Why* had she done it?

She blinked hard, dispersing the tears. She had to keep going, she had to keep telling him, because if she waited too long she would lose the impetus, the strength, to see it through. She took a breath.

'He left me with unpaid bills, no job, my vision gone, my dreams ripped up ...' A vision of coming home to a bare house flooded her mind. She swallowed. 'Nothing left.'

———

As she uttered the final two words he couldn't help himself. He reached for her. To lose her mother so young was one thing, to come through that and lose everything she had left was unfair. His fingers made contact with her arm.

'No, Yan, not yet.' She withdrew it from his reach.

'Ellen ...' he started.

'I haven't told you everything yet and I really need to. You said I hadn't told you the stuff that matters and you were right.' She met his eyes with hers and he saw the sadness mingling with fear. He did not know what she was going to say but he was certain now, it would not change the way he felt.

'You want to go back to bar? To sit down?'

She shook her head. 'No, if I do I'm probably going to stop talking and I need to keep going.'

He watched her crinkle up the hem of her skirt in her hands, scrunching the material then letting it go.

She let out a sigh. 'After he took the money I didn't function for a few weeks. I didn't know what to do. He'd fooled me. I'd been gullible and stupid and I'd let my guard down. I'd always known that it wasn't the right time to find someone to share my life with. I'd forced myself into a situation I wasn't comfortable with and now I'd paid for it. I had to get a new job and I had to move. I'd left my job at a really nice firm to set up my own accountancy practice, but with no money I couldn't do that anymore. The banks wouldn't lend to someone with absolutely nothing, no matter how good my business plan.' She stopped and looked directly at him. 'Are you understanding all this?'

'I understand,' he assured her.

———

She blew out another breath. 'I got the job at Lassiter's really easily. I had great references but I was still expecting more competition, for me to have to do much more to get the position.' She looked to Yan again. 'Lassiter's is the company I work for. They're also Ross' accountants, in charge of the business and tax affairs of Keegan Manufacturing and its board members.'

She steeled herself, straightening her back like she was adopting a yoga stance. 'I had my own portfolio of clients and then for bigger businesses I worked alongside a partner of the firm. I made sure one of those businesses was Keegan Manufacturing.

It wasn't hard. I knew Ross' business plans inside out and I'm a good accountant. All it took was a few helpful suggestions to the partner and then I was running their bookwork unsupervised. I just had to make sure none of the letters were signed by me and that I was unavailable for any meetings. It was easy.'

Yan was completely still, transfixed by her words. What was he going to think when she admitted everything? It was most likely going to end their relationship. But in a couple of days it would all be over anyway. She'd rather they parted having shared the truth than leave each other on lies. This way he would know the real her. The person who had lost everything then gone on a spree of revenge and not told a soul.

'The one thing Ross was always terrible at was bookwork. He never kept receipts, never knew how things worked financially. He isn't a business man, he's an ideas man. That's why I knew, if I got it right, he wouldn't notice. He wouldn't look at the statements and schedules. He entrusted all that to Lassiter's and he had no idea I worked there.'

'What did you do?'

Yan's voice broke her train of thought and for a moment she thought she was going to bottle out. Even after everything she had told him she could still backtrack, there was still time to batten down the hatches and not say another thing.

She held herself poker straight. She was going to finish this. 'I stole my money back.'

———

The surf brushed the grains of sand, its tide darkening and moistening the sand near their feet. His stomach was contracting as her words impacted. She started to talk again.

'I started off with small amounts, just a few hundred here and there. It wasn't difficult and the thrill I got …' She wet her lips.

'The thought of taking something of his, something that would hurt him, almost as much as he hurt me, it was liberating.'

Taking money and making a new start. It was all too familiar. Perhaps they weren't so different after all.

'So I took more, thousands, all well timed, all hidden in the figures and before I left for Corfu I'd almost taken everything he'd stolen from me.' She sighed. 'And now he's found out. All those calls I've had from England are about a meeting at the office when I get back. Ross knows I work there, he knows what I've been doing. He's probably going to have me arrested.' She sighed. 'I just hope he doesn't ask the charities for the money back.'

He looked at her then, frown lines creasing his forehead. 'Charities?'

'Um, charities, how do I explain those. Organisations that help people for different causes …'

He interrupted. 'I know what charities is. I do not understand why they have money.'

'Oh, yes, well, although I'm living in a horribly tiny flat in a not-so-nice area, I couldn't take the money for myself. That really would be stealing. And I didn't want his money to set me up with a business. I'd never be able to forget him if I did that. So I made donations to various charities, causes I know my mum would have approved of.'

'Ellen.' Her name on his lips still felt so soft, so right.

He watched her shift her feet then direct her eyes to the beach, as though the soft sand could give her answers.

He didn't know how to tell her everything he was feeling right at that moment. She had finally opened up to him and he knew what that had taken out of her. She was trembling from the experience, unable to look him in the eye. Was she afraid he was going to reject her?

'I took money too,' he stated. He took his hands from his pockets, let them drop to his sides.

'I had to leave Bulgaria and I spent all I have on engagement ring for Rayna. When … things end, I take money from her father for air ticket to here.'

He looked back at her, watched her nod her head.

'As soon as I have enough money from pay, I arrange hotel to send back.'

He hadn't wanted to take anything from that vile man. He should have known the kind of luxuries the family had could only come from corruption. Gavril Danchev wasn't an intellectual man, he was a brute. He had seen enough men like him in bars and restaurants where he'd worked. He should have realised the similarities.

But it had been a necessity, a desperate need to get away. He knew his mother had nothing. He also knew, if he asked, she would find the money for him. And the very last thing he wanted was to see her in debt to someone like Rayna's father.

'I take the money for me. You do something good with it,' Yan told her.

—

'But I never had any intention of giving it back.'

It was the truth. She wasn't sorry for what she'd done. No matter what the consequences were now, she didn't regret a single penny she'd taken from him. Ross could do what he liked to her going forward. The police, the accounting association, she was ready to hold her hands up to her crime. The only thing that remained was to find out whether he was ready to own up to his.

'You used it to start again, to find some freedom,' she continued. 'Not like me. I've been trapped for so long with one fixed life plan, the second it all evaporated I had no clue what to do.'

'But now you are free,' he said.

'Until the police get involved.' She shuddered. Would Ross really do that? Would he have the nerve to prosecute her after what he'd done, after what she'd let him get away with?

'You could not go home,' he stated.

The words seemed to echo around the cove, bouncing off the olive and lemon trees, circling the bay, touching the water, reaching every corner and then coming back to her.

She swallowed. 'Stay here?'

He shrugged. Non-committal. Not giving any indication of his feelings one way or another. She shook her head, trying to rid her mind of the ridiculous notion.

'I can't stay here. Things are so up-in-the-air at home. Lassiter's, Lacey ...'

'Other people and your sister,' Yan remarked.

There was a tinge of disapproval in his tone that he hadn't bothered masking. Were they all just excuses? Did she hide behind responsibilities so she didn't have to make a decision?

'You always think of someone else,' Yan added.

The blue eyes were studying her and all of a sudden she felt self-conscious standing there on the edge of the ocean, her heart beating an unsteady rhythm.

'It is good to think this way, but not if you really want something else.'

Yan was still looking, not taking his eyes from her and a shock of desire bolted through her. She longed for him. And not just in a physical sense. Being with him, getting to know him, learning how different life could be for her, sharing moments with someone, it had filled her up. It had completed a puzzle that had always had some bits missing.

He shifted on the sand until they were almost touching. Body to body. He was so close that if she breathed too hard, let her chest expand, they'd connect.

'What is it that you want, Ellen?'

'You.' The words came out as a whisper but with every ounce of determination and sincerity she had in her. There was nothing else to say.

THIRTY EIGHT

They'd run, sprinting like they were being pursued, as if their lives depended on it. She was holding Yan's hand, her lungs bursting, her body alive, racing to get back to the hotel.

The second they were inside his room his arm looped around her waist. One fast motion and he had pulled her hard against him, her body flattening against his. She was finding it hard to take a breath, their eyes locked, her temperature rising as his solid form merged with hers.

The inside of her mouth was parched with anticipation, her lips forming a delicate pout, expectant for the touch of his. What was he waiting for?

———

Lust was pooling inside him, every nerve ending primed and reacting to his feelings for her. It was taking every ounce of self-control not to move, take her mouth with his, plunder with his tongue, stroke his fingers down her arms and under her clothes. But he knew this was not a moment to be rushed. This time together was a moment to take slower, to savour. It was going to mean so much.

He could feel a heartbeat thudding erratic beats against his rib cage, echoing its way through his body until he wasn't sure whose rhythm he was feeling. Her face was tilted up, her lips parted, her brown eyes studying his. She was just such a natural beauty. He swallowed, realising how much desire he had, not just to touch and caress every inch of her, but to protect her, to cherish her … to love her.

'Yan.'

Her whisper was one of deep longing that made her quiver underneath his hands. Going slow was no longer an option. His fingers were at the buttons of her gauzy blouse, unfastening, eager, desperate to reveal the skin beneath. He parted the fabric, touching her with the lightest trace. His eyes appraised what he saw, her collarbone, the throb of her heartbeat at the bottom of her neck, wavy sections of her hair just touching her bare shoulders. He hovered a hand above the strap of her bra, pausing.

———

Ellen was holding her breath, watching his hand poised in the air between them. Nothing but pure anticipation crackled under her surface. She wanted him so much. He moved his hand a centimetre and she could almost feel it on her skin. He held off, just millimetres from actually making contact but she sensed the heat. If he didn't touch her soon she would inch herself forward until there was nothing he could do about it.

But she didn't have to. With his next motion he pulled the strap off her shoulder, sliding it down her arm and using both hands to unclip the back. As he removed her bra she slipped her hands beneath his t-shirt. Slowly she smoothed the tips of her fingers over his abdomen, wanting to leave her trace on every muscular curve.

———

Yan felt her pull at the material with one hand, as the other caressed his midriff, on a path to his chest. He helped. He took control, easing his body out of the shirt until it was off. He discarded it and stood up straight as she looked at him.

Her eyes seemed to roam over every bare inch on display and it made his need tighten even more. Her perfect breasts, the nipples already tight and dark, swelled against his chest as she hooped her arms around his neck, forcing his mouth to hers.

Yan cupped her face, the back of his hand brushing against the softness of her hair. As she kissed him, with so much passion, her fingers circled the waistband of his jeans, jutting under the denim, tugging at the metal button.

If she started to loosen his jeans he wasn't sure he was going to be able to stop this. But why should he want to? He cared for her, completely.

—

Ellen wanted to see him, all of him. He helped her remove his underwear until he was right there before her. Bare. And as much as she yearned to touch, all she could do was look. Her eyes trailed down his firm, athletic torso until she found what she was seeking. Hard, proud, as turned on as her whole body felt. She wanted to hold him, feel the strength of his passion for her.

She moved her hand towards him but he stopped her motion with his. Interlocking their fingers, he spoke.

'Come with me.'

Yan took a step towards the other end of the room and she let him lead her, wetting her lips in anticipation of what was to come.

He halted by the glass doors, drawing back the curtains. Darkness, a few lights at the front of the hotel and the red beacon at the top of Mount Pantokrator greeted her. Not the ocean scene she had from her suite but serene and beautiful in its own way.

Ellen gasped as he unfastened the zipper at the back of her skirt. Easing it down over her hips he pulled it lower, past her thighs, until she was able to step out of it. Her cheeks flamed as she realised she was standing in front of a full-length window in nothing but her underwear. A flicker of heat coupled with bashful self-consciousness ran over her.

———

All that remained were her cream-coloured panties. Yan swallowed, looking at the triangle of cotton, beneath it the most intimate part of her. He reached out, his fingers slipping beneath the band of elastic. Before there was time to think or hesitate, he pulled them away from her body, edging them downwards.

He heard the intake of breath she gave as he rolled them down further until she had no choice but to step free. Bending back up he locked eyes with her, excruciatingly aware that she was completely naked in front of him, a neat tangle of brown curls tantalisingly near. He swallowed and put one hand on the balcony door. With a swift pull he wrenched it open, the balmy night overpowering the air-conditioned air in the room.

'Yan.' Her voice was tinged with apprehension as he'd expected. Quickly he caught her hand up in his and led the way.

———

What was she doing? Her heart was pumping like an engine about to overheat and she was naked, more open than she'd ever been with anyone and now he was taking her outside, onto the balcony, where just about anyone could see.

She took back her hand, loitering in the doorway, unsure, unsteady.

'Yan, I don't know if I can,' she whispered. She crossed an arm over her chest to hide her breasts. Adrenalin wasn't pushing her on, fear about giving in to what she wanted was winning out.

Yan faced her then, all six foot of him, there for her to drink in. She swallowed, her eyes roaming his sculpted torso again, the lean, muscular limbs and everything in between.

'You are scared?' he asked her.

She recognised so many sentiments in his deep baritone, concern, longing ... something more? What was frightening her the most? Being naked on the balcony with the chance of being seen? Or making love with Yan? Her chest contracted at the last thought. She did want this. Not just bodily but wholly.

She didn't answer him but took a step forward, her bare feet meeting the rougher tiles of the balcony. She watched his expression, then shifted her eyes to his chest, saw the rise and fall increase in pace as she neared.

—

Lithe limbs, womanly curves, female perfection stepped closer and it was his turn to hold his breath. Ellen stopped a few inches from him as he braced himself against the balcony wall.

'I'm not scared,' she whispered.

A tight coil inside him began to unfurl as the meaning of her words catapulted his heart.

He reached out, smoothing the flat of his palm down her hair, then across her shoulder, over the swell of one breast and down lower, across her stomach towards her vagina. He paused then, his fingers teasing the very outline of her most sensitive part.

'I do not want this to be about other people. The ones that hurt us.' He whispered the words as his fingers traced a gentle pattern.

He needed to say this. He needed to let her know the way he was feeling wasn't a rebound reaction or about anyone else.

'This is for us.' He paused, taking a breath, the heat from her spreading to the tips of his hands. 'Just for us.'

He slipped one finger lower, touching her. He felt her shift, her hand reaching for his shoulder and squeezing hard.

———

Ellen was lost already, on a completely different plain. As his finger swirled, so deliciously, each tiny latent sense of pleasure seemed to come alive. She braced herself against him, her hands on his shoulders, her breath on his neck as he took control of her.

She'd never wanted anything more, the sexual tension was writhing a path through her, sparks of conscious awareness tingling in her head as Yan brought her nearer and nearer to the brink of letting go. She was in danger of slipping down from the top of that tall slide, riding hard and fast, out of control. And suddenly she didn't want that.

'Yan,' she breathed, her voice wrapped up in lust. 'Yan, stop.'

If he touched her for a second longer, if he made her any wetter or moved further down it would be too late.

'Yan,' Ellen said again.

This time he met her eyes, the rhythmic motion of his hand stopping. He looked like he thought he'd done something wrong.

'I want you with me,' she told him.

Yan blinked, his dark eyelashes refreshing those beautiful azure eyes. Had he understood? She shivered, a slight breeze waving over her nakedness. Whether he'd understood the first time or not, she wanted to be frank. She didn't want anything to be lost in translation.

'I want you inside me.'

Her voice was so insistent, so need-ridden she barely recognised it as her own.

—

His finger was still inside her, still hot and moist from her, his eyes locked on hers. He hadn't thought it would happen this fast. He hadn't really thought it would happen at all. He was just relishing every second he had this close to her.

He stroked a neat circle and she cried out.

'No, I won't.' She panted. 'Not without you.'

It was a determined statement and the more she talked that way, the closer he came to buckling under the intensity himself.

'I want you, Yan,' she repeated. Her hand felt for him then and he clenched his stomach. He couldn't hold off, not now she had begged and he was teetering on the precipice.

He gently edged her back until her shoulders met the outside wall of his room. She let out a tiny sound, something between a gasp and a moan and it fuelled his passion even further. He wanted to feel her rocking against him, he wanted to fill her body with his.

He lifted her then, shifting her hips higher, bearing her weight. She was staring at him now, wide-eyed, her pert mouth open. He'd never seen a more beautiful image. His eyes fixed on her, he watched her expression as he made their connection.

—

The first contact took the breath from her. Her weight between the wall and Yan, she tilted her hips further, wrapped her legs around him, demanding more.

Ellen leaned back, feeling the brickwork digging into her bare skin and not caring that it hurt. She pushed her hips toward him, inviting him in further, wanting his every inch inside her.

'Ellen,' he whispered. The sound of her name on his lips sent delightful shivers through her. She braced herself against him, one hand around the back of his neck, the other on his chest as he moved inside her.

Then every atom was fizzing with an electric heat like she'd never experienced before. As they pulsed together, in a perfect fusion, she felt her body arch in response to a building ache, fanning out, wilder and stronger with every motion.

She didn't want him to stop. She wanted to gather up this feeling and never let it go.

———

Ellen's hair in his hand, every sinew of him glided backwards and forwards, slowly, teasing, then faster with a desperate need to fulfil a physical and emotional void. She felt so good, so right, tight, hot, intense. It was a union on so many levels it was destroying him. Nothing else was important now, their being together was everything.

'Yan, I'm …' The end of her sentence died in a sound he'd never heard from a woman before. It was a mew, then a cry of pure pleasure and he felt every single contraction. She clung on to him, damp, coming apart and his resolve began to crack. He was falling, second by second, towards his own release.

'Yan,' she breathed his name again and this time it was just too much. White hot heat surged through his body and he was forced to let it go.

———

Yan shuddered in her arms, his body tightening then slowly shaking to a stop, his breathing laboured, his skin dewy with moisture.

She was still quaking, her thighs wrapped tight around him, her insides spinning. But much more than their physical union, emotionally she was floored.

She opened her mouth to speak before the moment passed, but his voice, thick with feeling, beat her to it.

'I am in love with you, Ellen.' He took a moment and another breath. 'I am in love with you.'

THIRTY NINE

Ellen heard his voice, like a far-away whisper in her ear. Just the light lull of the words was enough to make her mouth spread into a smile and she became aware of holding onto the bed sheet around her. But she didn't want to open her eyes. She wanted to stay there, semi-conscious, remembering their night together, reliving the best bits like a movie trailer in her mind. And as she let herself drift into those moments she fell back into a contented sleep with nothing crashing about her brain, just perfect snapshots of the love they'd shared.

Her eyes snapped open at the sound of a cockerel. It was the sound they used on the PA system to start the day's animation. Just before ten o'clock. She checked her watch. Nine forty-five. It was nine forty-five. She couldn't be in bed, in *someone else's* bed at nine forty-five. Her heart was racing with panic when the door opened.

Worried it was a maid, she pulled the bed clothes up over her naked form and waited. A familiar figure dressed in his polo shirt and shorts uniform backed into the room. He turned around, kicking the door shut and revealing the tray he was carrying.

'Good morning,' Yan greeted her.

She swallowed, watching him place the tray onto the table, then focus his attention on her.

'It's almost ten o' clock.' It was all she could think to say.

'I know this. I try to wake you before nine but you do not want this.'

His velvet voice, so close yet so far away. She'd heard him but chosen not to wake, still revelling in the glow of the night before.

'I have breakfast,' he announced, indicating the tray.

Her stomach reacted to the word, swishing and bubbling and reminding her it had been a long time since yesterday's evening meal, even if she had eaten a mountain of all inclusive treats.

She tried to move in the bed but was so twirled up in the covers it was almost impossible. She stayed put.

———

'I did not know what you would like. I have fruit salad with bacon and sausage. And coffee.'

Yan sensed her lack of enthusiasm from across the room. It was too much. He shouldn't have brought her breakfast. Like perhaps he should not have told her he loved her last night. She'd kissed him hard, driven him back into the room where they'd made love again and held each other until they'd fallen asleep. But she hadn't answered, hadn't acknowledged what he'd said to her. Had he expected her to? He hadn't thought he would ever say the words again but the depth of his feeling for her had overridden thinking twice.

She was twirling her hair around her finger and looking directly at him. Her brown eyes were without their usual sparkle, because of lack of sleep, he guessed. He didn't know what to do.

'Thank you,' she finally said, still unmoving.

He nodded. 'I have water exercise at ten.'

'I know. That's OK. I should head back and find out how Lacey is.'

He nodded again. He didn't know how to continue where they had left off. Why, in the morning light, did things seem so much more complicated?

'I will see you later?' he asked. He knew there was a tentative edge to his voice because he *was* just that, tentative, concerned. She was leaving in two days.

He watched her pull at the bed sheets, loosening them so she could move. And then she stood up, winding the covers around her body and walking towards him.

Just seeing her slow, rhythmic stride sent an erotic message and he took in a silent breath, straightening his form, waiting for her.

Ellen reached him, stood just millimetres from touching, one hand clasping the white cotton around her, the other reaching up to his face. Her fingers caressed the faint covering of stubble on his cheek setting off shards of electricity right the way through him.

'I love you.'

Her voice was soft but clear and the sentiment was right there, echoed in her eyes. He put a kiss on her thumb.

'I should have told you last night.' She stroked his face again. 'Because I felt it just as much then as I do now.'

Yan didn't say anything, just carried on planting delicate kisses on each of her fingers.

'I think maybe it's because it's happened so fast and so unexpectedly and …'

'You do not have plan,' he interrupted.

———

She smiled. This man knew her so well already. They had only been acquainted six days and he could read her better than any man she'd ever known. It just went to prove that, in their case, time, language and status meant nothing when it came to matters of the heart. Somehow they matched and, as bizarre as that scenario was to her, she couldn't deny it was true.

'I'm not even going to use that word anymore,' she told him.

Yan nodded, the sides of his mouth upturning.

'You don't believe me,' Ellen stated. She couldn't help furrowing her brow. She could throw caution to the wind. She'd done it most of this week with Yan, and the mobile phone she usually glanced at every second was still switched off. She could turn over a new leaf.

'I think you find this hard,' he told her.

She snorted in response and folded her arms across her chest. The sheet fell sideways at the movement, revealing one half of her naked body, but she held fast, matching his gaze.

He laughed then. That deep laugh resonating from his belly and filling the room. 'You are beautiful.'

'That doesn't mean funny. You do know that, don't you?'

'I know what this means,' Yan stated, inching himself forward, looking deep into her eyes.

Mesmerising. There was no other word to accurately describe his perfect eyes.

Yan grabbed the sheet in two fistfuls and whipped it from her body.

'I have plan,' he breathed. 'I plan to be a little late for water exercise.'

———

Ellen could hear his voice, counting in English then German from the pool as she made her way back to her suite. She'd mentioned the phrase 'walk of shame' before he'd left her high and quivering from another soul-stealing orgasm. He hadn't understood and it wasn't really appropriate anyway. She wasn't ashamed of anything they'd done together. She was excited, happy, for the very first time in a long time.

Everything was heightened. The sky had never seemed so blue, the sun was scorching the skin on her arms in an exhilarating way and the piped music coming from the plants along the path was putting a spring in her step. She felt wonderful. Like she could achieve anything. As if the fact that a huge disaster was waiting for her when she got home just didn't figure.

She bounced up the steps to her room and as she reached the door, she slotted the key into the lock. She turned the handle and pushed, but it stuck. The chain was across.

'Lacey?' she called.

'Hang on! In the middle of a hair rescue pack!'

Her sister sounded better. She was talking and it was understandable. However, she knew how incapacitated Lacey was when she was hair rescuing. Not that she really had a clue what it was actually being rescued from.

Ellen folded her arms across her chest, trying to duck down into a spot of shade. As the seconds ticked past, the sun beating down turned from exhilarating to burning and the piped music went from sexy Enrique to irritating Los Lobos.

Finally the door whipped open and there was Lacey, hair embalmed in something white and foamy, face still looking like ripe rhubarb.

'Sorry about that.' She looked Ellen up and down. 'Well, what are you waiting for? Come in and tell me everything!'

The phrase 'tell me everything' was concerning. The last time she'd seen her sister, Lacey had barely known her own name. Now she was grinning like someone high on drugs as she led the way back into the suite.

Ellen watched her sit on her bed and pat the counterpane.

'Sooo, tell me everything!' Lacey squealed.

'Which bits can't you remember? You know Mark and Dad are here, don't you?'

She knew sunstroke was bad, could give you blinding headaches and sickness but she wasn't sure it affected memory. Unless …

'Don't be daft! Of course I know they're here. As soon as I was able to stand I left. Mark wiping my brow every ten minutes was doing my head in.' Lacey paused and tried to shake her hair. It didn't move. 'Your bed hasn't been slept in.'

Ellen swallowed, the heat rising in her face as though a radiator had just been turned up to maximum. Her sister, the sex detector.

She opened her mouth to speak but stopped herself. Her first instinct was to lie, to make something up about being at a nightclub or being at Bo's Bar all night. But in reality, those scenarios were just as ludicrous as the truth.

'Oh my days, you did it, didn't you? You slept with Yan!'

Somehow Lacey had made it sound like she'd sold British government secrets to the Russians. Her sister's hand was clamped to her mouth, her eyes out on stalks.

You slept with Yan. Yes, she had and she was glad and it was nothing to feel bad about. She nodded at Lacey with conviction, sitting down next to her on the bed.

'Yes, I did.'

'Oh my God, I can't believe it. After everything you said about me and Sergei,' Lacey began.

What? What was she saying? This was nothing like what had happened with Sergei. Lacey was … had been … engaged to be married. *She* was single, completely single and hadn't been looking for anything from any man. She hadn't flirted with him from the moment she'd arrived or made a beeline towards him when the Conga line started up. She had felt attracted, tried to keep her distance but things had just happened. Real things, feelings grounded in more than all inclusive *ouzo*.

'Good on you,' Lacey finished with a girlish giggle.

'It isn't like you think,' Ellen started. She wanted Lacey to understand.

'I do know what happens when two people spend the night together, Ells. Your copies of *Cosmo* and Nan's talk on chastity belts learnt me everything.'

Ellen shook her head. She didn't want Lacey demeaning it. She was talking about it as if it were a fling and it wasn't like that. Yes, it would be short-lived because they were going home but it wasn't just a bit of fun, it was something special.

'Stop.' Ellen raised a hand, then, realising it was very over-the-top, she set it back down on her lap.

Lacey was looking confused now. Like she had all those years ago when Ellen had had to admit Margarette had never sent her Christmas or birthday presents, that she, Ellen, had bought stuff and pretended, to save her feelings. The memory of that moment made her take a breath.

'It isn't like that,' she began.

Lacey was studying her every motion, like she was trying to suck up information from every slight nuance. It was off-putting and making her nervous. *Breathe. Remember how good you feel.*

But how did she explain it? And how was it going to sound when she actually said the words aloud?

'I'm in love with him.' She nodded, tried to feel bolder. 'I'm in love with Yan.'

And there it was. The statement about a man she had known six days. Was she certifiable? Had all the stress and anxiety over Ross Keegan finally caught up with her? Had she made a mistake? Were her decisions not really her decisions, just choices her fractured mind was making because she was under so much pressure? She shook her head.

Lacey parted her lips and let out a huge gush of air. It was like someone had turned on an oscillating fan.

'Fucking hell.'

FORTY

Lacey had suggested wine but Ellen had managed to persuade her into making two cups of tea. Now they were sitting on their balcony watching the activity by the pool, drinking in the comings and goings and not saying too much. A line of holidaymakers were dancing a *sirtaki* dance to Zorba the Greek coming from the PA system. They swayed in time to the movements of the fronds of the palm trees, splashing up water from the edge of the pool with their bare feet. A couple were playing ping pong across the water, children tussled with lilos and, on the sand court, Sergei was about to commence a game of volleyball.

'Does Yan feel the same?' Lacey blurted.

Ellen nodded. 'Yes.'

'Are you sure? Because men can be very convincing when they want something from you.'

She definitely knew that was true. But this sudden role reversal was sweet. Lacey was looking at her as if she were the naïve sister, the one to have the wool pulled over her eyes on matters of the heart. And she was right. Just not this time. She was certain.

'I'm sure,' Ellen answered. Her gaze fell to Yan, in the water with the residents doing water aerobics.

'What are you going to do? We've only got today and tomorrow,' Lacey reminded her.

'I know.' And every time she thought about it her stomach sank to her sandals.

'Are you going to keep in touch? Text and email and stuff? Maybe you could come over here again in a couple of months.' Lacey grinned. 'Maybe I could come with you.'

Animated Lacey had thought of things she hadn't even considered yet. She was so busy worrying about their imminent departure from Corfu, she hadn't explored the options of carrying on the relationship, coming back. She realised then, that although she cared so deeply for him, she'd assumed it would end. That it was a relationship to cherish but one to move on from. But did it have to be that way?

Lacey was pulling at one of her acrylic nails and kicking a flip-flop at the balcony rail.

'What about you and Mark?' Ellen asked.

The kicking stopped and Lacey picked up her cup of tea, cradling it in her hands. 'He came all this way because he couldn't wait to see me.'

Ellen nodded. She was worried this might happen. That Lacey would see Mark's arrival as a devoted action and go back on the decision she'd made. She knew, deep down, that coming to Corfu had probably been Al's idea, not Mark's.

'But I wish he hadn't.' Lacey sighed. 'It's just made things more awkward.'

'What are you going to do?'

Ellen was concerned for her sister. She didn't want her to be bullied, her thoughts and feelings dismissed, Al to bluster in like a steamroller.

'We're having lunch together at that little taverna on the beach. Away from everything here.' Lacey put her cup back on the table. 'He needs to get it all off his chest and I need to let him down gently.'

Ellen let out a steady breath. Was it possible to be pleased and sad at the same time? Mark and Lacey finishing would be the end of an era but she was glad Lacey was the one making the decision.

'And I don't want you thinking this has anything to do with Serg.' The feisty attitude was back. 'He was just the catapult.'

'Catalyst?' Ellen suggested.

'That would make an awesome cocktail name.'

Ellen couldn't help but laugh.

'What are *you* going to do?' Lacey asked.

That was a good question and at the moment it was one Ellen had no answer to.

'I really don't know.'

———

'Thank you everybody. I see you here tomorrow at ten.'

Yan pulled himself out of the pool and grabbed up his towel from the chair he'd left it on. Today was a good day. Today he felt worthy of this new start. Once he had the money for the church he could implement the same plan he'd had at home, with different children in a new country. He knew he could enrich their lives using the skills he'd learned. As long as he could avoid the skills he didn't have, the ones he couldn't master. Here, it didn't seem to matter so much. He knew, without any doubt, that he could make this work. Because he'd done it before and he'd done it successfully. He just needed to hold onto his nerve and obtain a longer visa. The latter was definitely going to be the most difficult bridge to cross. He just couldn't do that on his own.

'Lacey's father eat six fried eggs. Six, Yan.' Sergei used extravagant hand gestures to get his point across.

'He is a big man,' Yan responded, putting his polo shirt over his head.

'Do you think he knows?' Sergei adjusted his sunglasses, his voice just above a whisper, his eyes darting over every inch of the pool area in case the subject of his discussion was around.

'Know what?'

'About Lacey. About us together,' Sergei hissed.

'Why would he know this?'

'Yesterday she was in terrible way. She did not know what she say to anyone.'

'Her boyfriend is here now,' Yan reminded.

'She is not marrying him.'

'It is not your business. You should not have done what you did but now it is over.' He looked directly at Sergei as he said the last phrase to gauge his reaction. He couldn't read it.

'I ask you this before. Do you love this girl?' Yan asked straight.

'No! Of course not!'

The reaction was severe and just what he had been expecting. He wasn't sure Sergei had ever been in love. He talked of his girlfriend in Bulgaria but then he would flirt and lap up the attention of guests. That wasn't a sign of devotion.

Yan shook his head at his friend. 'Then why do you worry about the father?'

'Because she come here to arrange her wedding and now …' Sergei started.

'Now?'

'She cancel this because of me.'

It was hard not to laugh considering the mood he was in. This was typical Sergei. A woman spent a few intimate moments with him and he thought she decided to change the whole course of her life off the back of it.

He put an arm around Sergei and patted his shoulder. 'You worry too much, my friend.'

'Maybe,' Sergei nodded.

'We should get a drink before volleyball.' Yan led the way towards the bar.

'I need more than fruit juice. Have you seen Dasha this morning?' Sergei asked. 'He's organising karaoke tonight. Tanja's got some meeting in Corfu Town so you're in charge of song selection.'

Just that one sentence had his happy demeanour crumbling to the floor.

———

'Do I look OK?'

Lacey's meek voice had Ellen raising her head from her paperback. Standing in the doorway of the balcony was her sister, looking like she'd never looked before. Flat sandals on her feet, a pretty print dress that skirted the top of her knees, no make-up on her post-box-coloured face and her hair brushed flat, glossy and rescued.

'Oh, Lacey, you look lovely.' There was an acorn-sized lump in Ellen's throat and a welling up in her eyes she tried to blink away. She'd never been more proud of her than she was now.

'He's never seen me without make-up on before. I always went to bed in it and reapplied before he had a chance to wake up.' She smiled. 'Plus I still feel dodge *and* the amount of foundation it would take to dull this red face down would use up the whole bottle.'

'You look lovely,' she repeated. 'How do you feel about it?'

'OK. A bit nervous. I know he's going to be upset.' Lacey played with a tendril of her hair. 'I'm upset too but I know … I'm sure it's the right decision.'

Ellen nodded. 'Now, are you positive you don't want me to come with you? I can be discreet. I could sit at the back of the restaurant in my hat and sunglasses, behind a large menu.'

Lacey smiled and shook her head. 'No. I want to do this on my own.'

Her little sister was growing up right before her eyes.

'Will *you* be OK? Having lunch with dad?' Lacey asked.

Lacey had dropped that bombshell on her while she was taking the rescue and recovery pack off her hair. Would she mind keeping their dad occupied at the all-inclusive buffet while she had her heart-to-heart with Mark? That way she could guarantee Al wouldn't turn up in the middle of tears and tantrums at the taverna. How could she refuse?

Ellen also needed to clear the air. Al had arrived, trampling in as usual, opening his mouth before he thought about the consequences. But he was a good man. She loved him. They needed to stick together. The thought snagged on something inside her. If she really believed the sticking together part she would have told him about Ross and what he'd done. It was a bit late for that now.

'We'll be fine. Three kinds of potatoes and a lamb shank, I'll barely have to talk,' she responded.

———

Yan's mind wasn't on the game of volleyball, it was on karaoke. It was put on once a fortnight and on most occasions it was his job to hand out the song books and collect in the song sheets. Sergei would announce and Tanja would handle the laptop and sound system. He needed to clarify the roles with Dasha. If Dasha took over the announcing then Sergei could be in charge of playing the songs.

'Yan! Come on, wakey wakey,' Sergei called.

He hadn't even seen the ball come over the net. He needed to try and put this out of his mind until later. But it was easier said than done. If he didn't arrange something, what was he going to do? He shook himself, pulling his focus back to the present moment.

'I am sorry,' he apologised to his team. 'Go again.'

Sergei pumped the ball down the court and the teenaged girl next to Yan fisted the ball up in the air for Yan to batter down onto the sand.

'Very good,' Yan said to her. 'How was that, Sergei?'

Sergei replied with another thundering serve over the net, this time a high ball. Yan leapt up and belted it back with everything he had. His colleague and a new holidaymaker from Italy both went for the return but neither made proper contact. The ball skewed sideways, bounced off the top of a sun lounger and landed on a table.

Yan watched as a plastic cup tipped over into the lap of the man sitting there, covering his fawn shorts.

'Shit,' Sergei exclaimed, clamping a hand over his mouth.

'I will go,' Yan said, jogging off the court.

By the time he got to the table the man was standing up, trying in vain to brush off droplets of dark-coloured liquid from his shorts. Yan couldn't help noticing that he was wearing leather shoes.

Quickly Yan plucked a couple of serviettes from an adjacent table and held them out to the man like a peace offering.

'I am so sorry, sir.'

The man turned sharply, eyeing Yan with nothing short of contempt.

'What the hell do you think you're playing at? I only arrived here an hour ago and now I'm going to have to change *again*.'

The voice was hostile, his body language verging on threatening. Yan didn't know how to respond except to apologise again. 'Again, I am sorry. I am sure we can arrange for shorts to be cleaned at hotel.'

'Oh, you're sure, are you? You're sure that this hotel is going to be able to get Coke out of these in any way that's acceptable to me? These are *designer*. Do you even know what that means?'

It meant one thing to him. This man was rich as well as rude. Yan stayed still, didn't respond. If you said nothing confrontational you couldn't be accused of anything.

'No, I thought not. This *bloody* place.' He shook the leg of his shorts. 'I don't even want to be in this *bloody* place.'

'Would you like for me to arrange someone to collect them for cleaning from your room a little later?' There wasn't much else he could offer the man. He couldn't exactly rewind time and stop the ball from hitting the table.

'No I bloody don't. Just … just piss off.' The man wafted his hand in the air like he was dismissing an irritating mosquito.

Yan ground his teeth together and held his nerve. He wasn't going to let this man get to him. The customer was always right, even if they were very wrong. He made sure his voice was accented perfectly.

'I hope you enjoy rest of your stay at Blue Vue Hotel.' He left then, to the irritated mumblings of the holidaymaker ringing in his ears.

FORTY ONE

'Could you pass the salt?'

Al held out one of his giant hands across the table. Ellen put the porcelain pot into his palm and watched it almost disappear. Richmond sausages. That's what her dad's hands had always looked like to her. Fat, pink, squishy but dependable.

'Food's good 'ere,' he continued, chowing down on corn-on-the-cob, now slathered in butter and salt.

'Yes, it's really good,' she replied.

'I bet they'd 'ave done a great spread for the weddin'.'

She could barely contain the eye roll. 'Dad ...'

''old your 'orses. I was just sayin', that's all. It would 'av been a good ol' knees-up. Fillis would've loved it.'

'Dad, Lacey's going to tell Mark it's over.' There was no point beating around the bush. Al was straight-talking. He didn't do glossing over. He had to understand.

Al put his knife and fork down on the table and picked up his napkin. Putting it over his mouth, he let out a belch. 'Pardon me.' He cleared his throat. 'She's made up 'er mind then?'

'Yes she has.'

Al nodded. 'That's that then. Back at 'ome. Me worryin' about 'er every night.'

Ellen caught the depth of emotion in his voice and right then all she wanted to do was get up and put her arms around him. Instead she popped a piece of tomato in her mouth and hoped he would say something she could deal with a little bit better.

'Because that's what it's been like since you left 'ome. She never tells me where she's goin', what she's doin' or who she's doin' it with. Sometimes she doesn't get 'ome until the early hours. And I can't sleep 'til I know she's there. I'm laid out in bed there, re-runs of *Have I Got News For You* on the telly, listenin' for the door, eyes 'alf-open ...'

'Dad, she's a grown-up now. You have to let go.'

'That's easy for you to say. You moved out as soon as you could and left me to it.'

The feta cheese in her mouth turned sour. *Breathe. Focus.*

'I didn't mean that,' Al added. 'It's just when she met Mark it was like a forklift's worth of weight 'ad been taken off me. I knew 'e was a good lad, that 'e'd look after 'er and watch out for 'er and I thought they'd be 'appy.'

'They were happy, Dad. But some things aren't meant to last forever.'

Ellen saw the expression on her father's face change, like a solar eclipse had spontaneously occurred.

'Like me and your mum,' he whispered.

It was rare for him to talk about her. The only time he ever reminisced was Christmas, birthdays or when he'd had too much to drink. He'd get the photo albums out, his eyes would glaze over and then he would shut down again. There were no stories of their life together before Ellen had come into the world, no happy memories shared. It was as if it was just too painful to remember she had ever been.

'I thought we 'ad all the time in the world ... and then she was gone.'

Ellen didn't know what to say. She was worried that anything she said would break his train of thought, stop him talking about her mother.

'I've made so many mistakes,' Al continued. 'With you two girls ... and Margarette.'

'Dad ...'

'I just want to know you're both gonna be all right. I want to do the best I can to make sure you're looked after and safe.'

She swallowed a lump in her throat. His vulnerability was tangible and she suddenly felt guilty about all the secrets she'd kept from him. Should she have told him? Or would knowing that his elder daughter was incapable have given him a nervous breakdown? He might have understood. He definitely would have helped, but would the knowledge that she was as imperfect as the next person have tipped him over the edge?

'Lacey has to find her own path. And we want that to lead to the right person, don't we?'

Al nodded then, dabbed at his eyes with the serviette. 'Course. 'Course we do.'

'Then we have to accept that Mark isn't the right person for Lacey. That she ...'

Ellen stopped mid-sentence as a figure across the room at the central buffet island caught her eye. Her breath was already trapping in her lungs by the time she focussed. She recognised him from the shape of his back, the way he held himself, ramrod straight, his head high like he thought he was someone special. But it couldn't be him. It was impossible. She closed her eyes for a second as the panicked feeling started to rise up through her. This was stress. This was a classic overreaction to what was happening in her life – the phone calls from Milo at the office, Lacey ending the engagement, her dad being here.

Ellen opened her eyes again and this time she got a full frontal view. Her fork dropped from her hand. It *was* him. She wasn't imagining it. Ross Keegan was in the hotel.

FORTY TWO

'… and clap your hands together like this! Yes! Well done everybody!' Dasha applauded manically as the children from the kids' club finished the song.

Yan had waited through four renditions of the German song and now only had five minutes to get his message across. He stepped into the room as all the children began high-fiving the tall man dressed up as a mermaid.

'I will see you all here tomorrow or tonight with your parents for karaoke, yes? Tell them they must sing or they do not love you,' Dasha said, laughing.

'Dasha,' Yan stepped forward and touched his arm. Contact would hopefully draw him away from the legions of children who were still demanding his attention.

'Look, everybody, it is Mr Yan! Say hello to Mr Yan everybody!'

All the children turned to him and said hello in several different languages, with toothy smiles, red cheeks, bright eyes.

'Dasha … ' Yan started again.

'Do you think we should get Mr Yan to dress up?'

Dasha's expression was all too eager and, needing only a little encouragement, the children began diving for the dressing-up trunk and pulling out items of clothing. This was the last thing he needed.

'Dasha, can I speak with you about karaoke?' he tried again.

'I know! Karaoke is my best favourite and tonight I am in charge.' He wrapped a pink scarf around Yan's neck.

'It is going to be great night but ... could I collect song sheets from people? Sergei, he is better at laptop equipment than me.'

Dasha let out a booming laugh. 'Why you say this?' He shook his head. 'Sergei has top hat and suit for occasion like this. He has to be the announcer.'

'But ...' Yan didn't know what to say next. How did he explain without making too much of an issue out of it? He swallowed. 'Before you arrive I always go into audience to get them to choose songs.'

A boy aged about five tied a sarong around his waist and a girl slipped a glove onto his hand.

'Yan, look at me.' Dasha paused, pouting, one hand on his hip, his uniform shorts pulled high like hot pants. 'I was born to get people to do things they are not natural with. I am the crazy guy. How can anyone say no to me?'

How did he put up an argument against that? Out of the corner of his eye he saw a blond haired boy heading towards him with a rubber face mask. He quickly peeled the glove off and started to untie the sarong.

'You are nervous for this?' Dasha asked.

Now Dasha was looking suspicious, the very last thing he'd wanted to happen. Yan shook his head. 'No. I just want night to be perfect for you.'

The chance was lost, Dasha's decision made. He had no idea what he was going to do. That knowledge was sending unwanted pinpricks of fear across his back. He tried to keep his cool.

Dasha's face broke into a smile. 'Me too! We have so much fun!' He slapped his hands against Yan's face, squeezing his cheeks.

'I ... I have to go.'

Ellen stood up, knocking her knife off the table and onto the floor. She was floundering, stuck between trying to hide her presence and moving too quickly, creating attention. Her fork followed the knife's lead as she bent to pick up her bag.

'What? Go where? You've not finished your dinner,' Al remarked.

She nodded at him, moving a sheet of her hair over her face and turning away from the buffet. 'I know, I just remembered ...' *Think, Ellen, think.* 'I signed up for boules this afternoon and it starts ... any second.'

'Boules?' Al looked confused. 'Boules is more important than dinner with your old man?'

'No, of course not. I ...'

Her heart was racing, beating so hard in her chest and throat it was overwhelming her. It felt as if every blood vessel in her body was pounding for release. She had to get out of the restaurant, get some fresh air, give herself a chance to calm down.

'I think I'm going to be sick.'

No one argued with ensuing vomit. Ellen didn't say any more. Ducking her head down she raced, as inconspicuously as she could, towards the door, silently praying Ross didn't see her.

She hurried, like a speed walker, out of the lobby, and down the steps. Only when she hit the main pathway through the grounds did she stop and take a breath that almost sent her sideways. Ross Keegan was in Corfu. He was in the hotel restaurant, obviously looking for her. He had come to Greece to confront her.

At that thought, more panic rode like a surfer over her and a spinning feeling filled her head. This couldn't be happening.

Not here. Not now. She'd been telling herself that here in Corfu only good things happened, the real world was far behind her, thousands of miles away back in England. She'd been clinging on to the two precious days left here in this paradise, with Yan, not *forgetting* all her troubles but certainly being able to compartmentalise them for the first time. She leant against the low wall that bordered the path and tried to find some balance.

———

Yan was running on adrenalin and the fact that he had to get back down to the court for boules. He needed to think of another option to get out of the karaoke that night apart from running away or feigning sickness. He didn't like to let people down. But he couldn't let himself be compromised.

As he joined the central path he saw Ellen. She was leaning hard against the wall, her eyes closed. She was far from the carefree person he'd said goodbye to earlier that morning. She looked as though without the support of bricks and cement, she would be down on the floor. Something had happened. Perhaps Lacey was more ill than they had first thought. He picked up his pace.

'Ellen?' he greeted, reaching her.

Her eyes snapped open and there was an immediate look of fear on her face. But then her body sagged, relaxing a little, her palms flat against the brickwork as she leaned into the wall a bit more.

'You are OK?' Yan asked. He wanted to reach out and make contact but they were in the middle of the main path with residents passing them by both ways en route to the restaurant and the pools.

She shook her head. 'No, I'm not OK.' She shivered, her eyes darting over towards the restaurant.

'What has happen?' He was really concerned now. She looked like someone might have died. No colour in her face, eyes wide, brimming with, as yet, unspent tears.

'God, I don't know what to do. I mean, what do I do?'

She was talking as much to herself as she was to him and not explaining anything. He watched her put her head in her hands and shake it. He couldn't bear this. He reached out, rested his hand in her hair. At the motion she sat back up, forcing him to retract.

'Ross is here,' she stated, the frightened look still there.

For a second he couldn't compute what she'd said. Ross? Ross, the man who had asked her to marry him. Ross, the man who had stolen from her. Was here? The two things didn't go together.

'What?' He needed more explanation before he said anything else.

She shook her head again.

'He's here, Yan. I saw him in the restaurant. Ross Keegan. The one I told you about.'

That was more clear but still with no explanation. How was this possible? Yan swallowed, not knowing what to say to her.

'You see him?' he questioned.

She nodded her head.

'Are you sure?'

'Yes.'

'What did he say to you?'

———

It was a simple enough question and one she should have expected him or anyone else to ask. She didn't know how to answer.

'I …' she began.

Yan was looking at her, waiting for her to give him something. This wonderful man, this person who had changed her outlook on things in just a few short days. She shook her head and shrugged her shoulders at the same time.

'I ran. I left my dad and my meal and just left. I didn't want him to see me.'

As the words came flooding out she realised how they sounded. She'd fled, letting his presence dominate her, just like it had when they were together. She'd crumbled, just as she had when he'd taken her mother's money. She'd proved just how weak Ross' actions had made her.

Yan wasn't saying anything but was looking at her with pity in his eyes. This action was a perfect showcase of her shamefully vulnerable personality. She couldn't think straight but she needed to. She needed to get it together and think how to handle this. The hotel wasn't so big that she could avoid him for the next two days. Knowing him, he would ask for her room number and hunt her down if he had to. That was exactly his style and he wouldn't have travelled all the way to a Greek island, to the hotel she was staying at, just to top up his tan. He meant business. It was a serious situation and she needed to own it.

'He is here to ask about what you do with your work?'

She nodded, wiping at her eyes with her fingers. 'I guess so. He phoned me, a few days ago. Then Lacey had all this trouble with Mark and he kept ringing so we both switched our phones off.'

Had Milo tried to warn her? She could only assume it was him who had divulged her location. No doubt Ross had been into the office making threats and being thoroughly rude to everybody. She could imagine her secretary, Jolie, crying the second his voice was raised above kettle boiling level.

'This is such a mess,' she said, toying with her hands.

Yan shook his head. 'No. This is chance to tell him why you do this. To say that he deserve this. To tell him how you feel.'

She could do that. Couldn't she? What was the alternative? She let him ride roughshod over her again? Taking, stealing, grabbing hold of her life and turning it upside down? She wasn't that same person now.

'I am with you,' Yan said.

Just four small words but they filled her up immediately, made the panic lessen. Until she looked up and saw Ross leaving the restaurant and heading their way.

'I can't, Yan. I can't see him … not yet.' She took his arm and pulled him away from the main path, desperately shaking her hair over her face in a bid for disguise.

She saw Yan looking back at the person approaching as she hurried them through the complex towards the alternative track to the main pool. 'Yan, please.'

'This is him?'

His voice sounded edgy. She nodded. 'Yes.'

'I see him before. He was by pool today. We hit his table with volleyball and spill the drink. He is angry man.'

It was an acutely simple yet accurate description. She only wondered just how much anger he was going to show once they were face to face.

FORTY THREE

'He managed to get a flight back later tonight so reception have called him a taxi.'

The whole time Lacey was telling her the details of her heart-to-heart with Mark, Ellen was sitting at the dressing table, brushing her hair, waiting for the knock on the door. It was going to come. It was just a case of how long it would take Ross to track her down. He only had to ask at reception. She was surprised he hadn't turned up already. Or was it all about the game-playing?

'I think he knew I wasn't going to change my mind.' Lacey sighed as she paced. 'But it was good talking face-to-face. And you were right. I shouldn't have broken up with him by iMessage. He deserved better.'

Ellen nodded, her eyes out of the door and over the balcony, scanning the residents as they left the poolside.

'Is everything OK with you?' Lacey asked.

Ellen turned her attention away from the view to find her sister analysing her. Lacey had a penetrating look that instantly made her feel guilt-ridden. Ellen nodded her head again and straightaway regretted it. What was she doing? She had to tell someone about this. In hours, minutes or moments, Ross Keegan was going to find her and ask her what the hell she'd been doing stealing money from his company accounts. She had never wanted her family to know what he'd done to her but now that she was in danger of being in serious trouble, about to face this man's wrath, perhaps it was the right moment to let it all out and share some of the burden with the people that cared for her.

'Ross is here,' she whispered. Her voice was so quiet she wasn't even sure Lacey had heard her say anything. The quizzical look remained on her sister's face.

'Ross Keegan is here. The man who asked me to marry him,' Ellen repeated.

'Oh my days! To ask you to get back with him? How did he find you? It's a bit over the top, isn't it? Flying out here when you're on holiday. Some might call that stalker behaviour. What do you think?'

She thought she wanted to get on the night flight home with Mark, now that all the bad stuff she'd left in England had followed her here.

'There's more to it than I told you, Lacey.'

'Like what? You're freaking me out a bit now.' Lacey sat down on the edge of her bed.

'He did something awful to me. Something really awful.' She paused before continuing. 'I should have told you and Dad but I didn't. Instead I did something awful back to him.'

She looked at Lacey. Her sister was wide-eyed, hanging on her every word and she wondered how this news was going to change their relationship. The second she told her what she'd done she would go from being the sister who was always perfectly in control of everything, to someone who had made more terrible, stupid mistakes than *she* had.

'I want to know,' Lacey said. 'Tell me all of it and then we'll go and find him and I'll break his balls. Because whatever he's done to you, Ells, I'm going to have to kick his head in.'

———

The red cover of one of the karaoke books lay on the table next to the laptop. Yan opened it up and stared at the pages inside. Letters and numbers, hundreds of them, all merging into one big random mess. He couldn't do this. Who was he trying to fool here?

He turned the book back over and watched as guests began to gather at the poolside restaurant. He had just over an hour to think of something or everything would become abundantly clear.

And then he saw him. Ross Keegan. Overdressed in tailored trousers and a blue short-sleeved cotton shirt, making his way to a corner table. That angry man, the one who had stolen all that Ellen had left of her mother except her memories. He felt the tension move through his body and suddenly he knew exactly what to do.

Yan picked up a carafe of red wine from the tray by the bar and made his way across to the dinner section.

He wasn't quite sure how he was going to do this. The most satisfying method would be to pour the wine all over his head. But a vengeful act would get reported to Tanja and his job would be in danger. All he needed was a fuss, some commotion and this man was perfectly capable of making it without very much persuasion.

Yan walked with stealth, making sure he wasn't seen until the right moment. Silently, he pulled a chair across his path and, just as Ross Keegan reached his hand out for the glass of beer on his table, Yan faked a trip.

He aimed the contents of the carafe at the pale tailored trousers and fell to the tiled floor with an emphasised groan.

'Shit!' Ross was up and out of his seat. 'What the hell have you done?!'

Red wine dripped from Ross' crotch, down both legs of his trousers, pooling on the floor. He flapped his soiled hands around, spraying droplets of red liquid onto the tablecloth.

Yan got to his feet. 'I am so very sorry, sir. I fall over chair and …'

'I don't believe it. You're the idiot who knocked that volleyball into my table earlier and ruined my shorts!'

'That was not me. That was my colleague.'

He needed Ross to be slightly more irate, make more noise so the restaurant manager would come over. He just needed to be sent somewhere else for the night. He could deal with any reprimand, he just couldn't deal with karaoke.

'I bloody know it was you. Where's your superior? You're a liability.'

'I think you overreact a little maybe?'

'Overreact?! How dare you speak to me like that? I want the manager, I want the manager now and I want you removed.'

———

When Ellen had finished telling the story both she and Lacey had shed tears. It wasn't raking over it all again that had made her cry, it was the fact that as she told the story, she realised how wrong she'd been to shoulder it alone. And how Lacey might feel about that.

'I could get into real trouble, Lace. If he reports me to the police it's theft. If he reports me to the ACCA I'll never be able to practice accountancy again.'

Lacey shook her head, backwards and forwards. The movement and vacant expression reminded her of a doll their nan had brought back from Blackpool once. Scraps of hair glued into place, googly eyes and a head that rocked left and right. It had scared them both and had been resigned to the back of the cupboard in their bedroom. If only she could do that with her problems. Shove them in a black bin liner and lock the door on the wardrobe of her life.

'Why didn't you tell me? What was I doing when all this was going on? You had to move house and I never knew?! Ells, I'm your sister.'

She hadn't been expecting the hurt in Lacey's voice. She hadn't even thought about that when she was covering everything up and hiding the truth away. Was this how her dad was going to react, too?

'I know. I just felt so utterly stupid and you were in the middle of wedding planning. I …'

'You could have said something. I know I was obsessed with cakes and venues and white doves that wouldn't fly down and shit on everyone's heads but this is big stuff. He nicked your inheritance, Ells and you let him get away with that!'

When Lacey said it, it sounded so much worse. Her sister was standing now, her hands on her hips, lecturing her. Telling her she'd done the wrong thing. Telling her she should have offloaded the hurt and humiliation.

'I didn't let him get away with it. I …' Ellen began.

'You lived like a pauper for months, moved house, didn't tell your family …'

'I was ashamed. Dad thinks I can do no wrong. And he was always going on at me to find someone, settle down. That's the only reason I dated Ross in the first place.'

'You know what Dad would have done if you'd told him. He would have called the police and got your money back. And if he couldn't have got your money back he would have given the bloke a kicking and given you the money himself.'

Ellen nodded. She knew that's what would have happened. And that was another reason why she hadn't said anything. She had so wanted to stand on her own two feet. Prove she didn't need her dad's money to get on. That was also why the money her mother had left her had sat in the bank for so long. Because it wasn't something to use on everyday things. It was a nest egg to spend on her dreams. The accountancy business she was never going to have, now.

'And then …' Lacey took a breath. 'Then, when you had the chance to get even with him you gave all the money to sodding charity.'

'I had to do that. I'm not a thief.'

'No, you're someone who's let a guy walk all over you, let him take what's yours and then lived with the no Sky TV consequences.'

Ellen didn't know what else to say. Her sister knew everything and she'd never felt more infantile.

'You're so bloody annoying! I can't believe you didn't say anything,' Lacey exclaimed and she levelled a kick at the bedstead. 'Even if you didn't want to tell Dad, you should have told me. We could have keyed his car together or slipped some of his business cards into the menu holders at the gay bar.'

'You had so much on your plate already,' she protested.

'Well, I don't now.' Lacey picked up her handbag and moved towards her, checking her reflection in the mirror on the dressing table.

'What are you doing? Where are you going? We can't go out.'

'What are you talking about? Of course we're going out. We're going to find him and sort this out. If he's flown all this way to have it out with you then we need to get in first. We need to tell him what a low life he is and that if he dares contact anyone about your conjuring job with his accounts we're going to hang him out to dry with the cops over your stolen inheritance.'

'No, Lacey, we can't.'

The thought of facing him was driving spirals of ice through her. She wasn't ready. She wanted the two magical days back, the reprieve, the time with Yan in that fantasy bubble where everything was a little bit brighter, where she felt a little bit stronger.

'We're going to karaoke. Dad loves karaoke and it might be needed to calm him down once we tell him what this Ross arse has done to you.'

Ellen shook her head vigorously. 'No, Lacey, please don't tell Dad. Not yet.'

'Not *yet*? It's months too late as it is.'

'Please, Lacey.' She wet her lips. 'I'll come.' She couldn't really believe she was saying the words. 'But let me talk to Ross on my own. I got myself into this mess and ...'

'Lied to your family.'

'Yes.'

'And hurt your little sister.'

'Don't, Lace.'

She felt her cheeks heating up as the gravity of the situation truly hit home.

'Is it because ...' Lacey stopped mid-sentence.

'Because what?'

'Because she wasn't my mum too? Because we're not full sisters?'

'No.' The word was expelled forcefully from her mouth. The fact that Lacey could think that made her feel even worse.

'Your mum was so much nicer than mine. All those photos Dad has of her ... she's always smiling.'

Ellen nodded. It was true. She'd looked through those old photographs so many times, trying to remember something about her mother, even if it was just a sensation. Her arms around her, the sound of her voice. She stood up then and went to Lacey, desperate to make things right.

'You're my sister, full, half, it makes no difference to me,' she blurted out, closing her arms around Lacey. 'I love you.'

'I love you too, Ells.' Lacey sniffed, her head pressed against Ellen's shoulder. Then she broke the embrace. 'Right, I'm done.' She swiped a hand at her eyes. 'That's enough emotion. You need to toughen up to face the thieving git.'

Ellen gave a half-hearted smile and wiped her eyes with her fingers. 'Just promise me you won't say anything to Dad yet.'

'Promise me you'll tell that arsehole he deserved everything he got and more.'

Ellen mused over the sentence. 'I promise I won't let him off the hook.' Behind her back she crossed her fingers.

FORTY FOUR

Yan didn't know what to do with himself. He was walking up towards the main hotel, heading for the lobby bar, even though he wasn't sure what he was going to do when he got there. Have a drink? Have several drinks and try to quell the sick feeling in his chest as he thought about how close he'd come to having his secret exposed tonight?

Getting sent away from the entertainment area had been exactly the outcome he'd wanted, to avoid taking part in the karaoke. But it meant he wouldn't be near Ellen. That's if she came to watch the show at all. When he'd left her earlier she was still digesting the information that her ex-boyfriend was here, let alone what it meant for her or for them.

He wasn't sure what she was going to do about it. Or would the angry man force the issue? Put himself in front of her, demand a confrontation, perhaps even in public. Today he had learned that Ross Keegan wasn't at all shy about using his loud vocals to get his own way. What if he did that with Ellen? What if he embarrassed her in public? She would hate that.

Yan stopped walking and looked up at the bulk of Mount Pantokrator rising up behind the hotel building. Unshaking, solid, always there.

He couldn't let her face this on her own.

—

Ellen's legs were trembling and everything in her stomach was on a fast spin cycle, despite the half a dozen Kalms she'd swallowed.

'You're shaking! And you want me to leave you on your own with him? I can't do it,' Lacey said, clutching hold of her arm.

Picture that place where you feel at peace. You're warm. You're safe. Let that feeling grow, fatter, taller, bigger.

The words didn't make her feel any better. She shook herself. No mental reassurance was going to help in this situation. She just had to believe in herself and trust she was capable of seeing it through.

She carefully negotiated the steps down to the entertainment area then, once they were safely at the bottom, she closed her eyes and took a big breath, the type that fills your entire lung capacity and half your stomach too.

'What are you doing? Are you meditating or something?' Lacey asked.

She shook her head. 'No, I'm OK.' She nodded. 'I'm really OK.'

Saying it aloud felt better than she thought it would.

Lacey lowered her head into Ellen's space. 'Which one is he?'

She was already scanning the room before her sister spoke. Wanting to find him but not wanting to see him at the same time. Perhaps he wasn't even here. He'd never shown any interest in anything like karaoke before. Maybe he was up at the lobby bar or even in his room. But then her eyes came to rest on a dark-haired man sitting alone at a corner table half-facing the stage, half-facing the ocean view. Even from this distance she could see clearly it was him.

'There,' she said to Lacey.

'Where?' Lacey's head turned left and right.

Ellen turned to her sister and took hold of her hands. 'I need to do this on my own, Lacey.'

The slump of the shoulders and the pouting told her that Lacey had always expected her to give in and let her come. She wanted to support her and Ellen understood that need, but what *she* needed was to end this on her own, without help, just the way it had all started.

'But, I can't just sit down and watch. I mean, what if he has a go at you? You can't expect me not to want to leap up and brain him.'

'I do expect you not to do that.' She gave Lacey the benefit of her best warning look. One she'd delivered so many times before.

Her sister puffed out a sigh and looked at her watch. 'Well, I told Dad we'd meet him down here at ten so …'

'I'd better get a move on.' Ellen smiled, putting a hand out and patting her sister's arm. There was nothing else left to say.

———

Ellen's father was at the lobby bar, his vast body perched up on one of the bar stools, a short glass in his hand half-filled with amber liquid. The first impression Yan had got when the man arrived at the hotel was bad. Shouting, loud, quick to place the blame for Lacey's actions on Ellen. Yan stopped short, put a hand on the doorjamb that separated the bar area from the lobby. But, whether he liked him or not, this was Ellen's father and he had to believe that he would want to help her. That he would want to know about this and stop her having to go through it alone.

Al could do more about this situation than he could. And that's why he had to go to him. For Ellen.

'Mr Brooks?'

Al turned at the sound of his name, then looked Yan up and down. 'Yes?'

'My name is Yan. I work in animation team.'

'I can see that, son. You 'ave a name badge on your chest.' Al laughed, before taking a swig of his drink. 'You don't have to badger me you know. I'm gonna come down and sign up for the karaoke when I've finished this drink.'

'That is good.' He nodded, trying to convince himself it was the right thing to do. 'But …'

Yan stopped, torn between carrying on and saying nothing more. He knew Ellen might not thank him for telling something so secret, so private, something she had shared only with him. They had so little time left together as it was. What if this changed things between them? Broke the trust they'd built up?

'But?'

Al was staring at him now, like he was a highly infectious disease being observed under a microscope. He needed to decide what he was going to do.

'It's Ellen, she …' He'd started but he didn't know where to go from here.

Al's expression changed immediately from confused to concerned. "as something 'appened? Is she all right?'

Yan nodded quickly. 'Yes, she is OK. I am sorry. I did not mean to make you worry for her.'

'Then what is it?'

He took a breath before levelling his voice. 'We go to sit down on chairs. Here is more quiet.'

—

'Hello, Ross,' Ellen started.

He hadn't noticed her approach and she was glad because every single step she had taken had empowered her. Now, responding to her calling his name, he was looking straight at her.

She watched the acknowledgement of her presence reach his features. His eyes narrowed and his mouth turned into a hard, bitter line. Slowly, he rose up from the chair and stood, hardening his stature, broadening his body, looking down on her.

'I wondered how long it would take you to realise I was here.' His voice. That deep, commanding sound she had once found comforting and stabilising, sounded nothing short of sinister now.

She braced every fibre of her being, maintaining eye contact, holding her stance. It was typical of Ross to pull the attention back to him. He hadn't gone looking for her because he had known she would go to him.

'I was under the impression we had a meeting at the offices when I got home.' She kept her voice even. She wanted him to tell her what he knew. She wanted to hear, in blunt language, that he was fully aware of what she'd done.

He smiled then, but the mouth movement wasn't reflected in any other part of his body language. He put a finger to his bottom lip, opened his mouth to speak and then stopped, observing her quizzically.

Why wasn't he saying anything?

He slipped his hand into the pocket of his trousers and pulled something out. It was a small square object that was instantly recognisable. She had seen it so many times before. The prototype, the model, the very first example of Keegan Manufacturing's unbreakable packaging.

He placed it on the table, smoothing a hand over it, like a caress, before turning his attention to her again. 'Remember this?'

Was it really a question he thought she was going to answer? She didn't say anything.

'This is *my* dream. *My* dream that I had to work so hard to make a reality.'

The passion in his words was evident but it wasn't affecting her. She'd heard a few of his motivational speeches in the past and after a while they all blended into one. Because whenever he'd told his story, it wasn't to benefit the young entrepreneurs out there, it was purely for the spotlight himself, to be held up, admired for being someone who had had an idea and grown it into a million pound business.

She looked away from him, turned her eyes towards the stage where a resident in a Hawaiian shirt was being clapped onto the stage to perform a song. Instinctively, she looked for Yan. Beautiful, strong Yan who had no idea what a bank reconciliation was.

'You believed in my idea, Ellen. You told me I shouldn't give up until I made someone listen and they helped me make it real.'

She had said that. She'd said that when she'd been blinded by his charm, glad to have found someone herself to avoid being paired off with sons of haulage firm owners by Al.

'And now I'm told that lumps of money have been going missing from my bank accounts.'

He *did* know. There was no pretending anymore. She had to face this head on and see if she could salvage something from the wreckage.

'How the fuck did you manage to get a job at the firm I chose to handle my business accounts?'

His irate tone and the way he was leaning a little, almost towering over her, filled her with the anger she needed to finally respond.

'I got a job at Lassiter's because *you* stole from *me*!' She blasted the words out, fiery, venomous and enriched with all the hate she should have unleashed the moment he'd walked out of her life with her inheritance. 'You took everything I had. You *stole* everything my mother left for me. You knew I'd packed in my job, you knew about *my* dream, my dream to run my own accountancy practice and you robbed me of that to achieve your own ambitions.'

She was boiling up, shaking on the spot, the hurt and devastation leaking from her pores as she regarded the man who had hurt her so much.

'I asked you to marry me, Ellen. All you had to do was say yes,' he bit back.

She couldn't believe it. What was he actually saying here? That she should have married him to avoid having her money stolen? Her mouth dropped open in shock at his gall.

'We could have been …' Ross paused, as if searching for the right word. 'Comfortable. My new business, maybe your accountancy practice in the future and …'

Comfortable. Not blissfully happy. Not even happy. Comfortable. And a maybe. She shook her head, almost saddened instead of angered.

Ross carried on. 'Things could have been just the same. They needn't have changed. No one says every married couple has to have children. It would have been a partnership.'

She wanted him to stop now. She didn't want to hear anymore. It was bad enough that he was still talking about the proposal, but detailing how he thought the relationship would have developed was making her feel sick.

'So what were you going to do if I'd said yes? Ask me for my money to make an "investment" or just take it?'

'You said you were going to support me with the idea, that you were with me every step of the way.'

'I meant emotionally. It wasn't code for "I'm going to give you all my money".'

He shook his head at her, like she was stupid. As if he couldn't possibly understand how she could think anything else. As if she should have known what their relationship was all about from the very beginning. The truth was, she'd fallen for his fabricated affections and had jumped out not a moment too soon.

'You left me with bills I couldn't afford. I had to move properties, I had to sell anything that meant anything to me. I had no job, no savings and no dignity. And you did all that knowing I wouldn't have the guts to ask my dad to bail me out.' She held onto a chair for support. 'I told you how important it was for me to stand on my own two feet. I told you I didn't want to rely on my dad's success in business. You knew how much proving myself meant to me.'

'Well, you've certainly proved yourself now. My legal advisers tell me the way you moved revenue around in my accounts was nothing short of brilliant. The work of a highly-skilled numerist.' He scoffed. 'Such a waste, using all that financial talent to break the law. I'm sure you could have put those skills to use getting me some tax breaks or something.'

Ellen's skin flamed hotter as she narrowed her eyes at him. 'It took me weeks to pick myself up off the floor and realise what I had to do.' She edged closer towards him. 'Taking my *mother's* money meant nothing to you. But money in general, that's your whole life. You didn't create this ...' She picked up the unbreakable package from the table. 'This ... stuff because you wanted to make a difference in the world. You created it because you knew it could make your fortune.' She scoffed. 'So, I realised quite quickly how I could hurt you. I was going to take my money back from you and I was going to do some good with it in the process. See, I didn't use it to furnish my flat or buy back the things I'd had to sell, I gave it to charity. Charities I know my mother would have approved of. D'you know, I had no idea until my dad told me just last year that my mum loved donkeys.'

She could see he was gritting his teeth, his lips thin and brutal, his cheek pulsing. She was glad. He deserved to feel that way and worse.

'And I don't regret a single moment of it. I very nearly got every single penny back,' she spat.

He grabbed her arm then and used his other hand to point a menacing finger at her. 'As soon as my advisers have finished unpicking every single thing you did I'm going to the police.'

'I couldn't care less. Let go of me.'

'I'm going to make sure you're prosecuted and then I'll make sure you're struck off that accountancy register and can never practice again,' he hissed.

His fingers were pinching her so tightly she could feel her bones bruising under the pressure. She couldn't let him see he was hurting her. She had to stay in control.

'Let me go,' she repeated.

'Get your 'ands off my daughter!'

———

Yan had never seen such a large bodied man move so fast before. When he'd finished telling Al everything about Ross and what Ellen had done, he was exhausted. It had been so hard finding the right words, explaining it in English so Al understood, but he'd managed it. Then Al had got off the sofa and started moving at pace, out of the lobby and down the path towards the entertainment area. And they were here not a moment too soon.

'Are you deaf? I said get your 'ands off my daughter!' Al's words were like bullets, firing from his mouth loud and fast.

Ross let go of Ellen's arm and she put her other hand to the sore skin to soothe it. Yan wanted to step forward to her, move her away from Ross Keegan but he couldn't. Not yet.

'Dad, it's OK,' Ellen started.

'I'll agree to differ on that one. What the 'ell d'you think you're doing 'ere?' Al looked at Ross as if he were a stain on a much-loved shirt.

'You must be Ellen's father,' Ross remarked. 'We've never met.'

'Cut the crap, son. I know everything,' Al stated.

Yan swallowed as he felt Ellen's eyes move from her father and Ross to him. The intensity of her stare penetrated him. He shrank into himself a little. He felt he had done the right thing, the only thing, but her look made him unsure she was going to thank him for it.

'Everything,' she mouthed, so softly it nudged at his insides.

'Your daughter has been relieving me of thousands of pounds worth of assets,' Ross informed. He stood up straighter, puffing his chest out a little more.

Yan didn't know how he had the nerve to do that. He was behaving like an innocent, like a victim, like he had no shame.

'Is that so?' Al said calmly.

'Dad ...' Ellen began. 'It's true.'

Yan could hear the tears in her voice and he knew instinctively how she was feeling. She would hate that Al knew what she had done. That's why she had never told him in the first place.

'I know it's true.' Al looked to Ellen. 'I also know what 'e did to you.'

Al's voice was not quite so calm now and he was levelling a stony stare at Ross, his breathing laboured.

"ow dare you steal money from my daughter? Steal money 'er mother left for 'er!'

As Al's voice rose in volume Yan felt Ellen's eyes on him again. He looked up, connecting with the gaze and seeing what lay there. Her expression was questioning, silently asking why he had exposed her secret.

'I ought to kick you right into next week! I don't know 'ow you can stand there like you're the one who's been mistreated. Takin' everythin' my girl 'ad, leavin' 'er with no job, makin' 'er leave 'er 'ome!'

———

Ellen heard her dad's voice falter a little and she was over-whelmed by the feeling of shame that settled over her. Despite what Ross had done and how she had chosen to deal with it, the worst thing of all was keeping it from Al and Lacey. How could she have been so silly? There had been nothing courageous about it. She wasn't a martyr, she was just plain stupid.

'And now you're 'ere, chasin' 'er to Corfu acting spurned and vengeful.' Al waved a fist at Ross. 'I won't 'ave it. D'you 'ear? I won't 'ave it!'

'Dad, it's OK. I'm going to take the rap for what I did,' Ellen broke in. She had to do something. She didn't want Ross turning any of his anger onto Al. He had only just heard about everything, she certainly didn't expect him to take any of the responsibility.

'We could maybe take seat?'

At the sound of Yan's voice making a calm suggestion, everyone stared at him, including Ellen. The voice of reason. The soothing influence. The person who had divulged to her father everything she'd told him in confidence.

'I don't need a seat. I need to 'ear that 'e's packin' up his suit-case again and getting on a plane back to where 'e came from. You've got no business 'ere,' Al yelled.

'I disagree. She's taken thousands of pounds of Keegan Man-ufacturing's assets,' Ross reminded.

'The business you started from what you took from 'er? Is that right? The company you kicked off with stolen money? 'er money! From the mother she lost?'

'Dad! Calm down! Let me do the talking. It's not good for your blood pressure,' Lacey said. Her sister appeared, wading in and taking hold of Al's arm.

'My blood pressure is just bloody fine. Or it will be once 'e pisses off out of it!'

This was all going downhill. She'd been wrong to think she could have a half-sensible conversation with Ross. He was al-ways going to think he was blameless. He was always going to put a hundred per cent of everything on her. Had she really expected to be able to get him to feel any guilt for what he had done or any empathy at how that situation had made her feel? Even now he still didn't think he'd done anything wrong. In his eyes she had gone back on what he thought she'd promised by starting a relationship with him. He had truly believed that money was destined for him and when she had said no to mar-riage, he had just taken what he'd really wanted anyway.

'How much does that money mean to you, Ross?' The words had come from Ellen almost without her knowing it. 'Is this about the money or is it about saving face?'

Ross looked to her then, the person she'd lain next to so many times, the eyes she'd gazed into, the lips she'd kissed, all merging into something hard and ugly.

'That money is just a drop in the ocean now you've sold your idea. It isn't about the cash, is it? It's about power. It's about me getting my own back and you not liking it.'

A snorting sound came out of his nose and Ross turned away from her.

'Urgh!' Lacey exclaimed. 'You really are gross.'

'I can tell you right now, this ain't goin' any further. You try and prosecute my daughter and I'll come after you with everythin' I've got. And I can tell you, I've got friends in very 'igh places.'

'Dad …' Ellen said, touching his arm.

'Is that a threat, Mr Brooks? Ross asked.

'You're windin' up the wrong person, son. You'd better leave right now because if I get started there ain't no unbreakable packaging gonna save you.'

Ellen held on tight to one of her dad's arms, Lacey at the other, bracing him hard in the hope that he wouldn't throw a punch or worse still, think about using the table as a weapon.

Ross made to step closer to Al and Ellen's breath caught in her throat. A dozen spinning thoughts moved through her mind. What was he going to do? Would he hit her father?

—

Yan moved fast. He clamped a hand on Ross' shoulder and drew him backwards, firmly but with finesse – a defensive action rather an aggressive one.

'I think you need to go,' he suggested.

Ross turned towards him, his body language tight and threatening. 'Oh you do, do you? And you're going to make me?'

'Listen to yourself! You're a dickhead. If he doesn't make you bugger off then I will!' Lacey yelled.

Yan stood his ground, not feeling the need to say anything in response.

Ross' face was contorted, determination and steely stubbornness there for all to see. Then, breaking the tension, came the deafening strains of someone attempting 'Knockin' on Heaven's Door' on the karaoke.

Ross' shoulders lowered and he raised his hand, pointing a finger at Ellen. 'This isn't over.'

'Yes it is! That's exactly what it is. It's over or you're in for the fight of your life,' Al yelled.

'Move,' Yan said, guiding Ross forward, his hand at the base of his spine. 'Do not say more.'

FORTY FIVE

A tiny little Polish man was doing a reasonable job of a Frank Sinatra number on the karaoke. The bar staff were clapping along, watching him, while Ellen clamped her lips around a plastic cup of neat brandy.

Lacey had taken Al to sit down. He'd looked visibly shaken by the encounter with Ross. And so was she. But it was over. For now.

When everyone got back to England, what would happen then? She may have got her angst out tonight but he was still in control. He was still finger-poking and shirking all blame. Was that how she wanted things to be?

She slapped at her arm and a mosquito carcass stuck to her skin. She brushed it off with her fingers. Another blood-sucking parasite that needed putting in its place.

And that's what she should do. She shouldn't let Ross leave Greece with that power he thought he still held over her. She needed to be the one to tell him how things were going to be when they got back to the UK.

She drank down the brandy and, without looking to seek out Lacey and Al, she headed out of the entertainment arena on a mission.

—

Ellen raised her hand and knocked on the door of Zeus 206. Despite coming here at the last minute, Ross had insisted on a five star room. She knocked again.

The door swung open and there he was. His shirt was open at the neck, not tucked into his trousers, his hair a little dishevelled. Perhaps her words had struck some kind of chord.

'What do you want?' Ross said, leaning his weight against the door.

'I'd like to talk,' she replied, with a confident nod.

'The family floorshow not enough for one night?'

She didn't respond but stood her ground, waiting to see what would happen next.

He shifted his weight, dropping his hands to his sides. 'Come in.' He opened the door a little wider.

Ellen stepped inside a replica version of her and Lacey's room at the other side of the complex. Two of Ross' perfectly crisp formal shirts were hanging in the open wardrobe. As if sensing her scrutiny he walked towards it, then closed the door.

She watched him turn back to face her. He folded his arms, adopting a look of irritation. And then he spoke.

'Why did you do it, Ellen?'

Her mouth fell agape at his tone. He sounded like he was about to stamp his feet and cry in frustration.

'What did you think I was going to do?'

'Nothing. And certainly not this. Do you know how much this has cost me?' He threw his hands up. 'It isn't just about the money you took, it's about all the independent accountants and auditors, legal teams, you name it, I'm going to have to call them in.'

'And what about *my* money?'

He shook his head. 'I was going to give it back.'

'What?! You liar! You didn't answer my phone calls or my emails. That's the behaviour of a thief, not someone who borrowed something with honourable intentions.'

'If that's what you really believe, why didn't you contact the police?'

Ellen shook her head. 'You knew I would never do that. Not out of any loyalty to you but because of my dad. Because I couldn't bear for him to know that the only thing I had left of my mother was gone.'

Ross put his hand to his hair, twisting a piece around his finger. 'I needed that money, Ellen.'

'Most people apply for a loan rather than try the fraud route.'

'I'd exhausted those avenues already. I knew the business was going to take off but you know what it's like. When you start something up there are always unseen costs. I had to work at gaining contracts and the first few months is always about paying out more than what's coming in.'

She swallowed. 'Was that the only reason you proposed to me? To get your hands on my money?'

'No.' He shook his head. 'Is that really what you thought?'

'You as good as admitted it during the floorshow.'

'I was angry.' He met her gaze. 'I still am angry.'

'And you have no right to be.'

Ellen closed her lips, shocking herself with the volume and intensity of her tone.

Ross dropped his body down onto the edge of one of the twin beds. He raked his fingers through his hair before turning his attention back to Ellen.

'I don't know, Ellen. I just thought marriage was the next logical step.' He placed his fingers over his mouth, making a steeple. 'We worked well together.'

'We *networked* well together.'

A flicker of a smile appeared on his lips. 'You make that sound like a bad thing.'

'It isn't a bad thing, it's just not enough.' She paced towards the patio doors at the end of the room and looked out at the view. 'We only ever talked about our *business* future.' She sighed. 'There's so much more to life than that.'

'My God, I don't believe you just said that,' Ross responded. 'You're the woman who fell asleep with a copy of *Accountancy Age* over her face.'

She turned back to face him. 'And you left me like that all night.'

'I thought maybe it was a new absorption technique.'

She shook her head. 'We were never meant to be forever.' She looked directly at him. 'You know that.'

He shrugged. 'I know I'm single-minded and I'm definitely not perfect but I did think we could make something together.'

'A business. *Your* business. You said so to the strains of Paul McCartney.'

'Yeah,' he answered softly.

'If you really felt anything for me you should have asked for my investment.'

He looked up, toying with this fingers. 'I knew you'd never give it to me. You'd earmarked that money for your accountancy practice and ...' He paused. 'I knew how much it meant to you.'

Tears were pricking her eyes but she kept herself in check. 'And that's why you should never have stolen it.'

He dropped his eyes to the floor, looking pitiful.

Ellen pulled in a long breath. 'So, this is how it's going to go.' She waited for him to look up then she pointed a finger. 'You are going to call off your auditors and your investigators and whoever else you've employed to scrutinise what I've done.'

'I don't think ...'

Ellen stopped him. 'No. You don't get a choice.' She waited for her words to sink in before continuing. 'You are going to go back to England and you're going to call a halt to all of this. I don't care what you have to tell your board members but I'm not being held accountable for what I've done and I'm not asking the charities for that money back.' She took another breath. 'As far as I'm concerned we're even now, it's finished, for good.'

She swallowed, holding her frame steady as inside, her heart pulsed with adrenalin.

Time ticked by so slowly then, finally Ross nodded.

Ellen blinked away her tears, hardly daring to believe that she had done this. She pressed the corners of her eyes. 'We've both made mistakes, Ross. It's time to move on.'

He raised his head first, then inched himself upwards until he was standing, looking a little defeated.

He held out his hand to her, a visible tremor there. 'To moving on.'

She nodded, still trying not to let emotion get the better of her. She clasped his hand and shook it firmly. 'To new beginnings.'

FORTY SIX

Ellen's heart was still thumping when she joined Lacey and Al at a table near the back of the entertainment arena.

'Where's the drinks you promised us?' Lacey greeted as Ellen sat down.

'Sorry.'

'Lucky I got two rounds in. Here.' Lacey indicated a plastic cup of brandy and Coke.

'Next, we have singer from England! Welcome on stage … Lacey Brooks. Applause!' Sergei announced.

Lacey put her cocktail down on the table. 'Shit. I didn't think I'd get called up yet. I won't go, Dad.'

'Lacey Brooks, everybody!'

Ellen looked at the stage and saw Sergei waving his hand in the air, beckoning Lacey towards him. 'Go.'

'What?' Lacey looked confused.

'Go up. Go and sing.' Ellen smiled. 'What are you going to do?'

'Take That. Thought I'd give the real Gary Barlow a try.'

'Go on then. Before Sergei has a hernia,' Ellen said, pulling her up out of her chair.

'Do you mind, Dad?' Lacey looked to Al.

He shook his head and raised his glass of whisky to her.

'Lacey Brooks from England, everybody!'

Ellen watched Lacey rush past the tables towards the stage. Once there she jumped onto it and grabbed the microphone Sergei offered.

Ellen looked back at her dad. He looked deflated, as if he couldn't take any more shocks or upset from either of his daughters.

'She can't sing for toffee,' Al remarked, his eyes on Lacey, who was making tentative beginnings.

'I know, but she enjoys it.' Ellen watched her sister. 'She's never worried about what people think.'

Ellen watched Al lift his cup of whisky to his mouth and swallow down the whole double measure of scotch. He was going to shout any second. How could he not? He'd just found out she had kept so many secrets.

He looked at her and finally he spoke. 'So, what I want to know is, 'ow comes I 'ave to find out about all this from some bloke from the animation team?'

Ouch. This was worse than shouting and she didn't have an answer to that one at the ready. She hid her eyes and mouth in her cup and hoped he would say something else.

'Why didn't you come to me, Ellen?'

That was no easier than answering why someone who worked at the hotel knew more about her life than her father did. She took her lips from the cup and placed it down on the table in front of her.

'I don't know. I was stupid.'

She was so tired of telling this story. She had nothing left to give.

'Stupid! I'd say. I mean what the 'ell were you thinkin'?' Al blurted.

'Which bit?' She'd lost the ability to try and state her case.

'All of it! But first and foremost finding an arsehole like him in the first place.'

'Oh, well that question's easy to answer. I found him to stop you trying to find someone for me.'

She was past caring whether she hurt Al's feelings or not. She'd spent far too long trying to live up to this perfect image that he'd created and she'd embraced.

'What?'

'Oh, Dad, I know you thought you were doing the right thing but I didn't want to be set up with sons of your members of the Royal Square or whatever it's called.'

'The members of the Ambassadors Triangle are trustworthy people, Ellen. Their sons are straight-down-the-line, good businessmen, 'onest. All the things it appears that shit isn't.'

'Yes, well, we all make mistakes, don't we? Even me, Dad.'

'But your mother's money, Ellie. 'e took what she left for you. The money you put aside for your business.'

She nodded, trying not to let his words smart too much. 'I know.' She sighed. 'And that hurt me so much.' She took a breath. 'It was humiliating and I was ashamed and I couldn't tell you because I couldn't bear to let you down.'

—

Yan watched them from across the room. Sitting on the edge of the arena, next to the sea view he took a swig of the neat Metaxa in his glass. They were talking now, oblivious to Lacey slaughtering 'Shine'. He had to hope he had done the right thing and that Ellen was going to forgive him for making it his business. He had taken a risk. But he'd done it for her. Because he loved her.

'Hello, Yan.' A small girl with her hair in bouncing pigtails skipped up to him.

'Hey, Emily. You not dance to songs?' He put his drink down on the table to high-five her hand.

'You don't dance to the songs either,' she remarked, trying to climb up onto his lap. He put his hands around her waist and lifted her up onto the table.

'Not tonight. When do you go home?' He touched her nose with the tip of his finger.

'Next week.'

'This is good. Then we will have many mini-disco and dances together.'

She giggled and kicked her legs as he tickled her sides. 'Good!'

'Good,' he responded, laughing.

She took hold of his hands and adopted a coy expression as she looked at him. She had hair the colour of corn and brown eyes, a picture of youthful mischief.

'Do you have a girlfriend?'

'Emily! You cannot ask this.' He smiled. 'I could ask if you have boyfriend. Let me guess. I see you like to play with Hans at kids' club,' he teased.

'Hans doesn't speak very good English,' she replied, blushing gently.

'Sometimes you don't have to know all the words to make things work.' He stopped. 'With friends.'

A warm swell was growing inside him as he thought of Ellen. He didn't want to lose her. Tomorrow was her last day and everything was still up in the air. He had no idea what to do.

'So you *do* have a girlfriend.' She laughed. 'Yan has a girlfriend, Yan has a girlfriend,' she chorused.

'Sshh! You must not tell, Emily. Come on, let us find Mummy and Daddy and your brother.'

He helped her down from the table and linked their hands.

—

'So now you know how flawed I am. How dumb and stupid and not the person you thought I was. I've wrecked my career, I've not supported Lacey properly and made her break up with Mark. I trusted a devious, liar of a man.'

'I won't disagree with any of that.'

Ellen closed her eyes.

'But I can sort it all out. We can make plans.' Al reached across the table to gather up her hand in his. 'You wait, before you know it you'll be runnin' your own firm and things can get back to 'ow they should be.'

Ellen shook her head. 'I don't want that now, Dad.' Her voice was strong and filled with determination. As each day had passed here, something in her had altered irrevocably. She didn't need the planets to align to be certain that a powerful new position in business wasn't for her.

'What?' Al looked at her like she'd gone crazy. 'Why?'

She shrugged. 'This whole thing's changed me. When Ross took Mum's money, he took the dream too. Starting a business with what she left for me was what made it so special. Even if I saved again, even if I was able to start something after all this blows up, it just wouldn't feel the same.'

'But, it's what you've wanted for so long.'

Did she sound certifiable? Was this really how she felt? Was she really going to give up her life-long ambition? She planned, loved a strategy, it sounded ludicrous to think she was letting this go.

'I know. But I don't want to be the number girl anymore. Maybe I'll … I don't know … lead a more simple, less stressful life.'

As she said the words she thought immediately of Yan and *his* dream. Was that what she wanted? To help him reach his goal, to be with him when he did it? The feeling that shot through her almost rocked her in her chair. Excitement and fright, combined lethally with heat and adrenaline.

'You're not thinkin' straight,' Al said. He was looking at her like she'd just told him she intended being the next female on the moon. 'When we get 'ome you'll feel different.'

She smiled. 'I won't, Dad.'

'We need to talk to my solicitor. See where we stand with that ponce.'

'There's no need,' Ellen told him.

Now Al looked completely bemused.

'I've been to see him.' She let out a breath of relief that was long overdue. 'It's over.' The next smile came from the depths of her. 'I started it and I finished it.' She picked up her cup, downing the contents. 'Do you want another scotch, Dad?'

——

'I will pack up.'

Yan felt bad that he had left Sergei and Dasha to do the karaoke session on their own. They didn't deserve to work his share but he hadn't had another choice.

'Is OK. There is not much.' Dasha's reply was short and lacking his usual flamboyant over-the-top energy.

'Dasha, if we let Yan finish up we can head to Bo's Bar for drinks,' Sergei suggested. Neither of them made eye contact with him.

'I am sorry I have to leave but the English man, he insist I do not stay and …' Yan began.

Dasha made a high-pitched noise that gave the impression he didn't believe his explanation.

'We know you do not like karaoke night but you know Tanja is not here and with only two it is hard work,' Sergei responded.

'I know,' Yan said. 'I will make up. I will do extra boules alone or football,' he offered.

Dasha looked at him then, sizing him up from toe to hair. 'You will do new dance routine in show. In some lady clothes.'

Yan shook his head. 'Come on.' He should have guessed there would be a penalty to pay. 'Not that. You know you are better for this. I look like man in lady clothes. You look like …' He stopped.

Dasha took on an expression that signalled he had to get the next words right or he would be in trouble.

'They are right for you,' he finished.

Dasha folded his arms across his chest. 'That is the deal. You dress up in lady clothes for show or we tell Tanja what happen tonight.'

Blackmail. Wear women's clothes for a dance or suffer Tanja finding out what had happened with Ross Keegan? He didn't want to give Tanja any reason at all to scrutinise him and his work performance.

'This is not OK.' He sighed. 'But I will do it.'

Dasha let out a yelp of pleasure, slapping his hands to Yan's cheeks and rubbing them hard. 'I have just the right thing to make you look so sexy.'

Sergei started laughing and slapped Yan's arm good naturedly. 'I don't believe you agree to this! You hate to dress up like that.'

'I hate idea of other option also.'

Sergei patted his arm again, then picked up his denim jacket from the back of the chair. 'Come on, Dasha, let's go get te-quila.' He turned to Yan. 'You really are OK to pack up?'

He nodded. 'Sure, no problem.'

He watched them head off towards the path that led to the beach and Bo's Bar before he started winding up cables for the PA system.

—

Yan was so engrossed in tidying things away he didn't see her approach. Ellen loved how he got so involved in whatever he was doing. She reckoned a goat could break into the entertainment area of the hotel and he wouldn't notice until he'd finished whatever task was in hand.

'Yan.'

He looked up then, coiling an orange cable around his arm into a loop. He said nothing, just carried on winding the cord until it was in a tidy circle then dropped it through the hatch into the dressing room.

He was looking at her as if he didn't know what to do with himself. There were only a handful of guests left around the entertainment area, all half-cut, none of them interested in what she was doing. Finally he spoke.

'You are mad at me.' He sank his hands into the pockets of his jeans.

Her mouth dried then. Was that what he really thought? She shook her head quickly, before any more time went by. 'I'm not mad with you.'

He met her eyes then. Those blue pools like beautiful, bright, icy lights. 'I think ...' Yan began.

'I know what you thought,' she started. 'You thought I would be cross that you'd told my dad my secrets.'

He nodded, the tension in his torso blatant. 'I know you not want your father to find out but ...'

'Ross was here. The horse had bolted, really.' Her voice was low and resigned.

'Horse?' he queried, looking blank.

'Sorry, it's a stupid saying.' She gathered herself. 'I know why you did it. You knew what Ross was going to do and you knew I needed support. You also knew I'd never ask for it myself.'

Yan nodded again.

'Thank you,' she whispered.

———

There was a small table between them, on which the portable speaker lay. All he wanted to do was move around it and take her in his arms. He shifted on his feet but didn't make a step. He couldn't hold her here. There were still bar staff and guests and, given what had happened with the karaoke, he was already tip-toeing the professional line.

Instead, he moved a hand across the table, inch by inch, slowly but with purpose, hoping she would notice.

'I knew he would shout. I knew he would say things to hurt you. I want to be the one who protect you from this but … your father should be the one for this moment,' Yan stated.

He watched her lower her hand to the table and skim the surface with her fingertips. Every centimetre brought them closer to connecting.

'You did the right thing,' Ellen said.

He felt her fingers slip so easily into the grooves between his and he sucked in the emotion it drew out of him. *You did the right thing.* He had believed that at the time, truly believed it, but he had never been sure she would be ready to accept that or acknowledge the action as the correct one.

He gripped her fingers in his, wanting their connection to be something strong and rooted.

'I only have tomorrow.' Her delicate words attacked his heart. He knew it would come. Someone had to mention the fact that the day after tomorrow she was going back to her life in the UK. He had wanted to put it to the back of his mind, try to forget it was even happening, but as it drew closer it just couldn't be ignored.

'I know,' Yan responded, softly. He moved his fingers through hers, stroking her skin, easing her knuckles against his. It had happened so fast. It was all still so new. But he knew what he wanted.

'Tomorrow I have the afternoon free. We could do something together.' He looked into her eyes, gauging what her response might be before she gave it. 'If you would like.'

He watched her face brighten, all thoughts of leaving lifting from her expression. It was a reprieve. More time. Another chance to forget about departure.

'I would like that very much,' Ellen said, smiling.

FORTY SEVEN

'Sergei's invited me on a boat trip,' Lacey announced.

The women were walking from their suite to the restaurant the next morning, enjoying the slight breeze that was rustling the leaves on the olive trees. Even though last night had been one of the toughest nights of Ellen's life, today she felt cleansed. Before, she'd felt like she was carrying an Atlas stone on her back, now, she could stand up straight, walk a little lighter, hold her head up.

'Are you and he …' Ellen asked.

Lacey gave a vigorous shake of her head. 'No. Not like that. Well, not like anything really. He just asked if I wanted to go and I said …' Lacey stopped.

'You said?'

'I said I'd think about it. And I have been. What do *you* think?'

Ellen smiled as they passed a plant, the speaker hidden inside playing a Gloria Estefan number. 'Where's the trip going?'

'Is that what you're going to base the decision on? Where it's going? I was hoping for a decision based on Sergei.'

Ellen laughed. 'You're the one who knows him – far more intimately than me.'

'Ooo, get you!' Lacey smiled back at her sister. 'It's going to Corfu Town and some island they shot a film on. I hadn't heard of it. Wasn't anything with Henry Cavill.'

'You should go. Have fun with Sergei and do some shopping. Lots of designer shops in Corfu Town, I've heard.'

'What about you? I don't want to leave you on your own with Dad.'

A blush hit her cheeks as up ahead she saw Yan walking through the complex. Dressed in grey cargo trousers and a black crew neck t-shirt, his presence and his choice of outfit made her stomach spin.

'Actually,' Ellen began. 'I'm going to have to leave Dad to his own devices this afternoon.'

'You're going out with Yan,' Lacey guessed.

'Our last day together.' Ellen said the words quietly, not really wanting to say them at all.

'Your last day *here* together,' Lacey said. 'Or have you not discussed the whole email/text/snail mail way of carrying something on?'

She let out a sigh as they approached the steps. 'Not yet.'

'Why not?'

'I don't know. Everything here has been so full-on. What if, when all that's taken away, there isn't anything left?' She didn't believe that, not really, but she ploughed on regardless. 'When we leave there will be several plane loads of new holidaymakers who need attention.'

Lacey made a noise like a lemonade bottle being opened for the first time. 'You're making excuses because the last guy you put your faith in was a complete arse wipe. Yan isn't anything like Ross. Look at what he did last night. He went to Dad. Can you imagine the start of that conversation?'

Going to her father had been fearless. Ellen knew what a rough-around-the-edges exterior he had. Al wasn't someone you just approached. He took some getting to know before you realised that underneath the tough shell was a soft middle. To dive right in like that was like asking for a war to start with no flak jacket to protect you.

'Give him your email and your mobile number. What have you got to lose?' Lacey asked, jogging up the steps and striding towards the restaurant. 'I'm starving! I hope they've got loads of bacon.'

———

Yan held the sheet of paper in his hand, looking at the typed words on it. He had no idea what it said. It really was all Greek to him. He was going to have to get someone at the hotel to translate it and then, as long as he was happy with the terms, he was going to agree to it.

'What is this?' Sergei arrived at his shoulder, leaning against the reception desk.

'Nothing.' Yan whipped the paper out of sight.

'Come on, what is it? You have secret?' Sergei made an attempt to get the paperwork from Yan.

'I have no secret. It is private.'

'Something from Bulgaria?' Sergei queried.

He nodded.

'I ask Lacey to come on Corfu Town boat trip,' Sergei said, stepping back and shoving his hands in the pockets of his shorts.

'Yes? As friends or something else?' Yan asked.

Sergei shrugged his shoulders up. 'I feel bad for what happen between us and for her boyfriend.'

Yan nodded. 'Then it is nice thing to do.'

'What do you do today?'

Could he tell Sergei about Ellen now? Yan had kept many secrets for Sergei in the past; about his women, and the days when he had been too hung over to perform his duties. But part of him thought that Sergei shared these things with him because they didn't matter. He didn't want to allocate his relationship with Ellen to the same standing as being too drunk to play volleyball or a one night stand with someone you didn't care about. She was special, what they had together was special and he wasn't prepared to give that out yet. He was afraid if he said the words, told someone, they would not believe it, would taint it, paint it into something else, something trivial.

'I do not know yet. Maybe go to beach,' he answered.

'There is space on the boat trip. You could come with us,' Sergei suggested.

He shook his head. 'You enjoy last day with Lacey.'

FORTY EIGHT

'Do not fall down steps. Keep your eyes closed.'

Ellen felt completely disorientated. She had met Yan in reception and now he was carefully shepherding her out of the front doors and down the marble steps.

'I don't really like surprises. I'm sure I've told you that before.' She was finding it hard to just put one foot in front of the other when she had no idea where she was going.

'Just a little further. Keep your eyes closed.'

'This sounds too much like a cocktail game. Is that what this is? Are you using me as a guinea pig for future animation items?'

'You guess right. Is that OK?'

She laughed. 'Stop it.'

She felt her feet on tarmac and the heat outside hit her skin. It was another perfect day in Corfu; sunshine, blue sky, just a hint of a breeze and that smell, of the sweet flowers, the fir trees, sand and sea. Ellen breathed in, filling her lungs with the scent and the memory, hoping to embed it deep inside her.

'OK, stop.' Yan smoothed his hands down her arms. 'OK, open your eyes.'

She didn't snap them open like she'd wanted to when he'd started this game, she unfurled her eyelids slowly, taking time to adjust to the brightness of the day and what was in front of her.

'Mountain bikes.' She said the words mechanically, with no enthusiasm. 'Yan, I haven't been on a bike in years. I can't go mountain biking. I'm wearing a dress.' This wasn't what she'd had in mind for their last day together.

Yan let out a laugh then and passed her a helmet. 'You think I take you up hills and tracks?'

'Aren't you?' she asked, a flicker of hope in her voice.

'No.' He shook his head. 'We go to near village, Kassiopi. Just small kilometres.'

She hoped *small kilometres* was the same in translation. Her legs always ached after water aerobics, she could only imagine how they were going to feel after even a few kilometres on a bike.

'You look like you do not want to do this?'

His deflated look stirred her next response. 'No, no. I do.'

Ellen smiled. Yan had obviously put a lot of thought into this.

He laughed then, that deep, rounded sound that warmed her inside. 'You lie.'

'No, it isn't a lie. It's just I'm unsure about my cycling capabilities.'

She watched him throw a leg over his bike and start to strap on his helmet.

'You wish you go on boat trip with Sergei and Lacey,' he added.

'No. No, I don't. Not at all.'

'Then get on bike.'

Ellen looked at the bike, sizing it up like it was an enemy she had to defeat. It was all spokes and wheels and circular discs. There were levers on the handlebars. But how hard could it really be? It was a bike. She could ride. She didn't need to use the gears.

'Fine. Let's go on a bike ride,' she said, slipping the helmet on her head and attempting to do up the clasp.

'Make sure helmet fits,' Yan said. He reached down and pulled his backpack up from the ground.

'I know!' She started to fiddle with the adjustment at the side of the helmet. She tugged at the strap but it wouldn't move.

———

Yan got off his bike and went over to her. Her cheeks were reddening now with the frustration of trying to secure her helmet. The bike riding had been a spur of the moment idea. He wanted to take her somewhere special for their last day and he knew Kassiopi was that place. He'd only been there once, on a tour when he'd first arrived at the resort, but the village had made an impact on him. He wanted Ellen to experience that too.

'Here, I help you.'

Carefully Yan unravelled the material, turning it so it was straight and aligned properly. Ellen was looking at him, her cheeks pink, her beautiful eyes wide and dewy, her lips slightly parted. His fingers grazed the skin on her cheek and he saw her swallow. He wanted nothing more than to kiss her at that moment. A long, deep, kiss that would mean so much. He inched forward …

'Hey, Yan! Enjoy bike ride!'

He quickly stepped back from Ellen, waving a hand at Spiros from the kitchens. They were too close to the hotel and now the moment had gone.

'You can do this now?' Yan asked her.

She snapped the fastening together. 'Yes.'

'Then let us go.'

———

'This is it. The harbour.'

Ellen's back was aching, her thighs sore and she had a scrape on her left shin from a pedal incident, but seeing Kassiopi harbour melted everything else away. She got off her bike and pushed it up and over the kerb to get closer to the water. She unfastened her helmet and clipped it to the bike.

It was beautiful. Azure water dappled by the bright sunlight, fishing boats bobbing up and down with the gentle motion of the sea, a larger cruiser mooring up. Circling the harbour were little restaurants, terracotta urns of clematis and bougainvillea surrounding the seating areas, tiny shops selling holiday souvenirs. All around she could hear the sounds of relaxation – the chink of plates and glasses as people dined or enjoyed a cool drink in the shade, the hum of mopeds passing by, the lapping of the ocean.

Yan stepped up beside her. 'Look this way.' He touched her arm and pointed to the left.

The Greek flag flew from the top of ancient ruins. All along the highest point ran a wall of stones, like a castle, towers still standing strong.

'What is it?' Ellen asked.

'It is castle. It has been here for many thousands of years. It was built to protect the island but it has been with many people in all this time. Norman people I think, and Venetians.'

'You must have read a lot of guide books.' She smiled.

'No.' He paused. 'They tell us on tour here. I have good memory.'

'It's so amazing. Not just the castle, this whole place. It's beautiful.'

She didn't want to take her eyes off it but she turned to Yan. 'Thank you for bringing me here.'

—

This was what he'd wanted. To see how she would react to this place. To find out if she felt the same way about it as he had the first time he'd seen it – awestruck by its simplicity, spellbound by its magic. The Greek people going about their day, the holidaymakers feeding the fish from the low harbour wall, the quaint buildings, the greenery of the hills, all kneeling below the great mountain of Pantokrator. This was what he wanted from life. Peace, an uncomplicated life, nothing more.

'You are welcome,' Yan whispered.

With her helmet off, her hair seem to float in the sea breeze, wafting back from her face, leaving her skin exposed, that delicate area along her jaw … He cupped her face in his hands and drew her towards him. Here there was no one watching. Here they were free to be together. Here they could be just another couple in love, getting caught up in the Greek majesty.

Her lips met his with such passion he almost stumbled. Hungry, hot and sweet, they explored each other's mouths with a matching intensity. They couldn't have forever. They couldn't have anything past tomorrow. But what they'd had in this week was something he'd never forget.

He kissed her mouth, sweeping her hair back with one hand. 'I love you, Ellen.'

He saw the tears forming in her eyes and wondered if he should have said those words. The very last thing he wanted to do was upset her.

'I love you too,' she responded. She took a breath. 'Yan, I don't want to let you go.'

———

She let out a sob then and put her hand to her mouth, feeling stupid. She had promised herself all goodbyes were going to be left until tonight. After their day together. When she could go to bed and sob until the transfer bus came to pick them up at six a.m.

'Then do not let me go,' Yan responded. He wrapped his arms around her and held her against his body. The firm, muscular chest wall embraced her cheek and she breathed him in. That familiar scent of musk and lemon filled her nostrils and, like the view of Kassiopi, she tried to etch it into her memory's hard drive. A moment never to be forgotten. The man she had fallen in love with when she was at her lowest point. The man who had given her the strength to be the person she'd forgotten she was.

He let her go then, his eyes a little glossy, a half-hearted attempt at a smile on his face.

'Let us have drinks.'

———

They sat in a bar right at the harbour's edge. Ellen was so close to the water that if she leant a little to the left she could dip her hand right in. They'd ordered beers and olives and the combination of the bitter, salt taste and the July sunshine was making her more relaxed than she'd ever been. Here she didn't have to pace her breathing, imagine herself in a happy place or rub her arms up and down in the Havening technique. Here she felt lighter, brighter, existing happily without a strategy.

Yan opened his backpack and she watched as he placed some paperwork on the table between them. He pushed it over towards her until she picked it up.

It was all written in Greek, several paragraphs with bullet points and numbers.

'What is it?' she asked. 'I don't really know any Greek. I can just about order drinks now and say hello.'

She looked at the words again, trying to make out a word or two she recognised. She saw a familiar place name.

'Agios Spyridon,' she said out loud. 'Is this about the old church?'

The smile that appeared on his face spread across the whole width, his eyes lighting up at her acknowledgement.

'It is contract,' Yan said. 'I have no idea what it say but … I want to take this on. It will be hard work, I know this, but I think I can do this.'

Ellen put the papers down and reached across the table for his hands. She took them in hers, locking their fingers together and holding on tight. She wanted him to know how proud she was of him. To come to a different country to better himself for his brother's honour was so admirable.

'I'm so proud of you.' She pulled his hands closer. 'And Boy-an would be too.'

At the mention of his brother's name a faraway look replaced the joyous one. She wondered what his life had really been like back in Bulgaria. She suspected she'd only been given a snap-shot. She squeezed his hands.

'You're going to have your dream.'

———

The way Ellen said the words, so full of admiration and pride, hit him hard. Did he dare to believe that, after all he had been through, simple perseverance and hard work could pay off?

He held onto her hands. 'What of your dream?'

Ellen smiled. It was pure and serene, nothing artificial.

'I've got everything and nothing in front of me.' She laughed as he furrowed his brow. 'Ross left this morning. He's not going to press charges against me and I'm not going to pursue the issue of my mother's inheritance.'

He didn't know how to respond to this. He was glad the man was gone but part of him still wanted him punished for what he had done.

'It's OK,' she said. She unfastened their hands and softly brushed her fingers over the back of his hand. 'It's the right thing. We can both move on from everything with a clean slate.'

'To start again?' he queried.

She nodded. 'Yes.'

'Then you will go back to work for the money people?'

She shook her head. 'No. I actually don't know what I'm going to do. And for the first time in my life that doesn't scare me.'

Ellen took her hands from the table and slipped one into the small pocket on the front of the bottom of her dress. She took out a slip of paper and held it in her hands, looking at it.

She slid it across to him then picked up her bottle of beer and sat back a little in her chair.

His heart was thudding now as he picked up the hotel compliments slip and looked at it. Letters, numbers, lines of words. He felt himself going red from the soles of his feet and upwards, the heat taking over his entire body, boiling it without any let-up. What did he say? He couldn't get this wrong.

'I … don't know what I say,' he spoke finally.

'I don't want us to say goodbye at the end of my holiday, Yan. I want us to stay in touch.' She paused. 'Maybe see each other again this year. If you want to, that is.'

He swallowed down a lump of fear that was lodged in his throat and tried to stabilise his heart rate. He reached across to touch her hand again.

'Have I got this wrong?' she asked. 'Don't you want to?'

The concern in her eyes spiked his heart into action. He wanted that more than anything. 'I do want this. I want this very much.'

An excited smile crossed her face and she squeezed his hands again. 'Then let's not think of it as goodbye tomorrow. It's just goodbye for a while, not forever. Now you have my email, my mobile number and my address, we can stay in touch.'

Her email and address. She had given him these details because she loved him and she couldn't bear for what they had to end. He felt exactly the same. The trouble was, like the church contract, he couldn't read a letter of it.

FORTY NINE

They had walked along the headland, stopping at the castle and chasing each other through the ruins. Then they had lain on the pebble beach, letting the sea lap over their feet. He had never seen Ellen so light-hearted, so completely happy. And when they'd taken the bikes off the road, they had found a deserted olive grove, and made love so slowly, with such tenderness, both of them had cried and made promises to remember.

He couldn't bring that crashing down after everything else she had been through. He had kept the truth from her since the very beginning and, in all honesty, he didn't know whether he had ever planned to tell her. Despite wanting to be with her, wanting to love her, he hadn't thought further than those feelings, never dared to consider a future. He had let her in on so much of his life – Bulgaria, Rayna, Boyan – but there was still that one thing he was so ashamed of, boxed up and locked away. *You are worthless. You are stupid.*

Tonight was the Fakir show. He and Sergei would be swallowing fire and lying on broken glass for the audience's pleasure. It would require concentration, on the one night he didn't have it.

He looked into the mirror, tying the black bandana around his head. This afternoon he had felt like a man who had it all. Now he resembled someone about to lose everything. The look on Rayna's face when her father had told her the truth invaded his consciousness. It was going to happen all over again.

—

'God, I'm going to miss their puddings.' Lacey sat back in her seat, settling her hands on her stomach.

'Good food 'ere,' Al said, scraping cream from the bottom of his bowl.

Ellen smiled at her family, enjoying sitting together, eating, conversing. Life got so busy you put things off, worked too hard, ignored the most important things. She couldn't remember a time before Corfu where they had all sat together and enjoyed a meal. Last Christmas Lacey had gone to Mark's parents and it was just her, Dad and Nan. On Lacey's birthday, Dad had left after the starter when one of his units caught fire. They needed to make more effort to be together like this when they got back home.

'I love this hotel,' Lacey said, stretching her arms out behind her. 'If I was going to get married to the man of my dreams it would be here on that water platform.'

Her statement stilled the air between them and Ellen wasn't sure how to respond. Was Lacey having second thoughts or simply being philosophical? Neither option seemed quite right.

'Oh my days, the look on your faces!' Lacey laughed. 'I'm talking in the future, when I meet Mr Right. Just because I decided to end things with Mark and I'd thought about having *that* wedding here, doesn't mean I can't come here again.'

'You don't even have to have a wedding to come here. We could just have a holiday,' Ellen remarked.

'You're thinking about Yan. I knew it! You're going to stay in touch, aren't you?' Lacey clapped her hands together.

Ellen's eyes dropped to her plate. She wished Lacey hadn't said anything in front of their dad. Now she was going to have to say something. He was bound to ask questions. Any second now …

'The animation bloke?' Al's tone was sober.

'We're just friends, Dad.' She didn't want to have to explain. She didn't know what to say to him. How did you explain love in seven days?

'I think you're a tiny bit more than friends,' Lacey carried on. 'He's nice, Dad. Always polite, looks great in trunks and he and Ellen saved a boy from drowning.'

'What?'

Her fingers itched to pull Lacey's hair like she had when she was younger. It had always been the only way to stop her blabbering.

'It was nothing. A bit frightening at the time, but …'

'Nothing! Dad, according to everyone I spoke to, they were like a pair of paramedics. Ellen jumped in and pulled him out and Yan resuscitated him right on the poolside.'

Ellen could feel her father's eyes on her and she just wanted to curl up. She didn't want to be centre of attention now Lacey's life had calmed down.

'Why didn't you tell me any of this when I got 'ere?'

No one spoke and when Ellen lifted her head both Al and Lacey were looking at her for a reply.

'I … don't know. I suppose there was so much else going on I just …' She looked to her dad. 'You had a lot of other things on your mind.'

Al wiped his mouth with a napkin. 'That's 'ow this whole mess started with Ross. Not tellin' me things. Keepin' stuff to yourself.'

'I know, I'm sorry. I should have told you but, at the time, it didn't seem as important as Mark being here and then Ross and …'

'Well things are gonna change round 'ere.' Al put his napkin down on the table. 'Once you girls both move back in then we'll all be there to look out for one another.'

'Yay!' Lacey squealed, throwing her arms around Al's neck.

Ellen went cold. What had he just said? *Once you girls both move back in*. She wasn't going to move back home. She may live in a less illustrious area of the city but it was still her space and one she didn't intend giving up.

'Dad, I …' Ellen began.

'And I'd better meet this Yan. Properly, I mean.'

'Dad, there's no need. I mean we're going home in the morning and …' She stopped talking when she couldn't find the words to say next. Her mind was clouding up with both issues, her brain desperately trying to sort and prioritise which one needed to be dealt with first.

'So you're not going to keep in touch?' Lacey frowned.

'No. I mean, I don't know, maybe.'

'Well, 'e's in this fire show tonight isn't 'e? Maybe we'll 'ave a drink after,' Al suggested.

'Yes, Dad. We'll take you to Bo's Bar. It's on the beach and they do limbo. But don't worry if you don't want to, it's just for fun. Dasha will be up for it. He's the one who wears dresses, but don't let that put you off. He's such a laugh.'

———

'Tonight, we present for you, mystical and magical show. It take years of training to be able to perform these trick and illusion but here, at Blue Vue Hotel, tonight, Sergei and Yan will bring for you … Fakir!' Tanja exited stage right.

'What did she say?' Al asked.

'Fakir,' Ellen responded.

'Can you swear like that in front of children?'

She closed her eyes. Right now the only reason she was here was to support Yan. What Al had said about moving back home had shocked her. They'd talked about Lacey moving back in when everything fell apart with Mark, but how had that translated into *her* moving back home too? She was so grateful for her dad's support over Ross but she'd never even considered leaving her flat for a second. She knew she was old enough to make her own choices but she also knew what Al and Lacey were like when they ganged up. A heavy hint here, a three a.m. vomit trip from Lacey that Al couldn't cope with there, comfortable Sunday dinners where she ended up staying over the night etc. etc. As much as she wanted to spend more family time together, doing it permanently had never been on the agenda.

The lights went up and there in the middle of the stage were Sergei and Yan, bare-chested, wearing Harem pants, bandanas covering their heads. Both were looking out into the crowd, expressionless.

'He told me all about this show on the boat. It involves glass, fire and nails. Apparently one animation guy got impaled and had to be carted off to hospital,' Lacey told her.

—

When they looked out into the audience they were supposed to focus beyond them. They weren't meant to see the lights or any of the faces, just get into the character of their performance and the right mental zone.

The first thing Yan saw was Ellen. She was sitting only a few tables from the front with her father and Lacey. Her hair was tied back from her face and she was wearing a lemon-coloured top. He swallowed. He needed to bring himself back to the moment, back to what he was doing. Losing focus was a one way ticket to making a mistake and he didn't want to be making a mistake with a bed of nails.

Tanja and Dasha entered from stage right, both dressed in black, although Dasha had added sequins to his outfit. They set down the bed of nails in the middle of the stage. He heard the intake of breath from the crowd and he tried to block it out. He needed to find the beat of the music, the deep, resonating drum and the ethnic vibe.

Yan closed his eyes and tried to find his centre. But he couldn't clear his head. All he could see was a carefree Ellen, grass licking her legs as she ran through the ruins of Kassiopi castle. All he could hear was her laughter, that gentle sound that pulled at his heart, her calling his name as they'd made love under the olive trees.

'Yan,' Sergei hissed.

He opened his eyes. It was time.

——

'Ooo I don't like this. I'm not sure I can watch.' Lacey had put her fingers over her eyes as soon as the bed of nails had arrived.

'Are they really gonna do it, d'you think? Or is it some sort of illusion?' Al asked.

Ellen couldn't take her eyes from Yan. He looked haunted. Was it part of the act or something else? Their last day together had been so perfect. He had seemed so happy about the future, with the renovation of the church, and their decision to keep in contact. Now he looked somewhere between nervous and terrified.

She shifted on her seat, her bottom sticking to the chair. It was a humid night and every inch of her was moist. Al had lit a citronella candle on the table and although its smoke was keeping the mosquitos at bay it was drying up her throat.

'I can't watch,' Lacey said again.

Ellen moistened her lips and tried to remember that Sergei and Yan had done this all before. It was a show they performed regularly and neither of them had been hurt on any other occasion. She rested her elbows on the table and, without thinking about it, she crossed her fingers.

Yan leant back over the bed of nails and the crowd all held their breath as Sergei hovered nearby.

'He's not going to, is he?' Lacey remarked.

'I need another drink,' Al responded, crushing the empty cup in his hand.

Ellen was holding her breath as Dasha took hold of Sergei's hand and helped him to climb up onto Yan's midriff.

'Ouch!' Lacey exclaimed.

The team all stretched their arms out straight and held the pose as the audience burst into applause.

Ellen felt sick.

———

Yan couldn't fight the draw to her. He had to concentrate on something and pushing against what his mind wanted to do was just making things worse. As he lay there, the nails digging into his skin, pressing and bruising his shoulder blades with Sergei's weight on him, he looked at Ellen.

She deserved so much. Love, a bright future, someone who was truly her match. Could he really be that person? She was so clever, so full of knowledge. What did he really have to offer her?

He pressed his lips together as Sergei shifted and a wooden board was placed on top of him. He wanted her so much, wanted this to work, but after all the lies and deceit she'd had in her life, she needed nothing but the truth.

He felt two audience members climb onto the board and he held himself completely still, his breath stoic. What was anything without trust and truth? Whatever the fall out, he knew he had to tell her.

FIFTY

Flames shot out into the audience and Lacey let out an ear-splitting scream. The heat from the fire was intense as it flashed forward just stopping shy of the roped-off area. Every member of the crowd was clapping in time to the music as Sergei and Yan twisted and turned the flaming batons, blowing balls of fire and making swirling circles of light. It was by far the best show they'd seen.

Then the batons were put out and the performers took the applause and a standing ovation.

Ellen clapped hard, standing up and smiling at Yan. She had never seen anything quite like it and all that was running through her head were thoughts of what they might have together in the future. She glanced across at her dad and Lacey. Tomorrow, by lunchtime, they would be back in England and if Al had his way she'd be back in her childhood bedroom by the weekend. She didn't want that.

'Another drink, Ellie?' Al asked, standing up.

'Yes, I'll have a Metaxa and Coke.' She was getting slightly too accustomed to the local brandy. It was probably a good job she wouldn't be able to afford it when she got home.

'Lacey?' Al asked.

'Ooo yes, I'll have an Apricot Cooler. Actually, get two because all inclusive finishes at eleven.'

Ellen watched Yan and Sergei disappear backstage. She wasn't just going to miss Yan, she was going to miss the whole place.

It was so strange how you could spend only a week somewhere but become so completely embedded in it, like you somehow belonged.

'So what's going on with you and Yan? I thought things were sorted and you were going to make a go of it long distance,' Lacey spoke.

'We are.' She sighed. 'I just … don't want him meeting Dad in that way yet. I mean, I'm thirty, Lace, it isn't like I need his seal of approval.'

Lacey folded her arms across her chest. 'We're one of *those* families are we?'

'What?'

'One of those dysfunctional families. Father with kids by two different women, younger daughter with a broken engagement, elder daughter a victim of crime so turns to crime herself, no one tells anyone anything …'

'Hang on …'

'I don't want us to be like that. I want us to be close like we used to be.'

'I want that, too.'

'Dad needs to feel useful. You know that. He's been like that as long as I've been alive and I'm sure he was the same after your mum died.' Lacey let out a breath. 'All I'm saying is, you might not *need* his seal of approval but he might need to give it.'

Ellen nodded. She knew exactly what Lacey meant. It didn't matter if Al really approved of Yan, it wasn't his call to make, now she was an adult. But he needed to be asked his opinion. He wanted to feel necessary.

'Besides, when you move back in I'm going to need you to be in his good books for all the tales you're going to have to spin when I come in late and slaughtered.'

—

Yan was on edge. He had busied himself dancing with the children for the rest of the evening, knowing that what he had to say to Ellen couldn't be said here, with other people around, with her sister and father nearby. It had to be said in private, away from any distractions.

'Hi, hi, hi! Amazing show tonight! Tanja is buying drinks at Bo's Bar!' Dasha slapped his hand hard on Yan's nail-pricked back, making him flinch.

'Hey, Dasha,' he greeted.

'So you come now? To Bo's Bar? Drinks on Tanja?'

'I would like this but after show I am tired and …' Yan began.

'You hear me? Tanja buy drinks.' Dasha's eyes went wide. 'You are star of Fakir show.'

'I know this but …'

He couldn't help but look over to Ellen. She was stood up next to her table, collecting plastic cups to dispose of. The lemon top she was wearing brought out the sun hued tints in her hair.

'Ah, now all is clear,' Dasha said. He slapped another hand on Yan's back and performed an elaborate wink.

'What?' Yan asked.

'No need to explain. I understand. I see you tomorrow!' Dasha backed away, winking ridiculously and waving a hand.

—

'Go and get him,' Lacey ordered. 'Dad wants to meet him.'

'Come on, Lacey, this isn't fair.' Ellen stacked the cups into a tower and realised just how many drinks they'd all consumed that night.

'I don't see what's unfair about it. When I first started going out with Mark I had to bring him to Nan's for Sunday dinner. Don't you remember? We had all the old war stories. She even put on Chas and Dave.'

'You're not ashamed of your old man are you, Ellie?' Al winked at her.

There was just an edge of something in his jokey tone that hinted that he might be upset. That was the last thing she wanted. Al had swiftly dealt with Ross for her. All he wanted was to meet her boyfriend. *Boyfriend* sounded completely alien.

'Of course not, Dad. It's just that he isn't meant to "get close" to the residents and …'

'What d'you think I'm gonna do? 'ammer his thumbs to the table and demand 'e marries you?'

'No. No of course not.' Now she was sounding stupid. It was an overreaction. Why couldn't she introduce him? They were only going to talk, not plan the grandchildren.

'Go and get him over here or I will,' Lacey threatened.

Lacey on the loose after a bucket's worth of cocktails was something no one at the Blue Vue Hotel wanted. She would have to give in.

———

Yan saw her heading towards him and his stomach twisted. He couldn't do it. He couldn't tell her. His determination swung back and forth every time he set eyes on her. He loved her. He didn't want to hurt her. But would he rather lie? Hurt her when the truth came out in time? Because it would. If they were going to be close she was going to find out. Probably when he never emailed or called.

'Hi,' she greeted.

She was brushing her fingers down the front of her top as if she was self-conscious about something. All it did was highlight her neat figure, shoot memories of him caressing those curves, his lips delivering light kisses to every inch of skin.

'Hi,' he responded.

'Listen, this is a bit embarrassing but ...' She stopped, swallowing and recomposing herself. 'My dad wants to meet you.'

Like an avalanche, his mind was instantly swamped with visions of Rayna and her father. His tears when she wouldn't listen. Her father's smug expression. The rejection, the pain. History was about to repeat itself.

Before he knew it he was shaking his head.

He saw the look of confusion spread over her face. Her eyebrows furrowed, her lips together, a lack of understanding in her eyes.

'It won't be bad, I promise. I know you met him when you told him about Ross but Lacey told him about us and he's a traditional kind of man. He just wants to say hello.'

Yan shook his head again. 'No. I cannot.'

He couldn't think straight. All the visions from Bulgaria were impacting like he was stepping on land mines, the images more vivid and real as every second went by.

'Yan, what's wrong?'

He didn't deserve her concern. He'd lied to her. Even used her to keep the lie hidden.

'I have to go.'

'What?'

He couldn't say anything else.

———

Yan had left her; turned and walked briskly off, across the complex. She saw his disappearing form heading left, towards his room. She swallowed and took a look back at her dad and Lacey. They hadn't seen the scene. They were busy talking to the German couple who had been sat at a nearby table all evening.

She knew her father was domineering and opinionated, not necessarily someone you'd feel comfortable with at first meeting, but it didn't have to be half an hour spent discussing cranes and diggers. It could have been a quick hello, just a small acknowledgement of their relationship.

She looked back to Lacey and Al again. The German couple had pulled out a pack of cards.

She needed to fix this. She headed off in a bid to catch him up.

FIFTY ONE

'Yan!'

Ellen could see him just ahead, striding up the incline towards the block that housed his room. He must be able to hear her, which meant he was ignoring her. What had she done that was so wrong?

'Yan!' she called again. She was running now, desperate and getting out of breath as she tracked up the path behind him.

And then, just like that, he stopped.

She slowed a little, trying to re-establish a better breathing pattern, as she made her way up to him. As she neared she noticed the slump of his shoulders, the way his head was hanging. There was more to this than meeting her father. There had to be.

Yan turned then and faced her. 'You should go. You should be with your family.'

There were tears in his eyes, tension in his torso and emotion layering his voice.

'I'm not going anywhere until you tell me what's wrong.' She reached out to touch him.

He snatched his arm away. 'Me! It is me! *I* am wrong!' he yelled. 'I am wrong for you. I am wrong for everybody!'

'That's not true. Why would you say that?' Her forehead creased in confusion. 'Tell me what's happened.'

'What has happen?' He scoffed. 'What has happen is that I lie. I lie to you. I lie to everybody.' Throwing his arms in the air he turned towards the steps to his room.

'I don't understand,' Ellen said, following him.

'I know this. I know you do not understand because that is the way I want for this to be.'

—

Yan unlocked the door and pushed it open, depositing the key fob in the slot on the wall. He flicked on the main light. He had to keep moving, keep doing, keep running away.

He turned to face her. Putting his hand on the door he made to shut it.

'You're going to close the door? Shut me out?' Ellen asked.

The look on her face was tearing at him. Right at this moment she loved him, was concerned about him, worried. In a few minutes, if he told her, she would hate him for what he was and for all the lies he'd told. He needed to preserve the beautiful memories, hold on to what they'd had. He'd fallen deep, despite himself, and it was something to cherish.

His hand fell away from the door and he stepped back.

He saw her come into the room and watched her close the door behind them. She leant against it.

He was so hot. Perspiration covered his back. He pulled his t-shirt over his head and wiped his body down with it before discarding it in the corner of the room.

'Whatever this is about, Yan, you need to tell me.'

There was her voice. Her sweet, soothing voice, so soft and believable, so encouraging. With Rayna the decision had been taken out of his hands. Here at least he had a chance to use his own words. *His own words*. It was ironic.

He slipped his hand into the pocket of his jeans and brought out the slip of paper she had given him in Kassiopi. He took a step toward the table and placed it in the middle.

'You say this is where you live. Your address to send email,' he said, fixing his eyes on her.

She nodded. 'Yes.'

He nodded in reply. 'I do not know what is there.'

Again, the look of confusion. He needed to just say the words, to get this out and then watch her go.

'I cannot read this, Ellen.'

Her eyes changed in response to his words. There was light there, hope, a shift in the concern she'd had before.

'Is that all?' She smiled. 'I wrote it in a rush. I can copy it out again for you,' she said.

'No.' He shook his head. 'It does not matter how you write this. I cannot read, Ellen. I cannot read and I cannot write.'

———

She felt stunned, like she'd been stung by a taser, or electrocuted. Her heart seemed to stop beating, her breath wasn't coming, the door was pushing in on her back as she leaned harder.

Yan was pacing the room now, like a caged animal that didn't know what to do with itself.

'I don't understand …' she began.

She didn't. At all. How did this happen? And how did she not know? They had spent a week together. Surely, she would have picked something like this up. Her mind was already in action recalling instances where he had written or read. *He had got her to write the accident report when Zachary nearly drowned.*

'What is there that is hard? I cannot read or write.' He let out a sound of exasperation. 'And now you can go.'

He stopped walking then, his eyes meeting hers.

'Go?'

'Now you know I am stupid. An idiot who cannot write own name. You give me email address. How can I ever be able to write to you?'

There were tears now, desperate tears falling from his eyes as he sat down on a chair and crumpled over the table.

There was no hesitation. Ellen went to him, sliding her hands over the bare skin on his back and around his shoulders, pressing herself against him.

'Why would I go anywhere? Is this it? Is this why you were worried about meeting my father? He only wanted a handshake.'

He shifted then, pushed her off, sat up straight. 'You think that this is joke?'

'No,' she whispered. 'No, of course not.'

'Rayna's father thought it was joke and he use this. He use this against me.' He sighed. 'He want me to hurt somebody. To beat somebody for his business. I say I do not do this. Then I make mistake. I get into a situation I cannot get out of. He find out I cannot read or write and he tell Rayna.' He took a breath. 'And she does not want to be with me anymore.'

'Yan ...'

'And that is why I do not look for love again. Because nobody will want to share their life with someone like me. I am rubbish. Nothing. Worthless like he say.'

Ellen shook her head. 'I can't believe you're saying this. Do you really think this makes a difference to me?'

'How can it not make the difference? You are so clever. The work you do. The business man you have ... '

She coughed. 'Yan, you know what sort of person he was. How could you say that? He may have been literate but he was a dishonourable snake.'

'He own big business. He have idea that will change the world. I only have dance and skills with sports.'

She put her hands on her hips. 'You're hardworking, you're kind. You're almost fluent in English and German. You speak a little Greek. You saved a boy from drowning.' Ellen took a breath. 'When the children here see you they just want to hold your hand and spend time with you. You're everything Ross Keegan and his business aren't. That's why I fell in love with you.'

———

Ellen's words settled in the air and fell gently onto him. She was still here. He had told her and she was still here. When was it all going to fall apart? When was she going to leave? She would, wouldn't she? That's what always happened.

'This doesn't change anything for us.' Ellen pulled up a chair next to him. 'Because we can get you some help.' She lowered her voice. 'If you want to learn.'

Did he want to learn? No one had ever asked him that before. Did he? Was it possible to learn after twenty-eight years of not knowing?

'I want to not feel ashamed any more. To be able to stop telling lies to people.' He paused. 'But I do not want to go to school. How would that be?'

She smiled and gathered his hands in hers. 'You don't have to go to school. I'm sure there's loads of information on the internet we can download.'

'I have not computer.'

He couldn't believe he was saying this to her. Finally admitting this to someone, to somebody he cared about. And she was holding his hands now, telling him it was a problem that could be fixed.

'I have one. I can send you …' She stopped. 'Does anyone here know?'

He shook his head. 'A friend in Bulgaria fill in forms for animation team. I pay him to ask no questions. I have to hide this. If Tanja find out I will lose job. I need job to pay for work on church.'

He watched her nod her head. Her fingers were still stroking his hands. She was still with him. She said she loved him. She hadn't thrown him away like Rayna had.

'How have you done this? How have you lived with this all your life?'

He shrugged his shoulders. 'I do not go to school. I look after younger brother while mother, father and Boyan work. When I am old enough, I go to work. I make after-school club in village. Then, when I leave for city I learn to drive for better job.'

'You learnt to drive. What about signs and maps and ...'

'There is always way to get around things.'

'And you worked in bars and restaurants. What about food orders? Menus?'

'I have good memory. I get someone to read menu to me and I learn.'

Ellen smiled, shaking her head. 'And you think you're not clever. I don't think I've met anyone more capable. I can't imagine how you managed that.'

He closed his eyes before slowly opening them again. 'Ellen, I know this is not how you imagine me to be. You go home tomorrow. You expect to have letters and email. Now you know I cannot give you this.'

'Are you keeping anything else from me, Yan? Are there any other secrets? Is there anything else I should know?'

He shook his head with passion. 'No.'

'Then I'll just have to save hard and come back here as soon as I can.'

———

Yan's news had been a shock but it hadn't rocked her. Knowing that he had kept this hidden, not just from her, but from everybody his entire life only made the fact that he had told her more poignant. Now he was looking at her as if he couldn't believe what she was saying. Had he really thought she would run? Be horrified? Turn her back and leave? It was just a bump in the road, a blip, an obstacle that could be shifted, got over. All she felt about it was sorrow. Sadness that a boy had grown into a man and missed out on an education she had taken for granted. How must it have been for him? How hard had he had to struggle? How many lies had he had to tell in the name of self-preservation? Every day must have been a challenge, a worry, wondering if he was going to be caught out. Wondering what would happen if he was. How had he lived that way for so long and how had it felt knowing the one person he'd confided in, a person he'd loved and trusted, had turned her back?

'Are you sure, Ellen? I just tell you this and … you should take the time to think.'

She shook her head, determined. 'I don't need time to think. I know what I feel in my heart and it has nothing to do with education.' She squeezed his hand. 'By the way, those few words of German are the only ones I can speak.' She smiled. 'And as for DIY, forget it.'

'What does this mean?'

'It means there are dozens of things I can't do. If you're looking for someone to put up some shelves in your after-school club I don't think it's me. So you can't read or write … I can't handle a screwdriver.'

'You make joke,' Yan said, smiling.

'Yes, I'm not very good at those either.'

She watched the light come back into his incredible blue eyes and she knew she'd never loved him more than at this moment. He'd shared his vulnerability with her, the secret he had been keeping for years. In her mind it made him a better person, a whole, rounded person. When you bared yourself to someone, showed the pieces of yourself you were less proud of, scared of, ashamed of, you were truly free. And if that person accepted all those bits of you, loved you just as you are, it was golden.

FIFTY TWO

Yan hadn't let go of her hand since they'd left his room at five a.m. They'd walked down to the beach in the dark, strolling barefoot across the sand and she'd tried to drink in the feel and spirit of Agios Spyridon. Each grain of sand on the soles of her feet provoked its own individual memory of her time there. She'd let the soothing sound of the sea fill her ears, the rugged mountains of Albania fill her vision and the taste of Yan's kisses roll over her lips. She needed to be able to close her eyes when she was at home and recall these sights, scents and sounds. It would help her feel closer to Yan.

They'd stopped by the church, which was as rundown and crumbly as the first time Ellen had seen it, but this time Yan was even more enthusiastic about his plans to renovate. It was *his* now. He had a plan and a vision and the passion to make it work. She was going to help him when she visited and do any admin she could manage from the UK.

Now, they were walking up through the complex to reception, Yan wheeling her case for her. Neither of them had said a word since they'd arrived back on Blue Vue Hotel property. Their footsteps were slowing the nearer they got to reception.

Ellen finally broke the silence at the bottom of the steps to the lobby. 'My dad and Lacey are there already.'

She could see her sister in her Juicy trackies, hair wound up on top of her head, sitting on one of her cases, headphones in her ears. Al was looking out of the glass door to the entrance wearing his favourite casual slacks, a lightweight jacket over his arm.

'You do not want me to come?' Yan asked, letting go of her hand.

'No! No, of course I do.' She took his hand back, sliding their fingers together. 'It just means the coach will be here soon and I'll have to go.'

He put an arm around her shoulders and pulled her into his body. 'I do not care who see us now. Once key is handed in you are not holidaymaker anymore.' He kissed the top of her head.

'I don't want to leave you,' she said, her voice thick with tears.

'I know. I feel the same.'

———

He just wanted to hold onto her, the way he had in his bed last night. Exploring her body and knowing she knew everything there was to know about him brought a whole new dimension to what he felt. He had never been that emotionally exposed with anyone. It was as if he had spent his whole life trying to be something he wasn't and now he no longer had to pretend.

She'd whispered in his ear and he'd kissed her every part until she'd squirmed and scratched and screamed his name. And then they'd lain together, content, wrapped up in their own world, unafraid for the first time about what was to come. Except for this day. The one morning they just had to get over. As soon as Ellen was gone it was one moment nearer to her coming back.

'I should go.' She sniffed. 'The coach will be here soon.'

Yan squeezed her hand.

———

'She's here! Thank God you're here! I was thinking you'd run off into the sunset and weren't coming back. What would I have done then? I mean I need you at home with me. Back to back episodes of *Tipping Point* with Dad would do my head in.'

Lacey had pounced forward as soon as Ellen and Yan had entered the reception. He was still holding her hand and she was carefully imprinting how it felt on her memory.

She turned to Yan. 'Would you like to meet my dad?'

He smiled. 'I would like this.'

'You're in luck. He seems to be in a good mood today. I think it's because the restaurant manager gave him a loaf of that yellow bread to take on the plane,' Lacey said.

Ellen led the way over to Al, who was checking his watch.

'Bus is late,' he remarked.

'Stop going on. It'll be here,' Lacey said.

'Dad, I know you've met already but, this is Yan.'

She let go of Yan's hand and he quickly offered it towards Al.

'Hello, Mr Brooks. It is very nice to meet with you.'

Al looked Yan up and down from his trainers, up through his Blue Vue Hotel uniform, to his shaven haircut, unspeaking.

'I hear you saved a young lad from drownin',' Al remarked.

'Yes, sir.'

'And I already know you've been lookin' after my daughter.'

'Ellen is very strong. She does not need anyone to look after,' he responded.

Ellen's heart swelled with affection at his comment. He really knew how much her independence meant to her. They were going to be a partnership, an equal partnership, no matter how hard things got.

Then her stomach dropped. The coach was crawling up alongside the hotel darkening the reception area. For a split second she didn't know what to do. Lacey was already strutting towards the door, dragging one of her cases while Al started adjusting his holdalls.

'Come outside,' she begged Yan.

'Ellen, it will be so hard. I should go now.'

'No, please. Come outside. Wave to me.' She tugged at his arm. 'I want you to be the last person I see when the bus heads down the hill.'

——

Yan could see the tears in her eyes were close to spilling and they were forming in his eyes too, the more he looked at her and realised the significance of the moment. He brushed her hair away from her face with his fingers and placed a delicate kiss on her lips.

'I will come,' he whispered.

He picked up Lacey's second case and, pulling Ellen's, he led the way outside.

The sun was just coming up and the air was cool, the sky an inky blue. Other holidaymakers who had congregated on the steps outside were handing their cases off to the driver.

'Be careful with that one, it's got a litre of brandy in it,' Lacey called to the driver as she handed over her case.

'I wish I could stay,' Ellen said.

Yan turned to look at her then. She was shivering, her arms pimpled with goose bumps, her hair buffeted by the breeze. He wished this could be over. He had to concentrate on her coming back. She'd said a couple of months. It wasn't that long. He had his job and the church repair to take up his time.

He unzipped his fleece jacket and removed it. Slipping it around her shoulders, he moved in front of her to fasten it. 'Take this. It is cold this morning.'

'But it's your uniform. Have you got another one?'

He shrugged. 'It does not matter.'

'Ellen,' Al called.

—

How had all the people got onto the coach so quickly? She was the last person left, standing on the marble steps next to the man she loved. The man she had to leave.

'It is OK,' Yan said, taking hold of both her hands.

She shook her head at him as the tears fell. 'It isn't. It isn't OK.'

'You have to go back. Find for me the information for learning. I will use every moment I have to practice this and when you come again …' He lifted her chin with his finger. 'I will write for you.'

His words made her sob out loud but she nodded.

'Ellen, come on, love, people are waitin',' Al called again.

'You have to go now,' Yan told her.

She knew it was inevitable but that just made it worse. She threw her arms around him. How long would it be before she got to hold him again?

Yan drew her face towards his and their lips met in a slow, deep kiss she couldn't bear to end.

'Go,' he told her, tears snaking down his cheeks. He unfastened their hands almost brutally and edged her body towards the coach.

—

Yan couldn't do this. He couldn't stand there and see the coach depart, knowing it was taking her away from him. He didn't want to wave. He wanted to turn his back now and head to his room.

Instead he watched her climb the steps on board and make her way down the aisle to a seat by the window. As soon as she sat down she put her hand to the glass, as if she wanted to reach through it and re-engage with him. This was torture.

The coach driver released the brake and the vehicle moved forward smoothly, slowly drifting away.

He waved a hand, the tears still falling, but then he could no longer look. It was killing him. It was physical pain like he'd never known. One week. This one week had completely changed his life.

And then there was a screech of brakes. He looked back to the road and saw that the coach had stopped just a few yards from the entrance to the complex, the red lights locked on. Seconds ticked by and still nothing happened. He was just considering movement when he heard the door release.

His heart leapt up into his throat, wondering, waiting, not daring to think. And then he caught a flash of chestnut brown hair and the turquoise colour of his fleece. Ellen.

She started running and he went to her, rushing down the steps of the hotel to meet her.

'I couldn't do it, Yan. I couldn't leave,' she cried.

He wrapped his arms around her, swinging her in the air and holding her tight.

'I don't want to leave. I want to stay. I belong here … with you,' she said.

He put her down and gazed into her tear-flooded eyes. 'Then stay.' He smiled. 'Stay.'

'I love you,' she cried, placing a palm to his cheek.

He kissed her mouth, stroking her hair back from her face. 'And I waited for you.'

EPILOGUE

She could hear the water softly lapping, brushing the stones at the shoreline smooth, every wave altering their composition a little more.

Head held up, facing the sea and the mountains of Albania, slightly worried for the delicate white flowers woven into her hair, she filled her lungs with the rich, salty air.

She was barefoot. Petals of all different colours – shocking pink, deep purple, hues of orange and lemon – caressed her soles as she began to walk the length of the water platform. She squeezed Al's arm and looked up at him. His mouth was clamped shut, his glossy eyes directed forward, emotion threatening to spill.

A *bouzouki* started to play a mid-tempo folk song and her heart soared. This was real. This was happening to her. She was about to become a wife and pledge to share her life with the man she loved. He was waiting.

———

Yan turned around the moment the first chord of the instrument was struck. And there she was. Ellen. Dressed in a long, light, white gown that skimmed over her body, shimmering in the sunlight. She looked beautiful, so beautiful. He wanted to look at her forever and today that's what he was going to promise.

He turned to his younger brother, Viktor, and patted his arm, instilling encouragement.

Today the best man had more nerves than the groom.

'Flowers,' Lacey hissed as they reached the priest.

Ellen turned to her, not understanding and was almost blinded by the glare from the neon pink bridesmaid dress.

She'd let Lacey choose, not seen the frock until that morning and, although it wouldn't have been her first choice of colour or design, it was a hundred per cent Lacey. And today she didn't want it any other way.

'You're meant to give me the flowers now,' Lacey repeated.

'Oh, yes.' Ellen quickly passed them over, a nervous laugh escaping.

Then, as Al delivered her to Yan's side, she looked at her husband-to-be.

Hair freshly cut, skin that tan-coloured brown he'd turned the last year. Crisp white shirt and linen trousers, barefoot. But it was those eyes she centred on. Those bright, clear, azure pools of light she'd always felt could see right inside her. They were gazing at her now, so full of adoration.

He reached for her hands and, as the priest began the service, she knew right now, life couldn't get any better.

Yan wiped a tear away as she finished reciting her vows to him. She had said so many perfect things about her love for him and their life in Corfu. He hoped that what he had to say would be enough.

He cleared his throat and slowly slipped a piece of paper from the pocket of his trousers. The breeze fluttered the page as he unfolded it, perspiration forming on his brow.

'I have not learned the words to say.' His eyes went to Ellen. 'But I have written them and I will read them.'

He looked to the paper and concentrated hard.

'Ellen, you came into my life and changed everything about it.' He paused, a balloon of emotion starting to expand in his chest. 'You took me for who I am and could see who I wanted to be.'

He blew out a breath as he refocused, trying to ignore his swelling heart and the tears reforming in his eyes.

'I learn to love, with you. I learn to trust, with you. I learn the value of myself and today … today, I give all I have and all that I am, to you.'

He took a moment to collect himself before looking up.

———

She couldn't stop the tears and she didn't want to. The fact that Yan had written those words, understood what they meant and had read them out in front of everybody in the congregation was unbelievable.

In just a year he had made such progress. She was so proud of everything he'd achieved personally and professionally. While she had taken over the running of the office at the Blue Vue Hotel, he had got his after-school club off the ground. Twelve months had changed so much.

Not waiting for the priest to say anything else, she threw her arms around him and held on fast.

———

Twenty-five children, each with a basket of hard boiled sweets, waited by the archway leading back to the hotel complex. They were his children. They came every day after school to learn sports and dance, to fish from the beach, to enjoy life. The church had taken six months to renovate, Ellen had helped him gain a childcare qualification and now everything was perfect. The church was finally alive again. Full of the sounds of laughter, boisterous fun and happiness.

'Congratulations!' the children chorused.

'Did you teach them that in English?' Ellen asked him, waving at the children and giving the nearest ones high-fives.

'Yes, Mrs Aleksandrov, I do this. And later, tonight, I will teach you how to say it in Bulgarian, Greek and German. I will even write this down.'

'Ah, and what else are you going to teach me?' she asked.

He laughed then, catching the glint of mischief in her eyes.

'Traditional dance with no clothes. I think it is popular all over the world.'

He smothered her lips with his, pulling her close and the children laughed, clapping their hands together in celebration.

THE END

ACKNOWLEDGEMENTS

Thank you to my wonderful agent, Kate Nash for believing in this story and pushing me to make it the best it could be.

Huge thanks to the team at Bookouture for taking me into their fabulous family and enjoying this escape to Corfu so much they bought it.

A big thank you to the Rokas Family of the Mareblue Beach Hotel, Corfu. Their wonderful hotel and the amazing holidays I've had there since 2012 inspired the fictional Blue Vue Hotel in the novel. I can't wait to see you all again soon for more Apricot Coolers and gorgeous Greek cuisine!

To all the friends I've made in the animation teams over the years who work so tirelessly to make sure holidaymakers have a great time. Mary, Ginny, Teo, Nikolai, Tisho, Ebo, Tommy, Rico, Gill, Chu-Chu to name but a few. I hope I've done justice to your hard work in the novel.

My crazy friends, Rachel Lyndhurst and Susie Medwell have to take a bow now. They are a constant source of all the good things a girl needs on the writing train. Thank you so much for all your advice, laughs, email/text/messenger/hugs. I can't wait to share wine and pork scratchings with you later this year!

Thank you to my husband, Mr Big and my daughters, Amber and Ruby. There are times when Mummy has to be on the computer more than she is cooking/cleaning/cuddling/watching trumpet and ukulele practice. You are patient (most of the time) and you understand (some of the time) and if you let me write more, think of all the holidays to Corfu it might pay for. Fingers crossed!

But the biggest thank you of all has to go to my street team, The Bagg Ladies, and all the wonderful readers and book bloggers who support me every time I have a new book out… and beyond. You do an amazing job and without your passion for books and spreading the word to the world I wouldn't be lucky enough to write for a living. Thank you from the bottom of my heart!

LETTER FROM MANDY

Are you crying? Are you smiling happily for Ellen? Or are you still laughing over Lacey's antics? Whichever it is I want to say a huge THANK YOU for buying Truly, Madly, Greekly!

Corfu is one of my favourite places in the whole world and the Blue Vue Hotel was inspired by the hotel I stay at on the island. I hope the setting, the characters and the story took you away to a little piece of European paradise and perhaps made you want to visit.

If you enjoyed the book I would LOVE you to leave me a review on Amazon. Hearing what readers think means everything to us authors. Who was your favourite character? Do you know someone like Ellen or Lacey? Are you Team Yan or Team Sergei? Was it a perfect holiday read? Reviews can spread the word to so many more readers – and I think delicious Yan needs to be shared!

And, if you liked this book, perhaps you want to read more! I love connecting with readers on Twitter, Facebook, Goodreads, Pinterest – in fact Truly, Madly, Greekly has its own Pinterest board full of gorgeous guys, yummy Greek cuisine and beautiful beach scenes. Come and join me!

To keep right up-to-date with the latest news on my new releases just sign up at the following page: www.bookouture.com/mandy-baggot

Here's to more feel-good reads and scrummy heroes!

Mandy xx

@mandybaggot
mandybaggotauthor
www.mandybaggot.com

Printed by Amazon Italia Logistica S.r.l.
Torrazza Piemonte (TO), Italy

10845900R00222